OTHER WORKS BY PETER STOCKWELL

ADULT FICTION

Motive Series

Motive

Jerry's Motives
(Coming soon)

Historical

Jesus and the Rich Man
(Coming soon)

MIDDLE GRADE BOOKS

Puddle Jumper Series

(Coming soon)

Off to New York

Seattle is Home

San Francisco Rocks

NONFICTION

Stormin' Norman –
The Sermons of an Episcopal Priest

Blog
www.wordpress.com/peter.stockwell

MOTIVATIONS

A Story of Love, Family, Betrayal and Redemption

Markie,
Pleasure to
meet you *Peter Stockwell*

PETER STOCKWELL

Peter Stockwell
PO Box 3847
Silverdale, WA 98383

home: 360 697-4099 - cell: 360 509-3651
stockwellpa@wavecable.com

Published by
Westridge Art, USA
PO Box 3847
Silverdale, WA 98383

First Printing 2015
Copyright © Peter Stockwell

10 9 8 7 6 5 4 3 2 1

ISBN 978-0-9886471-1-4

Printed in the United States of America

Publisher's Note

Cover Design by
Marsha Slomowitz
Images from Shutterstock.com

Distributed by
Epicenter Press Inc. / Aftershocks Media
6524 Northeast 181st Street Suite #2
Kenmore, WA 98028

DEDICATION

*My wife, Sandy, continues supporting my efforts
to write with any credible ability and recognition by a
literate public with sagacious comments. As an avid reader
of varying genre, her wordsmithing improves any manuscript
I create. I dedicate this book to her diligence and hounding
which push me onward to the completion of better stories.*

"NEVER QUESTION ANOTHER MAN'S MOTIVE.
HIS WISDOM, YES,
BUT NOT HIS MOTIVES."

———————————

DWIGHT D. EISENHOWER

TABLE OF CONTENTS

PART 1 LOVE

PART 2 FAMILY

PART 3 BETRAYAL

PART 4 REDEMPTION

PART
ONE

LOVE

1
CHAPTER

Roger Waite

"I just met the most beautiful girl I've ever seen. She has the face of a model, a porn star body, hair which shines like the sun and a personality." My roommate, Brian Russell laughed. "What are you laughing at?" I had returned to our apartment on Campus Way from a detour through the Holland/Terrell Library at Washington State University.

"Roger Waite, you sound like a naive freshman with a hard on." He put a hand on my shoulder. "Come on, you've dated lots of girls around here. What makes this one so different?"

"I tell you, I've never seen such a girl before." My hazel eyes glazed for a moment remembering the golden tresses and radiant smile.

"Have you been drinking?" Brian looked around the room as if searching for bottles of Johnny Walker or Bacardi. "Nope, no alcohol. You vowed to never let a woman stand in your way of fucking everyone in a skirt."

"Yeah, yeah, yeah, I know what I said, but I tell you this girl is different." I had bumped into her, literally, excused myself, and then fumbled for words to continue a conversation. "She spoke in ways I hadn't heard from anyone of those skirts, as you called them. We had a wonderful beginning."

"Oh, don't tell me you asked her out." Brian's head shook in disbelief. "Your thinking's gone whacko."

"Very funny, I mean it. I think this girl might be the one." I thought about all of the other girls I dated, whose hearts I left in shambles, whose lives I altered with abandon. What was so different about this girl? Why did I feel like giving up my old trials, my usual habits, or my current lifestyle?

"How long have you known her? An hour and now nuptials are in your future. Man, this girl better be the Playmate of the Year." I sat on Brian's bed and smiled. He was right. It wasn't rational.

"Well, if Hefner wanted a fresh face and outstanding body, he couldn't do much better. I'm meeting her at the SUB in half an hour. Come along and judge for yourself."

"You plan on sacking her tonight? I'll stay with Joanne."

"I just met her and I have this stupid fear, if I make my usual move, I'll lose her." Lose her? She had what no other female exhibited. I just wasn't sure what it was.

"Yeah, but what happened with others didn't upset you, so what's different about this girl? By the way, what's her name?"

"Mary...Mary Johnson. Odd isn't it. Her name is so plain and she's a Venus...with arms." My eyes acquired a faraway moment. "Ah, I don't know. Something's different." The gaze returned and the conversation waned. I stood and grabbed my coat. "Are you coming?"

Brian nodded and we left on an excursion of discovery.

Brian and I formed a plan for him to enter before me. As we entered the CUB, I saw her sitting at a table, cautious eyes flitting around the room. He didn't know who to observe. As he scanned, an expression of realization coursed his face. He looked at me and smiled. I sat beside her; Brian sat nearby but remained observable. His hand fanned, indicating a hottie. I grinned.

"Who are you looking at?" My face burned, so I touched her hand, endeavoring to proffer assurance my attention was for her alone.

"My roommate's over there. I would be remiss if I didn't introduce him." He strolled over when I waved at him. "Brian, I'd like you meet Mary Johnson. Mary, this is Brian Russell."

Brian extended his hand expecting the usual amenity. Mary appeared reluctant, but obliged. "Nice to meet you."

"Nice to meet you, too. Watch out for this guy. He's a lady killer." I frowned. Mary winced. "I'm kidding. He's a nice guy. Take good care of him." Brian turned to me. "I'll see you later." He winked and left.

"Forgive him. He's being funny for my sake." Mary smiled, but I saw doubt in her eyes. "Hey, I want to get to know you. So ask me anything and I'll answer, but I'm curious about you, too."

"Alright, have you lived in Wendlesburg all of your life? Do you have any brothers or sisters? What are you planning to do with the rest of your life?"

A stupid grin crossed my face. "Well." I hesitated, deliberating with intentionality. "I was born in Wendlesburg, have a brother and a sister, and I plan to work in real estate with my father. Now, what about you?"

"There's not much to tell. I have a brother who is older and a little sister who is thirteen. I live in Seattle and I don't know what I am doing when I graduate."

"What are you studying?"

"Sociology and psychology."

"I'm studying business. I'll get my real estate license and become a broker like my Dad. Would you have dinner with me tonight?"

Mary looked at me, curiosity shaping her face. "Dinner with me? You must have better things to do."

"Not really. Is something wrong with me?"

"No, I just believe most guys want me because of my looks and body. What do you want, Roger?"

She had a point. I had a hard time ignoring her assets. "I just want to learn as much as I can about you." I smiled again. "Well, how about dinner?"

"Okay, but nothing more."

"Of course, of course." *I'm an idiot blathering about a girl I hardly know. What's the matter with me?* "I'll pick you up at six. I've never understood this eight o'clock stuff in the movies. Seems so late to be eating." *I'm blubbering again.* "Mary, have you dated a lot of guys around here? I'm mean…um…ah…I've seen you before today, but we don't cross paths very often. Are you seeing anyone right now?" I blushed, embarrassing myself with each muddled word.

Mary furrowed her brow at me. Was she upset by the question? Time crawled along, seconds turning into imaginary minutes. "I've chosen not to be part of the dating scene, but I'll take a chance and get to know you. By a lot, are you referring to your many conquests?"

Boy she gets right to the point. "I've dated several women in the course of my years here, but I...wouldn't...uh...call them conquests."

"So, no sex for you?"

No one questioned my moral standing and most of the girls I slept with were just as willing to use me as I was to use them. Why did I even care what she thought? Yet, my infatuation transformed my shallow relationship-building to a deep foundation of compassion. Her eyes sparkled when she spoke. Her hair glowed with several colors of blonde and a hint of red. Her lips invited touching, as did the nape of her neck. My eyes trailed to her bosom.

"Hey," Mary jerked me back to reality. "What about it? Are you a sex maniac or just a guy who found a girl unwilling to be seduced on a first date?"

"Guilty."

"Oh, please." Mary stood. "I'll see you at six and I agree eight is too late." She left me sitting with lasciviousness drained from my soul and her address written on a napkin.

I stood to make my way back to the apartment. Before I could escape, an interruption halted my progress.

"Well, she looks to be innocent enough for you to ruin." I shuddered as I realized a former girlfriend sat at a nearby table.

"Hi, Monica. What's up?"

"Good, good, you haven't changed since we broke up. Any girl, anytime, anywhere. Nice to see you still hustling the uninitiated." Monica Atherton stood and approached. "Mind if I give her some sage advice before you bed her?"

"I get the feeling you're mad at me. You broke it off with me, remember?"

"I wasn't as willing to share you as much as you were willing to share you. Don't forget about that freshman last year." She closed in and kissed me a lustful kiss recalled from better times. She pressed her physique into mine. Monica smirked when she caressed my crotch. "She's going to lose this before you ever get to put it to her."

"Oh, come on, Monica. Don't be mad at me."

"Are you going to explain to Miss Priss what your main goal is?" She grabbed my hand, winked at her friends, and pulled me out of the SUB.

"All right, make me happy for old time sake." Her body was persuasive and argued for attention. Our sexual romps had been satiating and protracted, but she wanted something I had been unwilling to give, commitment. Our break-up had complications and I wanted nothing more from her.

I separated and said. "Sorry, I'm not doing anything with you. We're finished."

"Yeah? We'll see." She stormed away.

———⊗⊗⊗———

"So bro, tell me about this new girl?" My brother, William, a high school senior in Wendlesburg, aka Willie, Billie, dirt bag, scum bag, etc., goaded me as we talked on the phone. He knew which buttons to push to get a reaction, and he pushed them with frequency. He seemed genuinely interested when I told him about Mary. He liked Monica but understood her possessiveness as a bridge burner for me. I explained her intrusion after meeting with Mary but left out her attempt to rebuild the bridge.

"She's great. Her face radiates when she smiles. Her body has all the right curves, although she wears clothes hiding most of them. Her hair is sunny yellow and shimmers even in low light. Her eyes sparkle as in a pool of pure water. I want to grab her and hold her close to me so I can feel her body, but I need to take it slowly."

"Man, you're smitten. You never talk about girls this way. It's always how fast you bed them and how great the sex was. Are you sure about this girl?"

"Billy, it's more than her looks. She has a way of climbing into your soul and filling a void. I didn't realize how much I wanted someone like her. We're are going to dinner tonight." I wanted her to know my family.

"Are you looking for an out in case it blows up?" I imagined him screwing up his face in doubt, his usual response.

"What makes you think this will fail?" William said 'Goodbye' and agreed this single date would not be a fiasco. I punched the end button on my cell and thought about Monica's proposal and subsequent threat.

It was midafternoon, getting later because of my unwanted run-in and calling my brother. Monica was not happy with me and her possessive behavior cured me of any desire for sex. I needed to shower and ready myself for the evening. She was history and my future awaited dinner at a nice restaurant. If I could prevent it, nothing was going to mess this up. I undressed and proceeded to the bathroom in my shorts.

The warm water soothed me and I forgot about my chiller with Monica. As water cascaded over me, I relaxed. No more difficulties for this day. I turned off the spigot, got out and toweled off. Noises in the living room signaled Brian's return.

I put on my robe which hung on a peg by the door. I went out to confront the invaders of my solitude. "Well, hello, you two. How are you, Joanne?" I liked Brian's girlfriend, a tall, athletic type, who attracted attention because of her height. She was pretty and proportionate, not very endowed, because she had no fat cells in her body. She played volleyball for the college and kept Brian on his toes.

"I hear you have a new girlfriend." Joanne and I were friends, even flirtatious, but I wasn't interested in her. She was a couple of inches taller than me and intimidating. I liked my women more agreeable to my terms and we didn't have terms. Brian was infatuated and being as tall, though not as athletic, he exhibited no fear of her. He told me about her bedroom skills and exacted a promise never to reveal to Joanne our conversations. I relented, but related his loss of experiences with other women by explaining what he was missing. My tales were accepted as compensation.

"What time is your dinner date?" Brian asked.

"Six. Are you two planning some escapade tonight?" I figured Brian wanted the apartment to himself.

"Well, if you're not going to be here, Joanne and I were planning on ordering a pizza and watching a movie."

"Sounds exciting, I'll keep Mary out late so you can finish your cinematic experience." I returned to my bedroom to dress for an evening of exploration.

My college clothing consisted of jeans, polo shirts, and tees. I wore them every day and thought nothing of picking up women dressed as a fashion misfit. Tonight was different. I chose the one outfit I never wore, saved for Sundays and church, so it never left the closet. The one tie I owned stayed off my neck, but the tailored wool sport coat and khaki Dockers were a must.

Checking my watch, I had plenty of time before needing to leave. I figured Brian and Joanne were experimenting with new volleyball moves, hard to do in a confined bedroom, but volleyball had little to do with the moves. I exited my room, hoping to evade prying eyes.

"Well, dapper Dan is alive and well." Brian and Joanne were sitting on the couch. So volleyball would wait for my departure.

"Yeah, well, sometimes I need to wear this stuff to air it out. It feels abandoned in the closet." Brian laughed.

Joanne chimed in with her own banter. "I think you look nice. This girl must be something special. Even I might want to have dinner with you."

"Right," I responded, "because the clothing makes the man. Sorry, Brian, your girlfriend's in love with me." He fired a pillow at me. I caught and returned it. We laughed and I left them alone; my journey of discovery began.

Sitting in the car I wondered what I was doing. *I graduate in the spring and leave campus for good.* I had made a promise to myself, bachelorhood until graduation. With the milestone approaching, I guessed matrimonial instincts were kicking in. No previous companions invoked ideas of them as wife material. I pursued the conquest and didn't regret the heartaches I caused. Mary, however, elicited a different emotion. I wanted a long term commitment, but I wasn't sure how the process worked.

I don't even know how old she is. Maybe she wanted to complete her degree before marrying. Not a question for this evening. My thoughts were a conflict of emotions. I started the car. My heart christened a convoluted range of passions, none of which attracted a sense of sexual satisfaction. Why was this girl so important after such a brief acquaintance?

2
CHAPTER

Victoria Johnson

"Mary, I don't know if I like boys enough to want to go out with them. Mom says I should take my time." My big sister had returned from Washington State University for a short visit. Having my brother, Ben, and sister, Mary, at college is strange. I lived a quiet life with my parents, attending middle school and learning about people. Dad ignored me most of the time, but Mom and I developed a closer relationship. Mary was leaving too soon for me.

"She's just protecting you." Mary involved me in her life. "I think you'll do just fine. Remember boys only want sex with you."

"What happened after New York?" My curiosity had peaked. The scars were visible on Mary's wrists. Now 21, she had not tried suicide since long ago. College has been an escape for her, but I know she doesn't have many friends. I'm her closest confidant.

"Do you remember when you saw Dad in my room touching me?'
"Yeah."

"Well, he can't do to you what he did to me."

"Did he ever have…you know…ah…sex with you?"

"What?" Mary's eyes widening. "No, he touched me is all, but it's still wrong and I don't want him to come near you. Ben says he'll hurt him if he does."

"I know. Ben and I've talked about it. Mom shushes me when I ask her about Dad."

"Let's not talk about it anymore." I sensed the sadness in her voice, the shame within her.

"I'm so sorry. I remember you and Mom painting and I still have all of the drawings you did for me. Maybe you should take it up again."

"No, that part of my life is over. I don't want to be reminded of those awful times. Besides, I've met someone and we're dating. He lives near here and I really like him." The darkness faded and a sparkle developed as she spoke. Had my sister found her elusive happiness at last?

"Are you going to introduce us, or keep him a secret?" I grinned.

"I'm scared to bring him home. I know Mom would be happy for me, but Dad won't like him." A familiar darkness revisited.

"If he likes you, he must be very smart. You're beautiful and kind and elegant. I know I'll love him if he loves you. Bring him home so we can meet him. Ignore Dad." Anything my sister wanted, I wanted. I watched her entire life be unhappy and sullen. Now a spark of excitement exploded in her. My euphoria was genuine.

"I'll ask him to come home with me next time." Mary had been at school for three years, and not dated. She tried to keep her beauty muted so guys would leave her alone. Meeting this guy was a big step for her. I'd made friends and tried the boyfriend charade. Most of the guys just want in my pants or want me in theirs. I wasn't interested. I guess Dad soured me on that part of life. But Mary needed happiness and seemed to have found it.

"So tell me about him. What's he studying besides you?" We laughed.

"He's studying business and plans to work with his father in the family real estate business in Wendlesburg. He's rather athletic but doesn't play any sports. He's tall and has dark hair. You know how Mom said I'm Helen of Troy? He's my Paris and I love him." Having seen the movie TROY with a couple of girlfriends, I now understood the references. Yes, Mom was right. Helen of Troy and Mary both launched ships. I've heard I look like her, but I don't see it. If I can be like my sister when I'm twenty-one, I'd be pleased.

"Uh, have you and Roger done it yet?"

Mary groaned. "No, I've gone out with him a couple of times. I'm not sure he's into me. There's this other girl who told me he was hers and I should leave him alone. Roger explained how he and she were history, but she isn't letting go." I doubted Roger's sincerity.

"Dad's left me alone." A change of subject seemed appropriate.

"Good, he doesn't need to teach you anything. If you have questions ask me. Read books. Go on line. Just make sure he doesn't touch you." I tried experimenting with myself, but I sure didn't understand the attraction.

"Let's go to Westlake Center and Pacific Place. We can hang out and watch people." I enjoyed my sister's time and pressed to leave the house. Dad would be home soon and I wanted Mary away from him. Funny, to have this compunction for protecting my older sister. She warned me about Dad's nighttime adventures, but I hadn't experienced them. I now comprehended what I saw so many years ago. I'd never told anyone, but no guilt pervaded my psyche.

"What do you propose we do besides people stalking?" Mary giggled.

"I need to finish shopping for Christmas. I don't know what to get Mom or Ben. Dad's getting his perfunctory tie. I've already taken care of you."

"My, what a grown up word for you to use."

"I learned it in school and I've waited for the right time to use it." I stood and walked to the door of my room. "Let's go." Mary followed, hesitant for a moment. I looked at her but still did not see a resemblance. I had grown two inches since she had returned to school in September. I would be as tall as her by the end of the school year. My body performed the miracle of adolescence with unwanted speed. I didn't regret the growth of breasts and the beginning of menses. It was inevitable and I wasn't early or late compared to others in my class at school. The older boys were interested more now than last year, but I still considered them immature and self-centered. Mary drove her car and we enjoyed a relaxed ride into downtown Seattle from our home in Magnolia.

"Mary, do you want to have this guy make love to you?" My question reflected a middle school temperament. Her years through middle school had been a torture, a sullen period of time which left scars on her psyche, as well as her wrists. I watched her change from a euphoric moment to sullen deep darkness. She could ruin a good time just because the wrong word was expressed. Gloom emerged when Dad was near. I helped the best way I could, but nine years is a huge age disparity.

I hadn't understood her diagnosis until recently but wanted to help her control the mental gymnastics she endured since adolescence.

"None of your business," but a smile betrayed her. "I've thought about it. I guess I have to let someone fondle me so I can move on with my life."

"Is this something you've learned from a psych class?" My internet research taught me most psychologists were searching for cures for their own psychotic anomalies. Mary fit the definition. Dad hadn't touched her since middle school, but once Mary entered high school the lectures began: about keeping a moral standard, not embarrassing the family, presenting a dignified manner. Our morality was a fabrication and Mary kept to her room when not in school. She had no friends and upheld her part in the façade built by our father. I wanted to do something wicked just to torment Garrett, holier than thou, Johnson, but I wasn't interested in drugs, smoking, or criminal activities. Mom instilled an ethic and I wanted to please her. Dad benefited by proxy. Someday, though, I knew I had to be a bad girl.

"Well, as a matter of fact, yes. Now don't think me a lunatic yet. I'm much more rational and cogent than I've ever been. And the medicinal assistance has helped." We laughed, but I knew my sister's mood pills kept her stable. She began taking them after a diagnosis of anxiety. I had turned seven and watched with alarm as my sister became more depressed and aloof. Her attitude about living in hell changed to palpable sanity through high school and into college because of the pharmacology. Maybe this new guy might erase the last vestiges of a corrupted sanity.

Our time in Seattle was precious. I was as alone in the family as Mary since my group of friends was small. Was I destined to descend into the chasm of mindless grief? We sat on the third floor of Pacific Place and watched the people ascend and descend the escalators. I'm happiest with Mary. Ben was a good brother; he even talked with me, but I knew his secret and promised to keep it. Dad would never understand and Mom would need time to adjust. Mary didn't have any secrets worth the privilege of hiding, so I could tell her anything and she told me about her life. I didn't have secrets, I suppose because Mom and I had an understanding about what had occurred in this crazy family of ours.

"Do you ever wonder about people?" I broke the silence because of boredom. "I mean, people have lives of their own and I like to make up stories about them. I write them when I get home and have time to myself. Would you read them sometime?"

"So you're being creative. Does Dad know you're wasting your time with these stories? After all everyone knows you can't make a living as an author. Just ask Dad. Creativity means getting a job which can't support you." Mary put a finger in her mouth and made a gagging sound. I laughed attracting attention from others.

"You're so right. I'll die in poverty and embarrass my father who lives a righteous life and does no wrong." Mary hushed me. I burned a look of indignation into her.

"Let's go. I want to see what's in Westlake Mall." We rode the escalator to the first floor and walked the two blocks to the other shopping center. I bought some small gifts, finishing the seasonal requirements. Ascending the escalators to the food court, we bought nourishment and sat to watch a different class of people as they milled about the dining area. Two blocks made a difference in the clientele of stores, although I saw some of them at the other mall.

"I hope this Roger guy is nice to you. You deserve to be happy." Mary smiled but said nothing. I watched her gazing nowhere in particular, lost in thought. I realized we did resemble each other. My hair was longer and my breasts were not as reputable. Mary's hips accented her curvature in a sensual way which I sensed in my body. Sometimes I stood in front of my floor length mirror and stared at the magnificent changes from young straight line child to curvy adolescent. I wanted what Mary had. As a child I watched her dress. Her development awakened my interest, but I kept my questions. Mom told me I would change but not much information was exchanged between us. I wondered if any of my friends thought as I thought and guessed they did. I wasn't so different from other people, was I?

3
CHAPTER

Roger

"Roger, are you ever going to let Mom and Dad meet Mary?" William and I were returning home from Washington State University for a much needed break. He flew over to Pullman so we could be together without the intrusion of parents. This occasional escapade, encouraged by Mom and Dad, was an adventure.

He was a different sort of person, and introducing a girlfriend to him, because of his exacerbating ability to spill the beans, let the cat out of the bag, and tell the tale, created mistrust. He kept no information confidential, a trait which was not genetic. I loved but wondered about him. So Mary remained an enigma until a later time.

The drive was not complicated. Most of the roadways involved the interstate highway system. I had driven it many times knowing the course in my sleep. Once in a while I let Will behind the wheel and slept, ignoring or hiding from his abhorrent ability to extract fear and possible road rage. My next trip home would include Mary and my brother would stay home. I wanted to meet her family and introduce her to mine. We could see how the future looked when we ascertained our familial reactions to those introductions.

"Why do you ask? Are you thinking of telling them before I have an opportunity to broach the subject?" I stared at him a moment before returning to the road view. "I'm going to bring her with me next time I come home. We've talked about it and you will not fly here to be my companion." I wanted to disregard what I knew would be coming, but the dirt bag surprised me.

"Fine with me. I think you two need time alone to hatch your plot. If my girlfriend was anything like what you've told me about Mary, I might want to hide her from Mom and Dad."

"What's that supposed to mean?" I glared at him and almost drove off the road. The road turtles on the side pavement reminded me of my primary activity. I repositioned the car. "What's wrong with her in your little pea head?" If I had a James Bond button, I would have ejected him.

"Well, according to you, she's beautiful and has a great body, so I understand the attraction. But sometimes I notice you're like a predator with girls, she might be cold to your advances." His brow furrowed in an attempt to lessen my anger. He could redirect a conversation with his face causing people to relax when convulsed. I reciprocated. He continued. "Do you love her? I mean, I understand the lust of wanting to be with her. But you've never acted this way with other girls. All you've wanted to do is find 'em, feel 'em, f*** 'em and forget 'em. What's so different about Mary?"

He had me. I didn't know what struck me about her. I retained my personal "lust" as William called it. I wanted sex with her but we had not progressed to such a point. For some unappreciated reason I wanted life with her to begin on her terms. I wanted the All American dream, the 3-bedroom rambler with the white picket fence, the dog and two-point-three kids. I didn't know what to say. My feelings went beyond the obvious beauty of her face. Those golden tresses, azure eyes, offset with the sensual curve of her mouth, inviting kisses. Her anatomy encouraged exploration, a Greek goddess carved in flesh instead of stone. I ached, wanting to feel her skin, explore her womanhood.

"I don't know." I mused. "I just feel different about her. I think about being with her, not just physically, but with her. With her spiritually, I guess, emotionally." I pictured her in front of the car and almost missed the curve.

"Hey, if you're going to kill us, let me drive." I returned to sanity before inflicting any mortal wounds. We laughed and continued on our way. Home was close, within two hours. The mountain pass had been clear for once and weather bearable. Lunch at the summit included romping in the snowdrifts and consuming hamburgers at our favorite spot. I missed Mary already, just hours from my last encounter with her. Billy knew her not, but suspicion of a history hidden from me because of my blind love for her may have haunted him. We might agree on my fascinations, but this woman represented a challenge. I ignored the obvious and declared 'love conquers all'. I knew we had the proverbial something different. I recognized her coldness as strength in her because we knew each other for so short a period of time. Billy didn't profess to understand girls and maybe held a jealousy for me. His last girlfriend broke his heart and he hadn't yet resumed dating.

"Let me tell them about Mary." I implored. "Scum bags are silent when asked, aren't they?" I smiled. Billy nodded but the look in his eyes hinted at skullduggery. He would breach a promise in truth not offered, just because he wanted to. The competition for supremacy of maleness in the Waite house never rested. I needed to occupy his time and tell Mom the news before he leaked it.

"How was your break?" Mary and I ate lunch at a restaurant downtown, an off-campus hangout. We sat alone in a corner, away from the few other patrons. I called her when I returned hoping her interest in me still existed. She arrived a day earlier than me. I wasn't sure why she didn't want to extend time away from school, but I was euphoric when I heard her voice. Seeing her again fueled my desire for her. I wasn't going to destroy it by pushing too hard. A sense of fragility, initiated by William's caution about her, caused some anxiety. But I didn't care. I wanted to know her, wanted more than physical pleasure. I desired a mental connection, emotional and spiritual. No other girl elicited such yearning. I gazed at her like a forlorn puppy.

"Fine, but I'm glad to be back." She smiled. Her azure eyes reflected the lights, creating intensity in her face. She seemed to be controlling her emotions. I wasn't sure why but realized nothing advanced beyond this meal and conversation. Classes resumed in the morning, although I had nothing to study, except Mary. Was she disappointed in me? I wasn't certain.

"What did you do in Seattle?" The ice dammed our conversational river. Mary looked at me as if I was quizzing her. I doubted my question but wanted to break the jam. What if she didn't want to share with me?

What if this severed our future? Could I repeal the comment? I braced for the chill.

"My sister and I hung out together. We're close and I want her to learn about how the world works. She's young and doesn't yet have a grasp of the complexities of life."

"I know you told me before, but how old is she?" My inquiry didn't dig too deep into the jam.

"She's thirteen and thinks she knows more than she does. But I love her and we share our secrets with each other. I think you'll like her when you meet her." The ice was my imagination. "I want you to meet my mother and brother, too." The river flowed free.

"I would like to very much. I told my family about you and they're anxious to meet you as well. So, am I a secret?" Her mouth curled and her eyes gleamed. I fell in love with her right then. She reached out and held my hand giving a slight squeeze.

"Not any longer. I want to ask you something, but, please, don't think badly of me for asking it." My curiosity peaked. What could she want of me for which I engaged bad thoughts? My mouth exposed doubt along with my eyes. Mary continued. "I am not very experienced in this inter-action between males and females. I understand from people to whom I have spoken; some by choice, others not; you have…" she paused a mo-ment, "extensive experience in the physical sharing between people." The river had flowed into an ocean.

"I guess so." My past caught me off guard, an ignored warning now revealing itself. Monica cautioned me about my actions causing extreme heartache. I didn't believe anything could derail my life. Now a simple statement of truth and I withered, not sure of what she would accept and what I could endure. To change my perceived future depended on honesty regardless of consequences. "What do you want to know?"

"I think I'm ready for a relationship with someone and I like you." My heart sank. My love was unrequited. I wanted to guide her to loving me as much as I loved her. "You can teach me how to relate with men and what they want from me as a woman." The blood rushed to my face, an-ger boiled from unexplored depths. She cannot in all seriousness think I would accept this and watch her leave me for another man. I peered at her through narrow slits. My jaw set tight, seething disgust welling up. Teach her just to lose her? I rejected the question and remained silent. "Have I offended you?" *She perceives my thoughts. I find it difficult to hide anything in my soul from her.* It hurts to think she would use me just to gratify herself. Who does she think she is to abuse my love for her?

As sudden as a racing car circles the track I realized her intent. I relaxed and wanted to cry. She pierced my heart to open my mind to my own actions. This woman, who claimed little understanding of people, contained a wealth of knowledge exceeding any I gleaned in four years of higher learning. She would teach me, instead of my educating her. I knew what she wanted. I no longer burned with anger. But a heartache grew anyway, unburdening pent-up desires of lust for a more appropriate craving for a relationship. Mary exposed my selfishness and now I perceived my creativeness in causing pain to women with whom I engaged in wanton sex. Of my conquests how many were hurt? I would never know. But this simple inquest tore open my own pain, something I didn't enjoy.

"No, I'm not offended. I like you and I guess my reputation precedes me. You just called me out. I'm not interested in another conquest. I'm interested in getting to know you and developing a long term relationship. Stupid as it may sound right now, I think I love you. I want you to love me. You may not, but can we see where we might go with each other?"

"Like I said, I want to learn how to relate to men, not just about sex. Truth?" She smiled again. "I saw you several weeks ago. I've been hiding from people most of my life, because my family history is complicated. You asked about meeting them and I want you to, but my father is not a warm person. He and I have…well, let's just say…a turbulent past. I'm not close to him and I fear what men want most. I'm taking a chance with you. Your history with women notwithstanding, I am attracted to you. I don't know if love is part of it, but I want to be a whole human being. When our first encounters pleased me, I discovered something about me." During our conversation she held on to my left hand. I reached for the other.

"Thank you. Thank you. Thank you; for understanding me better than I do. It will be my honor to lead you to wholeness. I guess we will lead each other." We had finished our meal. The waitress left the billing slip and ignored us. "Let's get out of here. We can continue talking." I separated from her hands and reached for my wallet. Placing two twenties in the folder, I stood and assisted Mary to her feet. Our journey had just begun in earnest. We left the restaurant hand in hand. My lasciviousness was in the past. My future would be one of faithfulness.

Mary squeezed my hand. Anxiety or anticipation, I did not perceive. The walk to my apartment, though short, stretched time beyond Einstein's Theories of Relativity.

As we stood in the living area, an attempt at kissing was rebuked, not for fear of it but to leave her free to explore my habitat.

"So this is how a lothario ensnares his victims, in a den of iniquity and squalor." She radiated with teeth exposed as lips parts from each other. "I think it needs a female's touch."

"Do you want to move in and provide the necessary care to make this abode more inviting?"

"Not so fast, hot shot, not so fast. Where's your roommate?"

"He's probably with Joanne." Would her first lesson in womanhood commence soon?

"So we are alone. I suppose with other young ladies your moves begin to entice them into the boudoir. Am I to be regaled with the witticisms which cause females to swoon?"

What was she doing? Creating a lesson for me? Or asking for one? "I'm at a loss here. Do you expect me to begin teaching you about womanhood now?" Her smile said maybe. Her eyes screamed no.

Victoria

"Mom, tell me about Mary when she was younger." I sought empathy. I knew about the suicide and the night visits, but Mary was a conundrum. She hid from life and anyone who came near her. I seemed to be the one person to whom she related. Why couldn't she be like others? What went wrong? "Mom?"

Mom's eyes welled up. "Oh, honey, why do you need to know?" I guess I didn't, but curiosity instilled a deep desire to understand her. "She's a complicated person. When you're older, you'll understand more." Mom hugged me like it would be the last time. I returned the sentiment, forgiving any further inquiry. We separated; Mom left me alone in the kitchen.

I rose from my seat. I knew Mary's secrets, but did Mom understand her? I believed she thought she knew, but nothing was clear. Mary warned me about guys and getting too close to people. I accepted her philosophy remaining free of the rush to join the throng of "going out together" pairings prevalent at school. Mary needed happiness and maybe this new guy could provide it. As I contemplated my situation and Mary's I walked to my room.

My computer beeped as I entered; another message from my girlfriends or an update from Mary? I sat at the desk and opened my mail box. Mary wrote to say her date with Roger had enlightened her. She thought him handsome, gracious and a gentleman. I replied about meeting this wonderful person as soon as possible. Mary replied she would ask him to stop in Seattle before going to Wendlesburg. I replied I was anxious to meet Roger and overjoyed for her. We signed off.

I didn't feel any urgency to have a boyfriend, I wanted to be more adventurous. I had heard about a girl at school who got pregnant by a guy in high school. I didn't know her but I realized I shouldn't be doing something stupid. Mary had to realize the complications of changing her life by incorporating a man into it. Would she be sure to keep safe? I hoped she would.

I spent most of my days alone in my room, reading, studying, and writing letters to Mary and Mom. I never sent any of them. I just wanted to transcribe my feelings, my thoughts, and whatever ate at me about my life. Fantasies caused no harm and entertained me. I accomplished my chores and schoolwork, and no one suspected my aloneness was more than a middle school anomaly or quirk of nature. Dad avoided talking to me and Mom acted civil but aloof. I kept researching and learning about love and sex through books from the library and surreptitious magazines I acquired. Mom stayed out of my room since I cleaned it and laundered my own clothes to be sure she had no reason to enter.

Time crawled, anxious as I was to meet Mary's boyfriend. I satisfied urges for companionship with occasional dalliances, dating some of the boys from school, not letting anything get out of hand, so to speak.

Finally, winter turned to spring and another break came with the promise of a new acquaintance. As planned, Mary was coming home with her boyfriend, Roger Waite. Restless, I bided my time.

But who was this man? How did he win my sister's heart? What did I want from him? Is it true when a woman meets someone, they look for a person similar to their father? Was this Roger another Garrett?

4
CHAPTER

Roger

"Mary, I'll drop you off at your house, meet your family, and then head on the Wendlesburg." I explained my plans to her the week before spring break. I wanted everything to go well. Mary had become so important to me I scared myself thinking about how I would destroy my happiness. "Do you want to come to my house and meet my family?" We sat on my bed, half packed suitcases nearby. Travel time arrived as scheduled.

Mary turned to me and kissed my cheek. "I would love to meet your parents. We don't have to stop in Seattle first. There's nothing there for me, well, except I want to see Vickie. She wants to meet you, too. Ben may not be coming home this time so you might have to wait to meet him. I love my mother and sister, but my father is not worthy of meeting you." She turned away but I noticed a tear forming.

"Mary, contact Vickie and we'll pick her up. Will your mom care if she comes with us for a couple of days?"

"Her spring break isn't the same week as ours." Mary tried to dry her eyes without letting on, but I discerned her pain caused uncontrolled emotions. Sometimes a rage was stifled. This time I needed to defend her from her fears. I put my arms around her waist pulling her close. Her hair tickled my nose but the scent of flowers thrilled my heart. She reached back for my arms and then held my hands leaning into me. She drew them to her breasts and whispered, "Make love to me. Teach me the gentleness of sharing. Touch me so I can stop fearing what in truth I want from you. Hold me tightly and caress me. Warm this cold heart of mine."

"I love you." I refrained from expressing my desires for her, accepting the chill I sensed with each kiss I gave. She was harmed as a young woman in a way I did not comprehend. I languished in my own dishonorable history of destroying young women's trusts. This time had to be special. I craved her body, but withheld. I ached for her touch, waiting with patience. She reciprocated my advances with a contrived kiss of her own, careful to retain control of a wrath deep within.

I stroked her, sensing the response within her shirt. I moved her hair and kissed her neck. She turned to face me. Her eyes penetrated my spirit. I observed lust in her gaze, a long withheld desire. She kissed my lips fondling my face with her hands. My body quivered, excited by the eager affection from this beauty. She did not express a love for me, but it mattered little. My demeanor cascaded into an insidious frenzy matching her hunger for satisfaction.

I had wanted this moment from the beginning and now I could quench my fire without reproach. I wanted this more than any other desire I experienced with another female. Mary exposed my innermost mania. "Touch me anywhere you want," I implored. "I am your palette. Paint our future." Mary unbuttoned my shirt and kissed my chest. An inferno consumed me leaving ashes of my former salacious behavior. No other woman could satisfy me from this moment.

Mary detached from me and disrobed to her underwear. She was shapelier than I imagined and my yearning ignited. I stood admiring her face, her body, her very existence. "Well, do you want me or not?" Shaken from my unexpected stupor, I removed my shirt, unhooked my belt and pants, stepping out of them. Mary's eyes widened as she scanned my body. I pulled her to me kissing her, exploring her with my mouth and freeing her from the constraints of her bra. She stroked my back as if testing a rose petal surface.

My impatience exceeded imagination. We removed the remaining raiment of modesty and shared each other's anatomies. I became aware I hadn't experienced making love with anyone, but now educated about the difference between sex and intimate love, I repeated, "I love you."

Mary smiled, "I love you, too." Her eyes shone as on a cloudless day when forgiveness becomes human. "I'm not just saying it because this is my first time. I'm thankful for you and I want to be with you." I held her close, kissed her, imagined our future. Her warmth penetrated my heart. No problems could sway our success as a couple. No person would divide us or ruin this passion. I knew an inner calmness as never before. An hour passed with nothing said. We rested intertwined and content. Mary slept peaceful after our shared time. I'm sure I dreamt but remembered little of it. We rose from the bed and showered. Desire for her produced another indication of the pleasure. I embraced her. She smiled at my predicament and moved her body to revive her craving. After a release of mutual tension, we finished our cleansing, turned off the shower, and toweled our bodies dry.

"Mary, I need to meet your family, to understand who they are, so I can know you." I was dressing. Looking at her I perceived a fear, unknown and unappreciated by me. Her eyes darkened. Her appearance stiffened. Had I stepped into a mental minefield? Had I detonated a charge destined to destroy what I had just discovered? *No*, I thought. *Don't venture there.* Aloud I backpedalled. "I'm sorry. I didn't mean to offend you."

She relaxed. "No, you haven't offended me. I just know if you meet my parents all of this will implode, this excitement will wither and die. I'm ready to meet your sane, normal family. And I want you to meet my mother and sister. Maybe even my brother. But can we forgo the introduction of my father until a later time?" I smiled, nodding an acceptance of her request without a perceptive why. With modesty restored, I completed my packing and we left for my car and her apartment. Our life altering journey began. Where it would take us would be far different than I ever imagined.

A question haunted me which I left unasked. What had her father done so egregious as to compel this beautiful woman to become so ugly with rage at the mere mention of his existence? How would this affect our relationship as we corralled the demons inside?

———∞———

"What did your dad do to earn your wrath?" We were driving toward Seattle in my car. Curiosity may kill the cat, but I chanced proverbial death with my question. I experienced a normal youth and a productive adolescence. Could her father be the ogre she implied?

"My father is a complicated person. I don't want to talk about him right now." Her composure tighten, her azure orbs deepened their color. I had begun to comprehend her moods and realized her sensitivity needed careful handling. I appreciated this, as well as a need for kindness from me, something I ignored with my previous feminine interactions. I nodded my acceptance.

The trip contained little conversation, my reluctance to offend and her reticence for exchange about families. *I love her*, I thought. *Her family can't be too abnormal. I'll enjoy meeting them.* My imagination conjured up a clan of good people, misunderstood and unappreciated. I sometimes didn't get along with my dad and questioned whether I would dislike her father as much as she appeared to hate him.

Mary slept as I drove. Awakening rested and relaxed prompted a smile from me. "Roger, I'm sorry about my father. We can meet him if you want. I'm sorry for my attitude earlier. I guess I should be quiet about what I think."

I smiled again. "Mary, I want to know what you're thinking. How am I to get to know you if you keep secrets?" The gas gauge indicated a need to stop. "Let's get some lunch and gas." We arrived at a truck stop frequented by college travelers as well as truckers. The food satisfied and refreshed our bodies. Mary remained quiet throughout the meal.

After eating, I smiled as sweet as the pie in the refrigerator near us without reciprocity. I reached across the table for her hand. She moved it to her lap.

"What's the matter?"

"Nothing; I was just thinking about the rest of the drive. If you want me to drive for a while I will." Her eyes were darker than usual. What bothered her? I plunged into a morass better left for others.

"Mary, are you mad at me?" She looked at me apparently irritated by my inquiry.

"If I'm mad at you, you'll know it."

"Well, something's bugging you. You look mad. It's why I asked. Is it about your family and not wanting to go home?"

She stood up from her seat and walked to the restroom area. I didn't pursue. This woman was an enigma, but I wanted nothing more than to understand who she was. Asking her anything seemed dangerous to our continuance as a couple. "Tread lightly," I whispered.

Mary returned; her countenance appeared calm. I ventured a query. "Do you want to skip going home and come to my house?" I expected nothing more than a simple response. "We can rest and go to Seattle tomorrow."

Dark clouds accumulated in her eyes. Her body tensed. "What are you saying? You don't want to meet my family?"

"No, if you want to continue to your house, we will. I do want to meet you sister and mother. We can have dinner and then go to my house in the morning. I'll stay in Seattle."

"Alright, let's go to my home, and you can stay there tonight in our guest room." Clouds dissipated almost as fast as they gathered. A bright smile shined bright as an unfettered sun. "We'll have dinner and they'll get to know you."

What just happened? I left the incident alone as an anomaly of the drive. "Sure, sounds fine. Do you want to listen to some music? I have some CDs in a case on the backseat." We walked arm in arm as though no divergence occurred. I must understand her intricacies, her complexity, and the elusive facets of her personality. So much to learn; so little time to do it.

"I have some CDs with me. Can we listen to them?"

"Sure, you don't need to ask."

At the car I opened her door for her. She smiled and then kissed me. "I love you." Her face radiated as a sunrise on a clear morning. She entered the car and I grinned like a silly child with a new toy. I sat in the driver's seat and responded, "I love you, too." We continued our trek across the state into an unknown future and unexpected misfortunes.

As the afternoon passed and her music tethered her emotions in a stable realm of calm, silence reigned. The snow covered mountains reflected the sun's radiance, warming the interior of the car and adding to the warmth of my heart. I looked at Mary, enthralled by her beauty. She looked at me with sunlight of her own beaming into my soul.

Leaving the mountain pass behind I continued through the small towns and into the larger cities on a forbidden trail of wonder about what impelled this woman. I longed for her touch and to share myself with her. I thought of the many young ladies I left behind in an emotional desert I created. Conquests with little sentiment now became a passage through rich fields of craving and passion for one person. Mary consummated my existence.

She enlivened as we started across Lake Washington via the I-90 floating bridge. But her smile faded with each rotation of the wheels. I asked, "Do you want to stop before we go to your home? We could go to Pike Market and get some flowers and wine as a peace offering." She giggled.

"A peace offering...good idea." The sun relit in her eyes.

"Okay, Pike Market; here we come."

For a Friday afternoon traffic seemed light driving through downtown Seattle. The baseball and football stadiums welcomed us as the Symplegades met the Argonauts. The Mariners began a dismal season again and the Sounders were struggling. *I need to take her to a game. I wonder if she is a sports fan.* The waterfront bustled with people. A ferry disgorged its contents adding to the foot and automobile traffic. I drove to the Pike Market parking garage.

Patrons and tourists swarmed the market eager to gain some of Seattle's fame. We mingled with the crowds searching for the best flowers and finest local vintages. I held Mary's hand as we wended our way from booth to booth. The aromas lifted our spirits from any previous doldrums. Mary sparkled throughout our quest. Negativity vanished.

We stopped to watch the fish toss at the Pike Fish Market. Mary sat on the nearby brass pig and I took her picture with my phone, sending a copy to my brother. He enjoyed the market. "Are we expected for dinner?" I asked.

"Why?" She responded. "Did you have something else in mind?"

"We could dine here at Maximillian's and then head to your place."

"Can we do it later? I want to see my sister." I smiled. Her mood remained light and bubbly.

"Okay, but sometime while we're home, let's eat there and celebrate." We moved to the flower shop across the arcade. I picked up a bunch of chrysanthemums and daisies. "Do you like these?" They accented the blue of her eyes and the yellow of her hair.

"Those are beautiful. Mom will enjoy them." She held them as I paid the vendor. "What will we be celebrating?" A wry smile coursed her face.

"I would like to celebrate our love and friendship. I want to share my life with you."

"Are we getting a little ahead of ourselves here? Are you asking me to marry you?" I blushed and then stammered.

"I…I…meant…I, well, I want to finish school and set up with my Dad in his business. You finish your schooling and in a couple of years we can make a decision."

"So you don't want to marry me? Or are you afraid of what might happen if I dump you and find some other hunk to hook up with."

"No, I love you and if you want to get married, we can as soon as we graduate." A warmth but not because of the air or a flush in my face. An anger rose and I wanted no part of it.

"Oh relax. I'm yanking your chain. We might want to go to grad school. You get an MBA and I'll get a Masters in my field. We could get married before we finish school. I have enough money and we can get part-time work."

We walked back to the wine shop and picked out a local Chablis and Merlot. As we returned to the car, I said little. I could see confusion in her eyes, so I stopped and turned to her. "Mary, we haven't known each other very long, but I am in love with you. I've never met anyone so smart and beautiful. You've captured me and I don't want to escape. When we get back to school, we should talk about our future. I like to plan things out and be sure what happens. If you want to get married, we can work it out and then let our families know. I'll apply for grad school and stay with you." My hands were occupied with packages, but I leaned in to her and kissed her magnetic ruby lips. "I love you."

Her eyes brightened and she returned the kiss. "I love you, too." She smiled and said, "I'm not ready to get married now and I know Mom would not want me to jump into it too soon. I think she regrets being married to Dad, although I think she loves him. He's good to her and hasn't strayed or anything. Let's forget about marriage for now and just get know each other and our families."

We entered the car and left for Magnolia. My angst amplified as I closed near to her family's home. I thought about what transpired at the Market. What would life with her be like? My mind delved beyond the obvious physical attraction to a layer foreign to my experiences. The brain is a complex organ which imagines the unimaginable, constructing strange scenarios never to be lived. I traveled this unfettered avenue experiencing nothing resembling reality.

The house sat above a cliff overlooking Puget Sound and Bainbridge Island. I hadn't any reason prior to meeting Mary to venture onto this magnificent part of Seattle. The two-story Georgian, built of white brick with a large portico, graced the tree lined street with an accolade not yet affiliated to the occupants. I admired the obvious financial success of Mary's father; her loathing of him restraining my judgment of him as a father and a man. We parked on the street sitting a moment to gather resolve for our incursion. Mary heaved a sigh and said, "Well, I know Mom will be happy to meet you. Ben and Dad can just warm up their charm and accept the idea I have a boyfriend."

"What about your little sister?"

"Vickie? She's going to love you. Well, not the way I love you. But she and I share most feelings, so I'm not worried about her liking you." Mary beamed as she spoke of her sister. I released any anxiety and steeled myself for the intrusion into this outwardly respectable family. She held my arm and the bouquet peace offering. I transported the wines boxed in their carrying case.

The door opened as we walked up the pathway and up the three steps to the porch. A woman bearing a similar countenance to Mary appeared first. I estimated her to be in her late forties, but she manifested a youthful glow when she saw her daughter. An understandable connection permeated the atmosphere. Mary introduced her, "Roger, I'd like you to meet my mother, Marion Johnson." We shook hands.

"I am very pleased to make your acquaintance." Another person burst through the doorway, a young twin of Mary. Her blonde tresses billowed as she bounced onto the scene.

"Hi, I'm Victoria." She announced with an uncommon boldness. "You must be Roger." She stuck her hand out for me to accept. I realized her confidence exceeded mine and what I perceived in Mary. "Mary, you certainly did capture a cute one."

"I'm very pleased to meet you, as well. I'm Roger Waite." Her hand continued clutching mine as a person unsure of the prize just won. She studied my face, smiled, and freed me from her grip.

"Come in, please." Marion stated. We entered the foyer. I observed the living area to the right and a dining area to my left. A central staircase led to a landing which split into twin staircases leading to the second story bedrooms and bathrooms, I assumed.

"These are for you, Mom. Roger calls them a peace offering." Mary glowed in the presence of her female family members. I held out the box of wines.

"I offer a local Chablis and a merlot as my gift for your hospitality." Vickie made a point of taking the box from me, touching my hand as we transferred the bestowal. I sensed an attentiveness not solicited. Her youthfulness belied any attraction from me.

Vickie disappeared through the dining room. Marion guided us after her. The room manifested a comfortable aura for eating, albeit formal. The oval table was set for six. Three red candles accented a simple but elegant centerpiece. Aromas attracted my body's hunger as we entered the kitchen. I smelled fresh bread and pastry. The room was well lit for cooking sumptuous meals. I anticipated a dinner to delight my gastric desires. Vickie placed the box on the counter near a double sink. The counter was tiled in granite framed in wood which matched the cupboard doors. I could smell a roast cooking in an oven. A salad was being prepped by the sink.

Marion placed the flowers on a central island which served as a chopping block and storage for utensils. She opened a cupboard in the island and fetched a vase to display our gift.

Mary spoke, "Is Ben going to be here?"

"He'll be here about six-thirty." Marion responded as she filled the vase with water. "Your father is on his way home as we speak." She arranged the flowers and placed them on a table in a dining area behind the kitchen. A counter separated the two areas and I noticed stools for seating.

Mary's countenance darkened at the mention of her father. Vickie noticed and gave her sister a hug. I heard her whisper something but couldn't decipher it. Marion then led us into an open area off the kitchen. This room contained a fireplace, sofa, chairs and tables, a large television and a stereo outfit built into shelving which also held an extensive library. I sat on the sofa with Mary close to me. She hugged me and smiled again. Her father's anticipated arrival no longer a concern. Victoria sat across from us and studied me as a person studies an experiment in a laboratory. Marion occupied a matching chair on the other side of a square table with a lamp on it.

"I'm very glad to be here with you. Mary has told me a little about your family, but I look forward to meeting the rest and getting to know you." The usual tension of first encounters abated as the conversation continued about school and how we met. Mary wrapped her arm in mine and cuddled closer to me. I sensed her calm and enjoyed the moment.

A door opened somewhere in the house and tension pulled on my arm. Mary's breathing increased. A man about fifty with dark blond hair and dark eyes entered the room. I disengaged from Mary and stood to introduce myself to her father.

"Mr. Johnson, I'm Roger Waite." He shook my offered hand and grunted.

"So you're the man corrupting my little girl." A wry smile crossed his face. I didn't understand the humor. He removed his coat, placed it on one of the stools and rejoined the group. "Have these people regaled you with our family story?" The relaxation evaporated as steam from a window. I sat with Mary.

"Well, we've been talking about how we met at school and what we've been doing when not studying for classes." The air chilled though heat flowed through the air ducts. I smiled a false sense of security. My conversations with Mary about her father left a void as to how to interact with the man.

"Mary is a wonderful young lady. I love her very much, so be careful with her." Marion stood and signaled to the girls who left for the kitchen with her. I figured a grilling of my intentions was to follow. "What do you intend to do with your life after graduation?"

"My father has a real estate business in Wendlesburg, where I live, and I plan on going into business with him as an agent. He's been somewhat successful as a broker."

"Do you expect to marry my daughter or just break her heart like most of us guys like to do?"

"She and I haven't talked much about it." *Odd comment.*

"But you have talked about it." He glared at me. I decided honesty might not be the best option at this point.

"Well, we haven't gotten to know each other as much as I want before deciding to broach the question of matrimony." I adjusted my seating.

"So the one thing she's good for to you is sex. I want the truth about you two."

"Sir, that's between me and Mary."

"I suppose if she gets pregnant you'll just abandon her to us and disappear."

My defenses rose. "If she gets pregnant, we'll be married." Mary was not to be a pawn in this invidious game of chess. "She and I'll finish school. After graduation I'll decide to pursue an MBA or go to work."

He stood, glared at me, and left the room. I sat wondering how I would ever again want to have a conversation with him.

Victoria

Roger and Mary arrived. I had bounded out the door wanting to wrap myself around my sister. I hadn't seen her for months and wanted to catch up on secrets. Astonished by the sight of her new acquaintance, I halted. "Hi, I'm Victoria. You must be Roger." I offered my hand for him to accept. As I squeezed his hand I said, "Mary, you captured a cute one." I snickered and released my catch after studying him.

Mom led us into the house. I caught up to Mary and wrapped my arm in hers. I whispered to her. "He's cute. If you don't want him, can I have him?"

"Very funny," she responded. She then handed a bundle of flowers to Mom. They smelled as sweet and alluring as my sister. Roger presented wine which I took and then disappeared into the kitchen. I thought about the boys at school and wondered if I would ever have a boyfriend I liked as much as Mary seemed to like Roger.

As my family caught up with me, I watched the intruder with interest. I knew little of the relationship developing between my sister and this man;

I would glean the truth out of her as soon as we could be alone. My own boy-girl experience eluded me by personal choice. I wanted to understand boys but had little interest in the juvenile behavior they exhibited around me. Several asked me out. I engaged in a short disappointing interaction, less interested in the romantic pursuit and stuck with my female friends. I knew my body attracted attention and I had been told more often than desired how pretty I was. Why were these young studs so unappealing? Now Mary came home with a different sort and my curiosity peaked.

"Is Ben going to be here?" I heard my sister ask. I listened to my mother's response. My defense mode rose when Mom mentioned my father. I observed Mary for any telltale signs, holding her as they manifested. I whispered in her ear. "Mary, I love you. Dad can't hurt you anymore. Roger will keep you safe." Her building gloom dispelled. After Mom arranged the bouquet, we sat in the family room. I watched as Mary and Roger fused while sitting on the couch. Roger's face glowed as he relaxed. The very closeness of a handsome person raised my wonderment. His feelings for my sister seemed genuine, and therefore, I accepted him and loved him for it.

Enter the dragon to dispel any particle of calm. Father returned. I watched Mary tense. Roger stood and introduced himself. Father grunted something about corrupting Mary. I didn't get the joke, or maybe one didn't exist. I relocated to Mary's side. Roger defended his position with ability but was outwitted. Mom stood up and we recognized the cue to follow. The kitchen shielded the grilling I knew commenced upon our departing. Why must Daddy always assume the worst in someone? His precious reputation was not threatened at all.

"Mary, I think your friend is nice." I smiled as I spoke. "I sure hope Dad doesn't scare him off." Mary hugged me.

"He's pretty strong willed. I think he can handle Dad. Come on; let's get my luggage up to my room. Roger's spending the night in the guest room." I followed her into the hall. Before picking up any bags, I delayed a moment, and then hugged her.

"I am so happy for you. I wish I trusted a guy enough to date, but I don't and so I avoid them." I apprehended two of the smaller cases and started up the stairs.

As Mary lugged her large bag up the stairs she responded. "Hey, there are plenty of guys who might want to go out with you. Has Dad left you alone since I went back to school?" I nodded in the affirmative.

"Have you and Roger…uh…you know…," My face heated up for asking the question.

"You're funny, sis. I'm not one to kiss and tell." The grin coursing her chin and the glint in her eyes belied her answer.

"Ok, I won't ask you again, but tell me when you want." We entered her room and placed her gear on the bed. I sat next to the bags and asked, "What's he like?"

"Well, he's not anything like Dad. He's kind and thoughtful. He's tender and attentive, unlike Daddy in every way." The warmth of her words endeared him to me. I wanted what she found. I didn't understand the complexities, but I experienced the physical demands of adolescence. No natural incentive pushed me to experiment.

"Then I like him already." I stood and studied Mary's posture. She was relaxed. She unpacked clothing not returning to school; I helped her. We remained quiet for several minutes. She stopped, stared, and then turned to me.

"We talked about marriage on the way here." The announcement shocked me. I didn't realize how fast a relationship could develop. Was Mary rushing into this? Or did she desire something not experienced by us as a family?

"Who brought it up?"

"I did, but just to see how he'd react." Mary grinned. "Boy was he surprised."

"Do you want to marry him?"

"He's the one guy I've dated at school, but I don't want to be a lonely old lady." She frowned and continued. "He has a reputation. I guess it was one of the reasons I wanted to meet him. I was curious about what a man would do to get me into bed. I wanted to be touched without fear."

"What happened?"

"He treated me with respect and kindness. He told me about his past exploits with other girls and how he wanted more from me than shallow sex."

"So you haven't done it yet?"

"You promised you wouldn't ask." I blanched.

"It's ok." We laughed. "I think he was so worried about how I'd react to any sexual overture, nothing was happening. To be as blunt, I seduced him. So yes, we've done it."

My body reacted, puberty betraying me. "What's it like?" My blush must have shown since Mary laughed again.

"Do you want all the sordid details or just a recap of the basics?"

"No, don't tell me anything." I blushed again. "Someday my turn will come and then we can tell."

We finished and rejoined the clash of personalities downstairs. This man Mary seduced stirred in me a pot of unknown contents. Who was he that I might want to explore?

5
CHAPTER

Roger

Mary and Victoria descended the stairs with Cheshire grins on their twin expressions. Like Daniel in the lions' den, I had retreated to find a hideaway in the foyer and to retrieve my bag. "Mary, where did you go?" The conversation with her father still haunted me.

"I'm sorry, Roger. We took my luggage to my room." They laughed. I thought I noticed a glint in Victoria's eyes of knowing something I shouldn't. "Follow me. I'll show you to your room."

As I began my hike Victoria reached for my bag. "May I carry this for you?" She took it from me before I could speak. We ascended the stairs; had I intruded on a secret nest of spies about to discover the answer to the question: 'Who's Afraid of Virginia Woolf?'

"You have a nice house," I said to dispel the thickness of the air surrounding me. They were giddy to be together again. Nothing about closeness with a sibling occurred in my history. My brother, sister and I talked at regular intervals, but I saw in these two a camaraderie shared by few. Victoria seemed more intelligent than any thirteen-year-old I knew. My neighborhood contained some and I and my brother were not far removed from the age. But this girl was not what I remembered girls being like at Wendlesburg Middle School. My interaction with girls at college did not delve into their psyche; explore the physical and not the intellectual. Meeting Mary modified my course of action and now another female stirred an intrigue of who she was as a person. My love of Mary grew as I watched her interact with her sister. I smiled as we entered my haven for the night.

"The house is nice, yes, but who is in the house is more important." Victoria placed my bag on the bed and sat beside it. Mary turned to me and hugged me like a vise. "Do you like my little sister?" she whispered.

"If she's anything like you, I'll enjoy getting to know her." Mary released me from her grasp and sat with Victoria. Except for the difference in age a person would not distinguish between them at first glance. Mary exuded a security I hadn't seen before. Her sister appeared to provide a shelter from the family storm which I began to suspect aggravated much of their lives. I understood little of the dynamics of Mary's history as I sat in a chair and watched these playful sisters tease each other. We were interrupted by a shout from below. Ben had returned home. I was anxious to meet the last of the Johnson clan and build knowledge of the family I was invading for the sake of relating to a woman who confounded my life. Peace and bewilderment at the same moment. I was not about to trade it for any other existence.

We returned to the kitchen. Ben sat on a stool and spoke of the day he had at work. Technology was changing with lightning speed, and he was in the thick of it. I gleaned some of what he said but understood little. He looked away from his mother, then stood and came forward to shake my hand. "You must be the intrepid soul who dares enter the lair of the lioness. I'm Ben, Mary's older brother."

"Roger Waite. It's a pleasure to meet you." We sized each other up for a moment and then I continued, "I understand you're a computer genius."

"You've been misinformed by my little sister. I do I.T. work, and enjoy it. What are you studying besides my sister?"

Odd question. "I'm studying business. My father's a real estate broker in Wendlesburg. I plan on working with him when I graduate." The conversation lagged for lack of interesting fodder.

Ben changed subjects, looking toward his mother. "What's for dinner? A time honored Johnson meal to celebrate?" I decided I could like Ben. He was nothing like his father and exuded an aura dissimilar to the rest of the family. I couldn't put my finger on it, but he was different; like two peas from the same pod but not shaped or colored alike. His blond locks and the shape of his face reflected familial traits, but his persona had a casual quality. Tension in the house eluded him.

"We are having roast beef and vegetables with potatoes au gratin and apple pie for dessert. Mr. Waite has brought wine which you can open, please."

"Uh, Roger, call me Roger. My father is Mr. Waite." An uncomfortable grimaced crossed my face.

"Yes. Ok, Roger then." Marion appeared tense.

"Where is Mr. Johnson?" Immediate regret for asking shot from me. The barometric pressure signaled a severe storm approaching.

"Perhaps my father's in his den escaping the compelling conversation here in the kitchen." Ben's comment cleared the air. *What precipitated this family anxiety for a father?* My thoughts must have reflected from my face as Victoria came up to me and smiled.

"Father is not a crowd person. He likes to have his house be a certain way. You're an intrusion. He'll have to adjust to having you around," Victoria explained as she hooked on to my left arm. Mary locked onto my other arm and the girls escorted me into the family room. We sat on the couch as close as sardines. "Are you going to marry my sister?" I furrowed my brow, looking first at Victoria, then at Mary, and again at Victoria.

"I...guess...I...that's something for Mary and me to decide." I looked at Mary quizzically realizing she and Victoria kept no secrets.

Mary said, "Keep it a secret, little one. We've only just begun investigating how we feel about each other."

"But you have talked about it. You said so." I detected a disappointment in Victoria.

"What are you conspirators up to now?" Ben entered the room and sat across from us.

"We're not up to any conspiracy." Victoria defended. "We are three amigos in search of a quest." Victoria held my arm closer, seeming to protect her new found prize.

"I'm glad Mary and you hooked up. She needed to find someone." Ben's comment surprised me. "She's a wonderful person who's suffered indignities no one should suffer." My brow wrinkled.

Mary glared. "Ben, don't talk like that. I haven't told him everything about me, yet. You're scaring him."

"I'm not scared. What haven't you told me?" Curious as to what he meant I looked at him as if the next chapter should be told.

"I'm sorry." Ben stood. "Look, I'll leave you guys alone. Vickie, come on. Let them alone for now." Victoria resisted vacating the area but then stood and followed her brother into the kitchen.

"Ben means well. I haven't explained as much about my father as you should know." Mary sat closer. "I'll explain after we leave tomorrow." I nodded.

"I should call my parents and let them know where I am." I kissed her and then rose. Walking down another hallway to the foyer, I avoided the kitchen, ascended the stairs to my room and connected with my family.

What more needed explaining? Garrett was cold; I observed the lack of interaction. The question remained. How had it damaged Mary? And could I cope?

As the phone rang, I thought about these two females who sought my attention in similar and different ways. My thoughts were interrupted by my mother, Nancy Waite. "Hi, Mom," I said. "I'm in Seattle at Mary's parents." I listened to the questions of when I would be home and what her family was like. I satisfied my mother with my responses and we ended the call.

Returning to the downstairs I heard the invitation for dinner and entered the dining room. I was seated at the end of the table with Mary to my left and Victoria to my right. I had a direct line of sight to Garrett and his gaze on me. *Is he checking my manners?* I decided to pay attention to the other family members, close attention to Mary when the conversation warranted. Victoria whispered to me off and on about school and my meeting Mary. Dinner progressed with enthusiasm. *Garrett isn't much of a conversationalist. He looks like he wants to be somewhere else. He pays no attention to any of the discussions.*

"Roger, I understand you called your parents." I was jerked back to attending to the people around me. "I'm sure we would like to meet them this weekend, if possible." Garrett was talking to me. I was surprised by the content of his words.

"Ah, sure. I'll see what we can arrange." I didn't want to have him meet my family and judge my worthiness. "Did you want to meet here or in Wendlesburg?" *He'll decide about me if we meet at my house, and it won't be good.*

"Call us when you're at your parents and let us know what you have planned. We'll accommodate your family for you." *Why's he being nice? Did I form an incorrect judgment from what Mary said about him? Or maybe he's changed.*

"I'll do that." I looked at Marion and said, "This meal is delicious. My Mom is a great cook, too. I'm quite satisfied." Victoria stood and collected dishes to take to the kitchen, "Here, let me help." I began bussing the table as well. I spied a smile on Victoria's face. Her blue eyes provoked a memory of my first encounter with Mary. Were they alike in personality as in physical appearance?

⸻⧈⸻

In the family room Mary and I sat alone evaded by family members. Vickie made an excuse for me to leave the kitchen. "Mary, your sister is very sweet. I guess she thought we needed some alone time. What did she whisper to you?" I put my arm around her.

"She said you wouldn't be unfaithful to me like the guy in the movie."

I leaned in close and kissed her mouth. "I love you. I could never want another woman in my life." I stood up. "Let's go upstairs and get some sleep." Mary nodded and turned off the television. We walked hand in hand to our rooms. I kissed her again and opened her door. "Good night, my love." She disappeared into the room. I shut the door and moved on to my sanctuary. All remained quiet as I prepared for sleep. I needed the bathroom and left my room to brush my teeth and complete other chores. Finished, I heard a noise in the hall and peeked out to see Victoria enter her sister's bedroom. I waited a moment and then left for the guest room.

Victoria

"Mary, can I talk with you?" Curiosity demanded details. Her experience revealed a new and wonderful part of her. Reconciling her past with today bewildered me.

Mary smiled and waved me to her bed. I sat at the foot and waited for her to finish preparing for sleep. "Whatcha want, baby sister?" She unbuttoned her blouse and removed it. I imagined developing the way she had. *She's so pretty.* I thought, but then I asked her.

"What's it like?" Mary stopped for a moment. "You know, having a person who's not family love you so much." Mary slid off her pants and considered my question while standing in her underwear. I admired her shape and again hoped to be like her.

"I don't know. I guess it's like morning after a great night of sleep. I've awakened from a nightmare and found he's real. He came into my dream and led me away from a monstrous realism. Now I live in the dream and I don't want to awaken." She removed her underwear and put on pajamas.

"But isn't a dream, just a dream? Won't you wake and return to what's real?" I stood and hugged Mary. I was now almost as tall as her. "Stay in the dream." I whispered.

"Vickie, all of life might be a dream and we can't control what our minds create. We have to accept the ugliness we invent and the ugliness which happens to us. There's no more past for me. You're my little angel and I know you'll stay with me for all time. Now let's get some sleep. I'm tired." I left her room and walked toward my room. As I passed where Roger slept, I paused and wondered. *Who are you and why is my sister in love with you? Will I love someone like you, too?* Another tingle snaked through my body. In my room I climbed into bed anxious for my own dream.

6

CHAPTER

Roger

Morning is a wonderful time. Sleep had been blissful and I wanted to see Mary. We had another short drive, a couple of hours, to arrive at my home and introduce this amazing woman to my parents and siblings. I needed a shower and grabbed a towel and my travel case. Habit is a funny part of us. I almost forgot where I was, but I robed myself before leaving the room. In the hall I saw Victoria enter the bathroom. *I hope she hurries.*

I leaned against the wall and imagined the life I opted to embrace. I looked at my wrist and realized my watch was still on the desk in the guest room. As I straightened up with a jerk, Mary opened her door, smiled, beckoning with a wriggling finger. I returned the smile and headed for her.

"Good morning, beautiful." She shushed me and pulled me into her room. Her lips pressed mine with a passion I wanted more than ever.

"Make love to me right now." She whispered. "I want you to touch me, caress my body, now, in my room."

"What's the urgency? We can wait until we are away from here." I countered. "I'm sure your parents wouldn't be happy, if they caught us."

"I need it now to prove to myself what my father did is not going to hurt me anymore."

My brow creased as I said, "Listen, if we were married we wouldn't have sneak around. We could have sex and no one would question it. It wouldn't be good for you if your father caught us. And what about your little sister? It's not best for her to think you might be doing something immoral." The air cooled, a dramatic shift in atmosphere. Mary's eyes darkened and I doubted my decision. I hugged her and reminded her of my love, but her body tensed.

Victoria

Where is he going? Leaving the bathroom I spied Roger enter Mary's room. Sneaking near her door I put my ear to it trying to discover the results of this morning tryst. I feared betraying my sister and tiptoed away and entered my own room. What explorations did they pursue? A tingle grew provoking my inner desire.

I dressed and left for the kitchen to see if anybody else was up. Mom was fixing breakfast. "Good morning, Mom."

She turned and smiled. "Good morning." She continued to mix pancake batter. "Would you set the table, please?"

I opened the drawer containing utensils and grabbed enough for all of the people in the house. I whistled as I set the places.

"You're in a good mood today." Mom smiled as she spoke.

"I'm glad Mary is home and Roger seems like a very nice guy. I haven't seen her this happy in a long time."

"I agree." Mom responded. We continued our chores in silence. Ben soon entered the room. He asked Mom. "Has Dad left for work, yet?" He sat down in his usual seat.

"No, he's upstairs getting dressed. Why?" Mom answered.

"Just wondered. Are Mary and Roger up?"

I chimed in, "I saw him when I went to the bathroom. He was going into the guest room." No reason to betray their morning tête-à-tête. I changed the subject. "Do you think they want to get married?"

Mom stopped her preparations and turned to me. "I think it's a little early in their relationship. If they want to, they'll let us know."

"I like him. Mary's happy now and I don't want it to go away." I sat next to Ben smiled and then said. "Are you glad she's happy?"

"Alright, munchkin, what are you up to? You're acting like you have a secret and can't wait to say something."

I slugged Ben's arm, not hard, but enough to show contempt. He just smiled and returned the favor. No pain from his retaliation.

"You two stop right now." Mom chided.

"Ben, what's it like to be loved by someone else? You know; somebody other than family."

"It's an odd question for a little girl."

"I'm not a little girl, or haven't you noticed." I pouted.

"I'm not interested in leering at my little sister, but yes, you're getting older and I'm sure you're finding out stuff about guys. Just remember they want one thing from you."

Mom interrupted our conversation. "Please, stop before your father hears. You know he doesn't want lewd language in our house."

"Well, I don't think falling is love is lewd and I want know what happens when two people meet and fall in love. You and Dad are already married so Ben is the one other choice I have right now."

Ben answered, "I'll let you know when it happens to me. But I'll bet Mary is a better source than I am."

"We've talked a little. But she is almost always with Roger."

A noise in the hall interrupted our discussion. Fearing the worst, silent befell the kitchen. Roger sauntered in exclaiming, "Good morning, everyone."

We responded in tandem, "Good morning."

Mom asked. "Did you sleep well?"

"Yes, the room is very comfortable and I smell something enticing."

The breakfast preparation continued in silence for the next few moments. Roger sat next to me, brushing my arm as he sat. I blushed, hoping no one saw. "Is Mary coming soon?"

"I just checked on her and she's about ready." Roger said. Dad then entered the room. Silence befell once more.

Without speaking to anyone he poured a mug of coffee which, earlier in the morning, percolated in the automated coffee maker. He stared at Ben and Roger, ignoring me. Then he spoke, "Ben, I want to meet with you and Mother about your plans after your graduation." Although Ben was two years older than Mary, he continued schooling to achieve a Master's in Integrated Technological Communications and Data Storage and Retrieval. I didn't understand much of what he studied, but he interned at a company in Seattle while studying and was going to be employed full time with the company after school finished. Dad perhaps wanted him to move out as soon as possible. They didn't get along, avoiding contact. I just wanted him happy.

"Sure, I'll be here the rest of the day." He looked uneasy, edgy. He stood and helped Mom serve the bacon and pancakes. I poured juice for each place setting. We all sat down to eat.

"Is Mary joining us?" Dad probed. "Or is she hiding as usual?" His barb cooled the air.

"I'm right here, Father." She entered; eyes blackened by a suppressed rage I recognized from previous venomous pronouncements by our male parent. She glared at him from behind.

To quell the storm, I stood and went to her, held her arm, and guided her to the seat next to Roger and me. "You look fantastic, today." My input intended to dispel any aggressions worked well enough. Her demeanor calmed as she sat down and with a deliberate move, leaned into Roger kissing him with passion.

"Where did you sleep last night?" Father queried.

"In my room, whether it's any business of yours. Mary anticipated his next comment. By the way I was alone."

"Good" was all she got in return.

I looked at Roger, whose eyes widened at the argument, but he sat very still. He ate little of his breakfast.

"Garrett, you can trust these young people to be…"

"Stay out of it, Marion," he interrupted. An icy air muddled our meal.

———

Mary's happy. I love the idea he makes her feel good. I think I'll love him, too. Another brother is good, I guess. I watched the packing proceed and anticipated the emptiness of the house with their departure. I enjoyed having them home, our family whole and healthy. Why couldn't it be this way always? "When are you coming back?" I uttered.

Mary looked up from her task, "Don't miss me. We'll be back soon." Roger smiled and I blushed for asking. I knew they had their own things to do, but I wanted to be near the man who pleased my sister. I wanted to experience what she had, even if it was a vicarious experience. He had, in such a short period of time, become important to me, a man who was not my father or brother, but was someone who exuded a caring about which I had little understanding.

"Can I help carry anything?" Mary held out her overnight case. With glee in my heart I grabbed it, feeling wanted. I looked at Roger as he picked up Mary's other suitcase, as well as his own. *Would Dad or Ben be so obliging? He's perfect. None of the boys at school are nice like this.* "I look forward to your return." We sauntered into the hallway, Mary leading the intrepid trio. I followed, while Roger brought up the rear. Downstairs in the foyer, we said our goodbyes. I gave Mary a tight hug. "He's wonderful." I spoke in a muted voice to keep my words for my sister. Mary then hugged Ben and Mom, while Roger shook Dad's hand and thanked everyone for their hospitality. Mary opened the front door, picking up her bags so she could avoid a compulsory farewell from Dad. Ben and Roger exchanged handshakes, and then Mom offered her hand. Roger took it with a smile. My turn came, but I wasn't accepting only a hand. When he looked at me with his pale blue eyes, I ignored his hand and embraced him. "I love you for loving her." His muscled body, so different from Ben's or Dad's, I released him before I embarrassed myself for my familiarity.

7
CHAPTER

Roger

I've got to remember I am not marrying her family. I had sat stunned by the exchange between Mary's parents. *Is she like them?* I had excused myself from the table explaining the need to pack up so I could continue on home to Wendlesburg. I imagined holes burned in my back as I left the room. In the guest room I had hesitated by my suitcase. I loved Mary, but doubts about a relationship with her cracked any resolve to be her partner in such dysfunction. *Am I wrong about her?* I completed my task of packing as the door to my room opened and Mary entered.

"I am so sorry for what you witnessed down stairs." Tears cascaded down her face smearing her mascara. She closed the door. "You now have an idea of what goes on here. My father is not a nice person. You represent a threat to him. One of the reasons I wanted to have sex with you this morning was to shatter any illusions of control he might exhibit over me."

As my own eyes dampened, I reached for her and held her to my chest and whispered, "No more monstrous behavior." I released my grip and placed my hands on her cheeks and kissed her. "I am so sorry you have had to endure such irresponsible, vile behavior. I will not leave you alone with your father ever again." I smiled and said, "I love you even more now than before."

"Let's leave right now. I don't want to stay here any longer." The pleading look in her eyes contradicted the fear in her heart.

"Of course, we can."

"Thank you for loving me." She kissed me again. "Let's get my things and leave."

"What about your family, Ben and Vickie, your mother? I know we talked about going to Wendlesburg, but are they expecting you to stay here with them?" My emotional desire for her welled up within me, thinking about being alone with her far longer than anticipated.

"They'll understand. We can return in a couple of days and then return to school. At your home satisfy the desire for me you're exhibiting." I blushed. She noticed my arousal. "I want you, too." She mewed. I picked up my suitcase and we left for her room and the remnants of her life. *What an enigma!*

Vickie was waiting outside the door when we opened it. "Don't leave. I haven't gotten to know you."

"We'll be back in a couple of days." Mary answered. She dragged me down the hall to her bedroom. Vickie trailed behind like a kicked dog. We entered the room but the door remained open. Vickie stood in the doorway watching Mary pack.

<hr />

We drove a couple blocks before exchanging any conversation. Mary spoke. "Wow, am I glad to be out of there." I nodded; glad to be alone with her again.

"I hope my family comes across as congenial to you. My Dad is nothing like yours. Mom is going to adore you. My sister and brother, well, they just have to accept you." We continued on in silence. As we approached Wendlesburg, the carefree mood in the car evaporated like morning dew. An anxiety appeared on Mary with each mile we migrated. I watched her breathing shallow and hasten. She seemed to be fighting a mental unease I didn't understand.

"I need to stop somewhere and go to the bathroom." I knew of a rest stop a few miles onward.

"We can stop just ahead. Are you okay?" My apprehension must have been overt. Mary held out a hand to my leg placing it without moving it.

"I just need some time to compose myself. I know your family isn't like mine, but this is hard for me." *I put up with your family, especially your father. My family is kind. What's the problem?*

"There's a rest stop about five miles from here. We'll stop and recuperate. I could use a bathroom, too."

"Can we stop at a restaurant? I want to sit awhile and talk about what to expect." *What to expect? Are you kidding me? I stepped into your morass without much warning.*

"Sure, there's a Denny's in Tacoma on Sixth. We can stop there." The traffic thickened with each additional mile. Her disquiet diminished even as the highway bulged with more automobiles and my own anger rose. *This highway interchange project has not solved the problem. Where are these cars going? I'll be happy to see how the new roads alleviate congestion.* "Have you been to Wendlesburg before?" I asked to break the boredom of stop and go traffic. It seemed most everyone wanted to leave the highway at my exit. *Damn construction.*

"I went there once for a basketball game. We were in the state playoffs against your team. As I remember it, your team beat ours pretty badly. But I'm not much of a sports fan. I just wanted to get away from home for a while, and it seemed a good way to do it." Mary twitched as if remembering an unpleasant memory.

"Hmm! I remember a playoff game about six years ago. So you and I were at the same game and I missed an opportunity to meet you. I wish I had met you then. Maybe College would have been less adventurous and more fulfilling."

"From what I've learned about you, fulfillment of your lurid satisfaction was an adventure." She smiled and continued, "I hope I don't end up as just another adventure." I realized her mood softened and warmth returned.

"Very funny, but as an adventure it had better be life long and fulfilling." I leaned over to kiss her but a horn honked behind me. The slow traffic moved toward the exit for my journey to a future I perceived as good but knew not where it would take me. I returned to the task of maneuvering my car.

She responded to my romance. "Later, my horny little imp. I want to get some coffee and learn all about Wendlesburg. Then I will be ready to assail the Palace of Waite." I dared not question the change in atmosphere for a dearth of understanding kept her moods in a murky part of my brain. We arrived at the destined booth and ordered refreshment. Our conversation lagged for lack of a starting point. I held out a hand and she accepted.

"What can I tell you which will supply courage for this coming assault on my palace?" I grinned expecting a retort as wily as I mine had been. I was not disappointed.

"As a person of such discernment as you have purported to be, you can be assured I have no intention of ransacking your fortress for anything other than the treasures of your history and my future." Her face exuded cordiality, an approachability not exhibited in Magnolia; a passion for life I had failed to discern prior to this. Did my desire to embrace a future with her burst all fears of emotional distraught displayed by her? Or does love truly conquer all?

—⊗⊗⊗—

We arrived at my parents' house in Wendlesburg with settled minds and refreshed bodies. The excursion into Tacoma did its job. Mary remained unperturbed about meeting Walker and Nancy Waite. I parked the car in the driveway behind my mother's car. Not seeing my father's Lexus, I presuming he was showing property, a customary Saturday event. I started to exit my car, but Mary hesitating saying, "Do you think they'll like me?" I turned to her and smiled.

"They're going to love you." Touching her shoulder to reassure her, I cocked my head, and kissed her lips. "If they don't, I'll just have to set them straight about you."

"Okay, then, let's get this over with." We left our luggage in the car, but before we could get to the front door, Mom came out to greet us.

"Mother, I am pleased to introduce you to Mary Johnson. Mary, this is Nancy Waite, my mother." Mary extended her hand, but Mom embraced her. Mary looked startled, but relaxed as the hug concluded.

"Thank you for coming to visit us," Mom said. "Welcome to our house." She turned to me. "Roger, I'll take care of Mary, while you get your things." I hesitated, but Mary nodded and wrinkled her brow like all was well. I returned to the car as they disappeared into the house.

I hope nothing happens before I get in there. I retrieved our bags and hurried in to find out if the environment remained calm. My older sister, Peggy, and her boyfriend arrived as I approached the house. I glanced at them and hiked my head acknowledging them and then entered. I placed the bags near the stairs to the second floor. We were all standing in the foyer, where Billy had latched onto Mary like a new found sister. Her demeanor remained calm. His sophomoric conversation with her contained questions about our relationship and his obtaining another sister, which he thought was a benefit to him.

"Hey little Brother let her get acquainted first."

"It's okay," Mary responded. "It's nice to have an enthusiastic reception." I thought about the day with her family and realized this was a contrast Mary enjoyed. I relaxed. Peggy and Hiram crossed the threshold hand in hand to enlarge the party and crowd the room.

"Come on, everyone, let's go into the living room and sit down. I'll get some refreshments. Roger, you stay with Mary. Bill, you come with me." I was grateful Mom sensed his intrusion might be challenging Mary's emotions. But all remained sublime as we moved to our right past the stairs to the warmth of the living room. I introduced Mary to my sister and her friend. She shook hands with each and we sat, four people not sure of what was to commence.

Peggy began, "So my brother at last has been corralled and his lascivious life of grime has come to an end." My mouth dropped at this, but Mary caught on.

"I believe he found the one person at school who is not enrapt by his charming nature as much as he is ensnared by a conniving wench whose charms are much more revealing and provocative." Peggy stared for a moment and then burst out laughing.

"Well, it's about time someone smarter than my brother outwitted him. Roger, she's adorable. You had better hang on to her or I'm going to hunt you down and castrate you."

"Ouch," Directing my comment to Mary, "I guess it means we are stuck with each other."

She grinned. "Oh, you better know it." We all laughed at this. Hiram had dated Peggy long enough to comprehend my sister's ability to gauge a situation and interject humor in a subtle manner. He sat in silence watching the banter between these beautiful women who sought no competition for attention.

"So, Hiram," Attempting to gain a foothold on the conversation before I became a casualty of witticisms in which I fared poorly. "How's the new house coming along?"

"Fine, I just finished with the upstairs master bedroom. Peggy has everything she wants in the way of colors and fixtures. The master bath is next on the list. We have to finalize the features for it."

Peggy interrupted to update Mary. "We're getting married in three months and want to have a place to live. Since we both have our own money and his parents and mine are helping with the initial financing, Dad found a wonderful fixer-upper and Hiram and I are remodeling it." Peggy menaced me with a look and continued, "And you can help as soon as school ends next month." *Sure, it's what I intended for my summer project.*

"You know I'm not good with tools." My gaze moved from Mary to Peggy and I smiled.

"You're such a liar. He's very good with tools and even helped us with the kitchen this last winter when he was home." Mary looked perplexed. I figured she did not grasp the nuances of our family, since her family seemed dysfunctional to me.

"Alright, I'll see what I can do. Can Mary and I see what you have done so far?"

"I would love to show Mary our house." Peggy gleamed.

"Are you two living together, already?" Mary asked. The question constructed an awkward silence which seemed interminably long but lasted only a second or two.

"We're living at the house as we refinish it. My parents weren't pleased with the idea, but they're accepting it since we're close to getting married."

"My parents are acceptant as well." Hiram said. "Their biggest challenge was accepting a Christian instead of a Jewish wife. But it's all behind us now." Mary took all of this in and I thought she might be thinking about how her parents would accept our living in sin.

Mother entered with Billy in tow. They carried trays of drinks and cookies and cakes. My mother was a fabulous cook who enjoyed sharing her skills in the kitchen with guests. She placed her tray on a sideboard, while Bill put his tray of drinks on the coffee table in front of the sofa. I stood and asked if anyone wanted coffee or tea, and dispersed each requested drink. Mom picked up plates of cookies and petit fours, delivering them to each person. Silence won the moment as we enjoyed the food.

Victoria

"Mom, do you think Roger loves Mary. I mean, does he really like her and want to be with her?" I missed my sister even though only two hours had elapsed from their departure. "I want her happy." I sat in the kitchen watching my mother clean up from the breakfast fiasco.

"Here, put these away." She handed me some of the washed dishes which did not fit the dishwasher. I did as she asked. "Mary and Roger seem very happy together." Mom handed me another large bowl. "You mustn't worry about her because he's going to take good care of her. She needs a strong male who will give her what she wants but can influence her moods."

I heard enough. "She's not crazy, you know." Mom dwelt in a fantasy land of my father's creation. I believed they shared some kind of love. I just didn't want any part of it. Mary's experience with Dad created aloofness for any male companionship. "I'm going to my room to read." I left before any response included more time with my mother.

I sat on my bed after locking my door to keep out unwanted intrusions from family members. Ben and Mary were the two people I trusted, but Mary now had another person in which to confide, a man who enjoyed her body as well as her mind. *I wonder what it's like to be with a man.* I explored my curiosity.

A sense of satisfaction left a hollow in my mind about the reality of romance. What I didn't see at home I could watch on television and in movies. But nothing I observed taught me the intricacies of the physical aspects of love. *Mary, you have to tell me what it's like. I want to understand. I want someone so different from Dad, but I'm scared.* I changed my clothes and left my room. When I saw Mom, I informed her I was going to a friend's house. I had a couple of girlfriends, but I didn't confide in them as much as they seemed to confide in me. One friend, Andrea Collins, flirted with boys, and the rumor she was intimate with a high school sophomore intrigued me. She never told us about it, but when confronted, she did not deny it. I wanted to ask, not to be nosy, but to learn; so I left the subject unmentioned. As I headed to her house four blocks away from mine, I thought maybe today I would screw up enough courage to become an educated woman.

Approaching her house, after a leisurely walk planning my strategy, my breathing increased and became shallow. *Anxiety? Why? I've got to calm down.* I walked up to her front door and knocked. Her mother answered the door. "Hello, Mrs. Collins. Is Andrea home?"

"I think she's upstairs. Let me find out." She left me standing on the outside of the house. I fidgeted, looking around like a guilty criminal. *Maybe she's not home.* Mrs. Collins returned and opened the screen for me to enter. "She's upstairs. Please, go on up." I thanked her and ascended to the second floor bedroom.

"Hi, Andi, what's up?" I entered her room addressing her by her school nickname. We were friends who knew each other but shared little about who we were. I wanted to learn about her secret affair or affairs with boys. I knew nothing but cared much about what they wanted and how to get them to do what I wanted. Andrea would be my tutor, although not yet hired. What could I offer her which could entice her to help me learn?

"Hi, Vickie. What's up with you?" She was sitting at her computer which sat on her desk. The desk was away from the wall in a corner; I surmised she wanted privacy from prying eyes when anyone entered her room. I sat on her bed on the opposite side of the room. The bright pink and light lavender colors of the walls and bedding exuded a feminine quality I admired. By contrast my room was stark and neutral.

"Oh, my sister was just here and I'm feeling alone. She has a new boyfriend and I think she may want more time with him than me now."

Andrea giggled, "Well, I understand. Is she…you know…doing it with him?"

I blushed, but recognized my entry into forbidden Eden. "I guess." I paused. "She told me she had, but I don't understand anything about what it means." I leaned in awaiting a favorable response. And was not disappointed.

Andrea stood up from her desk and closed her door with a sliding lock on the inside. She slid it into place and came over to her bed and sat with me. Andrea placed a hand on my leg, startling me. I sensed a responsiveness again. "What do you want me to tell you…about boys, I mean?"

I turned to face her, my leg rising, curling on the bed. Andrea's hand moved with me. "What do you know about…sex?" There, the subject was broached. I would either find out about her liaisons with the sophomore or I would be learning the foreplay of lovemaking. I didn't care which because any information was more than I possessed now.

"You've heard the rumors, haven't you? You know, about me and Ryan Billings." Andrea placed her other hand in mine and said, "You've got to swear to never say anything about this."

"I swear." And I meant it. Her secret was gold to me and I wasn't about to share the wealth. If this vein was the mother lode, I wanted to mine it for all I could. I wanted the secrets to controlling men.

"Ever since we started going out, he's tried getting in my pants. But I toyed with him leading him on until I was ready. We made out of course, from the beginning, and he fondled me through my clothes. But I made it clear I would decide when and where, or even if, we would do it." Andrea stopped, removed her hands from me and said, "I don't know why I'm telling you this. I just don't want it to get around school. My mother would just kill me, I'm sure. She's such a prude." She paused a moment reflecting on the sagacity of telling a secret. "I've done it with Ryan."

"I'm not the telling type. I just need to know what it's all about so I'm ready when my turn comes." I squirmed. "The rumor's out and I figured you were my best hope for finding out what I'm missing. My parents are worse than your mom when it comes to intimacy. I don't even think they do it anymore. My dad is so worried about his precious reputation he's not going to tell me anything. And Mom is afraid of Dad." This time I held her hands and moved in close. "They haven't even had the talk with me. I'm not a little girl any more. When my period started, Mary was home from school and she got me through it. She explained to me what Mom never told me. I guess I was lucky it didn't just sneak up on me. I would have been mortified."

Andrea squeezed my hands. "Alright then, first, what do you know about your body?" I must have looked confused because she said, "Have you, ah, you know…touched yourself and aroused pleasant feelings?" I explained my experiments to her and she nodded. "Did you feel a throbbing in your body, you know, a bunch of muscle twitches and heat?" I nodded. "That's an orgasm. I get them when I play with myself, but Ryan is so hot to trot I never feel anything with him. I want him to slow down but it's not going to happen." She paused, "I think I need an older man with more experience than this kid." I was surprised by her candidness, but I pressed for more.

"So what does he do to get you in the mood?"

"I think I'm always in the mood. Has anyone ever…touched you? You know, fondled your breasts or put a hand on your…you know?" I wasn't sure about 'you know', but I thought I knew what she meant.

"No." She unhooked one of her hands from mine and placed it on my right breast. I gasped, but didn't remove it. My breathing intensified as she manipulated the flesh under my clothing.

"Kiss me," she coaxed. I didn't want to, but curiosity overcame fear. Was I gay like my brother? I placed my lips on hers. She opened her mouth and her tongue caress my lips. The deep stirring in me amplified. My reaction surprised me, aroused me, this other person's intimate touch. Suddenly, it stopped. Andrea removed her hands and face, the lesson concluded.

"Well, I guess that pleased you." She smiled, "And don't think I'm gay or anything. It's just experimenting. Why can't we experiment?"

I looked at her. "I…guess. I realize now, I want to learn more." Eden was now within my grasp, the Forbidden tree notwithstanding. More. I wanted more and we made a date to explore. But what was it I wanted?

As I sauntered home more gratified than before, I thought of how I could apply this new knowledge at school. An added level of experience changed my goals far more than I anticipated. Andrea provided an impetus to investigate what boys might respond to. My fourteenth birthday next year would now include seduction to some degree, depending on my curiosity and willingness. I wondered who else could offer familiarity about males. Andrea and I agreed to meet in two days, my angst about what was next added to the exhilaration.

I turned onto my street gliding rather than walking, my house no longer an abysmal entity. If my father approached my room in nightly sojourns for 'hands on' education, I would fight him. Mom had to know what happened to Mary or I would inform her. Entering the house, it seemed abandoned. My sanctuary, my bedroom, remained invasion free. My father entered the hallway. "Where have you been?" I disregarded his inquiry and kept walking upstairs. "Don't ignore me, young lady." I turned.

"What?" I glared at him, thinking of how Mary cringed with his hands on her. I knew the fantasy of another person touching without the horror of unwanted infringement. I despised him more than ever.

"Where have you been?" he repeated.

"At a friend's house." My hiss deterred him. "May I go now?" I bounded up the stairs to gain asylum. The hatred of my father swelled from his loathsome actions and attitude of superiority. He was worse than any of the males I knew, which were precious few. The boys at school were not an attractive lot. My brother Ben had confided his orientation when I confronted him a few weeks ago. I wondered why he had no girlfriend but lots of male friends. One guy, around the same age of twenty-five, like my brother, seemed closer to him than any of the others. So I asked. He wanted me to keep it confidential. I agreed.

I relocated to the bathroom because of the available lock on the door, stripped off my clothes and beheld my form in the full length mirror. I compared myself to my sister, whose body I admired. I knew people thought of me as a younger twin, and as I developed, I began to realize why people believed it. My face resembled hers from pictures I saw when she was my age. The contours of my body had grown to a shape imitating hers.

As I grew, I learned the features which invited male leers at school, and they would continue to enrich my allure. My hands moved across the contours of my body. To recognize another person could arouse pleasure in me was sufficient. I imagined Roger in front of me and wondered what he and Mary were doing with each other which sated this new appetite in me.

Since my twelfth birthday I investigated and stimulated myself. Andrea would supply the basis for enlightening my inquisitiveness. Her experiences would be my guide. I finished what had begun as an investigation.

My uncontrolled longing and unabated desire had an outlet to control my urges. I dressed and returned to my room, but who would satisfy my cravings. A more mature boy at school? Perhaps a friend of Roger's or maybe....

8
CHAPTER

Roger

Sitting in my bedroom I asked, "Mary, how are you doing? You seemed so comfortable with my sister, Peggy. I guess it has to do with her being closer in age, unlike your sister, Victoria." She stood next to the window and I watched a smile course her lips. I wanted to kiss them just as she answered.

"Your sister is wonderful. I guess her age has something to do with it. All the girls I've met at school are so focused on classes or getting laid. I haven't made any close friends. She seems so comfortable with Hiram, but I am surprised by her choice of husbands."

"He's a great guy once you get to know him."

"Where did she meet him?"

"He crashed into her car a couple of years ago. He asked her out, she went, and the rest, I guess you could say, is history." She sat next to me on the bed. "She had been dating another guy but never connected like she did with Hi."

Mary stood again, turned and looked into my eyes. "Do you truly love me? I mean, so much nothing can interfere, not my parents or my history, not my attempted suicide. I want to have what your sister has. I want the white picket fence without the deception. I want to be loved without feeling an obligation to be something I'm not. I want to know you will stand by me no matter what." Her urgency caught me off guard for a moment. I stood and clasped my arms around her. My lips closed to hers and we engaged in a passionate moment, not with arousal, but containing an intimacy to shore up her fragile trust in other people. I released her and stroked her golden locks.

"I want nothing more than to spend a lifetime sharing my mind and soul and heart with you. I want to become the one person who knows you so nothing can sever our bond. Your family is not important to us and neither is my family. Your history has created you and the result is marvelous. Suicide is a moment of regret and sorrow, a past which is not repeatable as we create new moments of serenity and impenitence." I held her upper arms at her side and squared my vision to hers. "Yes, Mary, I love you. I will stand by you and protect you and be your companion. Nothing will interfere. If you want an honest home with an honest picket fence, then we shall have it."

Mary listened, cheerful and relaxed. She wept and then kissed me again as I concluded. Intimacy fueled passion. She lifted her lips from mine and unbuttoned my shirt. I abandoned any inhibition at being home with parents and siblings nearby. I forgot about the door having no lock to protect my secrets. My mind and body wanted to consummate the deed now commencing. Mary unbuckled my belt and released the button of my pants. As the zipper descended sanity returned. I placed the desk chair under the knob of the door preventing unwanted intrusion. Mary disrobed, her body inviting my touch. No one disturbed our assignation while I traced the outline of breasts and waist, her skin silky and soft. She sustained my enlargement and she guided it into her. Before long we had satisfied our hunger, dressing a few moments after embracing each other on the bed.

Nothing was said as I removed the chair from it locking position. Mary held my hand a moment. I turned and kissed her again. We left to find other people hoping our privacy maintained. We had been discreet and quiet, but courage is misplaced on those who abandon discretion for unbridled lust.

"Roger, are you two settled in upstairs?" My mother's inquiry meant nothing, but I noticed a quizzical look from Mary, as though she suspected ulterior motives from the question. *Can't she just relax? No one is probing for indiscretions.* We were in the family room, a TV silenced with our entry.

"Yeah, I put Mary's stuff in the guestroom."

"How long are you staying?" Mary's demeanor remained dark and muted. Confused by her countenance, I put my arm around her. She resisted for a moment, but then cradled into my shoulder. The darkness subsided.

"Oh, we'll be here for a couple of days and then it's back to school. We're nearing finals." I relinquished my confinement of Mary whose mood vacillated from our exploit upstairs. The return to sanity calmed my anxiety. "What's for dinner?"

"Your father wants us to come out to town. He's made another sale and wants to celebrate and meet Mary. So let's get ready. Billy, go change your clothes to something cleaner." He frowned but left as requested. I noticed Mary remained calm, serene, a dinner away from the house providing a sanctuary. Peggy, can Hi join us?" She had just entered the room.

"For what? He left a few minutes ago to get parts for the bathroom."

"We're going to dinner at Luciana's. Your father closed his big house on the hill and wants to celebrate. He's also interested in meeting Mary."

I'll call him. I'm sure he can join us when he's done." She left with cell in hand.

I said. "We'll freshen up and meet you there."

Luciana's was the premier eatery in Wendlesburg. The chef had worked in San Francisco, Chicago, and New York, and speculation surrounded his landing in our town, but food critic reviews praised his culinary artistry. After ingesting succulent crab linguini marinated in a red wine tomato sauce, salad swimming in light raspberry vinaigrette, enough wine and liqueur to ease the palate, and garlic bread, we decided dessert was meant for another time. My father rose from his chair and said, "I would like to toast this successful day in business and the meeting of a charming young lady who has enthralled and tamed my son." Clinking glasses responded to the toast held by gleeful people. I looked at Mary who exuded an aura of warmth. She found a family which would not betray her or berate her decisions.

"I want you all to know I appreciate the warm welcome." Mary's eyes glistened as she spoke. "Roger is a Godsend to me and I do hope with all my heart you all are as well." She sat down; I leaned into her and kissed her cheek. I loved this woman more than I ever expected to love anyone.

When the waiter brought the reckoning, I offered to pay Mary and my portion of the bill. Hiram and Peggy likewise offered to share the expense. "You kids keep your money. This deal today will bring comfort to this household for several months and since I intend to keep buying and selling property, life will continue to be comfortable." We chortled at his attempted humor.

Having returned home, I sat with Mary in the living room explaining the real estate business which engaged my father's attention. He had begun as an associate of a local firm and quickly became the leading sales representative. He attained his broker's license in the early nineties and stepped out on his own, taking a large share of clients with him. A lucrative practice grew larger each year until the World Trade Towers attack in 2001. His business property holdings pillaged the community for a seven figure rental income which sustained his brokerage and fueled the homeowner market. Commissions, set at a lower level than other firms, attracted clients. His reputation for honesty and integrity contrasted a market full of charlatans. Mary listened, knowing I intended to join him when school finish in the next few weeks. Her father had made money in foreign exchange and investment markets using other people's capitol to enrich his life and his family. I didn't discern any shadiness to his endeavors, but Ponzi schemes had rattled people in the past.

Billy entered the room and sat with us. "Do you love my brother?" I threw a pillow at him. He caught it and continued, "If you don't, I'd like to date you. I like older women." He braced for another onslaught but none came. Mary smiled.

"Sorry, Billy, I know high school is devoid of attractive, alluring girls who only want you for your body." Her quick wit caught my brother off guard. "I find you very attractive and if it weren't for Roger, you'd have to defend your honor. As it is, yes, I love your brother."

"Man, are you lucky." Billy retorted to me. "Well, I guess I should leave you two alone." He stood. "Don't do anything I wouldn't do." Mary grinned as I chuckled. Billy glided out of the room but said as he left, "Do you have a sister?" He disappeared before an answer came forth.

"My parents are probably upstairs consummating the enriching of our family." I squirmed at the thought. "It's hard to think of them getting it on."

Mary stood and reached out her hands to me. "Let's go upstairs." I clasped them and stood with her. "Maybe I can have a consummation of my own before sleeping."

I smiled and nodded. "Your room is next to Billy's room, across from my parents, so we'll have to be quiet." We ascended the staircase, listening for any intrusive sounds from other rooms. I stepped into my room and removed my shoes and socks. We then continued to the guest room, passing Billy, a stereo blared but not loud enough to attract parental interference.

After closing the door, Mary turned to me, kissed my mouth, my cheeks, and my neck. I fumbled to loosen my belt and pants. She stepped back and stripped out of jeans and shirt, standing in her underwear, alluring, yet coy. She wore a lacy bra which matched her panties, a light yellow with white trim. Her breasts, cradled in the cups, peered through the sheerness of the cloth, her nipples erect. A rigidity of my own endeavored to free itself. Mary assisted with the removal of my legs from the jeans I wore. As she knelt on the floor, she bathed my member finishing its enlargement. I stifled a moan fearing attention from across the hall and next door. Mary stood up and I unbuttoned my shirt and removed it. She parted with her remaining garments. I leaned into kiss her and held her softness next to me. I wanted to enter her and satisfy us both. We moved to the bed where I laid while Mary cradled my body. We explored each other for several minutes and then achieved our objective.

After dressing, I kissed Mary and left the room. Billy was coming out of the bathroom and saw me. "Ooh, what have you been up to?" I glared at him.

"None of your business," I fumed.

"Hey, I'm just kidding. If I had a girlfriend like her, I'd want to spend all my time with her, too." He winked and entered his bedroom. I went into my room. I smiled, knowing Billy was right. She was so attractive, I couldn't resist her. I wanted to hold her and kiss her; her moods would not dissuade me from living a lifetime with her. I stripped off my clothing, put on a robe and went to the bathroom to prepare for sleep. Mary was entering it as I came out of my bedroom. I hurried down the hall, catching the door before it closed.

"Hey, can I join you. It'll be like we're married and we can watch each other prepare for bed." She looked at me with a perplexed countenance, coolness charged the atmosphere. It dissipated as a momentary silence commenced with my intrusion. I started to leave.

"Wait, I'm sorry. You caught me off guard. I think it would be nice to have a companion watch me brush my teeth. But maybe you're not ready to watch a girl tinkle." I blushed. "After all, I've not watched a guy pee since I was very little and Ben took me with him into the men's room because he was watching over me."

I entered the room and closed the door. We prepared for sleep as any married couple. I averted my eyes as she sat on the toilet. She was right. This time teased me like an intrusion. I had avoided such intimacy with girls I dated at school because they meant nothing to me, but this phase of life meant everything. Fortunate for me I suffered a momentary shy bladder, escaping another blushing moment. We parted ways from the bathroom. I reentered my room and climbed into my bed. Sleep was welcome and came with ease. I mused about her reaction to my initial request for using the bathroom with her. What caused such a response? I slept before discovering any semblance of an answer.

Victoria

I woke early enough to avoid my parents. I had overheard my father in their bedroom talking to my mother. "She's not very respectful of me. All I wanted to know was where she had been and she acted snippy with me. I never wanted another child. I'm not sure I even wanted the older two. There's something wrong with our son and Mary is so moody. I'm glad she's gone to school."

My father's comments had pierced my heart deeper than any nighttime intrusion. I had stood in the hall, angry tears filling my eyes, but I brushed them away with my sleeve. My own mother offered no defense, another betrayal. Why didn't he love me? Why wouldn't my mother defend me? Nothing about my parents now seemed normal. I wanted to run away and find a happier environment, but who would take in a teenager without wanting to return me? I had no money and no options. In silence I ate a bowl of cereal and moped about the unfairness of life.

After placing my bowl in the dishwasher, I returned to my room. Sunday was a day for church and Dad would not let me skip. I prepared for this inconvenience mindful of my loathing. No god should want me living in this thankless environ, so I misplaced any belief in a higher power. I went because my future independence was near and I would endure it until I could leave. I descended the stairs to the family room to await the impediment to my imagined freedom.

Could I be the only one who endured such irrational parenting? I must be vigilant and watchful for opportunities to prepare for emancipation. Education outside of the classroom became the best path to adult autonomy.

Andrea and I planned on meeting at my house after church, another educational opportunity awaiting. My parents had obligations away from the house. The preacher droned on about hatred leading to darkness, leaving each of us with no recourse about life. I figured he didn't know what he was talking about. I could explore my life full of light even if detesting my father's attitude. I wanted discovery and nothing about hating interfered. Another song interrupted my thoughts. Soon after, the service ended.

"I want you with us at the Jenkins house this afternoon. I don't like leaving you home alone." I explained I was grown up enough to be trusted on my own and Ben was stopping by later. Mom acquiesced and my father's face looked relieved. Being with my parents was more tedious with each passing moment.

At home I bid my parents adieu when they left and fixed a quick lunch. I called Andrea, who was eager to experience a rapacious life and came over after hanging up her phone. I thought of Mary, whether she attended church. She was much more spiritual, surprising because of her history in this hypocritical family.

"Andrea, do you think I'm naïve?" We realized the strength of character each of us could use to empower our leadership in school as well as life. We were lying side by side on my bed, sharing in depth far more than either of us had before.

"No more than me," she answered. "I'm just happy you had the guts to confront me about Ryan. I broke up with him."

"Why?"

"It wasn't fun anymore."

"I didn't mean to come between you two."

Andrea turned on her side and looked at me. "You didn't. I knew it was bad. I just wasn't sure how to leave until you butted in. Again, thanks." She placed her hand on my crotch and leaned in to kiss me. I smiled and met her mouth.

A noise interrupted any additional activity. "I think my brother's here," I whispered and stood up. Andrea remained on the bed.

"Do you think he might be interested in doing it with me?" Andrea's face wore a whimsical look. I furrowed my brow.

"He's gay," I responded.

"I was kidding," she countered, but I wasn't sure. As she stood, I left to discover the source of interruption. Downstairs I found Ben in the kitchen making a cup of tea. He turned when he heard my deliberate heavy tread.

"Oh, I didn't think anyone was home." He stirred a lump of sugar in the cup. "I came by to pick up my laundry which I left here yesterday."

"I thought you didn't want Mom doing your stuff anymore?" I retrieved a cookie from the jar next to the refrigerator.

"It's the last load," he said. "What are you doing here alone?"

"I convinced Mom and Dad I'm old enough to be here without a baby sitter to watch me." I sat down on a stool and continued, "Besides, you're here and I told them you'd be coming by." A sound in the hall grabbed Ben's attention.

"Who's here with you?" He moved to the doorway and looked out into the hall. As he stepped back into the kitchen, Andrea followed him.

I blushed but introduced my friend. "Ben, this is Andrea Collins. Andrea, this is my brother, Ben. She lives a few blocks over from here. We go to school together."

"Nice to meet you." She reached out a hand. Ben took it with caution, and looked at me.

"Same here. So what are you two up to?" My mortified soul wondered if Andrea would come on to my brother here in front of me, even after telling her about his preference of partners.

"We're studying science together." Andrea jumped into the void. "We have an anatomy test on Monday, so we're cramming." Shame reared its ugly head, again.

"Oh, well then, don't let me interfere with your learning about the body." I wanted Ben out of the house as soon as possible, but nothing seemed to promote my wishes.

She rejoined his comment, "Vickie says you're a computer whiz. I find it fascinating." She moved closer to him before he could pick up his bag of clothing. "Tell me, is computer stuff exciting or does it make a guy nerdy and uninterested in girls? That's what I've heard." I figured she was baiting me rather than Ben, but I didn't know how to stop her. She continued, "You're a cute guy; do you have a girlfriend?"

Ben looked at me and then Andrea. "What has my dear little sister told you about me?"

"Oh not much, but I thought maybe you weren't the type of guy to get too nerdy. Vickie isn't a nerd, even though she's one of the smartest kids I know." She smiled at me. I glared at her.

"I'm too busy at work and school to have a girlfriend right now." Ben replied. I didn't want the inquisition to continue but wouldn't have been able to stop it. She nodded her head and sat next to me on another stool. "Well, I'll see you two later." He picked up the bag and departed the house.

"What was that all about?" I shrieked. "What if he thought we were… doing…what we were doing?" I left the stool moving toward the sink and turning. "I don't want anyone knowing about us…"

Andrea smiled. "Relax; I was just messing with you. He is cute, though. Maybe I can flip him."

"What? Stay away from him. He's like, ten years older than you."

Andrea laughed.

We walked to her house. In her room with the computer humming, I thought about what she had said to Ben. *Can a guy be turned into a hetero if he's a homo?* "Andrea, do you think my brother is weird because he likes guys?"

She stopped. "Nah, he just swings different than we do." She cringed.

I blushed. "But what if a guy you like wants to…ah…" I didn't finish.

"Nobody's going in there." I forgot Andrea's presence until she said, "You're thinking about it, aren't you." She closed the browser window and deleted the search history. "Mom's not home right now. Are you up for some fun?"

"Sure, what do you have in mind?" I should have guessed. She locked her door. Education is a funny thing. It happens all the time, even when we think it's not. Mine now included another person. Neither of us reviled the awareness we gained.

I left for my house detached from my parents being upset with me or not. I knew a kindred intimacy I would not have with them, one of sharing passions and emotions. If only someone like Roger was my age and interested in me, I would gratify my lust and satisfy his concupiscence, my newly found word of the day.

Guys at school did not have the maturity I wanted, and waiting four or five years seemed so long. Where was a mature man who could make me a woman?

Entering the front door, hoping against hope to circumvent interacting with either of my parents, Mom appeared from the dining room. "Victoria, where were you?"

I answered as sweet as needed to soften the blow. "I was at Andrea's"

"You said you'd stay here. I don't like not knowing where you are. She seems like trouble."

"It's alright, Ben stopped by after you left. I called Andrea so I wouldn't be alone and we went to her house." I smiled as to defray any more investigation of my life. "I'm sorry; I should have left a note."

"Well, thank you for your honesty. What do you see in the Collins girl, anyway?" The probing began in spite of my effort. I changed the subject, pushing the so called envelop and delved into the girl stuff so often avoided.

"Mom, do you think Mary and Roger can have a good life together? I mean, does he know about her background and stuff?"

Mom crinkled her forehead, "She must have explained her wrist scars; they're so visible. I guess she's answering any questions he has."

"He seems to like her. What happens when two people want to be together? I mean, you know, uh, when they want to…" I couldn't finish, but I figured Mom would. So I ended my talking for a period of silence and modesty.

"Well, I guess it's time we sat down and had a girl to girl talk." Bait taken meant I could probe the mysteries of men and women without related interrogation of my own sex life. She could explain. I would listen, and then I would be safe and appear to be the proper and appropriate daughter I was supposed to be. Mom led me to my room and closed the door.

"Where's Dad?" I asked to be sure of his absence in the discussion.

"He's doing some work in his den." Mom then began with her ignorant explanation of the birds and the bees. Many birds and bees failed inclusion in our talk.

We had an early dinner without much conversation other than the safe ones of weather and school. No one broached the budding relationship which came home two days ago. I excused myself from the table and cleared my dishes. I went to my room and worked on assignments for classes. Picking up my cell phone and dialing Mary's number, it went to voice mail. "Mary, please call me on my cell. I need to hear your voice. Say hi to Roger for me." I clicked off and prepared for bed. Oh Roger, if only you had a younger twin brother.

9
CHAPTER

Roger

The light rapping on the door seemed like a dream in which I was tapping on wall boards looking for a secret panel. I wanted to uncover the long lost treasure of Santa Maria. At last the wall creaked open and a hand reached out and touched me. A silence screamed erupted from my mouth. Another touch and the dream melted away as a cloud on a warm day.

"Roger, wake up." I trembled at the sound of my name, but escaped from Morpheus arms. "Roger, Roger." I heard again. I opened my eyes and an angel hovered above me, then descended and kissed me, a gentle hint on the mouth. Consciousness completed its journey.

"Mary, what time is it?" My lips flubbed the words.

"It's a little past six." She lifted the covers and slipped in with me, nestling into my naked body. Her skin contacted mine arousing my cognizance she must have been wearing something when she entered the room but had discarded it before lying with me. "I wanted you to hold me." She did not move in a sensual way as much as she comforted herself. I sensed the usual response in me but sought not the quest. The warmth of her touch was enough. "I want to get married as soon as we can. I don't want to sleep without you." The comment startled me, but I remained calm.

I wanted to surprise her with me kneeling and presenting the ring but now I was caught in a paradox of emotions. Her body enticed me as well as her wit, but the occasional moodiness added salt to the mixture.

I had to be prepared to help her and love her. My declarations sealed my future, though, and I answered her with a simple, "Yes." She kissed me on the neck and her arm moved under covers to my erection. I inhaled as she grasped me moving up and down. I placed a hand on her breast feeling the nipple. I kissed her as she repositioned herself on me. Her slow sway, her breasts rocking on my chest; willed me to sustain the pleasure but I was compelled to finish. Mary continued moving until she enjoyed her own pleasurable explosion. She lay on me not letting any of my body escape her. I began moving again rising to another successful conclusion for both of us. No one had awakened as far as I knew so we slept for a few minutes entwined around each other.

Mary woke first and slipped out of bed. I admired the shapeliness of her anatomy, the shimmer of her hair, and the sparkle in her eyes. As she wrapped her robe around her waist and tied it, I asked, "Do you want to announce our engagement?" She smiled, but remained silent. Lying on my side, I propped my head in my hand and kept watching her. With a finger to her lips, she opened my bedroom door, peered out, and left.

I lay staring at the ceiling, wondering how this complex entity infiltrated my life, so quickly and with such depth. I was a mere bug in her web to be consumed at her leisure. I accepted the fate bestowed upon me.

As time marched on I reflected on the morning foray, believing she knew what she wanted and how to get it. *She's a conniving wench for sure.* My thoughts were not derogatory. Enjoying the pleasure of her physique, entranced by her mental ability to ensnare me in a web of exotic sensuality, I had no reason nor desired to find any deprecating memoirs. She seemed as simple as any woman who favored to use sex against a man and as complex as an intricate machine with parts unseen and unknown, but imaginable all the same. Her mind's complications challenged my sensibilities about rational people who have few problems which interfere with daily life and ride a sensible path of action; for nothing about this woman elicited a sense of simplicity.

I rose from my wanton bastion of pleasure, showered, and dressed for a possible sojourn to church. It dawned on me I had no idea about Mary's religious bent. While attending college, I relaxed the parental stranglehold inflicted upon me as a child regarding ritual stimulus on a week to week basis. However, for Mary's sake and the future of my family ties, I prepared to satisfy any possible infliction of religion on me or Mary as requested by Walker and Nancy Waite. I could offset possible questions of religious background by changing subjects as soon as possible.

In the kitchen I found my mother and father, dressed for church, eating a simple breakfast. "You're on your own for food," my mother said. I nodded and hunted for necessary objects of consumption. "Are you joining us for church?"

"I guess. I'm not sure about Mary's religious beliefs, but we'll come if she wants to go." I sat with my breakfast and ate in silence. My parents left the room to drive to church. I didn't know if Billy was with them when they left the house, but I assumed he was. Mary entered as I finished the cereal and juice I garnered. "Hello, again, my love." I stood up and kissed her. "Would you like some breakfast?"

"No. Thank you, though." We held hands and looked into each other's eyes. I noticed an impending storm, but had no perception of a source. A second later the sun burst through and she smiled.

"Hey, are you guys going to church?" My parents left without Billy. "I was hoping you could take me with you."

I frowned, a perturbed creature caught in a web. "I don't know." I turned to Mary and asked, "Would like to go to church?" She curled her arm in mine.

"I think it would be nice to see how you two view sanctity and religion. I, myself, am a Lutheran. What are you?"

Billy jumped in before I could answer, "We're Episcopalians." I scowled at him. Had Mom and Dad left him behind as a spy or chaperone?

"Mary, I'm glad you want to go with me."

"It's my pleasure."

"Billy, let's get going."

We left the house, climbed into my car and drove the ten minutes to St. Augustine Episcopal Church, where we met up with the rest of the family. Peggy came without Hiram. I still fumed at Billy being left for me to transport, but Mary comforted my angry soul by saying, "I like your brother and we can keep an eye on what he may have discovered about our morning rendezvous."

"You're right. Let's just get through this and head home." Church proceeded without incident and my parents appeared pleased with the family gathered together.

Mary and I drove home without Billy. "Thank you for taking me to your church. I'd have skipped it at home. Your family seems to be well regarded there."

"Dad and Mom make a show of it with money and time. It's not so much the belief as it is the status." We continued to the house without any more conversation. Mary placed her hand on my shoulder, as if to say something, but changed her mind.

At the house she asked, "Do you like going to church? I mean does it have any meaning for you?" She and I sat in the living room awaiting the remainder of my family.

"I guess. I never thought about it, but I've gone most of my life and it makes sense to me, in a way. Why?"

"I suppose there is a loving God or something, but why do we suffer so much. Can't this God just end the misery?" Mary sat on the edge of the couch and stared into my dumbfounded expression.

I watched her as though I could see into her soul and experience her mind working out the details of the woeful existence of humanity. She presented a comprehensive thesis for which I had no riposte. There was intensity but no storm in her countenance, a willing debate about the merits of religious tenets. "I don't know. I've not been asked this before." I grinned as much as the Cheshire cat, but without any guile. "I think we create our own misery." The intensity dimmed into a quagmire of anger as quickly as flipping a switch on the wall. I tread where no man should who wished for peace and harmony in a relationship.

"You think I desired my father's vile exploration of my body? Do you think I created the loathing he seems to have for his own children?" She stood and vanished from the room leaving me perplexed. She was correct, of course, since no one I knew would want such undesired interaction by a parent. I didn't appreciate her world. My life was perfect for me and I wanted her in it, so her life could be perfect as well. Together we'd forget the past and build a future. Was I so wrong to want it? I stood and followed her upstairs.

As I ascended, the front door opened and my parents entered with Billy. "Roger," my mother asked, "will you and Mary be joining us for lunch?"

"Sure," I hastened to answer not knowing Mary's attitude at the moment. I continued my sojourn after her. Did I need to apologize?

Mary sat on the bed holding clothes in her lap, her travel bag beside her. She looked at me as I entered the room. I didn't see anger or wrath, but a forlorn, disappointed expression. "I am so sorry. I didn't mean to imply you wanted what happened to occur. I'm an idiot and I don't deserve you. Please forgive me."

"Roger, I want to go home." She dropped the clothing into the bag. I approached her, but she held up a hand and said, "I want to be alone right now." I hesitated, to say something, but decided I better not; I left her room and went to my room to pack my suitcase.

Mary entered my room. "We can't leave yet," she said. "We need to talk to your parents about us. I don't want to fight with you." I stopped my packing. Her cell phone buzzed. She checked it and let it go to voice mail. "I realize you didn't mean to imply I wanted my father to abuse me, but if we are to have a future together, I need you to understand my family is dysfunctional and I haven't exactly enjoyed the good life. You have been wonderful to me, but I don't need to be reminded of my past."

"I get it." I moved toward her, fearing the worst, wanting the best, and hugged her. "I'll support you anyway you want. I love you." She didn't reject me, but the tension didn't reassure me. "I want to marry you this summer. Can we tell my parents before we leave?"

"Yes," Mary said.

We left my room to speak with my parents. I sensed an anxiousness as we descended the stairs. Our future needed a solid alliance, a united front. I believed I had it but wondered about my new fiancé.

Victoria

As days passed into weeks, Andrea and I researched the intricacies of our femininity. She explored her newly acquired knowledge with a boy from another school. My own ventures in the dating world were often a disaster of my own creation. What I wanted was not fulfilled by pubescent guys.

Mary and I talked on a regular basis, and I was thrilled when she and Roger had stopped by the house to announce their intention to be married in August.

"Mom, when school's over and Mary comes home, will we have time to put together a wedding?" I asked because my fourteenth birthday loomed soon and I figured it was a lost cause. Maybe fourteen wasn't such a big deal, so being in a wedding sure had to be.

Mom beamed her half smile at me indicating a worthy answer. "Yes, she and Roger want a small intimate affair with family and a few friends."

I guessed my big day would be turning fifteen or sixteen. Maybe by then I could find a compatible male to turn me into a woman.

Roger and Mary becoming husband and wife was exciting and terrifying. What if Roger was like Dad? And Mary was hitching up to the wrong cart, so to speak? *I must get to know this man better for Mary's sake.* "I guess this means we have to start planning, right now." I gleamed at the idea of learning more about the man who intrigued my sister so much.

My birthday came and went with little fanfare at home, as predicted. Andrea and I celebrated on a double date which became a contest about which of us would dump our male companions the fastest. "I'm sorry about setting you up with this guy," she said. "I thought he might be fun without wanting to paw you so much."

"It's ok. I want to get out of here and go to your place." We had escaped the dinner for a moment of restroom relief from the two older males at the table. Andrea had been seeing one of them but not yet consummated her lust. His friend had ideas beyond a level of civility I decided not to cross. We were stuck with them for transportation to Andrea's, my evening destination. The sleepover did not include other guests, who perhaps hoped it did.

"If we leave too soon, they're going to suspect something's wrong. If we wait too long, they're going to expect something more." Andrea nodded at me as she spoke.

"Do you want to have sex with Ronnie? I can call my brother."

"No, I promised you a night with me and we'll get rid of them at my place. We should get back and finish dinner." We left the bathroom.

"You girls want to get out of here and go somewhere quiet and private?" Andrea's date pushed the obvious on us almost before we could sit. The look of anticipation in his friend scared me.

Flustered, I began to speak. "Well, I think we should go home, soon." I half smiled at my date, trying not to look ready for the next move.

"I know this place where we can be alone and get to know one another." Andrea's companion leaned in with a garish smile and the raising of his eyebrows. I wanted to gag and flee at the same time. Andrea rescued the evening.

"We ladies are not yet ready to consummate our friendships with anything which might be considered unacceptable." She sounded so mature I thought the boys were going to need dictionaries. "Ronnie, would you be kind enough to return us to my house. We've had a lovely time but nothing further is going to happen which might lead you to believe we are ready for any intimacy."

I sat agape as did my date. Ronnie answered in disbelief. "What? I thought you liked us and might want to put out. At least, it's what I've heard."

"A vile rumor and so not like us." Andrea stood up and spoke to me. "Vickie, these gentlemen are ready to take us home and await the satisfaction of their libido at a future date." I knew they needed a dictionary after her exchange. I stood up and thanked Connor for being a gentleman. We headed for the door while the boys paid the tab. "They think one date is payment enough for a quick poke, but I think we should play it out for another date or maybe more. They are so, like, not my type."

"You would do Ronnie after a few dates? It seems so cheap, you know, like we are accepting pay for play."

"He's ok, and I do like sex. You can let Connor do you and you'll know what I mean. Shush, here they come." I was intrigued by her candidness with me.

We arrived at Andrea's after a short debate about changing our minds. She took point on this and fended them off with her best argumentative skills. Connor did hold my hand. I let him because he seemed more nervous about the next move than I did. He turned to kiss me. I allowed a quick peck which he took to mean he could touch parts of me. I clasped his hand, as it cuffed my left breast, and removed it.

"Be a good boy for now. You never can tell what might happen in the future." Still holding the offending hand, I placed my left hand on his crotch expanded by anticipation. A groan escaped his lips. "See, you're ready, but I'm not there yet." I stroked his pants which became stained rather soon. "There, now you can relax and think about it."

I kissed him on the cheek, opened the car door, and vacated the back seat. Blowing him a kiss, I thought he might jack it right there in front of me. Andrea slobbered a kiss on Ronnie before opening the door, and exiting. We waved goodbye as we strolled up to her front door.

"I think we caused some heartache, tonight." Andrea said. She held my hand. I smiled, anticipating another terrific evening. What new act could I learn tonight?

10
CHAPTER

Roger

Mary and I lay in bed having enjoyed a night together. "I love you." I said.

"Of course, you do. I'm adorable." We laughed. School finals were next and our individual studies interrupted sharing time. This night marked our last together until graduation. Our families planned on being present at the ceremonies and having them around inhibited intimacy. Mary exited the bed and began dressing. "You need to go so I can study. I don't need any more distractions." She stripped the bed sheets from me exposing my nakedness at which she leered for a moment.

I jumped up and said, "Alright, but I'm taking you out for dinner." I dressed in yesterday's clothes, pick up my backpack of books and study materials, and bid her adieu.

I thought about my past and how different it was from today. I hurried to my apartment hoping to miss Brian. As I entered I heard, "Welcome home stranger. I guess studying went well for you." He sat on the couch, books spread out in front of him. His finals were as gruesome as any I had, and passing these tests was his assurance of graduation.

"Ha. Ha. So I stayed at Mary's. We're getting married you know. Have you decided about being my best man?"

"Oh, I was yanking your chain. Of course I'll stand with you." He looked back at his pile of notes and essays. "By the way, who's the maid of honor?"

"I don't know. She doesn't have any friends I've seen or met." I placed my backpack on the floor next to a chair in which I parked my butt. "She and Joanne seem to get along."

"Yeah, well since you dropped the bomb about matrimony, I've been feeling pressure from a certain person we both know and adore about my future. Thanks."

"I thought you liked her. After all, 'what's love got to do with it'?" My attempted humor hit its mark when Brian smiled.

"Well, I don't want to break up with her and she still has another year of school to fulfill her scholarship obligation. Nothing's going to happen right away." He replaced a heavy tome about engineering he'd picked up. I walked to the refrigerator and got out milk and juice. The old adage of having breakfast fixed for you after an evening date failed to materialize at Mary's.

"Want me to ask Mary at dinner tonight about having Joanne in her wedding party?"

"Gees, this is complicated. Let me ask Joanne if she might be interested. Of course, if I ask her and then Mary doesn't want her it would be awkward."

"Yeah, and if I talk to Mary about it and Joanne says 'no', we're both screwed. Maybe I'll just ask Mary what her plans are. After all, I just have to show up, right?"

"Sure, everything about after the wedding has been accomplished." We laughed. I poured a bowl of cereal, added milk, and proceeded to eat. I slurped juice from the container.

Studying commenced in my bedroom at the desk I had used for the last two years, a gift from the previous renter who graduated and wanted nothing but memories and a degree in accounting to go with him. Optimism about finals lacked a level of comfort about attaining high grades and passing, but writing one ten thousand word essay on the ethics of business practices in Washington State steadied my attitude. My grades were above average, even though diligence for the subjects hadn't engaged as it had for other students in my college of business. My real education would occur in my father's real estate office.

Morning slid into noon and then into middle afternoon. My stomach growled because of the lack of attention. I didn't want to eat much because of dinner with Mary, but a snack of nuts and a soda filled the emptiness.

I left Brian sleeping on the couch, a victim of late nights cramming a full semester into an empty noggin. My thoughts about the wedding occupied most of the travel to Mary's place. *How should I broach the subject?* I experienced enough mental anguish from Mary to question bringing it up at all. No man should have to be the preparer of his own wedding. *The difference between marriage and a date is marriage lasts longer, much longer.* My thoughts didn't shore up my doubts.

At our local hangout Mary and I ordered the easiest meals possible. "Mary, I must get back to studying. Thank you for coming out with me, though. How's cramming progressing?"

"Fine, but what's your hurry? I thought we could talk about the wedding." My face betrayed my angst for passing finals.

"Sure, if it's what you want."

A tempest brewed across the table. "If you don't want to talk about it then we won't." I misjudged our conversation.

"No, no. I wanted to ask you about our attendants, anyway. I'm planning on having Brian and my little brother stand with me. Brian would be best man." I hoped for tranquility and waited for a response.

"Do you think your sister would accept being a bride's maid? I want my sister, Victoria, in the party, as well." Her calmness reassured my mind.

"I'm pretty sure she would be honored." I plodded forward oblivious as usual. "Who are you thinking about for your maid of honor?"

"I don't know, yet. I really only know Joanne." Hope rose for an easy conclusion regarding wedding attendants. "And Monica, your ex, contacted me yesterday and asked how we were getting along." This conversation now headed toward an ice floe. "What have you and she been doing behind my back?"

"Nothing. She called you, yesterday?" I hit an iceberg.

Dinner ended, nothing accomplished. Mary stayed calm, but I figured a meltdown lingered. I drove to her apartment trying to avoid any mention of Monica. My karma betrayed me. "Monica told me you wanted to do a three way with me and her." Mary waited for my fumbling response.

"What? I…she does this thing…sometimes, when she's upset. She tells lies to people just to see what they do. I haven't talked with her since the day in the Sub when I introduced you to Brian." *Oh shit, wrong thing to say.*

"You spoke with her after I left? What else happened?" I had nowhere to turn. "Was she worth it?"

"She wanted to know if my relationship with you was tight. She wanted to make up with me, you know, but I told her we were finished and I only wanted you. She said she was going to let you in on a few secrets about me. That's all. I left her standing there. I love you. I don't want any three-way with her. I want you." I reached for her, but she removed her hand. *Another fumble?*

"So with whom would a three-way be acceptable? Me and my sister? How about Joanne, Brian, and me? Would it make you happy?" There was little to do but cower like a scolded puppy with tail between legs.

"Mary, where is this coming from? I want no one but you in my life." I stood frozen as she turned; a sallow appearance affixed to her, and she went inside. *'Me and my sister?' Why would she say such a thing?* I entered my car, overwhelmed and hurt, and drove home. I figured Monica had gotten her way. When I parked the car and got out, a shadow moved into the light. "Monica?"

Victoria

I woke early in the morning. Andrea slept like a puppy after playing with a toy, the bed sheets not quite covering her. I stood by the bed watched her for a moment. We had diverted our hearts and minds of any desire to be pawed by young stallions. I robed my body and went to the bathroom.

Mrs. Collins was in the hall when I came out. "Did you two have a good time last night?" *You have no idea.* I smiled and tightened the sash of the robe.

"We did. The guys took us to a nice restaurant and brought us home when we wanted." I smiled. "Your daughter is such a kind and thoughtful person. I enjoy her friendship." We passed by each other and I entered Andrea's bedroom. She was sitting on the edge of the bed, yawning the morning into existence. "Your mother is so like not there about you." I said.

"Yeah, I love her and all. But she's clueless. She thinks I'm still a little girl." Andrea stood and stretched. Sniffing, she said, "Yuck, I need a shower.

"You are such a hussy." I laughed.

"You're not such a sweet scent, either," she whispered.

"Yeah, well, let's do something about it." We laughed. She picked up her tee and boxers. Putting them on, she again whispered. "Let's finish this in the shower."

I nodded. "What does your mom think we're doing up here?"

"Got me. As long as she leaves me alone, I'm fine with whatever she thinks." Andrea approached the door. "She's good to me, but she doesn't pay much attention. What about your parents?"

"I don't know. I don't talk with Dad, but Mom and I have a polite life together. They think I'm a little girl. You know, like, I don't do anything wrong and they don't question whether I would or not." We headed to the bathroom and thankfully avoided Andrea's mom.

The water cascaded over my body. Andrea handed me the soap. I washed my torso front and back and then cleansed my abdomen and buttocks. I didn't feel any sexual allure but still enjoyed the closeness of my friend as she washed her body.

I left Andrea's surer of what my future with a man would include. And a man it would be. No boy I knew could satisfy my sexual ambition.

Mary and Roger would be home in another couple of weeks and the wedding plans would be completed. *Can life be any better than this?* My mind drifted as I walked, abandoning my current environment for a visualized Eden.

Yanked back to reality by an unknown source, I heard. "Hey, watch where you're going." A man's yell and a horn's blast woke me from my fantasy. I realized almost too late I had entered an intersection with traffic. "Are you alright?" said the man holding my arm. I looked at him, seeing a dream companion.

"What? Oh, I'm sorry." Aware of the real world again, I twisted my arm free of his grasp. "Thank you, I was daydreaming, I guess." His azure eyes and tanned face, the day's growth of a dark beard and his rumpled hair reminded me of pictures in magazines selling a new fragrance to attract a host of females. A sense of security pleased me as I looked at him, and I smiled. He returned the smile and I thought, *Is this the type of guy to be my first?* I hesitated to speak again and he drifted across the intersection.

"Vickie?" His voice sounded so young, so immature. *No, this isn't right. The time is wrong.* "Vickie?" I heard again.

"Stop," I yelled. "I'm not ready." Blind to reality, Eden dissolved at another corner of the street. Conner, my date from last night stood beside me.

"Not ready for what?" I realized my circumstances, the remnants of Eden faded away.

"Conner, what are you doing here?" I noticed azure eyes turning toward a house another block away.

"I was on my way to see if you wanted to go out with me again. And I promise not to try anything."

"What makes you think I want to go out with you?" I stared at him like a lynx ready to pounce.

"I'm sorry. I just thought we could start over without anyone else ruining a date." He fidgeted, nervous as hell like all the young boys around my age. He wasn't so bad, but I watched past him to the poster man wondering how he might act on a date. I smiled at the older person who entered the building. *I'm not with him.* I fought the urge to speak with Connor.

Dream man was a lost cause. "What do you want?" Connor blushed, doubtless thinking about his hand on my breast.

He stammered, "I like you and I want to go to a movie or something." His eyes pleaded for affirmation.

"Alright, you can take me out, but no one must know about it." I leaned near his ear and whispered, "No funny business." I then kissed his cheek and walked across the street, fantasizing about him wetting his pants. I continued on home, wishing for a different person to be in my life.

"Mom," I said as I entered. "Mom, can I talk to you?" I didn't hear any response and headed to my room. At the top of the stairs I found her in the hall.

"Hi, dear," she said. "What did you want to talk about?" I hugged her and looked at her with a quizzical look to my face. "What's the matter?" she said. "You look like you've lost a friend. Have you and Andrea had a fight?"

I smiled. "Oh, no. we're BFF. No, I want to know when I can go on a date with a boy alone." I dropped my backpack on the floor.

"Well, we have talked about this. You're only fourteen and your father and I don't want you to get into trouble."

"Ew, Mom, I not going to sleep with anyone. I just want to go out with Connor alone. He's a nice boy and I like feel I'm ready."

Mom put her hands on my shoulders and said, "Let me talk with your father and see what he has to say."

I twisted free and answered, "Mom, he's going to go off on you and tell you I'm too young. When am I going to be not too young?" I picked up my pack and stomped down the hall to my room. *They just don't get it.*

I slammed my pack on the floor by my desk and fumed.

I just need to escape this hell. Mary's words came back to me like an explosion. *Someday I'm going to be old enough to get out of here.* She had escaped. Now I understood the desire to be free of parents.

A knock on my door startled me. "What," I yelled.

The door opened and Mom came in. "What's this all about, Vickie?" I sat down. "Haven't we had an open relationship up to now?"

Tears welled up in my eyes. "I guess." Mom sat with me and put her arm around my shoulders. She sat silent. She waited for me to continue. "I want what my friends have. They're all dating and everything. I'm not a bad person. I just want to be normal."

"You are normal, and pretty, and smart, but you're my baby. I guess I'm not ready to see you all grown up."

"I understand I'm not grown up, yet; I know. But if I'm smart, then trust me to do what's right." My head dropped to my chest.

"Yes, you are. I guess I can talk your father into letting you go out on a date. He might want to chaperon you, though."

"Why? It's like he believes I'll embarrass him. I won't. But I do want to know what boys are like." I stood up and turned. "When did you first go out on a date?"

Mom smiled. "You're right. I know you wouldn't embarrass yourself or your dad." She stood as well. "And as for my dating, that's not what's at stake here. You deserve some respect, so I'll talk with your father when he gets home."

"Oh, come on, Mom, when did you get to go out alone with a boy?" I asked.

"I was fifteen and we went to the movies. He wanted to hold my hand and I let him. But he got no further." She winked leaving me questioning what happened on the next date.

11
CHAPTER

Roger

"Monica, what are you doing here?" Betrayed by this minx, I wanted to crush her skull open like a ripe melon. "Why did you call Mary? And how did you get her number?" Hands on hips, I stared.

She closed the gap and purred. "Is she upset with you?" She grabbed my hands and held them to her chest. "Maybe you need to reacquaint yourself with these." I hesitated reclaiming my fingers. Did she notice? As well-endowed as Mary, my mind recalled her curvaceous frame. The 'fight', or whatever it was, left me empty, angry and frightened. For the moment, Mary was no longer a part of me. Monica continued. "Come on, you're not telling me she still wants you, are you? Did she tell you what I said?"

"Yes, and you're a bitch. Why would you do this to me?"

"You don't get it, do you? You sleep with any girl you can and don't even think about what you may have done to them or me. And then you find someone you realize you like and all those other nighttime conquests are forgotten as if they never occurred." She seized the organ between my legs. "This was mine and until I say you can have it back…"

I wiggled free of her hold. "Leave me alone or I'll call the police."

"Oh, and what'll they do? I'll tell them about all the girls on campus you raped when they didn't put out fast enough for you." She leered at me. I thought for a moment maybe she was right about some of them. But most were eager and willing, so I slapped her face.

"I didn't rape anyone and you know it." She rubbed her cheek, but the smile prevailed.

"Sure, but it's your word against, what, maybe ten or twenty or more, girls?" She moved closer. "I know how you can fix this. You break up with her. Then you and I can start a life together. If you still want to marry her, I'll make sure it doesn't happen. We can realign schedules and meet regularly for old time sake." Monica snickered. I recoiled at the proposition of extortion. I wanted to kill her.

"Monica, I need some time to think about it." The calmness of my words surprised me as I'm sure they did my antagonist. "Can we leave this for now? I need to study for finals." I turned toward my building and walked away, fuming and planning severe and malicious revenge.

———◦∞◦———

"Mary, I spoke with Monica about what she said and I don't think she'll bother you anymore." I turned to Brian. "I don't think it'll work. She's pissed."

Brian nodded. "Yeah, but if you want her back, you're going to have to grovel, a lot." He put a hand on my shoulder and continued, "You know, Monica is pretty hot, and it's obvious she still likes you. You could do a lot worse than her."

"Very funny, I hate her. Would you live with someone who'd blackmail you for the rest of your life? Would you want to be controlled like a puppet?"

"Nah, I get it. But what're you going to do?"

"I don't know, but it's got to be soon and it's got to make that bitch leave me alone." I sat down on the sofa. Brian sat next to me. "Are you willing to help me get rid of her?"

"You know it."

"Outside of just killing her, I guess I need to show her I'm not a good match for her.

"Yeah, and then she'll use it against you with Mary, telling her you admit to being a bad person." A sentient silence slipped into our exchange. "Wait, I know. We spread it around campus she's giving it away for free. She's taking on all comers, male or female. She wants to set a new record for partners in a single night, no holds barred sort of thing." I cringed at the thought of ruining this girl, but I had little choice. She wanted to ruin me.

"What's next, then?"

Brian laid the plan out like a general plotting a strategic attack on a defensive position of the enemy. I listened as he spoke. "What needs to happen requires we get some guys to spread the rumor she's going for it at her apartment. I have some guys who will not be traceable to us or more important, to you." He looked at me. I responded with a shrug of the shoulders.

"Brian, I want her to stop threatening me." I looked at him pleading. "Is this going to work? She'll know I'm behind this. I just know she will."

"I don't know, but she sure will understand she should leave you alone."

"I want Mary back. How am I to do that?" I stood and turned. "How do I get through finals and pass when this is so distracting. I don't even feel like studying. Life means nothing to me if I can't have Mary be part of it."

Brian frowned. "Roger, it'll be okay." I didn't feel as confident as I imagined he hoped he sounded.

I stood and moved to the door. "Alright, but tell me nothing about it. I don't want to know." As I opened it I said, "I'm going to the library to study." My trek to study land was diverted by a shadow watching me as I walked. A sense of anxiety rose, sickening me with nausea. I walked quicker, but the shadow moved with me, keeping in darkness.

"What do you want?" I asked. "Why don't you show yourself?" I stayed planted to my spot on the library lawn, waiting for something to happen. "Who are you?" But the shadow turned and walked away.

Word cycled back that Monica left school. I conjectured the ploy did its job. My finals were going better than I expected, but Mary ignored me for three days. "She hates me, Brian." I said at dinner.

She doesn't hate you. She's just studying for finals. She'll call you as soon as she's done." I wasn't reassured.

"What happened to Monica?" I asked.

"The less you know the better. After all, we had nothing to do with her leaving. Remember, it happened for you." We finished our Stouffers meals and cleaned up.

I had one more test and a paper to complete in the next two days, so I departed for my room. Staring at the econ book, nothing sticking in my brain. I put it down and picked up my cell phone, started to dial and quit. *She doesn't want to talk with me.* I thought about her face and her body. I recalled our first time together in bed. I picked up the phone again but again could not complete the call.

The phone sang its ringtone from my brother. "What do you want, dirt bag?"

"Nice, real nice; I was wondering when you plan to come home? And are you bringing that delicious babe with you?"

"You're a real scum bag, Billy. I'll be done in two days and no, I won't be bringing Mary with me. She has her own family, you know."

"Ok, I'm sorry, but what's the matter. I hear it in your voice. What's going on?"

"Nothing, I just need to finish a paper and get some sleep."

"Nice try, but I know when you're hiding something." He paused. "Oh my goodness," he said. "You broke up with her, didn't you?"

"No." I stammered. "I just need to get back to studying."

"Did Monica have anything to do with this?"

'You're sick, little brother. Sick. Sick. Sick." I clicked off and threw the phone across the room. Whether it would ever see service again, I didn't care. I didn't want to speak with anyone.

I closed the book, grabbed a jacket and left the room. "Where're you going?" Brian looked perplexed.

"I need some air," Approaching the door, we heard the doorbell. "Shit."

"Campus police, please open the door."

Victoria

"Andrea, I'm going out with Conner this weekend, but I promise to be a good girl." I wanted reassurance I was ready, even though I would control what happened. Andrea knew all the answers, as far as I was concerned.

Andrea laughed. "What made you want to see him again?"

"I kind of like him. I don't know. I guess he's safe."

Andrea laughed and I blushed. "So he's promised to be a good boy?" She laughed again, but heat stirred in my face.

"I tell him what and when he can have any part of me."

"Okay, don't get mad at me. I just want you to have some fun and see what happens." Andrea held my hands. "If you call the shots then lead him on a little and then tell him what you want him to do. You can, like, let him kiss you and maybe touch your boobs again." She demonstrated an appropriate style of touching. I closed my eyes and smiled. "Don't close your eyes or he'll move on to other parts. Your eyes let him know who's in charge." I nodded. She continued fondling my breasts until a moan escaped which she warned against. I was like a misused doll.

"Stop," I said. "What if I want him to touch me in other places? What if he wants me to touch his...you know..."

"It's ok to say penis. Or cock, or prick, or anything you want. If he wants to get jacked off, you decide. If he wants to put it in you, you decide. He's going to try and convince you he's in love with you and tell you, if you love him, you'd let him do you." She put her hand on my crotch and said. "But this area is all yours. No one gets in there until you decide you want it. I don't think you want Connor to be your first, do you?"

"No, I want to know how guys act and he seems the easiest to control."

"Who do want to be your first?"

A picture of Roger deceived my mind, but that couldn't happen. I wanted someone like him, kind, mature, wise. No guy I knew fit the description. "I don't know; somebody a little older who cares about me, who I am."

"Good luck with that. Teenage guys just want to do it and go on to the next conquest. Older guys want young girls because they're perverts."

"Well, why did you let that older guy do you?"

"I was stupid and curious. But I can tell you now, it's not worth it. Find a guy you like; one who cares about you and get it on with him. If you can't find someone you're interested in, who's attentive to you. Be patient. Don't do what I did."

I hugged her and then said, "I have to go home. I'll let you know how things go with Connor." We hugged again and I left.

The week finished with a lackluster thud. Mary called and talked to me about Roger and his problems with his former girlfriend. I explained my interest in boys and she offered her advice about staying away from them.

We laughed, but I worried about her losing Roger to another woman and I would never see him again.

Saturday afternoon was the day to experiment with Connor. He and I decided on a matinee movie and an early dinner at a fast food place in the mall. I wanted a dark area to try out ideas. I was sure he had something in mind, as well. He hired a taxi to my house and escorted me to our destination.

As we rode downtown to Pacific Place he said, "Vickie, I don't want to screw this up. If I do anything bad, just tell me." I smiled and held his hand. He grinned awkward as a scared animal.

"Connor, you can do whatever I ask you to and I'll try to do whatever you want. Just remember I'm not like other girls who put out on the first date."

"This is our second date." I laughed inside realizing he hoped second base was ready for stealing. His hip touched mine as we sat, causing a twinge of interest and guilt.

At the Pacific Place Cinemas Connor purchased tickets, popcorn and sodas for us. With hands occupied carrying refreshments, his one recourse was to walk shoulder to shoulder. I reciprocated.

We seated ourselves in the rear of the theater. I figured fewer eyes would observe any indecent activity which might occur. The theater remained mostly empty as previews and the requisite warnings showed. I relaxed, thinking, no gossip around school about Connor and me being an item. This date was not the beginning of going out with someone. If my experiment succeeded another stage in the development of my sexuality might happen with Connor, but I wanted to be sure he was not a "kiss and tell" kind of guy.

The movie began after a few minutes. More people entered and sat, but no-one invaded our sanctuary. During a night scene the room appeared darker. Time came to push my agenda. Connor acted the perfect gentleman. I put my hand on his knee. He looked at me and reached out to kiss me. I offered a cheek and then sat back and removed my hand from his knee. He placed his arm around my shoulder. I looked at him but did not smile. I leaned toward him and he lowered his arm over my shoulder toward my breast.

"Connor, go ahead, touch it." I moved my right hand along his left thigh caressing the growing tension in his pants as his hand clasped my breast. I experienced no sense of shame or exhilaration. I stroked his bulge as he fondled me.

"Kiss me," I said. He turned to my face placing his lips on mine. Connor sighed and continued his lip lock. A tongue caressed the edges of my mouth. I thrust mine to meet his.

His joy eclipsed any excitement I desired. I wasn't disappointed for I learned a valuable lesson about boys. As we watched the remaining scenes of the movie, Connor held my hand.

We stayed in our seats until the credits finished and the lights came on. I giggled when I saw the darkened area on his pants. His face reddened while he tied his jacket around his waist.

"I got all the satisfaction and you got nothing," he said. I placed my finger on his lips and smiled.

"I got what I wanted." I was sure he wanted me to have more, but I had a safer place to satisfy my wanton desire. We left the theater and went to a clothing store where he purchased a pair of pants into which he changed and carried a bag of soiled attire out with him. We ate our meal in silence at a Wendy's in the food court. I now appreciated my lust for sex, but Connor was not going to be the lucky guy. My ideal man awaited discovery.

12
CHAPTER

Roger

"Brian, you open it." I moved away fearing what was to come. Brian frowned but opened the door.

"Are you Roger Waite?" the officer asked.

Brian stepped aside and looked at me. The officer followed the look and approached. "Mr. Waite, do you know a Monica Atherton?" I nodded. "She lodged a complaint against you for harassment and misrepresenting her to other people."

Brian answered before I could. "What do you mean, exactly?"

"You must be Brian Russell. She's named you in the complaint, as well."

"What are we supposed to have done?" My body heated with the question.

The officer faced me. "Are you and she dating, currently, or have you ever dated in the past?"

"Why? What does she want?" My heart increased its pulse joining my head's anxiety.

"Did you advertise around campus she willingly wanted sex with as many partners as possible?"

"What? That's stupid. Why would I do something so incorrigible?" I tensed defensively.

The officer handed me a document which clarified the complaint. I read it and handed it to Brian. "Are we under arrest or anything?"

"No," the officer responded, "but this activity is frowned on by the school administration."

"What activity, pulling a train or spreading rumors?" Brian's remark did not relieve the tension.

The officer scowled. "We understand students have their liaisons, however, excessive sexual activity which is advertised as this has been is not appropriate to the university's reputation or academic standing. You can be dismissed from school, permanently."

Brian said, "Yes sir, we understand. Although we are not the precipitators of the aforementioned activity, we are not ones to engage in frivolous pandering." I stared at Brian wondering about the legal sounding language.

"Your graduation may be forfeit if any more complaints of this nature are filed in the next week." The officer bid his leave and departed.

Brian howled. I worried about the implications of a vanished bachelor's degree. "She filed a complaint? What a hoot. Roger, I guess it worked. She's not going to have anything to do with you from now on."

"Yeah, sure. If she's filing complaints, she might just want to ruin graduation for me."

"Remember, she left campus yesterday."

"I know but somehow she seems to know how to get even. I must see Mary and straighten out our relationship. I'll see you later." I left. And Monica had shaken my confidence once again.

Mary answered the door after the second knock. "I know you're mad at me, but I can't leave it like this. I love you. Monica is nothing to me or us. She's gone. Can't we talk this out?"

Mary stood in the doorway preventing my entry. "Why should I? It's obvious, you have issues to resolve with her."

"I have no issues with her, but she probably does with me. I don't care about her. I love you and want to spend my life with you. Please. Let's talk. Please." She moved from the entry and signaled me to come in. I didn't hesitate. "Mary, I am so sorry. I have nothing to say except I love you."

Mary stepped back as I could enter. "I love you, too. I'm sorry for overreacting to your witch. She caught me at a stressful time and I made a big deal of it." She closed the door. "Are you done with tests?"

"I have one left and a paper. How are you doing?"

"I've completed everything, but I didn't want to interfere with your studying."

"Studying was hard thinking you didn't love me anymore." She came to me and pressed her lips to mine. I melted into her arms. "I love you."

The evening passed without many words. The love-making assured me our future was intact and as passionate as before. I relaxed for the first time in many days.

Finals ended without any more anxiety. Graduation held no interest for either of us, so Mary and I headed to our respective homes to complete wedding plans. The days and weeks of summer delivered no surprises, and our wedding day arrived.

Mary looked beautiful as she walked toward me along the aisle of the Lutheran church in Seattle. Before this day shone like the sun on Puget Sound, I knew not pride. Brian acted as best man. Billy and Ben accompanied me as groomsmen. Joanne stood with Mary as her maid of honor. Victoria and Peggy were the bridesmaids.

August in western Washington can be pleasant, warm with little precipitation. Today was a typical day. We celebrated our union and partied well into the evening. The few invited guests bid Mary and me best wishes for a wonderful life together and departed. I married the one woman who captured my heart those many months ago. All my exploits were history, Monica Atherton a faded memory. No Trojan horse existed. Mary was my soul mate. What could happen to ruin my future?

PART
TWO

FAMILY

13
CHAPTER

Victoria

As Roger paced the reception room, I wondered what it was like to love another person so much you wanted to spend a lifetime with them. He looked so handsome in his tuxedo. I realized, watching him, I wanted a man who would care for me as much as he cared for my sister. Mary radiated in her eggshell white wedding dress which accented her figure. Her hair coiffed up on her head with a flowered ringlet holding her veil highlighted her face. She was more beautiful than ever. *Will I be like her someday?*

During the ceremony I watched Roger as he responded to ritual questions. I imagined myself standing with him, answering the same inquiries. His brother, Billy, seemed nice and being closer in age to me than other members of the wedding party, I entertained the idea of his escorting me for the day. Maybe he was the lucky one.

"What's on your mind?" Mary approached me as I stared out a window in the reception hall. She held up well under the presence of so many people in one place. She interacted, smiled, and laughed with everyone. I had married a new woman this day.

"I was thinking about how you have found what you wanted. I was wondering about our future."

"You'll be fine. What about the boy you've been seeing?" Mary asked.

"Connor? Oh, he's nice and all, but he's not...like...my future or anything."

"You're young, yet. Some guy will sweep you off your feet and take you on a magical mystery tour." Mary hugged me. "I love you."

"I love you, too." I watched her walk toward Roger. He beamed like a kid with a new toy. Then he saw me and winked. I tingled all over.

Billy came over. "They sure are cute together." He grasp my hand. "Come on, let's get a piece of cake." I followed him. Nothing else mattered at the moment. Mary had her man. Billy placed the plate in my hand and we sat at a table away from the remaining guests.

"Do you think they'll be happy together?" My question lacked assurance.

"Sure, I can't see why not. My brother has never been this involved with a woman. He's told me about his college flings and no one filled his heart with so much love or lust."

"Gross. Why would you tell me something like that?" I placed my fork on the dish.

"I'm sorry. I thought you knew. I just figured you and she talked a lot about things. You and Mary are so alike." Billy was four years older than me but at times I found him to be immature. I liked him, but I didn't think of him as anything other than my sister's new brother-in-law.

"We do. But that doesn't mean I want to talk with you about it." I screwed up my courage. "Have you ever…um…you know…with a girl?"

"Now who's getting gross? That's none of your business, unless you want to find out yourself." I blushed but stared at Billy.

"Are you asking me to sleep with you?"

He blushed. "Well, you brought it up."

"How? Because I asked you if you'd ever had sex with someone?"

"All right, yes, but I was just kidding. Have you ever been with a guy?"

Anger welled up. "None of your business." I wanted to yell yes, lying to myself and Billy. "I suppose you think because you're an older man with needs and this is a wedding, you get to have sex with one of the attendants like in the movies."

Billy laughed at my crude analogy. "Yeah, something like that. But my sister is off limits and Joanne seems rather involved with Brian. That leaves you as the only unattached female." He leered for a moment. "You're now a member of the family and a bit too young for me."

"So I'm too young for you. How old do you think I am? I'm fourteen. I can have any guy I want including you, if I so choose."

"Yeah, well, when I turned eighteen, you became jailbait." I stood to leave. "Wait, I didn't mean to offend you. You're a nice girl and if you were older, I might be interested, although dating my sister-in-law would seem weird."

I sat again. "I'm sorry. It's just…guys are interested in me…like for only one thing. I want what my sister has."

"Be patient. Your turn will come." Billy kissed me on my forehead as he left the table.

My thoughts wandered back Andrea and then to Roger and Mary. "I wonder, Billy. I wonder."

Andrea laughed as I told her about my conversation at the wedding with Billy. We hadn't seen each other for several days and the wedding became a conversation starter. "It's not funny," I retorted. We sat on her bed, our righteousness intact.

"Sure it is. You're exploring now in a way which clears your head of your Roger fantasy." Her hands clasp mine as she continued. "Look, I enjoy sex a lot, but I can't just climb on any guy I see. I want to know I can take them for a ride and not get hurt. So I keep my emotions in check. It drives them wild to think a girl plays the game like they do. They want to control me and make me fall in love so they can break my heart. I won't let them."

I stood up and Andrea followed. "All they want is sex with you and leave?" I let go of her hands and turned to look out the window. Andrea came up behind me. "It's not fair. I want to have what Mary has. I want to love someone with such intensity I ache when they're not around." I turned to face my friend who taught me so much and yet left out the intimacy found in loving without boundaries.

She pulled me close and whispered, "You will."

What future was there in having sex with no emotional entanglements? Roger and Mary were emotional about their love for each other. I wanted it. I wanted it with the right man.

Roger

"Mary, are you happy? I ask only because I'm so amazed such a beautiful woman is my wife." On our honeymoon in British Columbia, the skies cooperated with sunshine and a light breeze. The Fairmont Chateau at Lake Louise created a marvelous atmosphere for any recently wed couple. Mary's and my parents sprung for the finest room at the lodge overlooking the lake. The bellman placed our luggage in the room and left with a healthy tip.

"I'm surprised my father sprung for this room. He's so tight with money." Mary stood at the doorway mesmerized. The room was large with a corner window looking out to the lake. An elegant salon, dining area and powder room provided a gracious and relaxing environment. At the top of a spiral staircase, a roofed, private balcony and en-suite bath embraced a secluded bedroom with a king bed; a lake view and a sitting area filling the space beautifully. A deck enhanced the scene which Mary and I were to enjoy for the next three days.

I placed the suitcases on the racks provided and turned to watch Mary gaze out the window to the lake and mountain vista. "Let's go out on the balcony," I said. The weather invited outdoor activity and the grounds provided many opportunities.

Standing at the railing, we watched people below carousing around the pool. Mary slipped her arm around me. "Thank you."

"For what?"

"For taking a chance on a crazy lady."

"Taking a chance is the least of why I want to be with you. I love you."

"Make love to me on that big bed. Make love to me like the first time." She held my hand and pulled me into the room. She kissed me as passionate a kiss as ever I received and placed a hand on my crotch. "You want me, don't you?"

I smiled remembering her sultry advance on that day in college many months ago. She had said, "Make love to me. Teach me the gentleness of sharing. Touch me so I can stop fearing what truly I want from you. Hold me tightly and caress me. Warm this cold heart of mine." Her body enticed me as no other woman. Her beauty, brains, spirit all conspired to lure me into a web from which I wanted no escape. I removed her hand from me and led her to the bed. As I removed my clothing, she danced around and stripped. I waited for her to finish and grabbed her waist, pulling her nakedness to mine.

We climbed onto the bed and explored our bodies until satisfied. I lay looking at her eyes, so blue and alluring. "I love you so much."

"I know." She gazed at me. "I'll be your sex slave and you can be mine." Cold eyes then darkened as though lost in deep thought. She turned from me unresponsive to my touch.

"What are you thinking?" I asked.

"I guess my father was right about one thing. All men actually want is sex. I'll never forget how he touched me. You touch me the same way."

"Does it bother you I want to feel your skin and play with you?"

Her eyes brightened as she answered. "A long time ago, yes. Now I enjoy everything you do to me. Make love to me again." I did as requested but mirrored her movements with a sense of concern. Had her comment hit my heart or was I overreacting? We rose, dressed, and unpacked our belonging. I smiled at her whenever she gazed my way. What she was thinking? I had no idea.

We wandered the grounds, exploring, as the summer air thrilled us. I dismissed the hint of anxiety and enjoyed Mary's companionship. The lake shore filled with other tourists so we returned to the hotel and sought a gracious dinner. Mary smiled and her face glistened, an indication of our stroll. "Did you enjoy our walk?"

"Very much so. I'm sorry about earlier."

"What about earlier?"

"I must forget about my father and his fetish. I'll appreciate what money he offers as recompense for past behavior."

We entered one of the dining rooms, requesting a window table away from the kitchen.

—— ⊙☙⊙ ——

Several weeks after our return from Canada, Mary said, "I'm pregnant." Dad and I had worked the housing market well enough to earn a comfortable living for my bride and me. Now a family sprouted. I hadn't prepared my life for a family, and yet, exhilaration seized my soul.

"So soon?" I flustered. Mary gave me the strangest look. "I mean...I... ah geez. Mary, this is wonderful news." I reached out to hug this magnificent being who stole my heart and returned it vastly improved.

"I went to see a doctor today who confirmed the pregnancy test I took on Saturday."

"When were you going to tell me?"

"I am telling you." Storm clouds circled the bedroom as I watched another decent into hell. I perceived these changes in emotion several times since our return from Canada. Sometimes I thought I imagined them.

"Yes, yes you are." I said. "I just thought maybe you wanted to let me in on your joyous news a little sooner. No, this is okay. You needed to confirm with a doctor. I get it." Blue skies returned.

"We'll fix the spare bedroom for our new family member. How about a nice pale pink?"

"Are we having a girl?"

"I don't know yet, but I think so. I don't know why I think so, but I want a girl. I can teach her all about goodness and mercy and things which are kind and sweet."

"I can't wait to tell my folks, and your family will be thrilled. Vickie's going to so excited for you."

14
CHAPTER

Victoria

"Vickie, you're going to be an aunt." I had returned from Andrea's and overheard my mother on the phone. Mom hung up as I entered.

"What? Why didn't she tell me? I'm happy for her."

"Mary wanted to connect with Ben. She said she'd call you right back. Your father is going to be so surprised."

"Yeah, I'll bet." I went to my room to wait for Mary's call. All I could think about was Roger having sex with Mary and her now pregnant. I sat at my desk trying to read, to take my mind off speculating Roger and Mary together. The history book was about the kings of England and the infidelities they had when married to wicked queens or beautiful ladies with brains. I thought of Roger. "It's not fair." I expected no one to hear.

"What's not fair?" Mom entered my room.

"Oh, you startled me." I turned to face the intruder of my imagined world. "I was thinking about Mary and Roger and how unfair it is for them to live in Wendlesburg and we won't be able to see them as often with a new baby." I turned my flushing face hiding the betrayal of any real motives.

"Your sister's on the phone." I snatched the instrument from my mother's hand as though a secret might escape and incriminate me. She seemed oblivious to my trepidations as she left and closed the door. At least she was attentive to my privacy.

"Hello, Mary? How are you feeling? I am so happy for you and Roger." We spoke for an hour about the needs of a new baby and her excitement about my birth so many years before. I asked if she wanted a girl, but she did not speculate. I heard the anxiety in her voice about becoming a mother and the change to a routine so newly established and now to be modified to fit the needs of an infant. "Mary, everything is going to be fine." I spoke to assure her and wished it to be true.

I clicked off the phone and called Andrea, the only person I figured who understood my predicament. Telling her about being an aunt didn't relieve tension created in my fantasy world. Mary sounded lost again in her own world of regret and sorrow. I lay on my bed and cried because of a misplaced dream.

Roger's parents planned a party for the end of the month at their home. Mary called again about her anxieties of motherhood. I assured her with my best phrases of support hoping to allay any fears before the imagined became reality in her mind.

As the weekend of the party came closer, Andrea and I saw each other often. She and I doubled on a date the weekend before without any experiments beyond kissing. I remained as pure as a snow pixie from some forgotten fairy tale. She abandoned me post date for her own satisfaction.

"Mom, is Mary going to be alright when the baby is born?" I asked. Saturday morning arrived as usual and chores simply wouldn't wait.

"She'll be fine. Roger is so good to her." My mother can be ignorant to what's happening right around her. She continued sorting laundry and writing notes about the party.

"Is Ben coming with anyone to Mary's party?" The folding and writing ceased for a moment. Mom tilted her head contemplating my inquiry.

"I don't think he's dating anyone right now. Maybe one of those nice young men he hangs out with can come and keep him from being bored." I just nodded my head appreciating my mother's perception which relegated her to an Eden lost to the rest of us.

Roger
Mary and I arrived at Mom and Dad's house an hour before the party began. I wanted to speak about the house my father and I procured for

Mary and me. It was located in a nice neighborhood and included three bedrooms, two bathrooms and a powder room off the kitchen. A sunken living room and dining room were to the left of a small foyer. The rambler style was reasonably priced and not yet listed.

I hugged my mother and left Mary with her to finish any of the details for the party. "Dad, I hope Mary likes the idea of moving from our apartment to a house."

"She will. I spoke with your mother about this and she's excited for you. I have all the paperwork completed through our mortgage company. All you have to do is show Mary the house and we can finish this on Monday."

"Great, I'll take her over tomorrow after church and we can go through it." We returned to the kitchen and helped with the finishing touches. The patio and family room looked festive with baby items scattered around to enliven the crowd. The doorbell rang, so I left to open it and let in the friends and family attending the party.

Mary's parents and sister, Victoria, arrived with Peggy and Hiram. Billy was not coming because of school commitments in Pullman. Members of the office staff arrived as scheduled and Mary's brother and a friend of his came just as drinks were being served on the patio.

Victoria approached and asked about Mary. "She's fine. I guess having a baby can change a woman's outlook."

"I hope that's all it is. She sounded anxious when I spoke with her earlier in the week."

"I have a secret for her. I'll let you in on it, but you can't tell her." I took Vickie into my dad's office and showed her the proposed house. "We have everything ready to go. All Mary has to say is 'yes', and we can close the deal next week. We can move in within a month. The inspection has been approved and financing is already in the works. What do you think?"

"Mary's not much for surprises, but this one might please her." I looked at this young teenager and thought how much she reminded me of my wife. I was delighted to have her for a sister-in-law. "When are you telling her about it?"

"I hope to show her the house after church tomorrow." Vickie nodded her agreement and we returned to the party.

After a meal of barbequed chicken, corn on the cob, beans, and Caesar salad, we consumed a chocolate cake like it was the last one in the world. Ice cream rounded out the dessert and coffee and tea settled the meal as we sat and talked about our lives and futures. I sensed satisfaction. Mary and I had embarked on a journey, which if care and love worked their magic, would end after a long life together and a couple of children to spoil. Time would tell.

15
CHAPTER

Victoria

Watching Roger express excitement about the house thrilled me. He looked so handsome in his jeans and blue polo shirt. His eyes flashed as he explained about each of the rooms and the possibilities for a nursery, but how would Mary react to a surprise?

We returned to the party and ate our dinner. I glanced at Roger on occasion and caught him looking at me once. I smiled as he turned to say something to his sister, Peggy. He looked back at me as he spoke. My heart fluttered.

We all said our goodbyes and left for Seattle. A ferry ride broke the monotony of driving the car around through Tacoma. Magnolia Heights was lit with many street lamps and homes blazing in the night as we cleared the south end of Bainbridge Island. The night air brushed my face as I stood on the foredeck looking toward the city. The Space Needle marked the Seattle Center's location, brightly lit from bottom to top. The tall buildings had lights burning with late night workers and cleaning crews. Condos along the waterfront cast their light into the waters of Puget Sound. I wanted to share this moment with someone, but had no real choice with the people around me. Ben and his partner decided to stay longer in Wendlesburg and were coming back to Seattle on the next ferry. As the boat neared Colman Landing, I returned to my parents and we descended to the auto deck and our car. Roger and Mary looked so happy together, I shouldn't be sad because of my hollow existence, but emotions are tricky. My heart hurt. My life, devoid of what I observed in my sister's life, was empty. What future did I have without my own Roger?

Roger

As church finished Mary and I said goodbye to our fellow parishioners. My parents were accompanying us on the visit to the house in which I hoped for Mary and our family to live. I opened Mary's car door, kissed her as she entered and then rounded the car to the driver side.

"What are you up to?" she said. I'm sure I looked guilty.

"I want to show you something." I smiled like a child with a secret.

She sat, calm but bewildered, as I began to drive. "You're not heading home. Where are we going?"

"Dad and I have searched for the right place for us to live and I think I've found it." A Cheshire grin coursed my face. "I hope you like it."

"You conspired with your father to discover a place I may or may not like, and I'm to be happy with your decision. Is that about right?"

"I don't mean to offend you, but yes, it's what I'm hoping." I drove into the neighborhood and asked, "Do you like where it's located?"

"It seems to be a nice area." After parking in the driveway of the proposed abode, we sat for a moment. Mary studied the yard and front of the house. My parents parked on the street behind us. "I hope I get to see the inside as well."

"Yes. Yes." I exited and came around to open her door. "May I present to you our new home? It has three bedrooms, two full baths and a powder room by the kitchen. The living room and dining room are near the kitchen, as well. The master bedroom is large and has a walk-in closet. We have a family room and a large deck off of it. The yard is in great shape. The three car garage can hold a shop for me and a second car for you."

Mary walked up the front steps and turned. "I see your parents are here." Her eyes deepened their color. "Can you make a decision without them?" I readied for an onslaught but nothing materialized. I unlocked the door and stepped aside so she could enter. As we toured each room nothing was said. I began to fear I had offended her. In one of the smaller bedrooms she faced me and said, "This can be made into a nursery for our baby." I smiled and we hugged.

My parents had waited in the kitchen for the inspection to end. When we assembled my father asked Mary, "Well, what do you think?"

"I like it. Roger, could you do me a favor and go to the car and get my coat. It's a little cool in here." Her voice had a coolness in it, as well. Did she trust my judgment?

Regardless of her feelings, I said, "Sure, we can turn on the heat if you wish."

"Just get my coat, please." I left the kitchen wondering about her attitude. I found her coat. As I returned I heard Mary. "I'm glad you helped Roger find this place, but is he doing okay in the real estate business?" What else had she said?

My father answered, "Yes, he is. He's quite good at showing the right places for each client. I'm very happy for him and for you." I entered the kitchen and the conversation died.

16
CHAPTER

Victoria

"Mary, the place sounds great. As your younger sister, I declare it your sanctuary. Roger is very thoughtful to save you the trouble of looking for a suitable house. After all, he is in the business." Over the phone I heard the plea in her voice for a reason to hold steady, but I feared she was falling into the depths of sorrow. A physical embrace to calm her fears and guide her to a better sense of mind was not an option.

My fifteenth birthday whirled ahead of me like a beacon far off and not getting nearer. To reach her before any serious collapse befell her, I created an excuse for a family gathering. Roger didn't understand her like I did. He'd known her for a little over a year. I had spent my life with her and grew to recognize the mental valleys and hills which she traversed.

"Mom, can we have Roger and Mary over for dinner this weekend?" I held the phone receiver covered by my hand so Mary couldn't hear my appeal.

"What a wonderful idea. Let me talk with your sister and arrange it." I handed the phone to Mom and waited for a positive reply. Mom handed the phone back to me. "It's all set. She has to speak with Roger, but I think they'll come on Saturday."

"Mary, I can hardly wait. Do you have some pictures of the house? I'm so anxious to see it. This is so cool." We finished our conversation and I sought my mother to find out the details for the weekend. Would

Roger accept my help keeping Mary on an even keel? The baby needed a healthy mother.

School helped drive the week toward Saturday and dinner with Roger and Mary. Andrea and I talked depression and how to help my sister through it. We researched what it meant and how it came about until I was comfortable discussing with Roger ways to keep Mary happy. He didn't understand her, so I had to be strong.

"Mom," I said returning from Andrea's house early Saturday afternoon. "What time are Mary and Roger coming?" The table in the dining room looked bare and I panicked. "Mom, why's the table not set?" What can I do to help?"

Mom came in from the kitchen. "Hello to you. You can set the table and they'll be here about 5:00." I nodded and opened the sideboard for the silverware.

"Are we using the good silver or the flatware? Which plates do you want out? And what glasses are needed?"

"Why this sudden interest in helping?" Mom just stared at me as I blushed.

"I haven't seen Mary and Roger in like forever" I pulled out the silverware and set the table. Mom left for the kitchen laughing. It was good to see her happy even for a short time. I finished the table and entered the kitchen. "Mom, what are we having for dinner?" I smelled a roast and figured out the rest of her standard meal.

"We are having prime rib with sweet potatoes and broccoli and cauliflower. And for dessert I made an apple pie."

My guess was almost correct. We didn't have prime rib except for special occasions. A new baby and a new house were.

"Mom, is Ben coming tonight?"

"I invited him, but you know how he is around your father. I'm not expecting him."

"Okay." I departed to change clothes. Better to look impressive and mature than to be an officious teenager. As I put on a clean skirt and blouse, I studied my figure in the mirror on my door. If Andrea found my shapeliness arousing so could a male, I thought. I didn't intend a seductive encounter, but any attention might prove my desirability. I left the top two buttons undone and inspected the presentation once again. Enough cleavage without seeming lurid caused me to think something I shouldn't. When I heard the doorbell, I smirked.

Roger

Marion answered the door soon after our arrival. Mary looked happy but a tension in her body and the tightness of grip on my hand whispered otherwise. This house had no affinity for her anymore. Only Vickie could make the evening pleasant enough for her to enter. She stated a genuine love for her little sister which I didn't oppose. I accepted the fact I might play second fiddle to this teenager who possessed a spell over my wife which I didn't understand. "How is everyone?" I asked as a politeness to quell impending storms.

"Roger, Mary, do come in." Marion said. We stepped into the foyer as Garrett came in from his den. The grip increased as the smile faded. His arrival exposed the lack of love.

Vickie descended the stairs coming into view looking rather sophisticated for a fourteen year old. She appeared to be more mature than our last encounter and looked so much more like her sister. Mary saw her and I perceived her relax a bit,

"Hi...uh...hello everyone. I am so glad to see you." She hugged Mary tightly and whispered something I didn't hear. Releasing her catch, she next pressed her body against mine challenging my sensibility. She whispered in my ear as well about needing to talk to me in private. She then kissed my check leaving an invisible betrayal.

Garrett shook my hand and we proceeded to the living room. Mary and Vickie, arm in arm, led the procession. A grin coursed my face. How alike they were, and yet so different. Vickie was becoming as tall as her sister, better shaped legs and hair a bit longer. I wondered if her personality possessed tempests rivaling Mary.

We imbibed and consumed aperitif and hors d'oeuvres to whet our appetites. Conversations stuck to information about our family expansion and new living quarters. After a while and several libations we enjoyed a sumptuous meal of prime rib and steamed vegetables. I wondered about Ben for a fleeting moment and dismissed his absence, an indication of the chasm between father and son.

Dinner eaten, I watched as Mary and Vickie assisted Marion with the clearing of dishes. I proffered my aid but was dismissed from duty. Stillness between Garrett and me could only be stirred by asking questions.

"So how has your week been?" I injected into the calm. I expected nothing but was surprised.

"You have no idea the problems I encounter in my business. I imagine you have your own set in real estate."

"Well, it can be challenging what with interest rates fluctuating and banks being tight with lending. We do alright, though."

"I hope so for Mary's sake. You two seem to be getting along quite well."

"I guess we are. I know I'm as happy as I've ever been. We are looking forward to moving into the new house. We'll have you and Marion over for dinner when we get set up. And Vickie is welcome, of course."

Garrett nodded, as the dessert entered with three beautiful ladies carrying all needed pieces. Marion placed the pie before Garrett. Mary had carafes of coffee and tea, while Vickie placed plates next to the pie. She placed her hand on top of mine, leaned in close to my ear and whispered. "You'll enjoy this dessert, I'm sure." A guilty twinge swept through me. Her blouse opened a little to reveal more than a man should view. By design or mistake I did not distinguish. It was only for a moment, as she continued to her seat on the other side of the table.

Mary placed an arm in mine as she asked, "What little tryst are you two conniving against me?" I blushed as I glanced at Vickie. Did she just wink?

"She said I would enjoy the dessert."

"You'll have to watch her. She hatches schemes to get what she wants." Mary smiled. "I, myself, have fallen for her wily ways." I looked across the table and watched her delicate motions as she consumed her pie. Her blouse lay open as she caressed its collar not looking at me but with furtive glances to be sure I saw the smooth silky skin of her cleavage.

After dinner we sat and talked for a moment drinking coffee and tea. I explained our house and what we needed for the newest member, yet to be born. After small talk waned, I volunteered to clear the remaining dishes so Mary and Marion could catch up on whatever women catch up on. Vickie followed me into the kitchen.

"Roger, I hope you won't feel I'm intruding, but I can help when Mary has one of her tirades. I know her better than she knows herself." He placed dishes in the dishwasher, and I filled the sink with water and soap.

"Thanks. I'll wash. You dry." I put the pots and pans into the suds and began scrubbing. "What did you say to Mary when we entered the house?"

Vickie smiled her crooked little grin. "I said she has a very handsome husband." She picked up a towel on the counter and began wiping the first pan dry.

"What is it about you which entices such flirting?"

"Don't you remember being an adolescent?"

A snigger escaped. "I do."

17
CHAPTER

Victoria

Roger and I finished cleaning the dishes and putting them away. Domestic chores bonded me to Roger more than I figured they would. He enthralled me. Mary had a great man for a husband. I wanted someone just like him.

"I'm sorry I flirted with you before dinner." I held his right hand in my left hand.

"It's alright. I didn't think anything of it." *Was he telling the truth?*

"Anyway, Mary is sensitive. We need to have a plan for keeping her from the crazies."

Roger folded the towel he held and placed it by the sink. "Vickie, she's just fine. Let's join them before they start talking about us." He turned from me and walked away. My eyes followed.

Roger

My head rattled irrational thoughts like some ill-conceived adolescent plot to rule the world. Vickie had the ability to be like Mary in so many ways. Her looks, her body, no tantrums, at least none I'd seen.

Joining Mary and her mother in the living room, Mary looked content, relaxed. I sat next to her. "What are you two scheming?"

Marion answered first. "We were just talking about the new baby and how much fun you'll have raising it."

"Yes, we are certainly lucky."

Mary surprised me. "Vickie, you come over anytime, especially when you convince Mom and Dad to let you drive."

"I'll catch the ferry and Roger can pick me up. I'll even babysit for you." Vickie's offering kindled imagination.

I said, "It's getting late. I think we should get going."

We all stood as Marion said, "Thank you, Roger for helping Vickie clean up the kitchen." I smiled and nodded. At the door with coats in hand I hugged Marion and then Vickie. I pecked her cheek and said, "Thanks for cleaning up with me."

"You're welcome." Garrett came out when he heard the commotion in the foyer.

"Are you leaving?" he asked. "Please have a safe trip home." He turned around and returned to his sanctuary, free from dealing with domestic interaction.

In the car Mary asked, "What were you and Vickie talking about in the kitchen?"

"Oh, you know the usual stuff about school and your dad. She knows an awful lot about human thinking for a teenager."

"Be careful with her; she is more ingenious than one might expect."

"Ingenious? She's fourteen."

"I know, but she's more intelligent and mature than anyone her age. Watch out. That's all I'm saying."

"It sounds like you don't trust your sister."

"I trust her more than anyone. Still when things come to a head, she tends be the one who finishes on top."

We caught the next ferry leaving for the peninsula, went up to the passenger deck and watched Seattle lights as we sailed across Puget Sound. What Mary said about Vickie triggered my thinking. Would she be so imaginative as to manipulate me while helping Mary? What would those meetings entail? We docked in Bainbridge at the Winslow pier and drove home to Wendlesburg. "Mary, are you happy."

"I wanted so much to see Mom and Vickie. It was okay Ben didn't make it. My father was his usual insolent self."

"I'm glad." We walked from the parking garage arm in arm to our abode. As we prepared for bed I probed another area of Mary's psyche. "Do you think Vickie was flirtatious with me?"

Mary laughed, "She's young and exploring her sexuality. She's just practicing in a safe environment. I wouldn't get too worked up about it."

"Good because I love you so much and I don't want anything coming between us." No storms brewed, and although Mary was gaining girth because of the pregnancy, we made love. I fell into a deep sleep which included an erotic dream of Vickie.

18
CHAPTER

Victoria

I endured a fitful sleep thinking about Roger. Dinner had been fun, especially clearing the table and cleaning the kitchen after dessert. I just wanted to be near him and watch Mary be happy.

I finished dressing for church, although I wasn't in any mood to listen to the pastor drone on about our sins and how we need to repent for the salvation of our souls. My soul was mine and I would be the savior of me.

Dad called out, "Breakfast is ready." I descended the stairs and entered the kitchen.

"What's for breakfast?" Mom turned to me and handed me a plate with scrambled eggs and toast. Another plate on the counter had pieces of ham. I forked one onto my plate and sat on a stool to eat. Father said grace before we consumed food. Nothing but silence dominated the room. We cleared the counter and left for church.

Sitting in the pew, I looked around at the other families and individuals wondering if it is indeed a sin to be fantasizing about someone. Thinking about someone unattainable. Neglecting reality.

After church we went downtown to the Edgewater and had lunch at Six Seven. The day was warm, sun shining over the bay. We ate on the terrace. Why splurge when we usually went home? Maybe to sweeten the day before exploding bad news on me? School was coming to an end in two months and I was leaving Our Lady of Fatima School to attend Ballard High School in the fall. I had petitioned them to attend a public school for more experiences. They seemed to have accepted my premise. Was this the moment of reneging on a promise?

"I sure do like the view of Puget Sound and Elliot Bay," My Father's comment came out of nowhere. "Look, the Victoria Clipper is coming in."

"Why are we here?" I asked blatantly, unsure if I wanted to know.

Mom responded before my Father, "We thought it would be a nice treat for all of us. Besides, after having fixed a big dinner, I didn't feel like doing it again."

"Is this about my going to Ballard in the fall?"

"What? No." My Father seemed genuinely surprised by my inquiry. "Look, I know I haven't been the best parent for you. If public school is what you want, then that's where you'll go. Besides, I hear it's a pretty good school." An imaginary burden of guilt vanished, guilt against my parents' change of heart but not any guilt because of Roger.

"Well, I guess I owe you both an apology. I thought maybe you were going to…Oh, never mind. Boy do I feel silly."

As the lunch progressed to a conclusion with little conversation to interrupt, I relaxed about my outlook. All was well in my life. I had more questions about what a boy wants from a relationship, but Andrea seemed to know everything there was to know. I reckoned it wasn't worth creating drama with gossip sure to follow.

We finished our meal but decided to wander up to the Pike Market. I enjoyed the fresh flower and vegetable stands. The fish market near the south end always put on a show throwing salmon and other fish back and forth. Rachel, the brass pig, was fun to sit on for photo ops.

"Mom, Dad, do you want to be grandparents?" My father got the strangest look on his face.

"Do you have something to tell us which your mother and I should worry?" My eyebrows rose to the top of my head.

"Not me, I was just thinking about becoming an aunt and wondered. I don't want to be that person who doesn't want to be around babies."

"You'll be fine. As for your mother and me, we are very happy about becoming grandparents."

Silence pervaded the conversation again. I thought about Roger being a father. If they had a boy, he would teach him about all the manly things Ben avoided, sports, hunting, fishing hiking. I pondered Dad and Ben not going anywhere together to do manly things. Dad taught me like I was the son he forfeited with Ben. I wanted to be there with Roger when he took his son on trips to the great outdoors. Mary never went with Dad or learned any of the manly things. Would she want to go now?

Roger

Mary turned in the bed as I watched her sleep. What was it about her sister who caused my mind to act so irrationally? Mary was a wonderful person. I loved her with all my soul. I rose from the bed and sat on the edge, thinking about last night. No, Mary's right, she's just trying out her wings.

I left the bedroom to find the newspaper. The time was early enough to glimpse the scores and read comics before breakfast and attending church. The dream faded into my mental history and vanished.

Having read the palpable parts of the paper, I left the room for the kitchen to fix a cup of coffee. The automatic percolator performed its function flawlessly. I grabbed a mug from the cupboard and poured a rich flavor filled amount as Mary entered the room.

"Good morning sunshine," I said as she garnered her own mug and poured a cup. "I trust you slept well."

"It's getting more difficult the larger this baby becomes. I'm not comfortable on either side, but lying on my back is not good for the baby."

I hugged her. "I will do anything I can to help you." She smiled and shook her head.

"I'll be okay." We ate a bowl of cereal and toast along with some cranberry juice before retreating to the bedroom. I treasured the fact she attended church with me. We discussed the issue and she agreed.

At church I had little or no urge to ask forgiveness for thinking about Vickie. I prayed for other sins I committed, but she was a member of the family and not a sin.

Days passed by slowly as spring ended and summer commenced. Mary's pregnancy progressed normally even when she had bouts of temper as hormone levels prepared for the onset of delivery. I knew not when or why she lost control, but I tried in vain to calm her squalls before the winds of depression howled incessantly.

Avoiding communication with the one person whose intimate understanding of Mary could turn her temperament to sunshine was a challenge. I had to learn how to function when the emotional tirades quelled the peace of our house.

Moving during the last weeks of pregnancy was probably not the best time. We could have waited, but with the delayed closing finally completed and additional space required, it seemed most prudent. A local moving company packed the few possessions we owned and shipped them across town to the middle class neighborhood which was our community for the next several years.

The house tripled our living space. Two more bedrooms meant expansion of the family, attainable without a future upgrade of quarters. We had the requisite two and one-half bathrooms, living room, dining room, and office/den. The kitchen provided more than adequate space to prepare any meal from simple to full party mode. A family room off the kitchen with connection to the living room acted as the main people area. A single floor provided the least amount of climbing. A three car garage enabled the purchase of a second vehicle and additional storage. A laundry room with sink and storage of dirty shoes and sundry other items completed the ensemble.

Cultivating harmony in our new home we shopped for additional furniture, filling the living room and dining room. Our parents generously cooperated in the endeavor, satisfying our new home with baby needs, a new television and yard care equipment.

Mary and I were now up to our eyeballs in debt, but increases of listings and sales fetched additional income. I spent more time away from home which precipitated intermittent tempests disturbing our love nest.

"Let's throw a party, to celebrate our move to this neighborhood." The idea for social interaction had good intentions.

"Are you sure?" she replied.

"Our new neighbors and family can help us have fun with our transition. We'll hire a caterer to provide the necessary foods and drinks and subsequent clean-up."

A muted harmony existed as the time drew near for our little offspring. Mary feared delivery so squalls, though small, raged day after day prior to the birth of our daughter, Rebecca. Delivery and recovery delayed the housewarming party.

19

CHAPTER

Victoria

School days ended and my private school experience at Our Lady of Fatima, as well. I wanted to visit Mary and Roger in their new home but anxiety haunted me. Andrea and I planned a double date for the weekend after school ended which allayed some of my feelings. Connor remained a friendly distraction to real passions for which I figured he was clueless and frustrated. He wanted what I did not.

The phone rang one Friday in June. School was done and Mary approached her due date. I hurried to pick up the receiver in my room and heard my mother answer.

"Marion," Roger said, "You are now the proud grandmother of a baby girl. My excitement for Mary remained muted, covert listening my goal. "We named her Rebecca Elizabeth. She's seven pounds, 3 ounces, 21 inches and healthy as can be. She's so beautiful. Fortunately, she looks like her mother." I could not hold my silence.

"Roger, congratulations," I exploded through the phone.

"Thank you, Vickie. I want you both to come over as soon as possible and see her. Mary and Rebecca come home tomorrow."

Plans for a Sunday trip to Wendlesburg commenced. I bade goodbye to Roger as he and Mom continued. Rushing to Andrea's house I stopped before it and contemplated the idea of motherhood and parenting a baby. A statue of thought, my fears of pregnancy cemented my determination for preventive measures before succumbing to the growing urges within me. Andrea opened her front door interrupting my deliberations.

"What are you doing?" She approached me dressed in pajamas and slippers. "What happened?"

"Mary had her baby this morning. Why are you still dressed in pajamas?" We transited the walkway and entered the house arriving in her room.

"Mom's at work and I didn't feel like getting dressed. Now tell me all about the baby." I explained what Roger had said and why I stood in front of the house. Andrea laughed at my imagined panic.

"No one should be getting knocked up. See a doctor for birth-control pills."

"My parents don't believe in it. They think I should abstain until I'm married."

"Is that what you want?"

"I don't know. I'm not ready to do it with anyone."

"Yeah, except Mr. I-can't-have-him." Andrea disrobed as I sat on the bed. She dressed in a paisley bra and matching panties, jeans and a t-shirt with a picture of the Space Needle on it.

"I'm going to see them on Sunday. We're headed there after church. Mary and the baby are coming home tomorrow."

We sat silent as lambs in danger of attack from predators. I lay on the bed looking at the ceiling with its cloud patterns and birds. "Why did you want to have your ceiling painted?"

Andrea looked up. "Mom thought it would amuse me when I was younger. I've gotten used to having them and don't pay much attention. Raphael asked me about it the other day when he was here." She had met him at Northgate Mall two months ago. His dark hair and brown eyes matched his light brown Hispanic coloring. He attended O'Dea and Andrea now plotted to change her fall entry to high school.

"Were you alone with him?"

"Mom was at work."

"Did you...?" I winced, thinking about a male body lying where I lay.

A wink answered my inquiry. I scooted off as fast as I could. "I just couldn't pass up the opportunity."

"So how many others have been welcomed here?"

"Don't piss your pants. He was the first to grace my bed. I growled at her insensitivity, or maybe I just didn't like knowing.

"When are you going to see him again?"

"Curiosity can be a good thing, I hear. He's coming over in ten minutes." Andrea looked at her watch. "Want to meet him?"

I grabbed my coat, frowned at my so called friend and left. She followed. At the front door the bell rang. Andrea opened it and admitted a tall, muscular guy who looked like a young Matt Damon. Immobilized by what I observed, I missed Andrea's introduction. "Vickie, wake up. This is Raphael."

"Uh, hi. It's a pleasure to meet you." We shook hands, his gentle with a slight squeeze to show strength. No boy at Fatima even closely resembled this young man. I left, wondering.

As I walked back to my house, curiosity invested much energy to convince me to return. I resisted, reminding myself I could not nor would not interfere in Andrea's quest to satisfy her appetite.

I entered the house to find Mom engrossed in a television show about cooking. I said 'hi' and went to my room. Lying on my bed I visualized Andrea with Raphael. I fell asleep interjecting my own fantasies into the scenario.

I awoke to discover several hours had passed and the afternoon sun shone in my room. I remembered smatterings of my dreams which were erotic and puzzling. Who was the amalgam of the male? Roger, Connor, and Raphael represented as one person with gleeful adulation at my ability to gyrate and embrace a powerful stamina. Nothing of the games played in Morpheus's arms embodied real experiences, but Andrea accentuated the absurdness by laughing while I was being despoiled.

The sun beat down fading the last visage of memory from me. I wanted nothing more to do with an ignoble life. I sat up from the bed to discover clothing rearranged during my delusional sleep mêlée.

My impending birthday had no distraction this year which would discombobulate plans for a celebration. Mary's birthing of Rebecca meant she would not interfere. No weddings or pregnancies would confiscate my turning fifteen with friends. I could have a small soirée, but the only real present I desired would have to wait.

Dinner was quiet as usual. Dad talked about the new member of the Johnson clan as though the world would be better for it. His displeasure for the name originated from a girl who dashed his hopes for her as a girlfriend in junior high school. Mom laughed and expressed her pleasure for the appellation. I remained the third cog in the conversation, adding little to the verbal exchange. I liked Rebecca and visualized her looking like my sister and me. I wanted to hold her and love her. I was now an aunt and proud to be so.

Saturday came and I woke early. "Funny," I thought. "School is done for the summer and I wake up anyway." I dressed in jeans and a pink and yellow striped blouse over my plain white underwear. I descended the staircase to find my mother already constructing a breakfast fit for a logging crew.

"Good morning," I said in as pleasant a voice as possible. Rested and ready to take on the world, I planned a movie with Andrea, Raphael and Connor for late afternoon. "Why such a big breakfast?"

"Oh, Ben is coming over with his roommate, Jackson. He wants to discuss some business with your father and me."

Ben and his roommate. Mom was clueless about their friendship. I knew my father would not accept it, but what business did they have to discuss? I let it go for now.

The doorbell rang, so I departed to open the way for my brother and his friend to enter. The fun was about to begin.

Roger

"How are you feeling, Mary?" I asked, not expecting a positive result.

"Roger, I feel like I've been torn apart and put back together with duct tape which is now tearing itself from my body."

"Can I get you anything?" I held our new baby while Mary adjusted her body to find any semblance of comfort before she fed Rebecca. I could not have imagined the joy one could have becoming a father. I hoped Mary might relish the same emotions.

"Give her to me." I placed our jewel in her arms and watched the feeding commence. "I'm not some freak show to ogle while I feed her. Get me some juice and another pain pill." I departed for the nurses' station. Mary had not returned to a happy disposition, as yet, but I knew she was going to love this baby and we would be a cheerful family. I returned to her bedside after informing the nurse of her request.

"I love you and Rebecca. What a nice name for our little girl." Mary smiled sardonically. I hoped the day improved when we returned home, scheduled for later in the afternoon.

The nurse arrived with a cup containing the requested medication. Mary procured the pill from him and a cup of juice from me. Satisfied with the actions she finished feeding our baby who then slept in her arms. I sat down and watched my two ladies. Mary closed her eyes endeavoring to rest as well. The nurse removed Rebecca from her arms and placed her in the bassinette next to the bed. Mary did not complain but dozed within a few minutes.

I rose from my seat to find the nurse. "How long will my wife be so miserable?" I asked.

The nurse looked at me smiling. "She'll be alright. It takes a couple of days for the body to recover from birth and about a week to heal most of the tissues which have been stretched. The doctor will prescribe pain and antibacterial medication for her."

"How about her moodiness?"

"It's not uncommon for some women to experience a post-partum depression." I nodded and returned to Mary. She slept peacefully as did Rebecca. Hunger pangs reminded me of a lack of food, so I departed for the hospital cafeteria, my worries about Mary's thundering forgotten in the moment.

Sated with the mediocre fare of the cafeteria, I returned and found Mary awake and happy. "I need the bathroom." She said. I helped her stand and walk. She shrugged me off at the door and entered. I turned to see Rebecca still sleeping quietly. She looked so pretty and proportional. I grinned. We were parents and I was proud.

The bathroom door opened and Mary emerged. I scuttled to assist her back to the bed, but she wanted to sit in the only chair. "The pain pill kicked in while I slept. You have no idea what a woman goes through to produce your offspring." I placed a hand on her head and stroked her blond locks away from her face.

"You are so beautiful." Her eyes lifted to glare at me.

"You are such a liar, but I like hearing you say it." No vestige of sullenness manifested for the moment. "I want to go home."

"The doctor's coming in this afternoon and we can leave after he sees how you and Rebecca are doing." I leaned down and kissed her lips. She responded meekly and I wondered when an inevitable storm might strike.

20
CHAPTER

Victoria

"Mom, I'm ready to leave whenever you and Dad are." I yelled up the staircase. We had returned from church and ate a quick lunch. Roger called last night to inform us of their return home. Rebecca was healthy and adjusting well to her new room and crib. Mary had gone to bed and slept for most of the evening. I had answered the call, giddy when I heard his voice.

Ben and my parents worked out a partnership for his return to school for another two years to complete a Master's degree in computer programming and technical support. He stayed a programmer for a small biotech firm but scaled back the number of hours of work. His friend had come to support the proposal for schooling since he had accomplished the same program earlier in the year.

All was right with the world. Andrea and I enjoyed Saturday afternoon without excessive fondling or satiation of primal male urges. Raphael drove us to the movie and a fast food restaurant before returning us to our respective homes. Connor adjusted to the level of attention he received because of the reputation of having a hot babe for a girlfriend. I'm sure he expected a breakdown of my defensive posture before too long a time period. I resolved to remain as pure as snow for the one person who would melt those barriers of ice and thaw my libido much as Andrea described.

We packed our bodies into the BMW C class sedan and headed for the ferry terminal. Ben was going to meet us dockside and ride with us to Roger and Mary's new house. We had not seen it yet and anxious minds reflected on the changes in our sibling's life. They married less than a year ago and already a new house, new baby, and new automobile. Events scurried faster than I thought Mary could handle.

With our car parked on the port side of the ferry, Kitsap, we climbed the staircase to locate Ben. He enjoyed a cup of coffee from the galley where we found him sitting with Jackson.

"I didn't know your friend was coming." Mom said.

"He didn't have anything else to do and he wants to meet my niece." Jackson Waterman and Ben had roomed together for the last two years, keeping their relationship quiet for Mom and Dad's sake. Paying for a Master's degree would be out the window if Dad realized the commitment they had for each other.

"Hi, Ben." I gave my brother a hug and kissed his cheek. He grabbed me and tickled my ribs.

"So what nefarious activities have you been up to?" I sat on his lap and hugged him again.

"None of your business, but I understand you are going back to school."

"Yup, with some help from Mom and Dad." He smiled at them. "Are you excited about high school?"

"Yes, Ballard's going to be a blast."

"Be careful of those young men buzzing around you as soon as you hit campus." I stood up and turned to him.

"I will. They cannot have any of this." I said with a sweep of my arms. Mother tapped my shoulder as if to say 'Don't be crude.' I sat in the seat next to Jackson. He was a bit taller than Ben with slender shoulders and arms. His build reminded me of a frail flower barely able to stand under the weight of the petals. He was attractive for an older guy, but I didn't think him handsome like my brother. Andrea would reject him as unsuitable for mating, the antithesis of Raphael.

The ride over Puget Sound was pleasant with no clouds for so early in the summer season. I didn't contemplate any at Roger's house either.

Our car was packed with Jackson accompanying us. We drove up the ramp to the street level and proceeded to Roger and Mary and the baby, Rebecca. Nothing could spoil this day for me, could it?

Roger

Mary woke on Sunday weary from a restless night of little sleep. Rebecca demanded much from us, or more so from her mother than me. I offered assistance but not being capable of breast feeding an infant I mistakenly turned over for sleep.

The morning's arrival dimmed the spirits of an already over-taxed family. Rebecca cooperated by continuing her sleep. Mary shook me.

"Some help you turned out to be," she lamented. "I can't do this alone."

"What can I do?"

"You can be the first one up to get our daughter and bring her to me, instead of my rising from bed."

"I can do that. What else?"

"You can change her diaper after I feed her. Then you rock her to sleep and put her back in the crib. Stay up until I am finished and then you can sleep."

I kissed my bride and nodded in agreement to the terms of my surrender to the night. "May I get you some breakfast?" I stood by the bed awaiting my orders.

"Yes, I want an egg and some of the ham in the refrigerator freezer. Defrost it in the microwave and bring me some juice, and coffee."

"Would you like a muffin as well?"

"Yes, yes, hurry up before our little darling disturbs my rest again."

I left to prepare a feast for the two of us. This day was to be magical when her family arrived in the afternoon. As the ham heated in the microwave, I poured orange juice for Mary and a tomato juice for myself. The coffee machine had accomplished its task, brewing as preset the previous evening. The muffin toasted quietly in the toaster as I began cracking eggs into the pan on the stove.

I heard a shuffling sound in the hallway. Mary rounded the corner, sitting in the first chair at the table. I placed her juice glass and coffee mug next to her. "I would have brought these to you in bed."

"I know, but I needed to get up and move." She smiled weakly attempting to lighten her spirits. Her azure eyes appeared darker than usual. Her blonde tresses tussled in the night with interruptions now flowed across her face obscuring one side. The ding of the oven reported warm ham and the toaster ejected another russet coloring of bread. The eggs crackled in the olive oil as they firmed to a proper consistency.

We ate our meal in silence, fighting urges to sleep as we sat. When finished I cleared the table and stacked the dishes in the sink.

"Why can't men put things in the dishwasher?"

"I'll rinse them later and do that. Right now, let's get you back to bed for some rest, while Rebecca sleeps." She didn't argue but scuffled back to the bedroom and warm covers. I checked the baby's room and smiled at the beauty who rudely interrupted the night for her own selfish desires. I wanted to lift and cradle her, but thought better of it. I joined Mary in the bedroom.

"I need you to be the mule until I'm well enough to pick up my part in this bargain."

"I know and I will." Her eyes had returned to a more temperate blue as I tucked her in and watched them close. I returned to kitchen duty and cleaned up breakfast's residue. The hallway bore the remnants of our return from the hospital, so I collected the dirty laundry and began a load. The suitcase was stored in the garage.

Reentering the house I heard Rebecca announce her awakening. I found mother and daughter rocking gently in the chair as Mary fed her. "Where were you?"

"I was cleaning up the house. I started a load of laundry and returned the suitcase to the garage. The kitchen is presentable again. I heard Rebecca but you got to her before I could." Mary's countenance expressed another storm. I hoped it to be short-lived for my sake and Rebecca's.

I changed Rebecca after her feeding as Mary returned to bed. We sat in the rocking chair looking at each other with an apparent smile on her face. My imagination probably, but I wanted to share this moment and cherished it. She released an ignoble throaty sound unworthy of her but expected after feeding. The illusory smile disappeared and she fell asleep. The warmth of her body seeped through the blanket wrapped around her and I cuddled her before placing her in the crib, kissing her forehead as I laid her down.

Going to our bedroom I found Mary sitting on the edge of the bed. "I'm sorry," she said. "I shouldn't take it out on you." I sat with her. "We're not ready to be parents."

"And yet, we are. So let's do this right."

She nodded and placed her head on my shoulder. I held her for a moment. We dressed during the lull of parenting and I finished neatening the house for her parents. All was ready to meet the newest member of our two families. My parents had visited the hospital and met Rebecca on Friday. They came on Saturday to help me with the transfer to our house and planned to stay away, letting the Johnsons have their time with their new granddaughter.

I checked my watch. Time approached mid-morning. My tired body rejected its lack of sleep, wanting a respite. I had no argument against it. Sitting on the sofa, I closed my eyes.

"Roger," I heard from a distance. "Roger, wake up. I want you to go to the store and get me some ibuprofen and ginger ale." I stirred from my respite.

"Anything else?" I said grabbing my coat and car keys.

"Yes, chocolate ice cream and Nilla Wafers." An odd assortment of items, but Mary needed caring and I provided it.

"I'm taking my cell, so call me if you think of anything else." Her moodiness seemed less prevalent as I left the house. I prayed for calm.

Her family wasn't expected for another few hours but lunch and an unplanned dinner awaited my return. No storm appeared when I returned to the house with her demands.

"What do you want for lunch?" Standing in the kitchen, I gave her the pills and put the other things in proper places.

"I don't feel like eating."

"You need something to help you recuperate."

She looked at me and responded. "What would you know about my needs? You didn't shove a basketball out your ass on Friday. I just want to be left alone."

"I know, babe, but I can fix anything you want when you want it. Just let me know. I'll heat some soup for me and if you want any just tell me." She stomped from the kitchen back to the bedroom. Rebecca remained asleep.

I consumed soup and a turkey sandwich, then visited our daughter to see if she had awakened. Her eyes tracked my movement to the crib.

I picked her up checking for the usual waste product. Changing her into a fresh diaper, I changed her clothes to look presentable to grandparents, aunt, and uncle.

Mary entered. "Don't put that pair of pants on her. Put this jumper outfit from Mom and Dad on her."

"Oh, good idea." Her storm abated for the moment. "Do you think she needs to be fed?"

"What am I, a milking machine? Why don't I just ask her if she's hungry?"

"I know this isn't easy, but until she's on a bottle I'm kind of limited here."

"Give her to me." Mary fed our voracious darling. "Fix me some soup, please." I assented and left for the kitchen. With soup heated and a warm cup of tea, I returned to Rebecca's room and set the lunch on the dresser next to the rocking chair. Rebecca continued her consumption. Mary looked at me as if to say I was an idiot, or so it seemed. I departed again to clean the kitchen simply to occupy my time and be away from any disaster pending in the bedroom.

Mary came in with Rebecca and handed her to me. She left. My baby looked at me with deep blue eyes penetrating my self-indulgence with innocence and unfettered love.

Mary returned with her bowl of soup and tea. "Do you think me overreacting to having a baby?" My furrowed brow tipped the scale of equanimity to one of sorrow. I regretted my expression.

"No," I answered. "We have this beautiful child who is your offspring and looks like you. I love you all the more for bearing such an incredible person."

"But I didn't want to be pregnant this soon."

"I know, but we'll survive and get through this."

"Get through this. You make it sound like an ordeal. Is it an ordeal? Is it?" The heat of the discussion upset Rebecca who whimpered at the increase of volume. Mary left before finishing her lunch. I calmed the baby as best I could and walked her into the living room to look out the window.

"Watch out there for your grandparents and Aunt Vickie and Uncle Ben. You and I need to talk with Aunt Vickie about Mommy." I whispered unsure of prying ears. Rebecca snuggled against my shoulder, let out a small burp and fell asleep.

Returning to the nursery to place her in the crib, I found Mary sitting in the rocking chair, tears welling in her eyes. "I can't be a good mother. I don't know what I'm doing." I sat on the other chair and reached a hand to her.

"We can learn together. We can ask our families for help and support each other when one of us is down."

"Down? Am I such a sorry person you think I'm not happy? I'm ecstatic about doing this alone. You'll be at work all the time while I take care of your child." Tears spilled over the bottom lids, cascading down her cheeks. This was worse than her usual storm. I stood to lift her and hug her, but she resisted. "Don't. Leave me alone." I changed course and headed for my office. Nothing was more agonizing than observing Mary's descent into Hell. How could I effect a better environment? What could I say or do to lighten Mary's mood?

21
CHAPTER

Victoria

We arrived at Roger and Mary's, emptied out of the car and walked to the front door. Roger opened it after Dad rang the doorbell. A foreboding eminence greeted us. Something was wrong.

"Welcome, everyone." he said, but his voice wavered. "Mary's in the bedroom. I'll get her and Rebecca." He left as we filed into the living room. I stood by the bookcase near the foyer. Was Roger near tears when we arrived?

As we waited for Roger's reappearance, our silence accentuated the tension apparent when we arrived. I walked toward the window only to hear my mother whisper to my brother. I couldn't make out what she said, but Ben nodded and looked at me.

Roger entered with a small blanket bundled around the cutest face. "Everyone, meet Rebecca." We gathered like children in a petting zoo. Mary strolled in as the oohing and aahing commenced.

I clasp my sister and said, "She is so cute, I know you must love her." Mary hugged me.

"I miss you." Her voice faltered as she released her hold. "I can't do this alone."

"You have Roger. I know he's going to be a great father." My assurance pathetic, Mary nodded agreement but her face refused to hide the doubt.

We each took a turn holding Rebecca. My father seemed more interested than I expected, probably because he wouldn't have to raise this child. Ben looked so happy holding his niece. Jackson watched with a smile on his face. I wondered again what Mom had said to him.

After my turn had completed, Mary took Rebecca and held her as she slept. She looked comfortable, but I wondered what Mary sensed holding this fragile human who depended on her for so much. Roger left the room, so I followed him into the kitchen.

"How is Mary doing?" I asked.

He turned to me. "She's okay, I guess. It's been hard on her, being pregnant and now the delivery. She just needs rest."

"She's not as strong as you and me." My hand clasped his arm before he could turn away. "I can help if you need someone. She trusts me and I know her better than anyone."

Roger gazed into my eyes. "Vickie, I don't know what happened. She hasn't been happy since we returned home. I though having a child would be a joy for her." He picked up a tray of cups and saucers and moved toward the doorway. "Can you help her be the radiant beauty I married?" He left for the living room.

I waited for his return to collect the coffee and tea which remained on the counter in pots. I picked them up, started for the living room, but hesitated a moment. He came in.

"Roger, I'll come over when I'm able." We walked into the living room where I set the pots down next to the tray of cups. He poured each person a cup of their request. Small talk about future plans for Rebecca dominated the time. I relieved Mary of her baby. Holding her was so fun.

Roger

I'm glad Vickie came today, I thought. *Mary looked happy to see her and she can help lighten her burden.* Mary's family stayed for two hours. I offered dinner, but Garrett declined saying he needed to get home to finish some business deal before the markets opened in the morning. Ben and Jackson looked apprehensive. I figured they kept a secret.

Mary returned to our bed while Rebecca slept in her crib. I cleaned up the dishes and prepared a light snack for my dinner. Mary declined to eat.

Working in the office, I prepared for the next purchase I planned to make, a house in the central part of the county. Renting it to naval officers would be more stable than my becoming a downtown slumlord.

The baby monitor reported Rebecca's stirrings. I closed my computer and went to my daughter. Mary still lay quietly in our bedroom. After changing Rebecca I carried her into the office and sat at my desk. What was I to do? Could I raise a child, care for my wife, and earn a respectable income, alone? I needed a miracle and only one person could promise its possibility.

22
CHAPTER

Victoria

Connor and I agreed to a cessation of our semi-sordid friendliness since what he wanted was not available and I sought nothing from him. Some allowed groping above the waist frustrated him as much as it dissatisfied me. He agreed to explore other ripe fruit.

Andrea and her mother found another house to rent on Capitol Hill leaving me without a source of information. Mary and I talked weekly and every couple of weeks I went to Wendlesburg to see her. The funk remained but in abeyance. She fought for sanity and a display of happiness, but the battle caused a greater strain in her than Roger or I could help.

"Mary, can I get you something to drink?" I heard Roger ask one weekend morning. I sometimes stayed during the week, because of the amount of time Roger was away showing property at night.

"No, stop fawning over me like I'm an invalid," Mary retorted. Roger slinked out of the room.

"Come outside with me and take Rebecca for a walk," I said. Mary agreed and we prepped for a foray into the warm July sun. I pushed the perambulator as Mary strolled along side. "What have you and Roger been doing for fun?" I asked.

"Not much, it's kind of hard to get out with a new baby."

"I can watch her for you."

"I'm not much for leaving the house right now."

We walked to a nearby park and sat on the swings. Rebecca slept covered by the hood of the carriage to keep out the sun. Mary slowly rocked in a swing while I sat still.

"Mary, are you feeling better? You haven't had much pleasure since Rebecca was born."

She looked at me with disdain but did not answer. Her feet dug into the sand and stopped the swing. Standing, she faced me and began crying. "I don't know what's wrong. I never feel happy anymore. Roger deserves better from me. He's been so patient and kind. Sometimes I feel like I don't want to live anymore."

"Have you seen a doctor?" I stood beside her.

"No, but maybe I should. I can get something to help with the moodiness, I suppose." She checked on Rebecca who continued sleeping. "Vickie, I feel like when I was your age and nothing fit." We walked again. I pushed the stroller following my despairing sister.

Rebecca awoke as we returned to the house. I picked her up and nuzzled her. "I'll change her and then you can feed her. How long do think you'll go before putting her on a bottle?"

"I don't know. Soon I hope; it's such a bother. My nipples are chafing and she eats at odd hours of the night."

We entered the house to find Roger in the kitchen preparing lunch. I went to the bedroom hoping Mary and Roger did not have any disagreeable exchange.

Returned with a wide-awake little girl clutching at me for her own lunch, I handed her to Mary. I sat and ate a meal consisting of a turkey sandwich, chips, and a glass of iced tea. Mary began to leave, but I asked her to stay. "You can feed her here, I don't mind." She bared her breast and suckled her baby. Roger and I ate our lunches in silence. Mary took bites as Rebecca nursed.

When Rebecca had her fill of both breasts, Roger took her from Mary. He said, "She is so beautiful, like you, Mary."

I watched my sister feign a smile which Roger accepted as a positive response. "I agree," I said as he left to rock his daughter to sleep. Mary left for her bedroom and a nap. I cleared the kitchen, and then went to find Roger.

Locating them in his office, I asked, "Is Mary's doing alright?" He looked up and smiled. Rebecca cooed delightfully in his arms.

"I wish I could say yes, but she's been so moody ever since coming home last month." Rebecca closed her eyes and slept. We walked to her bedroom. After placing the baby in her crib, covering her with a blanket decorated with kittens, he said, "I love your sister with all my heart." He walked out of the room and down the hall. I followed like a devoted puppy.

"Can you get her help?"

"She won't go."

"But she told me she wanted something to help with her moodiness."

"Well, I'm glad to hear that. Can you stay a few days to help with your niece?"

His words sent a thrill through me. "I need to call Mom and let her know, but I'm sure it'll be ok." I wanted to hug him, but refrained.

"I'll set up a doctor's appoint on Monday." I sat on the leather couch across from his desk while he wrote a memo in his calendar. Then he sat next to me and took my hand. "Mary so looks to you for a kind of stability I can't seem to give her." A bead of moisture trailed down the side of my head, thankfully buried within my blond curls. He kissed my forehead and said, "Thank you…for everything." The thumping in my chest shattered my emotional composure into a million bits.

Roger

Vickie and Mary returned from a walk as I finished prepping a lunch. "Oh, hello. I've fixed us some sandwiches." Vickie left with Rebecca who needed a change of diaper. "Mary, I'm so glad Vickie's here for you. She is so much help."

"I suppose you think I'm a total misfit." Mary sat in a chair.

"No, you're capable. I just think it's nice you and your sister are so close and she's willing to come here." I put a plate of food in front of her as Vickie returned with our daughter. She handed Rebecca to Mary and sat. I placed a plate in front of her. As Mary rose to leave, Vickie stopped her. Thinking of the luxury of having her with us, I ate my lunch in silent comfort.

Mary exposed one breast and Rebecca ate with us. Conversation lagged. After finishing our lunch I took my baby from Mary.

"She is so beautiful." I noticed a smile and accepted it as fake as it was. At least with Vickie around no arguing occurred. I went to my office as Mary rose to go to bed. Vickie cleaned the kitchen, and I wondered why she got most of the sanity genes. I rocked this sweet child born of two people who fell in love and cascaded into a chasm of despair from which escape eluded them.

"Rebecca, you and I have much to learn. I want to show you the world when you're older. We'll take Mommy with us and Aunt Vickie can come if she wants. You love them, don't you? You love them as I love them." My daughter stared into my eyes and made little noises like she understood all which I said to her. We sat looking at each other.

I smiled and swore she returned the gesture. As we enjoyed each other's company, Vickie entered the room.

"Is Mary doing alright?" She asked. I looked up and smiled. Rebecca cooed in my arms.

"I wish I could say yes," Rebecca closed her eyes and slept. Vickie followed me to her room. After placing the baby in her crib, I said, "I love your sister but she's so moody." I walked out of the room and down the hall. Vickie tailed along.

"Can you get her help?" she asked.

"She won't go."

"But she told me she wanted something to help her."

"Well, I'm glad to hear that. Can you stay a few days to help with your niece?"

"I need to call Mom and let her know, but I'm sure it'll be okay." I wanted to kiss her.

"I'll set up a doctor's appoint on Monday." Vickie sat on the leather couch across from my desk while I wrote a note in my calendar. I then sat next to her and held her hand. "Mary so looks to you for a kind of stability I can't seem to give her." A bead of moisture trailed down the side of her head. If she was nervous about something, I didn't fathom it. I kissed her forehead and said, "Thank you…for everything."

She twitched a bit. Was she actually infatuated with me as Mary claimed? She's so young and yet acts so mature. I see how people confuse her for Mary. If not for the age difference, they could be twins. I wondered if she knew how attractive she was.

23
CHAPTER

Victoria

I didn't want him to let go of my hand. He was such a good father and Mary deserved him. I stood up to go to her. I glanced back as he returned to his desk. He picked up some papers. I continued to my sister.

As I entered their bedroom, she faced away from me but said, "Do you love me?"

I wasn't sure if I was the intended recipient but answered, "Of course I do." She turned and looked at me with tears streaming down her face.

"Oh, it's you. I'm no good for them right now."

"Just remember, it is right now. Not forever. You can get help from a doctor and all will be better. Roger just told me he loves you so much, he'll never leave you." I sat on the edge of the bed.

"He needs someone to be here for him."

"That someone is you and don't forget it." She sat up next to me and I hugged her. "Nothing has to be forever, except how you feel about each other." I held her shoulders and stared into her eyes. "I just hope I find a guy as great as Roger. You looked a long time before leaping into this marriage with both feet."

"Can you stay another day or two? I don't want to be alone when Roger has to leave for work."

"Roger asked me already. I'll call Mom and let her know. I'll stay as long as you want." How was I going to live in this house with Mary carrying a load of pain and Roger lamenting her condition? I wanted to satisfy both of them and myself. I could not ruin everything with my sister. What did Roger want from this marriage? I shouldn't be providing any of it, even if I wanted to.

Roger

On Monday I tried for a doctor's appointment for Mary. Nothing was available until later in the week. We took a walk because I wanted time with Mary. Vickie stayed with Rebecca.

"She doesn't need to be with us." She retorted. I had asked if she wanted her sister with her at the appointment.

"I just thought you might be more comfortable with her present," I said.

"I like having her here, but she needs to go home. If I want her to come back, I'll call her."

Mary and I needed to be alone; Vickie was a third wheel with unacceptable aspirations.

"Look, all I want is for you to have a great life, with me, of course. You're so beautiful and warm when all is going well. I just want you to be happy. We'll see the doctor on Thursday. Maybe nothing's wrong."

Mary reached for my hand. We continued on without further speaking but love conquers all and this could be the beginning of a better life.

24
CHAPTER

Victoria

"Rebecca, your Mommy and Daddy are sure nice to you. I wish I had all these toys to play with when I was younger." She grinned or so I imagined. I nuzzled her tummy and blew a raspberry on her neck. She made a giggly noise.

"If your Daddy liked me like he likes Mommy, I would be happy. But I can't be your Mommy. Mary loves you and can take care of you," I said believing little of what I uttered.

"Daddy needs help with Mommy, so I'll be here often. I can teach you all I know about living. You have a wonderful family." Rebecca squirmed as I spoke to her. I hugged her and kissed her neck. She snuggled into my shoulder and fell asleep. Sitting with her I imagined her as my child although I wanted nothing to do with parenting. I had turned fifteen at the end of school and wanted to experience adolescence.

With Andrea missing, Mary was my best chance to discuss my feelings and emotions, but she contributed little considering her current mental state. Not understanding what I could do for Mary left me thinking about taking a course at a community college. I could enter the Running Start program when I went to high school in the fall.

I put Rebecca in her crib, covering her with the kitten blanket. Leaving the room, I roamed into their bedroom and stood by their bed. I departed for my room and reflection about my life. I was not going to ruin what took Mary so long to attain. She needed this life and I could wait, couldn't I?

The front door opened so I left my room to see how the walk went. Mary looked relaxed and stress free. "Hi, you two. How was the park?"

Mary smiled, "We had a nice time together. Thanks for watching Rebecca. Are you ready to go home?"

What did she say? I'm to go home? I thought she wanted me to help when Roger was gone. What happened?

"I...I guess. You don't want me to help you?"

"Vickie, I love you and you certainly have been a big help around here. I just think Roger and I need to learn how to live with another mouth to feed, and change, and watch. You know what I mean. We just need to become a family." What she said was not meant to be hurtful, but my heart ached with the words spewing forth.

"Alright, I'll get my things. Roger, will you drive me to the ferry?"

"Hey, I didn't mean you had to leave right now." Mary put her hands in mine. "This must have been hard for you to do."

I wanted to scream, but Mary acted rationally and I was not about to send her off the proverbial cliff ranting about insane behavior and lack of love. "No, you're right. I'll call Mom and let her know I'm coming home, tonight." My stomach churning with anger. How could Roger stand there and let her talk like that? He said he loved me.

In the guest room I packed the few clothes I brought with me. In the bathroom with closed door, tears formed. I wanted to stay for reasons I didn't fathom, but I was not the mother; I was Rebecca's aunt. I grabbed a tissue, dried my eyes and opened the door.

Roger stood in the hall with my suitcase. The look on his face expressed disappointment, but in whom? We got in the car and headed for the terminal.

"Did I do something wrong?"

"No, your sister wants to try it alone and see how it goes." Roger answered without looking at me once.

"Are you mad at me? I would be heartbroken if you were mad at me." My heart beat faster; my breathing shallow.

He didn't answer but looked at me while stopped at a red light. The light changed but he didn't start until the honk behind us startled him. More silence kept it weird until we pulled up to the terminal drop off spot.

I opened the door. "Vickie, I was glad to have you here for Mary's sake. She wouldn't have been able to cope without you. I wouldn't have survived, either. It's just…you and I…well, Mary doesn't want anything to interfere with our building this family thing we have to go through. You're not a problem at all, but…

I ignored him, retrieved my bag from the backseat, and didn't look back. He didn't need to see the waterfall on my face.

———⊗⊗⊗———

A few weeks passed since my inglorious departure from Wendlesburg. Roger and Mary seemed to be building their family thing quite well. The drugs prescribed by the doctor seemed to be helping with the depressive anxiety she experienced after Rebecca's birth. She and I spoke occasionally, although not as often as I wanted. Something seemed incongruous although I couldn't put a finger on it.

Roger came to Seattle on business and asked me to meet him at my parent's house. Mom thought it a good idea he and I endeavor to keep Mary healthy.

I hid my exuberance as best I could. Did he sense any wicked passions? He explained how Mary had tried to befriend the next door neighbor's wife. He already knew and spoke with the husband.

"He's a nice guy, and I like his wife. So I'm glad Mary tried to be friendly. It didn't go well for her. The lady had other friends over and Mary got jealous."

"Yeah, she does get possessive."

"Well, the guy started a fence between our properties. He and his wife don't have much to do with us anymore."

"I'm so sorry for you, Roger." I wanted to hold him and reassure him about Mary. He only saw the surface of the roiling caldron he married. She had her man, but all was not well with her psyche.

"Do you think I should come over and stay with her for a while?" The summer was passing by and we had no family gatherings. Maybe it was time to have a barbeque in the backyard and watch ferries and container ships pass through Puget Sound.

"Mary doesn't want to burden you."

"Is she taking her meds?" A burden no fifteen year old needed to feel. Reversing roles with Mary converted my life into a travesty of trials. I mothered her instead of her being the one to comfort me.

"She says she does, but I don't know for sure. I called the doctor and got a prescription for a sleep aid to help her at night. With Rebecca on a bottle, I give her a nightly feeding. It helps that she sleeps through most nights."

"Let me come over and stay with you. I can help with Rebecca and can talk with Mary." I hoped he would say yes. He stood up.

"I have to catch a ferry, but I'll call you when I've spoken with Mary." He hugged me lingering longer than before. Was he missing this human contact at home? I wanted to remain in his arms, but he released me.

"Alright, I'll wait to hear from you." I turned from him and called out to Mom. "Roger's leaving."

As she entered the hallway, she said, "Roger, I do hope you and Vickie were able to plan a strategy for helping Mary." The urge to kiss him remained unfulfilled.

"He's going to call me when I can go over and stay with them to help." He shook Mom's hand and waved bye to me as he walked out the door.

"He's such a nice man." Mom said.

You have no idea, Mother. You have no idea.

Roger

At the ferry dock, I thought about Vickie and her willingness to help. Mary was not getting better, again. She understood her sister so well I could comprehend why it was wise for her to visit. And I wanted assistance with Rebecca.

"What a body," Lurid words said aloud to no one. She had become a young woman and now challenged Mary for height, beauty, and shapeliness. They truly could pass for twins, except for the mental state. She had all any guy wanted in a woman, apart from the fact she was an adolescent. She had a maturity beyond her years and a sense of how to listen and interpret a man's unconscious requisite to be manly around her. She exuded the sensuality of a twenty-something woman.

The ferry from Bainbridge arrived, disgorged its load of cars and passengers, and loaded the return trip people and vehicles. I left a fantasy realm to reenter reality. How would I find Mary this time? And now Rebecca was an added dimension. Irony filled life; the fates conspiring against my happiness, a happiness not available for me, but within shouting distance. I put it out of my mind to call home.

The car sensed my apprehension moving at a plodding pace toward home. My hesitation to return came at a price. I entered the driveway to find Mary standing in our doorway, holding Rebecca, a grimace coursing her face.

"Where have you been? I expected you sooner."

"The traffic downtown was awful and it took a while to get off the boat." She handed me Rebecca, whose odor indicated my next task. "I'm sorry if you think I'm late." I walked to my baby's room to change her diaper.

"Did you stop and see Vickie?"

"Yes, she wants to come over and stay with us for a while. I think it would be good for you. I can get more business done and you can have help and companionship. Your sister is a considerate person." I picked up Rebecca who smiled at me with unabashed love. At least one person didn't care about my lateness.

"I suppose it would be alright. Do you think she's prettier than me?"

"Actually, you are two of the most beautiful women I have ever met. She is a young girl, though.

"A young girl, which means, I'm getting older and less desirable? You probably think she's better than I am. So you want some fantasy high school girl in a short skirt? You men are despicable."

My daughter whimpered at the volume increase. "I did not say that. I love you and yes, she is young, too young." I regretted my words.

"Oh well, let's wait until she's older and then you can exchange sisters, a sane one for this crazy one." Mary stomped out of the room to our bedroom and slammed the door.

Rebecca squirmed. I retreated to the kitchen, found a prepared bottle in the refrigerator, and heated it. She reveled in sucking in her meal as I contemplated Mary's tirade. And the implications of making such a swap.

25
CHAPTER

Victoria

The ferry slowed as it approached the Colman dock. The crowd coming off the boat was small for an early morning transport across Puget Sound from Wendlesburg. I figured I missed the commuters by one boat. The sun warmed the air; my heart burning to see Mary and Roger again. Although, Roger had stopped by just two days ago, this trip to stay for a week thrilled me.

The ride across the sound offered a vista of the Olympic Mountains. Tourists remarked about the beauty of the Cascades with a panorama from Mount Baker in the north to Rainier south of Seattle. I sat on the sun deck out of the breeze caused by moving through the water. What a glorious day it was.

I looked at the new cellular phone my dad got me to use if I needed to call for help. Strict instructions about use of minutes came with the acceptance of the phone. I practiced texting Mom as we sailed on the water. I knew dad had an unlimited plan, but his warning about calling and texting randomly to my friends was heeded. I needed my own plan regardless of the lack of money to pay for it.

The ferry docked with a minor bump. I guessed a trainee was at the helm. As we waited for the ramp's placement on the deck, I thought about calling Roger about whether he arrived to pick me up and dismissed it.

Roger waved at me as I walked up the ramp into the terminal. My heart fluttered. We hugged and strolled to the car which he parked in the underground garage next door.

"How was the trip?" he asked as we walked.

"Fine, the tourists are here in droves and talking about our mountains, as usual. How is Mary doing?"

"She's okay. We had a bit of a squabble the other day when I returned from Seattle." He started the car but didn't drive. "She said something about me wanting to exchange a crazy sister for a sane one. I'm worried about her." I cringed. Was my desire too overt? "Does she think me so shallow?"

"She's being paranoid like usual." My heart burst hearing Roger's words. *Shallow? She couldn't know my feelings for him, could she?* "Let's get her to take her medicine regular like."

"I don't keep tabs on her, but it's a good idea." He began the drive across town to the house. I wasn't happy hearing Mary's tirade. What if he thought it possible for us to be the happy couple? No, she's paranoid about losing the one person who gave her a normal life.

At the house I found my sister rocking Rebecca in the nursery. "Well, hello, you two. I'm so glad to be here." Mary handed my niece to me as we hugged and shared a greeting.

"Vickie, I've missed you so much. I live closer to you than when I was in college, but it was so different then. We need to talk more, be together more."

"Oh, you just want to keep me out of trouble. After all, I'm starting high school next month. I'll meet some cute guy and be swept off my feet."

"He should be so honored to have you for a girlfriend."

"We'll see."

"Was Roger a perfect gentleman?"

"He always is." Love him, Mary, or lose him.

Rebecca snuggled in arms; her warmth triggering a yearning in me for other affection. The morning progressed to noon. Rebecca played with her mobile as she lay on the floor on an adorable blanket with lots of African animals. Roger watched her while Mary and I fixed lunch.

"Mary, are you taking your pills as the doctor ordered?"

She hesitated, and then answered. "Usually, I do, but they make me listless. I feel like a failure. I act so crazy without them and so useless with them."

"Maybe something else would be better for you."

"I don't know, maybe."

I finished with my sandwich constructions and placed them on the table for Roger and me along with a bowl of chips and some pickles. Mary fixed a salad with a cup of soup. We poured iced tea. I departed the kitchen to announce lunch was ready.

Roger

"Mommy can't believe I would leave her for Aunt Vickie." Rebecca eyed me suspicious as if a great conspiracy developed. Or she had to burp or poop. "You are such a good girl. Come on, I'll change your diaper and then we'll have some lunch."

Vickie was the stable one. When I talked with her, the magic of those years in college with Mary flooded my mind. I wanted that back. I needed that back. So much happened in so little time, I despaired of ever recovering my beautiful wife.

Rebecca cooed as I picked her up from the changing table. "You two are a perfect pair." Vickie startled me.

"Thanks a lot, I almost dropped her." I smiled at the loveliness gracing the doorway. "Mary, ah, Vickie, man you two are beginning to freak me out." What a mistake. Did she smile at me or my faux pas?

"Lunch is ready," she said without hesitation. She reached for Rebecca. The touch of her hands on mine chilled me, an anxiety not invited. "Come my little princess; let's allow Daddy some time to eat his lunch before he goes back to work." I held my breathe letting a slow exhale calm my soul. So much for the little girl I met when Mary brought me home not so many years ago. Somebody's heart would be shattered in the next few years. I followed her watching the figure filling blue jeans invitingly. She turned as if knowing of my dalliance.

"This is delicious and just what I needed. Mary you fix a great sandwich." I said without a hint of the reaction to such an innocent remark.

"Vickie made the sandwiches." Blue eyes clouded into darkness.

"Yes, I did. But Mary, I couldn't have done it without your guidance." Another storm abated before growing to fullness. "She made sure all of your favorite items were placed in it."

We finished our meal without banter, for a winter blast may be short but kill so much. Vickie cleared the dishes while Mary and I took Rebecca for a walk in the warm sun.

"I'm sorry for snapping at you about the sandwich." Mary slowed her pace placing an arm in mine as I pushed the stroller. "I just don't know what comes over me. You tried to complement me and I took it wrong."

I stopped and kissed her. "I love you. We'll get through this together. If your medicine is so horrible, we'll find another which works better. Vickie'll be a big help for us. I have a lot of work this week and I'm glad she can be company for you." What would happen without her at the house?

"I love my sister, but she cannot give up her life for me. She needs an opportunity to live better than I have."

"Your life is pretty good. We're moving along quite well. We have a beautiful daughter, a nice house, enough money to be comfortable, and families who care about us."

Mary said nothing, so I quit talking. She continued to hold my arm.

Several other families frolicked on the swings and slides with their children. Our neighbors who built the fence ate a picnic on a blanket under a large maple tree. We acknowledged each other but the barrier between houses created a barrier between friendships. Mary and I stopped at the toddler swings. Rebecca had grown enough to be able to sit in the swing enjoying the movement.

"Roger, does my sister like you more than as a brother-in-law?"

"That's a funny question. Why?"

"I know she had a boyfriend while in middle school, but she seems to want you near her. I just wondered if she might like you more than as a brother-in-law."

"Well, a little teenage flirtation isn't uncommon, but I'm pretty sure she doesn't want to mettle with our relationship. She genuinely wants you to be healthy and happy." I pushed our daughter until the swaying motion lulled her to snooze.

"I…I love you. I'll take my medicine, but you have to be understanding. When you go to work I want someone to help me around the house. It can't be Vickie when she goes back to school."

"I'll ask Mom for recommendations." Mary nodded agreement to my idea. We sat on the bench near the swing set watching Rebecca sleep. I wanted this idyllic time to last forever; realizing personal climate was a matter of current relations over a long period of time. Challenges ahead could batter the most diligent of survivors into forfeiting Eden.

We gathered our charge and began the stroll back to our garden of hope where weeds and brambles waited in seed cases as yet undiscovered.

26
CHAPTER

Victoria

While Roger and Mary walked to the park with Rebecca, I explored the house. Curiosity wasn't snooping as far as I was concerned. I sat in Roger's office chair imaging him writing real estate proposals and completing land deals which produced millions of dollars. He and I would travel and explore the world.

My fantasy world shattered as I heard the lock on the front door turn. I rose from my place and returned to the kitchen pretending to fold towels and finish cleaning. Then I walked into the hallway which split the dining room from the kitchen and led to the back hall where I entered my guest-room. I sat a moment as the front door closed and I heard talking.

"Hi, you three. How was the park?" I asked feigning innocence.

Roger answered, "Fine." Mary unhooked Rebecca who fussed as she was lifted from carriage. I reached out for her.

Mary said, "Thank you, she needs changing and a bottle." Breast feeding had not been a popular activity for my sister. It ended before I arrived for the week.

"I'll take care of her. I love you guys." I departed for the baby's room and clean clothing. Roger followed me when Mary went into their bedroom.

"Vickie, can you be sure Mary takes her medicine while I'm at work next week?" I frowned listening to his plea, as I snapped the crotch of the jumpsuit on Rebecca.

"Of course. Isn't she taking it?" Rebecca wriggled as I handed her to Roger. He grimaced as if a pain stabbed his heart.

"I'm not sure. She says she is, but every so often she loses what little control she has." He followed me to the kitchen. I retrieved a bottle from the refrigerator, heating it in the bottle warmer on the counter. "She asked me a funny question while we were out." I looked at him. "She asked if you liked me more than as a brother-in-law."

"What?" My mouth gaped, shocked thinking my sister perceived more than intended. "I don't know what to say." I reached for Rebecca.

"You could say you like me as your brother-in-law and leave it at that." Holding my niece, I walked into the family room to feed her. "Well, do you?"

"Do I what?" I whispered. I sat in the rocker and placed Rebecca in the fold of my arm, held the bottle to her mouth and ignored Roger's stare.

"Do you like me more than as a brother-in-law?" He sat in the chair next to the rocker.

"No." I lied. The blood rushed to my face. "I can't believe she asked you."

"I couldn't either, but she did." He rose and then surprised me. "I can see how she might think it, though."

"What are talking about?" My whisper rose in tone approaching a normal voice. He sat down again.

"Oh, don't be so naïve. You two are so much alike other people might not even be able to tell you apart. She knows she isn't stable mentally. She knows you are. I'm not saying she's jealous or anything, but she realizes you're searching for something she didn't have at your age." My heart paced faster with each word he uttered. "I'm pretty sure you can have any guy you want, and yet you spend more time with us than a person your age typically would."

He stood again. "I'm just saying; you're an attractive, smart young lady and any guy would be thrilled to have you as a girlfriend." He left the room while I finished feeding Rebecca and quivered at the same time. If only he knew the truth of those words. Rebecca commented as a baby does after eating, closed her eyes and slept. I returned her to her crib and went to my room and closed the door. Tears enveloped my lids and spilled down my cheeks. Lying down I buried my face in the pillow on the bed, imagining how my cruelty to wish for something so wrong might not be hidden.

Roger

What did I say to Vickie? "You can have any guy you want." She could. If Mary had grown up as Vickie had, her problems would not exist now. I thought about what it would be like not dealing with this depression she suffered. Vickie needed to be here…to help Mary find a peace I found hard to provide.

I looked over a proposal for a small house I intended to buy as a rental property. A crazy idea crossed my mind, but she was too young. She needed to finish high school and she perhaps had college in her future. No, Vickie could not move to Wendlesburg and help me with her sister. It was a radical, insane idea.

Leaving my office, I went to the bedroom to find Mary sleeping. She looked so calm and sweet, peaceful. I closed the door, pausing a moment, reflecting on my earlier thoughts. Vickie and I had to find a solution so Mary could be whole and we could live a normal life. Looking in on Rebecca, I smiled. My life warranted everything I ever dreamed about, except for Mary's troubled brain.

Rebecca stirred, not waking, so I left her room. For a moment I stood by our guest room, wondering about what might happen to our guest in her future. Mary's question haunted me because Vickie reminded me so much of her. I liked my sister-in-law. She was fun to have around and to talk about life. Nothing bad could come from her here.

I raised my hand to knock on the door and thought better of it. If curiosity killed the cat, I was doomed to die if I entered this room now. Walking away I returned to my office to finish what I started.

Time passed without my recollection of what I had accomplished. Mary walked in with Rebecca. I looked up. "Oh, hi, did you have a nice nap?" I took Rebecca and we sat on the couch.

"Roger, I'm sorry about this afternoon at the park."

"What about?"

"You know, asking you about Vickie. I had no right. She's come over here to be with me and all I think about is her stealing my life from me. I love her and hate her at the same time."

"Come on, you don't hate your sister." Rebecca sensed the tension and fidgeted. "You're just letting your imagination get the better of you."

I looked into her blue pearls wishing I could unsay my last comment. Nothing changed. She remained calm but seemed uneasy.

"Do you believe a person can love more than one person?"

"I suppose. Why, are you in love with another man?" My joke collapsed faster than a balloon with a large hole. Her blue pearls deepened. "Hey, I was just kidding. I trust you love me."

"And I trust you. You have been the best man any woman could have the pleasure of marrying. I'm sorry for not being a better wife." I didn't refute her statement but sat mesmerized by her beauty and remarkable likeness to Vickie. I guessed nine years was not much of a difference within a family.

"Can I fix you something to eat?" Dinner time approached but I wanted to break the growing tension. Rebecca snuggled into my arms as if to say she wanted a snack, as well.

"No, you go ahead. I'll feed Becca."

Mary returned to the nursery. I went to the kitchen scrounging for something, indeed not wanting anything.

"Roger." I jumped out of my skin.

"What the f…" I turned to see puffy, red eyes framed with smeared mascara watching me. "Vickie, what's the matter?" I stopped my search for food. "Have you been crying?"

She sat in a chair by the table. I sat next to her. "Does Mary hate me?"

"What? No. She loves you. She told me so in the office. Why would you think such a thing?"

"You said she thought I liked you more than as a brother. I wouldn't do anything like that. It hurt."

I held her hands. "She isn't upset with you; she's just mixed up about life." I released her from my grasp. "Do you want to go home?"

"No, Mary needs help and you have to work. School doesn't start for another month, so I'll stay and help my sister."

"I do love you for being who you are. I love Mary so much that what she thinks about you doesn't matter. Stay as long as you can."

Vickie nodded. "I need to clean up." She left the kitchen. I hoped that Mary was wrong about Vickie, since I wasn't even sure about her myself. Could I survive living with a fragile woman, or resist another whose strength challenged my sensibilities. Rebecca's wishes paled in comparison.

27

CHAPTER

Victoria

Mary sat in the rocker talking to Rebecca. She looked up as I walked in. My face reflected a different countenance than in the kitchen. Looking in the mirror in the bathroom had been ugly. "Vickie, I'm glad you're here. Can we talk?"

"Sure, what about?"

"Are you infatuated with Roger?"

I sputtered, "What?" I tried so hard to hide my feelings and she asks this? "He's my brother-in-law."

Mary stared at me for a moment. Then looking at Rebecca, she continued. "I asked Roger if he thought you might like him. It was a stupid thing to ask. I'm sorry."

"Mary, I love you. It hurts to think you don't trust me." Panic grew. I wanted to run but was riveted to the floor.

"Oh, I trust you," she said. "And I trust Roger. I feel so mixed up all the time. I feel abandoned and yet here you are." She stood and handed Becca to me. Her eyes narrowed and darkened. "Don't ever get in the way of my marriage." Her mind traveled another dark road.

I held my niece, hoping for a cessation of Mary's troubled thoughts. She left the room for her bedroom. I sat in the rocker, stunned by the quickness of her mood swing. "Becca, we have to help mommy get better." I looked at the door across the hall. Roger deserved better. Rebecca burped and expelled gas. A check indicated a change of diaper was next.

After cleaning her bottom, I carried her out the family room and her play pen. Grandparents spoiled her with gadgets and sparkly attractions. She batted at the mobile of butterflies hanging from the edge of the pen. I neatened the room then sat and read a magazine.

From the hallway I heard hushed voices. I strained to hear the conversation but comprehended Mary sounded angry. I stood, moving to a better place to listen to them. Roger's words attempted to calm the storm raging in my sister.

He said, "She's not trying to steal anything from you, Mary. Don't be so paranoid."

"I can't have anything I want without someone trying to take it from me," Mary countered. I slinked back to the family room slipping into the kitchen to stay far from the fracas in the hall. Was I to blame for this meltdown? Her remark about me roiled inside. Exposed to the argument, I knew I couldn't stay, but I had no path of escape to the bedroom and my things.

A door slammed. I returned to the family room, checked on Rebecca, who played peacefully in her prison.

Roger entered. "I want to go home," I said. Tears formed pools falling on my cheeks.

"You heard? She didn't mean any of it." He moved closer. I shrugged.

"She thinks I am taking you away from her."

"She doesn't know what she says sometimes. She gets a mood and crazy stuff pops out. Please stay. Help her get through it."

He placed hands on my shoulders, kissed my forehead and said, "Thank you." Guilt burned as I flushed a sensation for wanton abandonment of Mary's wishes. Rebecca remained oblivious to the fractures in her life.

I left the room for my sanctuary. Mary was in the hall. I stopped, but she saw me and approached. Fear rose from deep within me. My body tensed as she hugged me.

"Vickie, I love you." She let me go. Looking at me she said, "Is Becca ok?"

Not sure of what was happening. "She's fine. She's in the family room playing with her mobile." Mary went to find her daughter. My heart raced with adrenaline, and I began to understand what Roger faced living with my sister. I was helpless to aid in her regaining sensibilities.

In the bedroom I pondered the uselessness of helping. She seemed more insecure and lost than I observed in our years together. I knew I loved Roger more than I should, but helping my sister meant being near him.

Roger

"Janet, can you come in here?" I called out from my office. When my secretary entered I said, "File these for me, please, and contact the seller. We have a deal."

Walker came in soon after hearing about the closing. "Well, young man, I guess congrats are in order." The last several months produced enough income to change Mary and my status. I now owned three properties which would bring in enough rental revenue to offset the mortgages and generate income. A large commercial building I purchased, repaired, and resold paid off the remaining balance of our own house. I ruled the world except for stormy outbursts at home.

My father didn't often celebrate by opening bottles of champagne. I knew he had a refrigerator with a supply, but I was the recipient for the first time and relished the feeling. I hoped for the same support at home.

"Dad, thanks for everything."

"You're welcome, but you've done all this yourself." We popped the top and passed glasses around the office. After a short party, staff returned to work and more sales.

"Roger, how are things at home?"

"Alright."

"I'm glad to hear that. How long will Vickie be at your house?"

"She's leaving on Thursday." Dad nodded and left my office. Was he concerned about my sister-in-law staying at the house? I dismissed the unintentional angst.

I picked up the phone and called home. The morning deserved a lunch celebration with the three females who occupied my heart. We agreed on a nice quiet place on the main drag in town. Manny's Bistro had great sandwiches for me and soups and salads I knew Mary enjoyed. Vickie could order for herself, although I would pick up the tab.

Just before noon I checked out of the office heading for my date. In the parking lot of the restaurant I found Mary and Vickie, voices muted, something was not right. As I approached, the storms of Mary's mind blew as teeth clenched, and cold flinty eyes stared at nothing. Vickie gathered Rebecca from the car seat. I took her as soon as I approached. "What's going on?" I asked.

Mary turned. "Leave me alone."

"Honey, I just got here. Can I help?" As time slipped away her eyes melted into blue pools softened by whatever controlled her. Vickie handed me the baby's bag.

She said to Mary, "Let's just go in and eat a nice lunch." We walked to the door which I held open for my ladies. I bit my lip hesitating at the door. I looked at my daughter fearing what she could become. "I promise to never hurt you like Mommy was hurt."

We ordered drinks and food. The silence echoed around us until I asked, "What happened out there?"

Mary looked at me as if I were a loathsome animal to be extinguished from the earth. Vickie said, "It was nothing. We were talking about Rebecca's next appointment. It's on Wednesday and I said I wanted to go along to help." She remained calm as Mary turned from me to her.

"You indicated I may not be capable of getting there without a catastrophe happening." Mary's words burned at her sister.

"And I apologize. You are capable. I just thought it would be easier to have two taking care of Becca."

Trying to ameliorate the situation I said, "I think having all of us present would be fun. I don't have anything that day."

Mary quieted as I spoke, but expressed, "I don't need any help."

"We can make a fun day of it," I said. "After all, Vickie leaves the next day." Mary smiled. We finished lunch in a calm atmosphere. I wondered, disaster averted?

28
CHAPTER

Victoria

Thursday came before I wanted. Yesterday had been joyous. My niece's checkup was superb. Becca grew each day and her development was on target, according to her pediatrician.

Roger, Mary and I spent a glorious day strolling the downtown board-walk. Rebecca delighted many a passersby. Mary's tantrums faded for the moment. Roger, kind and wonderful, accepted Mary and her challenges. He was such a marvelous person, a delight to be near.

As I stood on the aft of the ferry watching the dock fade where Roger and Mary and I said our goodbyes, I wondered about the kiss on the forehead. The ferry made one last turn before crossing Puget Sound to Seattle. My eyes refused to stay dry. "I'm such a fool." No one sat near to watch me dissolve into a puddle. Why did I care so much for someone who remained so far from any real life I might live? School started in two weeks. At least that distraction could help quell my anxiety.

I arrived home on the bus, surprising Mom who expected my dad to pick me up at the dock. I hadn't contacted him about a time because I didn't want to talk with him, although chances for that were slim even in the same car. "Hi, Mom. I going to unpack my things."

"Tell me about your sister and Rebecca."

"I will." I abandoned the foyer for my room, putting away my cloth-ing and placing dirty things in the hamper in the bathroom. I couldn't carry on an intelligent conversation with my mother at the moment, so I called Andrea.

Her mother answered. "Well, hello stranger," she said.

"Hi, Mrs. Collins. Is Andrea home?"

"Andrea, dear, it's Victoria Johnson," I heard her say. Silence ruled the airwaves until I heard a phone pick up.

"I got it, Mom." Andrea waited for the click and then said, "Hi, Vic, what's up? I haven't heard from you all summer."

"I know. It's been crazy. How's the new place working out?"

"Mom found out about me and my new guy. I'm restricted to the house until school starts. I'm surprised she's letting me talk to you."

"Maybe she thinks I'm a positive influence." We laughed at the absurdity. "I miss seeing you."

"Yeah, maybe you can come over and keep me on the straight and narrow." Awkward silence befell the phone again.

"I can do that. Let me ask my mom." The called ended with a promise to let Andrea know as soon as possible.

I was left to face the barrage of questions about my sister. In the kitchen Mom concocted another mystery dinner. Reading new cookbooks she began a quest for improving the quality of meals. The previous ones weren't abhorrent. I sat at the counter watching her nimble hands create as she perused the recipe.

"I called Andrea. I was hoping I could go over to her place tomorrow or Saturday. We haven't seen each other all summer."

"Tomorrow would be alright. Saturday we're hosting a family get-together with your brother. I invited Mary and Roger to come over. I think they're coming. I haven't seen Rebecca for weeks."

My heart raced a beat faster. Beads of moisture laced my forehead. "Now, tell me all about your week with your sister." I sat dumbfounded, lost in time.

Little by little, I related the wonder of Rebecca. "Mary is so good with her," A fabricated lie to prevent more questions. "She and Roger are so happy, and they enjoy Rebecca. I was glad to be there." My heart slowed to normal. I wiped the beads from my head with my sleeve.

"Are you alright?" Mom asked.

"Fine, why?"

"You look like you're feverish." She wiped her hands on her apron and touched my head. I dared not flinch. "I don't feel anything."

"Mom, you have to stop worrying about me. I can handle anything."

"You're my baby and soon enough you'll be leaving. I don't want to think about the emptiness." She sat with me. "You are so grown up. I forget you're just fifteen. Mary wasn't as world wise when she was your age. I guess we messed that up when we went to New York."

Mom's reminiscences halted the conversation. I remembered little of the day other than Ben taking me to the park. "That was long ago. Mary's fine now," I lied. "I'm going to call Andrea and tell her I can come over tomorrow." Before Mom could respond I left the kitchen. I thought, *"Why do terrible things happen to good people?"*

Roger

"Roger, Mom called. She wants us to come over on Saturday for a picnic. I said I had to talk with you first." She had relaxed while Vickie was here. I figured a trip to Seattle would benefit our family harmony.

"That sounds great."

"Ben's coming." I wondered if his friend was coming as well and how Garrett might handle understanding a son with a different take on life.

"Good, I haven't talked with him in a while. I hope your sister made it home, okay."

"Do you miss her?"

"It's nice having her here to help you with Becca." I averted gazing at Mary. My mind could betray my mouth.

"When school starts, we won't be able to see her as much." Mary stirred something in a pot on the stove. I changed the subject.

"What are you brewing for dinner?" I joked.

"Brewing? Am I now a witch with magic spells to entice you into my boudoir?" Her humor fashioned a calm seldom experienced of late.

"You had me hooked long ago." I wrapped my arms around her waist, kissing her neck and nuzzling her ear. "I love you." A smile course her face as her cheeks expanded.

She pivoted in my arms raising hers to clasp my neck. Our kiss, passionate, fresh, inviting, stirred the beasts within us. Still embraced, I reached down to turn off the bubbling cauldron.

"Love me, alone," she pled. "Love me always. Love me as no one has." I whispered she was the one woman for me.

"What about Becca?" I asked.

"She's still napping. Take me here and now." The kitchen was not the most comfortable venue for lascivious activities but this tick of time called for adjustments. We cleared a counter on which Mary sat exposing herself to me, a skirt without panties surprised me. My pants remained on with zipper undone. We satisfied primal urges, as she experienced an orgasm quelling her craving.

She hopped off the counter, turned to face it and said, "Again, from behind." I obliged her until she convulsed again and I released my juices. From far away a baby announced the end of our tête-à-tête.

"I'll take care of Becca," I said. Cleaning myself, I reassembled my clothing. Mary's smirk belied a witchy countenance that enhanced her beauty. Enrapt by this moment, I wanted more, later, in a comfortable setting. Becca called again for attention. Mary ignited the stove to finish whatever brewed in her pot.

"How's my sweet little girl, today?" I cooed. "Is Becca wanting up and wanting a change?" Her little hands reached out for me as I picked her up from the crib. "I think your mommy is horny," My words were just for me.

A daydream envisioned an older daughter entwined in the arms of a faceless boy. Then Vickie's face replaced my daughter as the boy became a man. My heart raced. Why? Why? What is this? I finished with Rebecca, carried her to the kitchen for dinner and reflection of my roving brain. Mary placed our meals on the table. We sat and ate without conversation. I fed Rebecca between my own bites. The spaghetti sauce did not suffer, nor did the noodles, cooked in two unceremonious stages. Was Mary's lust an attempt to focus my mind on her? Did she use sex to lasso it back to the corral? Did I want to escape? Did I need to be free?

29
CHAPTER

Victoria

I arrived at Andrea's house a little before noon. The Metro Bus system had a good cross town setup. Still, I endured three changes before getting close enough to walk from Broadway down the hill to her house.

The air was unseasonable for Seattle, the temperature nearing 90 for the third day in a row. A trickle of sweat ran down my back. I pulled the paper with directions and an address out of my rear jeans pocket.

"Andrea, how did your mom find out about you and Raphael?" We sequestered ourselves in her bedroom.

"She came home early one day.

"Did she catch you together? You know in the…act"

"No, but she suspected and I tried to lie my way out of it. It didn't work." I couldn't do anything but laugh. "So, Vickie, you think that's funny?"

I just smiled. "Actually, it's like insanely funny. I figured you and I'd be caught before anything else." Andrea burst into laughter with me. We hugged as we laughed.

A knock on the door halted our activities. "Are you two alright in there?"

"We're okay, Mom. Vickie told me something funny." My mouth hung open covered by hands. I giggled, but she placed a finger on my hands, shaking her head. We sat silent until the coast was clear.

"That was close. I thought Mom was coming in." A paranoia exhibited itself for the first time since meeting her. She was vulnerable, frightened.

"Are you okay?" I asked. She had moved to the door and pressed an ear to it. My own paranoid intuition told me something happened to Andrea in the months since we had seen each other. I thought of Mary.

She sat on the bed next to me. "Ever since the Raphe thing…" Her voice trailed off.

"You call him Raphe?" She looked at me like I was the crazy one. "I mean, like, you know, I never figured you to be afraid of anything."

"Mom means well. It's just, well, I thought she didn't care what I did as long as I didn't get hurt." Andrea laid against the wall feet curled up with arms wrapped around them.

I pulled myself to the wall. "She wants you safe."

"She doesn't knows what I want or how to make me happy."

"Do you know what you want?" I put my hand on her knees. She grabbed me and cried into my shoulder. I just sat, soaking up her tears.

"I'm scared. Mom doesn't talk to me anymore like she used to. We had some great times together and now…nothing. It's like I'm not her little girl anymore." I didn't comprehend her loss. I knew nothing else. I understood my mom's love for me and tolerated my father's lack. Roger was what I wanted, anyway, and he lived with my sister who was getting worse each time I saw her.

"Parents are the pit of hell," I said. "They want us to show off what we are, not who we are." How would my future be happy if I didn't realize what it looked like? Maybe Mary suffered from something similar.

"I've got to go. The bus ride takes a long time. I'm glad you're my friend."

"Do you love me?"

The question knocked me for a loop. "I guess, yes, but I'm not…"

"Oh, I'm not a lesbian," Andrea said. "No, I just love you like the sister I never had."

Downstairs we hugged and I left her at the front door to her house. What did I want in a relationship? What affection could fill the one void I missed with Andrea? Sixteen was just a few months away. Could I find the right partner for a sweet present? Or did I know him already.

Roger

Saturday began early with Mary and I awakened to the sound of baby talk from Rebecca's room. "Stay in bed. I'll get her," Mary rolled over and closed her eyes. I found Becca her on her knees hanging on the edge of the crib. "Wow, you are growing up fast." I picked her up, checked her diaper and put her on the changing table.

"I think you're the best little girl in town." I nuzzled her belly after cleaning her bottom, enjoying her giggle. Mary had laid out a two-piece pants and shirt with elephants and giraffes. I dressed her in them.

"Come on, and say hi to mommy." We entered the bedroom where I placed her beside her mother. She stirred but ignored us. "Let's leave mommy to sleep." I picked up her up and walked to the kitchen to find a bottle and milk. She sat in the playpen while I prepared her breakfast. Rice cereal looked like paste but she liked it.

Mary entered as I placed Becca in her high chair. "Why does she have to wake so early," I smiled. "It's not funny. I didn't sleep very well last night."

"What's the matter?" Innocence can be rewarded unless your wife is like mine.

"Nothing. She's a lot of work when you're not here."

"I know. I'm glad Vickie was here to help you this week." I sat with Becca and shoved food in her mouth. She chewed and swallowed, gleeful, happy, contented.

"You know nothing. You're never here. You seem to think I can work magic taking care of this house and your daughter."

"Honey, if you want help, we can hire someone to come in." Oops. Her eyes darkened. Becca looked at me waiting for another spoonful of cereal suspended in the air in front of her.

"I don't want anyone coming into my house who's a stranger. If you cared about us, you'd be here more and worry less about accumulating gobs of money."

Becca whimpered. I pushed the spoon into her mouth and watched her manipulate the food to her throat. Mary stormed from the room. "Wow, Mommy seems a bit tense today." She finished eating. I looked at the small pile of cereal on her bib and around her mouth. A wet cloth managed the mess. I placed her in the playpen with her bottle, which she worked to her mouth and drank, eager for the contents.

Going to our bedroom to find Mary, I wondered what her mind formulated. The tirade made no sense. "Are you alright?"

"Go away." I stayed. "Get out of here," she screamed.

"No, talk to me. What's wrong?"

"Nothing, go away and leave me alone. You and Becca have a nice little life without me." She pulled the covers over her head. With no response I left to get my daughter. A car ride might give Mary enough time to regain civility before our trip to Seattle to her parents. At least, I hoped so.

30

CHAPTER

Victoria

"Mom, when are Ben and Jackson coming." I set the deck table for a royal dinner. Nothing mattered much except being ready to see my sister and Roger again. Rebecca would steal my mother and Father would ignore all of us. Mom carried out a tray of glasses, plastic and unbreakable if dropped on the stone tiles.

"They should be here soon. I'm expecting them by two. Why?" Mom asked.

"I haven't seen much of Ben this summer. I miss him." I thought about Jackson and my brother doing the kinds of things Roger and Mary did. I shuddered.

"Well, he'll be happy to see you, too. I'm sure." She left to gather more stuff for the table and feast. I thought about Roger and Mary doing what married people do. It seemed much more appropriate. What might it be like to be with someone for a night? I shuddered again.

My phone buzzed in my pocket. Checking the caller ID, I almost dropped it. As I answered, I heard it click off.

What did he want? Was he calling to say they weren't coming? Or maybe Mary had another tantrum and Roger was cleaning up the mess left from the storm since I hadn't been there to quell her hysteria. Checking my watch, anxiety crept in. I heard the phone in the kitchen. Was it Roger?

"No, I understand. We'll see you when you get here." Mom hung up the phone.

"What's the matter?" I asked. She looked at me as if I interrupted her.

"Oh, nothing. That was Roger. They missed the ferry and will be late." Something else occupied her mind as she spoke.

"Mom, is Mary ok?"

"What? No, she's fine, I guess. Don't worry about it."

"About what? I want to know." The doorbell halted any further interrogation. Mom left the kitchen to greet Ben and Jackson as they entered the house. I had to find time to talk with Roger.

Roger

"Mary, come on. We have to leave, if we're to catch the next ferry." I picked up the baby's diaper bag and started for the door.

"I don't feel very good," Mary said. "I'll stay home. You go with Becca." She turned away running to the bathroom. The next sound turned my stomach.

"Are you alright?" A peaceful Rebecca sat in her car seat chewing on a soft doll. I dropped the bag as I entered the bathroom to find Mary kneeling on the floor.

"I think I'm pregnant, you bastard. How can this be happening to me?" Her pale face told the story. I helped her stand and she slapped me. "You and your fucking cock." She turned toward the toilet but nothing happened.

"I'll call your mom, again and tell her we aren't coming."

"No. Throwing up helps. Get me some crackers." I left to retrieve her request. The crashing sound scared me. I ran back to the bathroom to find a broken mirror and a ceramic cup lying in the sink.

"What'd you do that for?"

"It felt good." I reached for her. "Don't touch me. You make my skin crawl." She left the room, picked up her handbag and walked out to the car. I picked up the diaper bag and Rebecca and joined her. Little conversation journeyed with us to Seattle.

I parked the car in the drive of the Johnson house next to Ben's ten year old Honda. Mary left me with the tasks of baby and assorted baggage. "Mommy has to see her family," I said to Rebecca who cooed as if understanding my words. As I gathered my possessions, Vickie bounded out of the house.

"Hi," she said, bright as the sunshine around us. "Can I help?"

"Please do." She grabbed the diaper bag and the toy bag and stood like she needed another instruction. "Vickie, I need to talk with you. Mary's upset about something and I want your advice about what to do."

'Sure, what's up?" Her face reflected daylight as though it was meant for her alone. I admired her upbeat ability to live in a dysfunctional family. She was the most stable of them all and her beauty rivaled her sister.

"We had a fight before coming over and I'm not sure how to fix everything."

"Is she mad at you?" Vickie clung to the bags as I retrieved Rebecca from her car seat. Seeing her aunt, she reached out for Vickie, who dropped the bags and took my daughter into her arms.

"All I know is she's mad at me for doing something I didn't know I did."

"What was it?"

"I have to swear you to secrecy." Vickie's confusion halted my confession for a moment.

"Well," she said, "what's so covert?"

"Mary wasn't feeling well this morning, throwing up and all. She thinks she's pregnant."

"She's mad at you for knocking her up?" Recognition replaced confusion, and then a grin surged across her face. "You horny little bastard."

She blushed with my stunned look. "Well, I guess that's one way to put it. We best get in." I picked up the discarded bags and began the march to uncertainty. "You shock me sometimes."

"I'm sorry. Forgive me?" Her radiance melted any angst I brewed.

"I forgive you." We entered the house and found the rest of the clan in the family room. We moved outside to the deck and a delightful afternoon and evening of family time, such as it was in this irrational bunch. How was I to interact with nothing in common, except maybe for the youngest and brightest of them?

31
CHAPTER

Victoria

I was ashamed with my comment about being horny. But he forgave me and I revivified with his forgiveness. If people wanted to think we conspired to do something outlandish, I cared little. I didn't want to hurt Mary, though, and any misstep by me would be a fatal wound in her heart.

I carried Rebecca into the family room where she became the center of everyone's attention. Mom confiscated her from me. My father's attention to her existence exceeded any I had experienced.

Approaching Mary I said, "Did you have a nice drive here?" An empty question devoid of any concern for her since I wasn't sure about the subject of pregnancy.

"Come with me," she whispered. "I have something to tell you and I don't want prying ears to hear." We left the deck without much attention and walked around the house through the garden.

"What's with the secrecy?" She put her finger to her lips. I followed her to the greenhouse where we entered and shut the door.

"Roger and I had a fight this morning. I almost didn't come."

"What about?"

"I think I'm pregnant and I can't be right now. I can barely take care of Rebecca.

I wrapped my arms around Mary. "We can get through this. Have you tested yourself?"

"I don't want to get through this. I don't want to be pregnant. So you can't say anything to anyone." I understood her next thought.

"You can't do it. Mom and Dad would just die if you did."

"What are you talking about?" She scrunched her face and then enlightenment shown. "Oh, you think I want to abort this one. I haven't had time to think what I want to do."

"Well, call me before you do anything." She nodded.

"Don't tell Roger I told you. And please don't mention…you know… to him. He would have a fit."

A sudden knock on the door alerted us to the presence of another person. Had he heard our conversation?

The door opened and Roger entered the greenhouse. "What're you two cooking up?" He tried to be loose and funny, but I trembled with his being here and the possible discovery of our conversation.

"I told Vickie we needed to see her more often on weekends and vacations from school. I want her to help me with Rebecca." Roger did not solicit any desire to know the truth. Both he and Mary were playing a cat and mouse game with me as the unintended victim of their scheming.

"I must go," I said and left them alone. Tears, unwanted and acknowledging, filled my eyes. Could I be in the middle of an incessant drama building in Wendlesburg? Drying my lids I walked around the house to the front door and entered. I went to my room to clean up before returning to the deck and inquisitive people. Down deep I knew I had to build my life with my own guy. Could I?

Roger

I found Victoria and Mary in the greenhouse on the side of the garden. I watched but did not interfere. I couldn't hear what they said, but presumed Mary informed her sister about the baby. I opened the door and entered.

Vickie hurried from the greenhouse saying, "I must go." Upsetting her was not my intention.

"I sorry. Did I come at the wrong time?" I asked.

"You're such a boob, at times." Mary said. She moved toward the door. "I don't want this baby."

"Is that what you and Vickie talked about?"

"What she and I discuss is none of your damn business."

"Why are you mad at me? I didn't do anything wrong." An anger raged at her insinuation of my intervention. "Talk to me. Please, talk to me," I demanded.

Mary stared at me, her eyes blazing with wrath. "I'm leaving before one of us gets hurt, and it won't be me." She stormed from the building leaving me wondering what happened.

Was she still mad at being pregnant? Although Vickie was not the best help in the situation, she was the one available. I left the greenhouse and trailed her to the front of the house.

Ben and Jackson open the front door as I reach for the doorknob. "Oh, hi," I said in a startled voice.

"Hello yourself. What are you doing in front? The party's going strong on the deck."

"I was in the garden and came around this way to go back in." I passed by them as I entered. "Are you two leaving?"

"No, we need to get some things out of the car." I didn't really comprehend their relationship, but it didn't matter to me because Mary and Vickie were okay with it.

I stood in the foyer staring, wondering if I dared find Vickie. Marion entered the room and asked, "Did Ben and Jackson come by you?" I nodded, smiled and left for the deck. Vickie could wait. Mary's attitude threatened where our marriage headed. Was it salvageable?

32
CHAPTER

Victoria

I sat on my bed daubing eyes, smearing mascara across my cheeks. I gained nothing from anything he had. He and my sister were all I ever wanted. I opened the door to the hall, crossed over to the bathroom to wash my face.

Staring at the clown in the mirror, I said, "No one is so important to cause this much heartache." I realized what drove Mary to want an end to the suffering, peace, obtained by suicide. I comprehended and the enlightenment lifted a burden from me.

I washed the grime from my face and returned to my room to replace a lost identity. My resolve from this day forward had to be as pure and innocent as I could make it.

Returning to the party on the deck, I smiled, hiding any pain as best I could.

"How's everyone doing," Mom smiled. Dad ignored me while playing with Rebecca. Ben and Jackson walked onto the deck from around the house.

Mary approached, drink in hand. "I want to tell them about, you know."

"Should you be drinking alcohol?" Mary laughed.

"I'm drinking ginger ale and cranberry juice, as virgin as you."

We sidled away from the deck to the family room. "Why do you want them to know?" I asked.

"These hypocrites don't deserve any happiness, so telling them and then ending it will be the biggest hurt I can rub in their face."

"Mary, it will hurt me, and Roger will just die if you do this." I grabbed her. "How would you explain killing Rebecca's baby sister or brother to her when she got older?"

She twisted out of my grasp. "You know you're a smart ass. It's like you're the older sister and I'm the stupid kid who knows nothing." She walked to the patio door and turned. "Sometimes I just hate you, and love you even more." She went outside.

Roger approached from the deck. "Can we go somewhere private?"

"Come on. We can go to the living room. We'll hear anyone approaching." We walked out of the family room, through the foyer to our objective. "What do you want?"

Roger frowned. "I don't know what to do with Mary." He sat on the sofa. I sat with him. "Mary doesn't want to be pregnant and doesn't want anything to do with me." I reached for his hand but thought better of it.

"Has she said anything to you about what she wants?" He stood, walked away and turned. I followed. "What does she want?" I repeated.

"I don't know. That's why I wanted to talk with you." He reached for my hands as a tear coursed his cheek. "I do love her and I am happy about another child. It's going to be difficult, though, so I'm thinking, we…I… need you to help us."

The touch of his hands whipped my heart to a frenzy of mixed emotions. "I'll help you as much as I can." I pulled out of his grip. "We better get back to the party."

Roger

As Vickie left the room, I wondered about her. Why couldn't her sister be as rational? I followed. When I reached the deck, I found Mary approaching her father. "Dad, I'll take her, now."

She seemed calm, as though nothing negative happened all day. This was the girl I fell in love with at WSU. Rebecca cuddled next her mother's chest. I approached hoping for serenity.

"How are you doing?" I asked. She looked at me, smiled and handed me Becca.

"I'm fine. Really, I am fine." She kissed my cheek, but was it for show or did she mean it?

Dinner was presented soon after. We sat at the table on the deck and consumed our picnic. As evening progressed, I said, "It's getting late. I think Mary and I should head home."

Marion said, "Why don't you spend the night here."

Mary responded, "We have enough with us for Rebecca and I still have some clothing here. It'd be fun."

Why couldn't we just go home? I had no change of clothing. What got into Mary to stay in the environment which created her insecurities? Looking at Becca sitting in her high chair asleep, I decided staying was the right thing to do. Mary and I gathered our daughter and left for the upstairs and her old bedroom.

When we were alone, I asked. "Why stay here, tonight?"

"I need to be here with Vickie." So did I, but I wasn't going to announce it. We placed Becca in her Play N Pak and prepared for sleeping in a twin sized bed. Neither of us had been this close while sleeping since leaving college and the double beds in our apartments.

I wanted a shower, but putting on dirty clothes afterward repulsed my sense of cleanliness. I could survive until the trip home in the morning and refreshing at our house. Marion provided new toothbrushes and paste, towels, hand towels, and face cloths.

When Ben and Jackson departed, we came down to say our goodbyes. Marion was clearing the table so I intervened. "As long as I am staying here tonight, let me do this and you go upstairs and relax."

Vickie chimed in before Marion could answer. "I'll stay and help Roger, Mom. He's right, you've done enough, already." She hesitated, lingering, an interloper daring to trespass. She turned leaving us to tend to the chores we contracted.

"I can do this myself," I said half believing she might leave. Her smile radiated enthusiasm calming fears of intimacy. Mary was most important and this twin, this unwavering twin, held the keys to transforming my wife into a similar human being.

She picked up a dish towel and said, "You wash. I'll dry." Captivated by her willingness to help Mary reconnect with life created a strange silence as though we each wanted to say something and with reluctance held back. What was I thinking? Imagination conjured improbable scenarios as fast as I washed pots and pans.

When we finished we stood admiring our handiwork. I opened my mouth to speak, but words dodged transference from brain to mouth.

Vickie broke the spell. "I enjoyed working with you."

"Thank you," was all I mustered for a response. We stood an eternal moment, then I leaned toward her and kissed her cheek. My body's act wasn't a misconception. I left the kitchen before anything could happen. What would she think of me if I kissed her? I didn't want to find out.

33

CHAPTER

Victoria

The heat of his lips on my cheek aroused my body, nipples in my lace bra and a warmth between my legs. He can't be my first and yet I wanted it more with each contact. I was glad I stayed and washed the dishes.

As he left the room, I remained in the kitchen to be sure no escapade would happen. I ate a piece of the cobbler Mom made for dessert. After rinsing the dish and fork, I placed them in the dishwasher and started the cleaning cycle. Bed and sleep were next.

As I went to my room, I lingered outside of my sister's old bedroom a moment, listening to the silence of the house. All remained as it should, at least for now.

In the morning Roger and Mary packed their car and left for home. I did not get a chance to speak with him about her, but all seemed fine. She ate breakfast in a giddy mood which was missing yesterday. He looked perplexed about the woman he married whose personality changed like the fickleness of Pacific Northwest weather.

Mary's calmness held, for now. For Roger's sake, I hoped she maintained this blithe spirit for the rest of their lives together. My infatuation could not and should not destroy their evanescent happiness.

Weeks passed without any contact, and feelings faded as school intervened. At Ballard High School I expected nothing from the males and females who could become friends and acquaintances. Classes occupied the majority of my time.

Senior males accosted the new crop of female students with unabashed attention. I flirted with these roués but stayed aloof. Other girls succumbed to the allure of passion awakened by adolescence. Several activities and clubs garnered my attention. I discovered volleyball and math club.

Roger

"Mary, do you know where my red tie is? I thought it was hanging with the rest, but I don't see it." Life since the picnic in Seattle with Garrett and Marion and Mary's siblings, had been calm and rational. I catered to Mary's every need. Mondays and Tuesdays were good days. This Wednesday did not herald anything different.

"I got rid of it. It was hideous." I walked back into the bedroom from the closet carrying a blue tie instead. Seeing the tie she continued. "Much better."

Mary exuded the alluring ability to entice my every need. We were back on track. I knotted the tie around my neck and put my jacket on. Mary left to check on Rebecca who needed corralling since learning to scoot around the house on her bottom.

I went into the kitchen to fix breakfast. A scream from Mary startled me. I ran to find her on the floor of bathroom, blood everywhere. "Oh my god, what happened?" I checked for cuts or slashes reminded of the history conveyed to me about Mary.

"I've lost the baby. I came in here and then the blood started flowing. I need a doctor." I pulled my phone from my pocket, flipped it open and dialed 911.

Explaining the situation, I clicked off. "An ambulance is on its way. Stay calm. I'll get a blanket." Rebecca cried for an abrupt loss of attention when mommy left her room.

I covered Mary and retrieved Becca. Pulling out my phone again, I called my father. Mary came first. A sales meeting and two house appointments meant nothing now

The bathroom was a mess. I placed Becca in her playpen in the family room returning to Mary's side. I stripped off my coat leaving it on the bed. My next miserable comment failed. "I guess I could use the red tie now." The sound of the ambulance rescued me from the tirade about to break forth.

As the EMT personnel worked, Mary said, "I get nothing good in this life. Just when I think I have what I want, it's yanked away." She began crying. The medics carted her to the ambulance and transported her to the hospital. I called my mother and begged assistance. She agreed to watch Becca.

The bathroom was a mess of blood and extraneous medical discards. I began cleaning realizing my next child was lost. I hoped Mary was not.

The doorbell rang, but before I could answer, my mother found me. "Go to the hospital. I'll take care of things here." Tears spilled from me.

"I should never have believed it would last. We had it all going so well," I lamented.

"You'll be fine and so will Mary. These things happen and perhaps for the best."

"How can you say such a thing? Mary and I wanted this baby." Maybe Mary didn't, but I did.

"Go. We can discuss this later." I left for the hospital and an uncertain situation.

34
CHAPTER

Victoria

When I returned home from school on Wednesday news of my sister's miscarriage hurt. Mom and Dad acted so cavalier like nothing serious was wrong. Had Mary done something to cause it? I had to go to Wendlesburg even if it meant skipping school.

"Mom, please let me go to Mary. She needs me," I pleaded.

"Roger can take care of her," she responded with ice in her veins. I stomped out. Dad was not going to be any different.

In my room I picked up my cell phone to call Roger. Grunting, I threw it on the bed. What could I say to him? 'I'm sorry' sounded trite. I picked up the phone and punched in the auto-dial.

"Hello," I heard on the other end. "Vickie, I think you should come here," he said before I answered. "I need your help. Mary is so depressed and I'm confused, because I thought she didn't want this baby and now she acts like the world is coming to an end."

"Mom says you can handle it," *Lame*, I thought. "I'll see what I can do."

"Thank you. You're coming will be a lifesaver." I didn't want to be a lifesaver. I didn't know what he meant. He clicked off. I had to see him, to hold him so he was not alone.

I left the bedroom to find my mother and explain to her why I must go. She was in her bedroom placing clothes in a suitcase. "What are you doing?" I asked.

"I'm heading to your sister's. She'll need help with Rebecca while she recovers." Words wedged in my throat. Immobilized, watching her betraying me. I couldn't go, but she could? "You need to stay here and finish the school week. You come over on the weekend." I stormed out.

How was I to go to school? I could help Mary through her depression. I was the one who should be there for Roger. How much help was my mother?

Dad and I ate a simple meal alone. We didn't speak to each other except when I said, "I have to be with Mary. Please, let me go to them."

"Your mother is capable of handling this. You have school tomorrow and Friday. If your mother wants you, then you go. Until then you'll stay here." I finished eating without any more words. He was colder than mother. His comment about not wanting children resurrected itself in my head as I cleaned the kitchen after dinner.

As soon as I had enough resources, I was moving out. I was bent on emancipation. Three years of high school were not going to pass with sufficient speed. I left the kitchen for my sanctuary.

I tried doing homework without much success. I closed my math book and lay on my bed gazing at the ceiling. *What do they want from me?* I thought.

Roger

As I clicked off from my call from Vickie deteriorating emotions erupted. I needed a stable person near me. Mary was morose. Marion's imminent arrival did nothing to assuage my angst. My mother gave no assurance for satisfaction. I had no one who provided refuge.

"Mary, when your mom arrives I have to get back to work. I don't want to argue with you, but I have to go."

She turned away from me, lying in the hospital bed facing the wall. "Leave me alone." I turned and left. In the reception area I sat on one of the sofas, alone in a room full of others. I stood, returning to the nurse's station. "Is there a doctor I talk to about my wife's condition?"

"Mr. Waite, I can page your doctor, but her schedule is full. I don't know when she'll get back to you. Is there anything I can do for you?"

I shook my head, started to leave, but stopped. "Yes, I want to know how long it takes for a woman to recover from this." I didn't mean to be begging, but I was sure she heard it in my voice.

"I'll let the doctor know of your concern." Unsatisfied with her answer I nodded.

A phone call to Mom helped. "How's Rebecca?"

"She's fine and sleeping right now. How's Mary?"

"About the same. I can't get anyone to tell me how long she has to stay here."

"Honey, it takes time. As for your father and business, he will understand." We ended the call.

Retracing my route back to Mary, I found her still curled up facing the wall. She appeared to be asleep. I sat in the chair next to the bed, not knowing what to do. If Victoria visited would I get the sort of help I wanted?

A nurse entered the room, "We are discharging your wife as soon as the doctor sees her," she said. Mary rolled over.

"Did you hear?" I asked. "You can go home soon."

"I heard," she answered. "You said you have to get back to work, so leave me alone. Get out." The nurse raised an eyebrow and tilted her head. I leaned over the bed to kiss Mary, but she turned away.

After we left I asked the nurse, "Does this kind of thing happen often after a miscarriage?"

"It's not common." She walked to the nurse's station and left me wondering why I had to endure such hardship. I hadn't signed on for this. Mary's mother was due to arrive at any time. She could deal with her daughter's irrationality.

My phone buzzed. Looking at the ID, I answered with haste. "What's up?" I said and grimaced like a stupid teenager.

"I called to see how my sister's doing,"

"She's alright. They're letting her out soon as the doctor sees her. I understand your mom is on her way."

"Yeah, I can't come until the weekend when school's out. Is she really okay? I know this kind of thing dinks her mind."

"She's fine physically, but she's upset, which confuses me. At first she says she doesn't want it and now she's depressed." Hearing her voice electrified me. *What's wrong with me? She's my sister-in-law.*

"Roger, I'll get there as soon as I can. Mom will be able to help her until then." *Who's going to help me?* I thought.

35
CHAPTER

Victoria

As soon as school ended on Friday, I avoided anyone who might keep me from getting home. I called Mary on Thursday, but Mom answered the phone and told me Mary was not receiving. I figured it was a lie, but I didn't know. I called Roger's cell to ask him. The call went to voice mail. I clicked off without leaving a message. I wanted to pack and head to Wendlesburg. Nothing went the way I wanted.

At home I stood in the middle of the family room crying like a spoiled child. This large house echoed my life's emptiness, haunting me with memories of atrocities real and perceived. No one remained for me. Ben left when I was still young. Mary abandoned me to parents whose lives were encumbered because of me. Even Roger didn't want me.

Now I needed someone to share my feelings and Andrea lived across town. It was a wonder I hadn't attempted what Mary executed when my age. I picked up my discarded backpack full of a life I most often enjoyed now weighing on my soul as a burden hindering freedom. I went to my room.

Dinner was a frozen something or other which I was in charge of preparing with Mom in Wendlesburg. Dad would eat anything as long as he didn't fix it. Virile men didn't do women's work he might say. He was such a schmuck. I opened drawers to put clean clothing in an overnight bag, a blouse alluring enough without trashiness.

I heard a commotion downstairs and realized my father had returned from his daily sojourn to amass wealth. I stopped stuffing my bag and left to supply our meager rations for the evening meal.

"Hi, Dad. What do you want for dinner?" I asked when I entered the kitchen to find him staring at the refrigerator. He turned, startled to find me home, I guess.

"I don't know. Maybe we should order in and watch a movie." What was this? An attempt to purge his guilt for the many years of ignoring my existence? I shrugged my shoulders not willing to confront him.

He called a pizza delivery service. I asked, "Dad, what's bugging you?"

A whimsical look crossed his face. "I realize how much your mother does around here. I've not had to be alone in this house in a long time. I guess I rely on her more than I thought."

"But I'm here and I take care of things." My retort was not meant to incense him. He stared at me as though seeing me for the first time in his life.

"You're right. You're growing up, not a little girl any more. Your mother is the glue in this house and with her in Wendlesburg, it's eerie here." He left for his office. Unappreciated, I returned to my room to complete packing. Would he take me to Colman Dock after we ate our dinner? I hoped he would, eerie or not.

Roger

Marion arrived at the hospital in time for Mary's discharge. I was like a third wheel on a bicycle, since Mary still wanted nothing to do with me. I left to get the car from the parking lot.

I slunk along like a whipped puppy. I lost a child and maybe a wife. Rebecca needed me more now than ever and I needed her. Victoria had to save Mary. My cell phone sang its glorious song. I answered. *Shit. What now?* "Yes, Mom."

"Roger, dear, I'm having trouble with Rebecca. She's crying but does not want a bottle. She's clean and I've walked her for the last hour. She refuses to sleep." My mother raised three children, but this one exasperated her.

"Mom, I'm still at the hospital with Mary. She's being discharged. I'll be over as soon as I can. Is Billy available to help, or Dad?"

"Billy's at a college function and your father is out showing properties." The frustration strained her voice. I now had another crisis and no one to help. *Vickie, where are you when I need you.*

"Alright, let me get Mary home and I'll be over as soon as I can. Marion's here, so she can stay with her until I pick up Rebecca." I clicked off and found my car. The short drive to the entrance of the hospital left some time to reflect on the chances of having a normal life. Hopelessness cascaded my miserable existence in a state of depression the likes of which my emotions never experienced all of the years through adolescence and marriage. Finding Mary at WSU exuded an aura of satisfaction I realized now was an illusion. But I did love her even in this state of collapse.

As I parked the car by the entry, Marion and a nurse wheeled Mary out. At least someone other than me had finished the paperwork for her discharge. I got out, went around to the passenger side and helped my wife into the front seat.

Marion said, "I'll get my car and meet you at your house." I nodded and started for the driver side.

"Wait. Would you go over to my parents' house and get Rebecca? Mom's having trouble getting her to go to sleep. I think she's upset and wants to come home." Marion nodded and walked away.

In the car I tried to be upbeat, hiding my own frustration with the day's events. Mary still looked white as a ghost. "Do you want anything at home which might help you feel better?"

"Do you think food is the answer to every problem?"

"Well, I wasn't thinking about food as much as something to ease any pain you might have."

"I'm fine. I want to get into bed and sleep until nothing exists." She closed her eyes and put her head back against the headrest. The remainder of the drive was silent. Another tragedy for the stage wrote itself.

In the driveway Mary exited the car, leaving me with all of the baggage we took with us to the hospital. I had no idea what future lay before me.

In the house I found Mary in bed and the bathroom cleansed of the tragic end of our child. Nothing had transformed the house to happiness and tranquility, though. I went to my office and sat behind my desk. Evening erased the day just as the morning erased my serenity.

My cell sang again. Seeing the caller, hope rose in my heart. "Hello, you. Are you coming?"

Vickie answered, "I'll get there soon. Is Mom with you?"

"She went to get Becca. I came home with Mary. We're awaiting their arrival. When are you coming?"

Silence was followed by a heavy sigh. "I'll try and be on the 10:20 ferry. I have to get Dad to take me to the dock."

"I'm glad. I need you" *Maybe I need you more than I should, but I don't care.* "Maybe your mother will pick you up."

I could hear a sound of disappointment in her voice. "You can't come?"

"I would, but someone has to be here with Becca and I think with today's trauma, I should care for her." I was disappointed, as well. "Call me when you're getting close."

The call ended. Thinking about the strain a severe depression generated in our lives, would Mary try to end it all? Could I cope and not feel the accompanying guilt? Victoria had to come. No one stabilized her as much as her sister.

36
CHAPTER

Victoria

"Dad, can you take me to the ferry? I want to get over and help Mom with Mary." I stood in his office with my bag in hand. Time was getting later and later. "Please?" I begged.

"I don't understand why you need to leave tonight. Can't you go tomorrow morning?"

"Dad," I screeched. "Can we go?" His reluctance to be alone, I understood. Nonetheless he rose from his chair and walked out toward his car.

At Colman Dock I leaned over and kissed my father, an action seldom done.

As the ferry left, I called Roger. "I'm on my way."

"Great, Rebecca's finally fallen asleep, so I'll come and get you. Your mother has gone to bed in Rebecca's room. You can have the spare room." My heart fluttered.

"Alright," I wanted to scream 'I love you', but it remained unrequited. "I'll see you in Wendlesburg," I said. We clicked off. I wandered the passenger deck from the café section to the aft fantail, standing next to the outside railing, letting the breeze caress me.

The lights of Seattle shrank as the ferry crossed Puget Sound. School had been in session a few weeks and I uncovered no friends. The one guy who talked to me at school had yet to ask me out. Maybe my reputation as an ice princess thwarted him. I wasn't interested, anyway.

As the ferry docked in Wendlesburg, anxiety gripped me. What if Roger did love me and wanted out of his marriage to my sister? It was not right. My heart beat heavy in my chest. If I stayed on the ferry, I could return to Seattle without him knowing. But the announcement about all passengers must disembark meant I had to get off.

Walking to the passenger pickup area, I looked for him with trepidation. How could I break up his family because of my selfish curiosity? The guy at school might just become lucky after all.

My sixteenth birthday was months away, and I promised to explore more than holding hands. I wanted to share like Andrea and someone had to be first. But Roger? Doubts flooded my brain. "Hi," he said as he approached. "How was the ride?"

"Fine," I mustered. He took my bag and my arm leading me to purgatory.

"How was your week at school?" I wanted to ignore the simplicity of his question and confront him with my emotions to uncover his true feelings. Instead I repeated my last communication.

"Are you okay? You seem distracted."

"How's Mary," I said.

"She's asleep."

"Roger, what's to become of her if she doesn't get over the loss of the baby?"

"Wow. Is this what's eating at you?" He slowed for a light change. Waiting, he asked, "Are you worried she might do something drastic?"

"I guess." *I'm not worried about her, as much as I wonder about you.* The light changed and he continued. At the house, he sat a moment before saying, "I am glad you came over. I miss you when you're not here. You're the younger sister I didn't get."

A sister? "Glad to be of service." The sarcasm missed its mark.

"You're wonderful and how you work with Mary is astonishing. If I didn't know better, I'd say you were the older sister." *Old enough for you, Roger.*

He exited the car and entered the house with my bag in tow. Why did my fantasy have to be so darned handsome?

Roger

Seeing her on the ramp exhilarated me. "She must never see the thrill she causes," I thought aloud. I asked inane questions about the ferry ride and school. *Keep it light.* I must not ruin this for her.

We arrived at the house. My remarks about her being older sounded lame. And she is not a younger sister to me. *Don't be so dumb, Waite.*

I took her bag into the house. It was late and I was tired. Nothing about this day had gone as planned. Two days of Mary being hospitalized had not turned the trick. I needed sleep.

I placed her bag in the guest room and turned around. She stood in the doorway, blocking my escape. 'Do you need anything?" I asked her.

"No, I've all I need for now." She took off her coat. Her blouse revealed her undergarment. A deliberate show? Fifteen and better shaped than many others. She stepped into the room opening my retreat. We brushed against each other. She smelled even better close up. I left experiencing betrayal where none should be. In my bedroom, I undressed to undershorts and climbed into bed. I forgot to clean my teeth and wash my face, so I reversed course. Heading to our bathroom I glanced out the open door, which I hadn't closed, and saw a vision as sweet as the one first encountered at Washington State. A sheer teddy with matching panties. No robe concealed the body. Mary and Victoria exuded the same allure. She disappeared into the other bathroom. I closed the bedroom door and slipped into my bathroom to finish teeth and face cleansing and returned to bed. Mary turned toward me as I settled into position. Without even thinking she might get upset, I pulled her closer to me. A positive response helped me pass into sleep. Dreams were another matter.

37
CHAPTER

Victoria

I woke hearing people whispering. I didn't comprehend the conversation but recognized Roger and my mother. I found my robe and cracked the door of the bedroom.

"Marion," I heard Roger say, "if Rebecca wants to sleep, let her."

"Children need a routine," A routine? Some routine I got growing up with her. She ignored me, although I figured she'd deny such an accusation.

"Alright, but you're responsible for her," he said.

I had to intervene. "Can I help?" I asked.

"Oh, honey, we didn't mean to wake you," Marion said.

"It's okay. I woke when the sun came in the window," I lied. "Do you need me to watch Becca?"

Marion answered, "Thank you, but I'll take care of her. You help Roger with Mary and the house."

"What's the matter with the house?" Roger asked.

"Nothing, dear, but things get out of place and need to be straightened up after a while."

"Mom, we can do it." Neither of them needed to get into a pissing match.

Roger slinked back to his bedroom. I followed knowing Mary should be helped. "What are you doing?" he asked.

"I thought Mary might like company." The knot on my robe loosened. Roger turned away after a quick glance at my left breast. I closed it and retied the sash.

"I need to get dressed."

"Okay," I said. Mary stirred so I sat on the bed beside her. Roger disappeared into the closet. "Mary, are you awake?"

"Hi, sis. I guess I need to get up. How's Rebecca?"

"Mom's with her."

"Where's Roger?" She sat up, putting her head against the head board.

"He's dressing in the closet. I should leave so he can finish." I stood and walked out of the room. I entered the baby's room. Mom sat with Becca in the rocking chair. Her baby blues followed me as I sat on the edge of the toy box. She smiled.

"Mom, Mary's awake."

"Good. How is she?"

"She's alright, I guess. I had to leave so Roger could get dressed."

"I think you need to do the same. No need to tramp around in night clothing." *No reason to start an argument*, I thought, so I stood and departed for the other bedroom.

Roger was at his door watching me before he closed it. I went in my room and stripped off my robe and baby dolls. Standing naked before the dresser mirror, I stroked my breasts and smiled. *Roger would like these if he got to see them.* I then dressed in the lacy underwear and jeans and a light blouse.

In the kitchen I started creating pancakes and bacon to begin the day with vigor. Mom entered soon after, placing Rebecca who wore a cute jumpsuit with butterflies and bees in her high chair. "Oh good, you've started breakfast." She opened a drawer looking for flatware to set the table in the kitchen.

"Mom, the silverware's in the drawer beside the one you're in." I finished mixing the batter and checked on the bacon. Roger didn't need any distractions like fixing breakfast. I figured he'd ignore it unless someone fixed it for him.

Mary wandered in, followed by Roger. He was dressed in jeans and a t-shirt. Mary remained in robe and slippers.

I asked Mary, "How are you doing?" She smiled as if she had recovered from the shock to her body and mental instability caused by the loss of her baby.

"I'm fine. I'm sorry I've been such a bitch. I guess it hit me wrong to have a pregnancy and then to have it end."

Marion said, "Honey, we'll take care of you." Mary nodded.

Roger sat at the table with a smile unseen by me since last evening. We ate breakfast in an atmosphere of peaceful happiness. I relaxed but thought of the meltdowns in Mary's life. How long this abated storm would last, I wasn't sure.

After eating, I cleared the table while Roger took Rebecca for a stroll. Mom went to the bedrooms to strip and change bed linens. Mary stayed to help.

"I'm glad you're feeling better," I said.

"I just needed some rest. It was quite a trauma." We smiled at each other, like old times. "I love you."

"I love you, too. You dry. I'll wash." We loaded the plates and silverware into the dishwasher and hand washed the remaining bowls and pans.

"Is Roger being good to you?" Mary frowned.

"What an odd question to ask." She smiled at me. Was life back to normal?

Roger

"Rebecca, I love your mommy, and your grandmother, and I love your aunt, Vickie. She looks so much like Mommy and acts so much better. Do you like Aunt Vickie?"

My daughter smiled like she understood. I reached down to the stroller and kissed her. We walked on to the nearby park where I sat on a swing thinking about the three women at my house. How did they live together and end up so different? What could have been so horrific for Mary and so amazing for Vickie?

Rebecca whimpered as my mind ignored the obvious for a fantasy. "Oh, I'm sorry, sweetie." Unhooking the straps of the stroller, I picked her up and hugged her. "I never want you to suffer." I stood holding this miracle of mine, knowing the challenge of raising her. How could anyone reject this precious jewel?

"Come on. We have to return to the house." After strapping her in the seat, I rolled the stroller at a slow pace to my destiny.

Entering, I met Mary, She asked, "Did you two have a nice time together?" She kissed me. I cupped her face in my hands and returned the action.

"I love you. We had a wonderful walk to Never Never Land."

"You're Peter Pan, now?" She laughed.

"I may be. And you can be my Tinker Bell." I held her hands and grinned.

"I much prefer being Captain Hook, without having lost a hand, of course." A glimmer of mischief flickered in her eyes. Vickie came in.

"You're Smee," Mary said to her.

"I'm what?" she answered.

I answered, "I took Rebecca to the park. I called it Never Never Land. Now we are playing Peter Pan."

"I get to be Smee? Who's he?" Vickie asked.

Mary responded, "He's the pirate who runs with Captain Hook in the Peter Pan story. Remember? I read it to you when you were young."

Who was this person telling stories? Was she returned to the woman I met in Pullman? Would I have my Avalon after all?

38
CHAPTER

Victoria

The weekend concluded with Mary and Roger recovered for the moment. Mom and I returned to Seattle. Miracles did happen. Mary was cheerful and upbeat. Returning to Ballard High, I discovered a few new friends who gave me hope for my own redemption. Roger became an enigma for me to solve without causing pain for anyone. My father remained his usual supercilious self. Mom and I talked more and became closer.

After the weekend of Mary's recovery from her miscarriage, I jumped into school life with a vengeance. A sophomore named Jacob garnered enough courage to ask me to dinner and a movie. I accepted and we started seeing each other.

"How was school today?" Mom asked me one day in early October.

"Fine," I answered in as sweet a voice as I could muster. The day had been a disaster from the beginning. Although no classes were failed, the collapse of my budding romance and the rumor I had no vagina plagued my entire day. Jacob turned out to be a sex maniac by definition and got nothing from me except to hold his hand. He concocted the story of my being a not so anatomically correct Barbie. I concluded any friends I may have acquired were history and I was destined to regret ever breaking Connor's heart.

"That nice young man you've been seeing, was he at school, today?" *Oh was he ever.*

"Yes, mother. It turned out he's not so nice. We broke up."

"I'm so sorry. You must be devastated." Mother, you have no idea.

"It's alright. We had a difference in opinion about how many dates we went on before I became a slut."

"Vickie, don't talk like that."

"I'm sorry. He wanted more from me than he should have expected. After all, I am the school's ice princess." I turned around from the kitchen and recoiled to the foyer to retrieve my backpack and beat a hasty retreat to my bedroom.

I sat on my bed fighting the tears. Roger would never push me to do something I didn't want to do. The knock on the door interrupted my pity party. I wiped the wetness away with my sleeve and opened the door.

"Honey, I didn't mean to upset you," Mom said. "If this boy pressured you, you had every right to say no." She sat beside me.

"Mom, why is it so hard? He pretended he liked me."

"You did the right thing. If indeed he likes you, he will apologize and come back."

"I don't care if he comes back or even apologizes. I want someone who loves me without it being a condition." I gazed at my mother hoping for some answer to a question I couldn't ask. She sat looking back with a blank expression. "When did you and Dad decide it was right?"

"We waited until we got married. He was a gentleman about it. He wanted to, but I was raised to understand it is a marital thing and is not to be done except within marriage."

"You think I should wait until I find the right man and then marry him first?"

"Yes, but it is not easy to wait. I know you'll make a good decision when time comes." I figured she was thinking about Dad and his obsession with image. I nodded, but I knew what I wanted and knew I couldn't have it. I was going to be one of the best looking nuns at the cloister. *Those Catholic priests weren't getting any of this.*

The awkward silence repelled anymore interaction. Mom stood, walked to the door and hesitated. Without looking back, she left the room.

I thought about what Jacob had said at school, the coldest girlfriend a guy could have. I told him to buzz off and he did. The number of boys who would be interested in me from now on I calculated to be zero, something

I could live with. What I would not live without was being close to my sister. And Roger.

Roger

The weeks since the miscarriage had been good. Mary's buoyant personality and Rebecca's growth into charming young lady of one masked a turbid atmosphere. We planned a party for her first birthday. Then a hurricane whirled into our house on a Thursday evening in late May.

Mary's antic included taking too many sleeping pills and expelling them when her stomach rejected them. I had not expected her to act out.

"Are you alright?" I had asked.

"Leave me alone," she seethed. The door to our bedroom slammed shut, waking Becca who wailed.

"Mommy's not feeling well," I said as if she understood something I'm sure I did not. The phone rang. Picking up Becca I answered it in the office.

"Roger, how's the birthday planning going?" I winced, wanting to expunge frustration with a confession. "I know it's late." My watch read 9:41.

"Everything's fine."

"Can I talk with Mary?" Not happening. I changed the conversation.

"Mary's indisposed right now. How has school been?"

"Oh you know, the usual drama and such." What drama could she experience? I believed Vickie to be the most 'with it' person I had met in a long time.

"Drama?" I asked. "What drama is there at Ballard?"

She laughed. "Roger, you've been out of school too long to remember." The adjustment didn't track well so I tried another tactic.

"What are you planning for your sweet sixteen next month?" I figured some guy would take her somewhere special to celebrate. I was happy for her.

"Nothing yet. I wanted to help with Rebecca's party. Then I can set up something. Do you want me?" I wished I could. But did she have to know?

"I might. Let me know when you have something in mind."

Mary entered the office. "Is it Vickie?" I nodded. "Let me talk to her."

"Your sister is here." I handed the phone to Mary. Rebecca stirred in my lap, so I stood and left.

The pull-up diaper and plastic lined protective cover were still dry. "You are such a good girl." She smiled at me. I put her on the floor and held her hands so she could walk. Each day she was getting stronger and better. Soon she would be free of us.

We walked into the office looking for Mommy. She was still talking to Vickie, so our sojourn continued into the kitchen.

"Vickie wants to help with Becca's party," Mary said as she entered the room. "I think it would be nice to have her here." Who was this lady? The suicidal person disappeared, replaced by my wife. A tear formed so I turned away.

Facing her, I said, "I agree. She's lots of help. Rebecca loves her aunt." I wanted nothing more than for Mary to have the sane and ordinary life we planned. The evening escapade was history...for now.

39
CHAPTER

Victoria

"Mary, it's nice to hear your voice. We haven't spoken much since…well, that weekend."

"I'm okay." Her voiced rattled as if she just awakened. Had another week of raising Becca drained her? My plans interfered with offering any help for another couple of days.

"So is my niece walking yet?"

"Almost, which I'm dreading."

"Why? She's not going to be too much to handle, is she?" I knew the truth.

"I don't know. I was sick last night and I don't feel well today. Vickie, can you come over and help this weekend?"

"I'm already doing something else I can't get out of, but I can help with Becca's party next week. Mary, what made you sick?" Her voice sounded empty. I feared she did something.

"Nothing. I just got sick. Are you sure you can't come over this weekend?"

"Yeah, I promised to participate in something Ballard High is doing on Saturday. Maybe I can come over on Sunday for the day." I was not much for school activities, but this spring retreat for suicide prevention, to understand more about the psychology of people compelled to end it all for no apparent reason, intrigued me.

"I'll be okay. I guess I should find out what my dear husband is doing. Goodbye, Vickie." She clicked off before I could say anything. Was she mad at me?

Becca turned one in another month so I reasoned I would be in Wendlesburg often. School ended at the same time freeing me from the doldrums of being ignored by fellow students. Rumors about my lack of sexual interest persisted.

My birthday was another month and a half and I hoped to have a car freeing me from parent taxi services. Driver training finished. I had my permit. I drove Mom around some parts of town and nothing awful happened. I was ready for soloing. Dad didn't respond much to my inquiries regarding my own transportation. He never said no, but he hadn't taken me out to look for anything.

I had not dated anyone since Jacob pushed for more. I missed nothing, no heartaches or stressful breakups after losing virginity to a true love. Was I a frigid teenager? Other girls were dating guys and experiencing their ecstasy. Acting out fantasies for the thrill of it did not interest me. Guys left me alone except when they wanted help with math or history. I acceded to their requests at school.

Saturday came and I was excited about the suicide exhibition. At breakfast I asked, "Mom, can you take me to school?" The gym opened to the public at 10:00 AM, but I wanted to be first to arrive.

"Honey, it's eight o'clock."

"I know, but I need to be there to help with the booth I'm working in the afternoon. You know if I had my own car I could drive myself there."

"You can't drive alone until you are sixteen."

"I know. I'm just saying."

"I'll take you over at nine."

"Thanks," I went to my room to dress. Going to Wendlesburg after the exhibition was doomed. The next weekend included Memorial Day, a better time for staying with them.

At nine Mom fulfilled her promise. The morning sessions about suicide prevention and living the aftermath gave me hope for helping Mary. I ate the lunch my mother fixed and worked the booth for YSPP, Youth Suicide Prevention Program.

Mary was not a youth in age but mentally she acted it. Her past haunted her present. I was not going to let her future be a victim of it.

Roger

"Is Vickie coming over this weekend?" I asked Mary.

"No, she's doing something at her high school on Saturday. Next weekend is better since Memorial Day is Monday."

"All right. We'll finish party plans for Rebecca then. I'm so happy you're better."

"I don't know what gets into me. Sometimes I want to die." Listening for triggers which set her off, nothing was clear.

"Would you to see someone about your moods?"

"So you think I'm crazy."

"No, you need help with whatever is messing with your mind. I'm not a psychologist. I don't have the first idea of what to do for you, except love you." As I reached for her, she pulled away. I initiated another storm.

"I go crazy because you say stupid stuff. All you want is someone to sleep with you and fix meals."

"Mary, I want you to be happy and I don't think you're crazy." Oops.

"You're such a boob. Take care of Becca and leave me alone." I looked at our daughter who slept with peanut butter and jelly on her face. I missed Mary's next action.

My left cheek stung. No girl slapped me so hard. Perhaps I deserved to be from many of the women I dated, but why now? My nostrils flared as I bit my lower lip and hid my clenched fists. She had no right.

40
CHAPTER

Victoria

At the end of the suicide prevention conference at Ballard High School I had learned enough to help Roger with Mary. As promised, Mom arrived. I climbed into the car placing a bag of material on the floor. Clicking my seatbelt, I asked. "May I go over to Wendlesburg? I need to see Mary,"

"Vickie, this conference must have been very interesting. You have quite a collection of material," she said.

I know. It was so cool. I learned so much."

"Are you sure? Don't get into trouble with her." Mom, started the car.

"I don't think she'll get mad." We returned to the house in silence. I unpacked my bag and read them again. I was now an expert and who better to help Mary.

I found my cell and dialed Roger. The record message came on. "Roger, I'm trying to convince Mom to let me come over tomorrow. Call me or send a message." I clicked off, tossing the phone on my bed.

I found Mom in the hallway outside my bedroom. "Mom, please let me go over tomorrow. I have to be there to help Roger with Rebecca. Mary and I can figure out what to do."

"I'll call and ask." Mom walked away.

I stood frozen. How could she not understand? Mary was in trouble. Was Roger to be left alone with her and not get help with Rebecca? I returned to my room and checked my phone for messages. Nothing.

"Don't ignore me, Roger," I said. Placing the phone on the desk, I lay on the bed staring at the ceiling.

The knock on my door startled me. "Honey, dinner time." Afternoon gone? I must have fallen asleep.

"I'll be down in a minute," I answered. Orienting my groggy mind came at a snail's pace. Grabbing one of the brochures to convince my parents helping Mary could happen, I went down to dinner. I had slept for half an hour, but it seemed an eternity.

At the table the information sat in a noticeable place, ignored as we ate. Little conversation occurred except about a deal my father completed for another financial coup of some sort. I had my own coup to pursue.

Frustrated, I asked, "Mom, you were going to call Roger and Mary. Did you?"

"I called but didn't get an answer." *Not good enough.*

"May I be excused?" I begged.

"No," my father said, "we are not finished with our meal. Do not disturb your sister with these inane ideas of fixing her." He glared at me. I returned the same.

"You don't get it," I thought but said, "Alright, but Roger needs help with Rebecca. I want to go over tomorrow."

"Next weekend is soon enough," he growled like an angry dog missing a bone. Icy silence finished our meal. My father was so unsympathetic. All he cared about was his precious reputation. Had he written Mary off?

Roger

I checked her phone message, listening to Vickie's plea for information. I, too, wished her here for reasons other than helping. My heart beat increased and my breath quickened. I clicked the phone off and put it in my pocket, looking around for any unwanted eyes and ears.

Rebecca wailed from her bedroom as if abandoned on a train platform. I ran to discover her on the floor. The side of crib had lowered and she had fallen. Mary came in after me.

"What happened?" she asked.

"I don't know, but the crib side is down and she's on the floor."

"Can't I trust you to take care of her without letting her get hurt?"

I picked up our daughter and cuddled her. She was not damaged, except her pride. Her lips quivered and her breathing staggered as she calmed in my arms.

"She's alright. She's fine." I hugged her for reassurance of my medical diagnosis.

Mary snorted. Her eyes glazed and darkened. She stepped into the room and I stepped back. "Give her to me." I acquiesced.

With her free hand she blazed my cheek a second time. My fist quaked at the idea of returning the favor. I resisted.

They left. I examined the side of the crib ascertaining Rebecca had to be a magician to unlock both hooks at the same time. The locks to secure the crib side had not engaged. Mary had put Rebecca down for her nap.

I walked into our bedroom finding Mary sitting in the side chair with Becca. "The latches on the side must not have been secured," I said.

Mary's eyes narrowed. "I suppose because I put her in the crib, you think I failed to keep her safe." She stopped short of making another comment. I did not.

"I'm not accusing anyone of anything. I don't think Rebecca is capable of unlocking both sides of the crib. We need to be more diligent."

Mary glared at me. I turned to leave. "Coward. You think I don't know what's in your head. You think I'm incompetent."

"No, I think we need to be careful."

"No, you think I need to be careful. Don't lie to me." Rebecca whimpered with the screaming.

"Look I'm sorry. I didn't mean anything by it." I left this time without looking back as she answered.

"You're a bastard," I thought the better of returning to slap her for it.

"Vickie," I thought aloud, "I need you."

41
CHAPTER

Victoria

The next seven days dragged, anchored to the previous week. I couldn't be sure if my parents would keep their promise. I took a lead role at school handing out suicide information pamphlets each day, but the days still crawled. Roger didn't returned any of the messages I sent to his phone. Two days before the weekend, I spoke to my sister, a conversation entertaining the idea she was not happy with Roger.

"But Mary, what's he done?" I asked.

"He's an insensitive boor who cares only for work and money," she said.

"You might be thinking about Dad, you know." I waited for Mary to contemplate what I said. "Roger isn't a selfish person."

"You don't live with him," she countered and the phone went dead. What was wrong?

On Friday I arrived home from school to find neither parent. Upstairs I packed an overnight bag, hoping someone would return by the time I finished stuffing in clothes. Leaving it on the bed, I searched for Mom for a ride to the ferry.

I called a friend who had a car and lived nearby. Entering the kitchen I left a note for the missing parents and departed without permission, assistance, or comments, a confrontation not needed.

"Randy, thank you for this ride to the ferry?" He wanted to date me, which might be good experience, but I resisted. A fear of intimacy? Ironic since it seemed so much like my sister.

"Yeah sure, where are you going?"

"To my sister's in Wendlesburg."

I wasn't sure how I was to get to Roger and Mary without calling them. He could be my driver saving me time, but at what price.

"Is someone picking you up?"

"No, I'm taking the bus."

"I could drive you to their house."

"You don't need to do that."

"I don't mind."

"Thanks, I'll pay your way." I didn't want him to think he was on a date with me.

"Don't worry, I can afford it."

"Thank you, Randy. I'm ready whenever you can get here."

"I'm on my way." I clicked off and ran upstairs to retrieve my suit-case. I looked around for any forgotten items, and then left. As promised, Randy arrived at the curb as I walked down the steps. Had he been on his way when I spoke with him? I placed my bag in the backseat and entered the passenger side.

"Thanks, again for helping me." I smiled as he started the car on a road of destiny I wanted, but didn't deserve.

As we pulled away, Mom's car pulled into the driveway. I know she saw me and probably wondered if I was running away. I'd call her as soon as I got enough courage.

"Vickie," Randy said, "why won't you go out with me?" He looked ahead at the road and not at me. Warmth flushed my face and a tingle coursed elsewhere.

"I don't date." I looked out the side window hoping rapid words end-ed the conversation.

The light turned red. "You're afraid of guys, aren't you? I'm not like them. You're smart and beautiful. Just say yes and I'll prove I'm a gentleman."

I had no rejoinder. We spoke several times at school, but I did not pursue a relationship. "Will you go out with me? And this is not a date." I grinned.

"Alright, but just so you know, I'm Ballard High's ice princess." His face contorted and he laughed. The light changed and he drove on.

A call to Mom was proper. "Hi, Mom, I'm on my way to Mary and Roger's house." She questioned about the driver. "Randy is a guy I know from school."

"Your father is not going to be happy about you leaving like this," she said.

"I can make it up to you when I get home on Monday. Just cover for me until then."

The phone call ended and I thought about how little I cared whether my father thought ill of me. He mattered so little.

We waited for the 5:20 crossing. I checked my watch. It was 5:02, eighteen long minutes of intimate time alone with Randy. Unlike Jacob, he was an athletic person, a member of the soccer team and fairly popular with girls. He dated several over the months since school started in the fall. I heard a girl he dated say it was too bad he was gay, since he never wanted to make out. I wondered if dating me was cover for him.

He was handsome with high cheek bones and a chiseled jaw line. His skin was clear of blemishes and his eyes sparkled when he spoke. He wore long hair which framed his face with blond locks. At nearly six feet in height, he filled the space next to me.

I checked my watch again. The minute hand was not moving. I preferred analog for some quirky reason, but time was at a standstill. "Are you in a hurry to escape?"

"What? Oh, no."

"Well, you checked your watch twice within a few seconds. I thought maybe being here with me was uncomfortable for you."

A twinge of guilt scurried through me. I turned my body to face him, "Do you think I'm an ice princess?"

"I hope not for both of our sakes."

"What's that supposed to mean?" Eyes scrunched, not angry, confused.

"I know you aren't much for dating and, Jacob, the dweeb, spreading rumors about you doesn't help. I've dated a few girls and I guess broke their horny hearts. I'm not interested in a string of sexual conquests like other guys and I think you want a meaningful relationship with someone since you are not a slut like most other girls. So I hope for both of us we can find a real connection."

Thinking about Andrea and our interplay, I wondered if he indeed meant what he said or was trying another tactic to get me to loosen up. To experiment, I reached out my hands, caressing his face as I pulled it toward me. I kept my eyes opened as lips touched. He closed his while his hands cradled my back. His tongue traced my lips side to side from top to bottom. I warmed with familiarity. Then, it ended.

"You are not as icy as advertised." My face blushed.

"Without doubt you are not as gay as reported." We laughed. The boat began loading saving us from any further experimentation. I thought of Roger and how I fantasized. Was Randy a better candidate for fulfilling my womanhood?

Roger

Mary and I called a truce for the week. I left for work earlier and returned later. Rebecca received my attention making the time bearable. I refused to sleep anywhere but in my own bed. I wanted to hold Mary and apologize for being a senseless fool, but she had to make the first gesture. She was not malicious, but neither was she warm. We coexisted.

Vickie's call made me think I was better off leaving Mary and letting her find a better man who could understand her and help her. However, I enjoyed time with her younger sister and I knew she helped. Leaving my wife was not a good choice.

I didn't talk with my parents about my problems. They were not sympathetic to cries for help. I was marooned. Vickie could stay with me over the weekend and help Mary. "No, stay at the house with Mary and me. What was I thinking?" I blurted. She was not a surrogate for her sister. I married for better or worse.

Showing houses all day for six days kept my mind off of my troubles. It was now Friday afternoon and nothing hindered my leaving the office except thinking of interacting with Mary. Rebecca needed me, of course, so I packed my valise and drove home.

"Hello, is anyone here?" I said as I entered the kitchen from the garage. "I'm home."

Mary walked in holding Rebecca. I placed my valise and car keys on the kitchen table. She held out Becca to me. I took her and recoiled, waiting for the facial impact.

"Roger, I'm sorry about this week."

"No, it's my fault. I know it's hard to raise Becca and take care of the house. I'm here for the weekend. I don't have any shows to do." She moved closer and enfolded Rebecca and me into her arms. I placed my free arm around her waist squeezing her to me. She then kissed me with a longed for passion. I reacted as a hungry man would.

We walked to the hallway to the bedrooms. I placed Becca in her crib, being sure to latch the clips. I kissed her and put her favorite toys in with her.

In our bedroom Mary stood with her clothing removed. Her breasts rose with each breath and I tore at my jacket, shirt and tie. She placed a finger on my lips and said, "Slow down. I want to make love not just have sex." We embraced and kissed, her hands moved to the bulge in my pants. She unhooked my belt and trousers and slid the zipper down. She reached in. My pants fell to the floor.

She moved to the bed and lay on it. I removed the remaining articles of clothing tripping as I fumbled with shoes. Nothing remained of the storm which had lived in our house for the last week. We satisfied each other's lusts and in truth made love. The feel of her flesh against mine reawakened an adoration for her devastated by recent interactions. The girl I met in college was home.

42

CHAPTER

Victoria

On the ferry we limited our conversation to people we knew and school. Antagonism? He acted as if I had invaded his space.

"Randy, I didn't mean to be forward when I kissed you." The ferry was reaching our destination.

"Vickie, I wouldn't mind doing it again, but if you are not interested in exploring a long term relationship, I'm not interested in asking you out."

He had me. Did I want something which might release my inhibitions about sex and plunge me headlong into a maelstrom I couldn't escape? Or finding a proper mate with whom to raise a family?

"Dating you wouldn't be a bad thing." He reached over, took my hands in his, and leaned in close. I shut my eyes awaiting his warm breath and lips. He caressed my mouth with tongue. I reciprocated. My body quivered as blood swelled certain parts. The announcement for drivers and their passengers to return to their vehicles ended further exploration. Confused and pleased I sat silent as the boat docked. No betrayal, but guilt reared an ugly head.

"I need directions," Randy said as he started the car and followed the others off the deck.

"Turn right at the top of the ramp. Follow the street until you get to a light." He did as directed until we arrived at the house. I wasn't sure if he was staying or leaving. Silence was not an ally. "Thank you for driving me here." I wasn't sure what to do next.

Randy broke the deadlock. "I have to get back to the ferry terminal."
I reached across the seat and kissed him.

"Call me about a date. I would like to explore whether I can do a long term thing." I retrieved my bag from the backseat and walked to the front door. I did not look back as the front door of the house opened and Roger stepped out.

"Who was in the car?" he asked.

"A friend from school."

"Looked to me like he might be more than just a friend." He saw me kiss him. Anger? Or disappointment.

"He wants to go out with me." Roger took my bag and turned back into the house. Was he jealous? "How's Mary?" Silence.

In the foyer Mary had Rebecca. "Hi, Vickie, I'm glad you're here." She was dressed in her robe, which lay open a bit. Roger disappeared down the hall to the guest room. He likewise was under clad for late afternoon.

"I'm glad, too. You look great."

"Roger and I patched things up." I understood the lack of clothing.

"How's my Becca?" I asked. She smiled reaching for me. Mary handed her to me and we nuzzled.

Roger returned, "I put your bag in the bedroom." Was he cool to me?

"Thanks, Roger." He passed close and kissed his daughter. Touching her, he brushed against me. Did he mean to? I forgot about Randy.

Roger

Vickie had a boyfriend. I guess I shouldn't have been surprised. Why did it matter? She was a help with Mary who did matter. "Vickie, I'm glad you're here."

"Thanks, I wasn't sure I was going to make it. My friend, Randy, brought me."

Mary said, "I'll start dinner. Want to help, sis?"

"Sure," she said and handed Rebecca to me. The changes in my life burst forth around me faster than I comprehended.

In the kitchen I placed Rebecca in her highchair. "Do you want me to feed Becca?" I asked.

"Please do." Mary opened a cupboard and pulled out jars of baby food. "Here, give her these."

Watching these two young women working together, I admired the beauty each possessed. They not only looked like twins, they sounded so alike no person would distinguish the difference in their voices. The touch of their skin was soft and inviting. The scent they exuded enticed. I loved one and was curious if the other matched in sweetness as well.

Becca consumed dinner oblivious to conflicts surrounding her. I shoveled her food at her as she worked to aid her feeding. It would not be long before she fed her own face and surroundings.

As Mary took plates into the dining room, Vickie asked, "Roger, are you upset with me?" I shook my head believing I should not say a word. What was I to say? She had a right to enjoy the company of a young man her age.

Mary reentered ending any more inquisition. Vickie took the silverware handed her into the room to set places. "Roger, are you okay?" Mary asked.

"Why?"

"You were happy until Vickie arrived. Did she say something or do something to upset you?"

"No, but she arrived with a guy and it surprised me, I guess. I'm thinking she has a new boyfriend." Mary smiled.

"Are you jealous?"

"Now you're teasing me." Mary still held the allure I found in college. Mental sanity had such short stints of late. I desired stability, needed it, to continue this challenging marriage. Vickie returned. Finished with feeding Rebecca, I cleaned her and placed her in her playpen.

Aromas of sautéed onions, mashed potatoes, and broiled steaks whet my appetite. We ate well since success in real estate increased my income. Our home was a haven and I needed to remember all of the blessings I received. Vickie was part of it, but to what degree?

43
CHAPTER

Victoria

I heard Mary's question. Does she suspect how I feel about him, or does she think he feels something for me?

"Mary, you are such a good cook," I said. We chopped onions and sautéed them with vegetables and potatoes. Broiled steaks rounded out the meal. As we ate we chatted about high school and last weekend's seminars about suicide.

Mary asked, "What did you learn?"

My new found knowledge proffered plenty of information. "I learned about the difficulties some people have separating the realities of life from the imagined burdens. Sometimes problems are more misunderstood by family members than the suicidal person."

"I believe you're right." I watched Roger listen to Mary.

"I hope I'm not one of those who doesn't get it," he said.

"Vickie, without you, I would have died long ago." Mary smiled at me.

"That's a lot of pressure to put on your sister," Roger interjected.

"It's okay. I can handle it." My smile faded.

Glowering at me, Roger responded, "You don't need to be a savior for Mary. You have a life of your own to live." Mary frowned and her eyes darkened.

"Roger, I haven't been pressured to do anything I didn't want to. I love Mary." I smiled hoping to dispel any argument.

Mary seethed, "You aren't much of a help, Roger, so leave her alone."

A tear formed. "I'm sorry. I don't want to be a problem to anyone." Brushing it away I continued, "Please, change the subject."

"No," Roger said, "I suppose I'm not as informed as you, but Mary is my wife and I want to be there for her."

"You're not here. All you care about is making money. I want a real man not some cold fish."

"I wasn't so cold earlier today, was I? You enjoyed our afternoon soiree as much as I did and you initiated it."

"That was a mistake I won't make again."

"Please, you two are supposed to love each other." Tears flowed in spite of my attempts to stem the flood.

"I do love Mary, but sometimes she is unreasonable."

I turned to my sister, "Does this have anything to do with losing the baby?"

"No, I want to be normal and I can't find it."

Roger asked, "Did any of the literature address the changes which affect a pregnant woman?" Mary grunted at the statement.

"Yes, but not about the post-partum period."

Mary asked, "Anything about surviving a husband who is insensitive?" She sneered at Roger.

"Yes, but Roger's not insensitive."

"He leaves the house and doesn't come back until late. He's always working. Any information about inattentiveness?"

"Not as I remember."

"I could spend more time here and help," he snorted.

"What kind of help do you think I need?" Mary asked. "I can't handle it?"

"I'm hiring a yard service to do the outside." My head flipped from Mary to Roger and back like watching a tennis match.

"Too much time away from me can be a detriment to our future, so I'm happy to hear you come to a sense of reason about helping me."

The conversation seemed to have an undertone of sarcastic civility for which failure's imminent response coupled with the dangers of Mary's instability stood sentinel in the house. Who would concede the battle only to suffer the onslaught of the other?

"Do you have anything sweet for dessert?" I asked attempting again to quell the melee.

He had done nothing to deserve Mary's attack. Dinner ended without sweets of any kind. I retired to my bedroom, the kitchen left for Roger to clean.

Roger

As I finished cleaning the kitchen, I thought about Vickie's innocent conversation and the decline of my marriage. Mary was wrong about her sister. Vickie was young, not an expert with people's emotions.

Rebecca slept oblivious to any storms swirling around her enclosure. I picked her up realizing a need for a change. As we passed the guest-room I heard whimpering sounds. No sound extruded our bedroom. With Rebecca comfortable and placed in her crib, I explored the crying. A gentle knock received a welcome response.

Vickie opened the door. "Are you alright?" She had changed into sleepwear which was see-through lace and showed her underwear, also lacy. I averted eyes which wanted to probe the delicacy before me.

She turned to let me in. My valor evaporated as the fog when the sun warms the day. "I'm alright. I don't think Mary treats you very nice." Tears streaked her mascara. "I must look awful."

"You could never look awful." I kept eyes on hers. Her blond locks framed her face. In spite of smears her beauty was not diminished. The one clue I surmised as the difference between these sisters was Mary's age. "Listen, Mary and I will work through everything. She needs you to be her sounding board. I'm not much help."

Vickie embraced me, surprising me with the feel of her body which was more ample than Mary's. A lump formed in my throat and elsewhere. I returned the hug for a moment and then forced a release. "I must go. Get some sleep and talk with Mary tomorrow." Holding her shoulders, I kissed her forehead and left the room. As I turned to nod a goodnight, my eyes beheld the portrait before me of a person who doubtless understood her allure and its affect.

In my bedroom a woman of similar beauty carried no such allure. "Mary, I'm sorry for this evening. We should not be fighting in front of your sister." She lay on our bed wearing her robe, her slippers cast aside on the floor.

"You can't be insensitive to my needs."

"I don't understand what it is you want. I'm willing to cut back some on work at the office, but I have to go out and sell if we are to have a life I know you want. Let's make up again."

"You think sex will compensate for your behavior tonight?"

"I'm sorry. I love you but can't figure out what you want from me." The words fell on hollow ears.

"Alright, show me you love me." She opened her robe. I removed my shorts and shirt. "My goodness, you are ready for this." I was ready but my brain framed another liaison. My passion, fueled by 10th commandment violations, provided a platform to satisfy my wife. I consumed the fire of rebellion in heart and soul, feeding my lust for a surrogate.

44

CHAPTER

Victoria

My tears dried, Mary weighed on my mind. I was not against her marriage. I praised the idea she found what she lacked before him. Was I evil in wanting to share the prize for a short while until my mister right came forward?

I slept a satisfied courtesan of Italian literature in Genoa. No man touched me except in fantasy. He kissed me and peaked at my visage before leaving. Randy would not be a long term relationship if I consummated my womanhood with another.

The morning broke early when Rebecca announced its arrival. I placed a peignoir over my negligee and retrieved my niece. I changed her and we left for the kitchen and breakfast.

"You are such a good girl." She cooed. I placed her in her chair, opened a box of O shaped oat cereal and placed many on the tray. A shuffling of slippers alerted us to an invasion by other members of the household. Mary wandered in as I made a bowl of baby food for Becca.

"Good morning, sis," she said as if nothing negative happened the previous meal.

"Good morning." I placed the bowl on the counter. "Does Becca eat toast?"

"Yes."

I placed a slice of bread in each side of the toaster, one for me and one for Becca. Finishing the cereal, I placed the bowl on her tray and fed her. "Are you and Roger okay?"

"Yes, if it's any of your business. By the way, do you think you should be parading around in your underwear?" I blushed understanding my intentions.

"I'm not parading around in anything. This is what I wear."

"Please change for me then. Roger doesn't need distractions."

"Good grief, Mary, what do you mean?" She stared at me, eyes cocked in disbelief.

"Let me finish feeding Becca, You get dressed." The toaster popped. We gazed at each other not wanting to concede our positions to the other. Roger arrived to witness our standoff.

I stood and picked the slices out of the toaster.

Putting one on Becca's tray, I left with the other respectful of Mary's comment. Breakfast could wait. As I walked out I turned back. Mary scrutinized me, but he surveyed me. Did he appreciate what was leaving?

Roger

"My sister's growing up. Don't you think?" Was Mary asking interested in the adolescence of Victoria or probing for any hint of my attraction.

"I guess," playing it coy. Her body reflected the youth she was. Mary's body remained supple, firm. Its allure remained despite birthing a child and nursing. Victoria's body carried no fat or sagging flaps of skin. Although her breasts were sheltered from my wandering eyes, they framed the filmy clothing for the imagination.

"You seemed to notice as she left."

"Don't be jealous. She's a fifteen year old flirting for attention. I'm not interested in her or any other young lady. I want you." I hoped to be convincing.

"She'll be a sweet sixteen soon." I wondered about the boy who brought her to me. Or rather to us. Was she sweet on him?

"We need to finish planning Becca's birthday. We only have three weeks." Diverting the conversation seemed prudent.

"Vickie can help us as soon as she's dressed." I smiled. "What's so funny?"

"You're jealous and I think it's cute. She has what you had when you were her age. However, you are a mature and desirable woman."

"I didn't have the kind of body at sixteen she has. Nor did I exude such feminine wiles in the presence of men or boys. She knows more now than I did then and probably more than I do now."

Vickie entered with proper attire. Had she overheard any of our exchange? "Can you help us plan a party for Becca?" If she had heard she did not let on.

"Yes. Who do you want to invite? Family, of course, and any friends she has met at the park. Are there any other kids on the neighborhood?"

Rebecca sat in her high chair playing with the remaining pieces of toast and her sippy cup, oblivious to the intimate talk which concerned her.

"Slow down," I chimed, "we'll keep it simple until she's older." Neighbors reacted to Mary with indifference, a callousness to hospitality when we moved in. Now a fence separated us from the house on the south side and a row of bushes planted on the north side. We were isolated in a crowd. Every so often I spoke with them, but Mary remained aloof.

"Our parents and Ben, and your parents and brother and sister," Vickie offered.

I don't want anyone else coming." Mary stared at me as if I might continue the list of potential victims. Vickie obtained a paper from the kitchen junk drawer and wrote the names of all the people. "What do we want the theme to be?" she asked.

Mary said, "I think it should be an artistic theme with paintings of animals and scenes of gardens."

"She won't get it," I answered. Raging eyes surged toward me.

"I told you. You need to be sensitive to my desires." I retreated.

"Okay then we'll have pictures of animals and pastures."

Vickie offered another idea. "Why don't we have a simple theme of toys and stuffed animals? After all, it is for her we're planning this party." Becca looked up as if to say, thank you. "You are such a good girl," she said to her. Rebecca giggled.

"Alright," Mary said. "A simple party it is." How does Vickie calm her sister without any question?

45
CHAPTER

Victoria

"You are such a good girl," I said, and Rebecca giggled. Mary agreed and we calmly continued our brainstorming. I wrote all ideas to be culled for the best.

Later, I sat on the deck outside the family room, holding Rebecca, talking to her about how much she was loved and what great things she would do when she grew up. I explained about how mommies and daddies were supposed to be wonderful all the time and she was lucky to have two parents who were.

"You have a nice mommy and a handsome daddy who take good care of you." She stared at me as if I was full of malarkey. Looking around to be sure we were alone, I continued, "I think your daddy is the best man in the world. Mommy loves him as much as I do." She smiled and burped. I cuddled her to me.

We sat for a few minutes and she fell asleep in my arms. Roger came out and sat in a seat across from us. "What's up?" he whispered. Rebecca blinked but didn't awaken.

"We've been discussing what a nice family she has. Although, I haven't introduced her to the benefits of aunts, uncles, and grandparents." Roger laughed and Rebecca stirred. Her eyes opened and she reached for her father.

"See, Becca, I told you. You have the best daddy in the world." He took her from me and she returned to sleep.

"I guess I should put her down in her crib." He stood and entered the house. I followed. Mary was napping as she often did when her daughter slept. I had provided an early start for her by taking Rebecca out on the deck.

After placing his daughter in the crib, Roger and I returned to the seating outside.

"Earlier today, when we were discussing the party, you calmed Mary from having a tantrum without much effort. Every time I try to have a civil conversation with her, it ends up being a fight. How do you do it?"

"I don't know. I've always been able to see her side of things and she's happy to be with me. I envy you having a loving relationship with her."

"Why?"

"She's not had it in her life, and I can't seem to find it, either."

"What about the boy who drove you here?"

"He wants to date me and I might do it." The next words out of my mouth surprised me. "If he wants more, I don't think it will last very long."

"What would he want?" A personal question. Why?

"You know, what guys always seem to want."

"You don't have to sleep with him."

"I know, but sometimes I want to experience what it is like. I just don't have the right guy, yet." My eyes connected with his.

"Listen, somebody is going to sweep you off your feet just like your sister did with me. I was one of those guys who wanted what you won't give out. Stand your ground for the right guy." I nodded and began plotting.

When I was dressing, I justified my perspective to have what I wanted without destroying what Mary had. Hearing Mary and Roger talk about me, I waited in the hall for a proper moment to break in, to be sure I didn't want to cross a line of respect I planned to cross in the future. How to get Roger to know was my challenge.

Roger

The weekend finished without any further outbursts. Mary and I said goodbye to Vickie who called a cab at my insistence. I gave the driver enough money to insure a safe and pleasant arrival at the ferry terminal. How she was to get home bothered me, but Vickie assured us she would be alright. She called Randy, her delivery service.

"I think we should surprise your sister with a party for her sixteen birthday." Mary looked at me as if I had small pox.

"She should spend it with her friends rather than her family."

"Maybe she wants both. She can hang out with friends and we can have a family celebration for her later." Wanting her back in my house, was flirting with disaster.

"Alright, but don't be surprised if she balks at the idea."

"After Rebecca's party we can ask her and see what she says." Mary shook her head and retreated to our bedroom. Rebecca was asleep for the night, or as much of it as we could hope for. I returned to my office to complete the paperwork for a house in the Seattle area of Capitol Hill. The house was small and built before 1960, but it had promise for flipping with some upgrades to meet code. Another idea invaded my head. A retreat from the hurricanes of Wendlesburg? A place to go for short periods of time. I could stay to complete business in Seattle before returning home the next day. I sold a few homes and business properties in the city and it made sense to me. Another idea probed my brain. "No, I can't." I said to myself.

After putting the papers in the drawer I closed and locked it. I went to our room to prepare for bed. It was still early, so I was not surprised to find Mary reading.

"What have you been doing?" The question had undertones of an inquisition.

"I was completing the paperwork for the house in Seattle. It can be fixed up and flipped for a nice profit."

"You're the supposed expert." It sounded like a personal crack at me. I went into the bathroom without responding. Vickie would have had a kind word for her. I couldn't think of any.

When I finished toileting, I came to bed, stripped off my clothes and climbed in. I turned out the light on my bed stand. "Goodnight," Inattentive to her I rolled away from her.

"You're such a coward."

Without facing her I said, "I don't know what you mean."

"What's the matter with me? You don't want me tonight? You wanted me on Friday, but Vickie isn't here to excite you."

I turned around with her comment about Vickie. "She has nothing to do with this. I'm tired and want to sleep," I lied. "You can stay up, but I have to get up early and go make money for you, as you are so quick to point out."

"Fuck me, and I'll leave you alone."

"Yeah, real inviting." I rolled over. The next move caught me off guard. Mary crawled over me, her naked body touching me tender and light. She used her breasts instead of hands.

"Is this more inviting for you?" I faced her as she continued caressing me. I responded and wrapped my arms around her pulling her close and kissing her. We consummated what she started. I lay back on my side of the bed.

"So, do you think Vickie could do anything like this to you?" Mary suspected?

"I wouldn't know." Wanting to know haunted me. Was she as sensual as Mary exhibited in her sane periods of time? "Why would you ask me such a thing?"

"I see how you look at her."

"If you haven't noticed, you two could be twins. It's uncanny how much you look alike." I propped my head up on my arm and looked at her. "She's not old enough for me or anyone my age. She should be interested in the guy who brought her here on Friday."

Mary sat cross-legged on her side of the bed. "Not old enough, yet."

I reached out and pulled her to me again. Talking about this excited me. We played for another half hour until drained, we collapsed and slept. I dreamt about two women vying for my affection, feeding the battle to find out who was the stronger. The younger one was alluring while the older one exhibited skills. I pitted them at each other. Which would prevail?

46
CHAPTER

Victoria

The end of the school year and a birthday party rounded out the month. I had not spoken with Mary since her reprimand of my sleep wear. Roger called me once about the party and we finalized plans.

Randy asked me for a date, which I accepted. We had an uneventful but enjoyable time. He treated me with respect and I kissed him good night as a reward. We talked at school and reputations died ignoble deaths.

One Monday morning after the end of my sophomore year of high school, I asked, "Mom, when do you know if a guy is the right one for you?"

"You must have had a wonderful date with Randy." She never gets it but jumps to conclusions.

"I did but that's not the reason I asked. I'm turning sixteen soon and I feel like I'm becoming a woman who has no idea what's happening." She would buy this fabrication more than my asking if I could experience sex on my birthday.

"You will meet many young men who are interested in you and who are interesting. I guess it depends how you feel about them."

"You and daddy met in college, right?"

"Yes, and he was a real gentleman. I fell for him very soon after we met."

"I guess I need to wait and see what happens." I hugged her and left for my room. A fateful decision done.

The rest of the week crawled along. I called Andrea to find out how she fared at parochial school.

"Are you and Raphael still together?" If I wanted a thrill, it was vicarious.

"No, he moved to Arizona in April. His parents kind of kicked him out of the house. He went to live with an uncle or something." Her voice weakened as she spoke.

"I'm sorry. I guess it wasn't meant to be." Why do I say stupid stuff? I bit my lower lip.

"Vickie, I'm not seeing anyone anymore, at least not until I grow up." I envisioned the tears cascading her cheeks.

"Can we meet up? I've a b party for my niece next weekend, but we could hook up afterwards at Westgate." I wanted her company and her voice cried for help. So a moment of reciprocity for all she did for me?

"Okay, I can get there on Monday or Tuesday."

"Good, cause we got gossip to push." I wasn't sure how I would get there, but Randy was as handy as anyone.

On Thursday Mary called. A sultry, soft voice oozed through the phone. "Who is this and why are you claiming to be my sister?" The chortle spoke volumes.

"Did you like it?"

"You sound like a 304." I wasn't sure she understood.

"Thank you. I didn't realize I was a hoe." Did I start a storm?

"I'm sorry, I didn't mean to upset you."

"You didn't. I've been experimenting with my voice to entice Roger. But I digress. Can you bring a table cloth with you when you come?"

"Sure, I'll tell Mom to make sure it arrives."

"By the way, Roger wants to talk with you." My heart stopped as did my breath.

"What about?" My words seemed jumbled.

"Here he is."

My mouth grew cotton, my face flushed. "Vickie, Mary and I want to throw you a sweet sixteen, but I thought it important to see if it was okay with you."

Okay? Could he unwrap the one present I wanted and still be a member of the family? "I guess. I mean, sure."

"We thought we would come to Seattle and you could invite some friends over and we'll barbecue and such."

"What about Mom and Dad?" Why did it matter about them?

He laughed, "Of course, they're invited."

"No, I mean, have you talked with them about it?"

"Yes, and they think it's a great idea. After all you only turn sixteen once." And you only have sex the first time once.

"Thanks." Nothing more to say, my mind blanked. Except for hands unwrapping me.

Roger

The party for Rebecca went off without a hitch. Dinner was simple, hotdogs and beans. Cole slaw tasted as sweet as a summer cookout should. When her cake arrived we sang and helped extinguish a monstrous candle. Cake makes a funny disguise. I kissed her cheek, tasting vanilla and chocolate. Cleaning her made me sticky.

Vickie and Mary stood together admiring our little one year old. It was as if one was a clone of the other. The timbre of their voices matched so much a person would have difficulty discerning them.

Sixteen was not the age to be fully mature, physically or mentally, but Vickie offered to anyone interested the requisites of an older woman. She appeared to be as fully developed as any twenty something. Her sensibility when interacting with Mary exceeded my own awareness of how to quell storms.

When the family entered the house, we alone remained on the deck. "The party was fun." I had no better words to introduce.

"Yeah."

"Mary seems in a good mood." She moved closer, stirring my concupiscence with a hint of gardenias.

"How are you and she doing?" Did she want to know the truth?

"We're fine." Her face radiated in the sunset glow. Her skin flawless, as was her sister's. I placed my hands on her cheeks and kissed her forehead. "Let's go inside and join the others." I turned before another could happen. She followed me into the living room.

Our parents had coffee and tea, which Peggy had fixed with Hiram. Billy sat on an ottoman. He invited a lovely girl of Hispanic background which didn't seem to sit well with Garrett. I wondered if he knew about his own son's liaison.

Vickie handed me a cup of coffee before I asked as if she understood my needs. Mary entered the room without Rebecca who needed a bath which Ben had offered to complete. He then would place her in her crib for the evening.

I raised my cup. "Here's to a wonderful evening." The celebration ended soon after. As everyone departed hugs abounded. Garrett refrained from closeness.

Peggy and Hiram left first. Billy kissed Mom and hugged Dad, Mary, me, and Vickie. He left hand in hand with his new girlfriend. Ben departed next thanking all for a grand evening. Garrett and Marion finished the parade without Vickie who lingered to hug Mary and whisper something. She then hugged me. Her breasts crushed into my chest as she stretched to my ear. "Take care of yourself and call if you need anything." I made no verbal response as she followed her parents.

Mom and Dad stayed to help with cleanup.

"Roger, you and Mary throw a mean party." Walker intended to be complimentary, it sounded odd. Nancy and Mary finished washing dishes as we cleared the deck of detritus.

"Thanks, I guess." Vickie had been a major contributor to the planning but no one need know. My parents left us at last so we retired to our bedroom.

"What did Vickie say to you?" Mary's words were calm.

"I suppose much the same she said to you. She thanked us for a great party."

A storm brewed as Mary undressed. "She asked me to be good to you." A glint of despair assaulted me.

"You are good to me." Notwithstanding any outbursts.

"She has a crush on you."

"She has a boyfriend. You know. Randy." The storm seemed to grow as she stood in her underwear.

"I have more to offer you than she does." I wondered what the other twin's capacity for offering might be, as I submitted to this offering.

47
CHAPTER

Victoria

Roger flooded my dreams. He kissed my forehead. I wanted more. Destruction of their family was not my goal. An experience with him transformed my sister's life. I wanted a similar transformation to complete me.

Andrea and I met at the Westgate Mall on Pike Street. We ate lunch at the food court on the fourth floor and talked for hours or so it seemed. As the day wore on we rode the monorail to Seattle Center. Andrea paid for a trip up the Space Needle to the observation deck.

"Andrea, what am I to do? I love someone I will not have, who is in my life forever." I locked arms with her wanting closeness. She kept staring at the city and Puget Sound.

"I want to have someone to love like you do." Her words faltered as tears formed. "My life is shallow and cold. Sex is fun but now it's meaningless, without joy." I realized she recognized consequences I had yet to experience.

"Mom says I'll know when the time comes. Did you love him?"

"Who, Raphe? I miss him. I don't know. He was the best in bed and he treated me like a real person. I guess maybe."

Squeezing her arm, "You see, you did love someone. At least you got to be with him. Maybe you'll hook up after you're done with high school." She leaned her head on my shoulder.

"He hasn't called or texted or anything. If I was in love wouldn't he be?" I pondered her question with no response. Silence finished the afternoon soiree of our ridiculous sex lives. I caught the bus back to Magnolia thinking about Roger and how he must feel. I was in love and so was he. With Mary.

———⟨∞⟩———

Birthdays are a strange ritual for which each person has expectations or disappointments. We expect gifts most of the time and are disappointed by the contents. We expect people to understand what it is we want and are disappointed when no one has any idea. I wanted Roger as a gift for which I had no real expectation. How could I?

The day and family arrived as expected. I invited Andrea and Randy and a couple of other acquaintances to round out the afternoon. Roger and Mary and Rebecca were happy together. I watched them interact and hated my existence for desiring a touch which destroyed a piece of perfection.

Mary had seen a psychiatrist about her moodiness. He prescribed a medication which had a side effect she didn't like, but Roger tolerated the condition because she remained rational. I found her robotic.

"I didn't take my medicine today." Mary confided to me. "I didn't take it yesterday or the day before, either."

"Why are you telling me?" What was I to do? Tell on her? She knew I wouldn't reveal her secret. It had to be another reason. "Have you told Roger? He may prefer you as a zombie to you having bouts of mania."

"I love you little sister, but sometimes you piss me off."

"Okay, so what? I know you love him, so why do you think it okay to berate him?" I said.

"Do you love him?" Faces should not screw into shapes which scare others. Mary looked at me awaiting an answer I didn't want to reveal.

"Yes, as a brother."

"Would you love him if he was single?"

I answered what I didn't want to believe. "He wouldn't even cross my path." I turned to go.

"He's in love with you." Stopping a moment to fathom her words, I continued my flight from her fantasy. Could he really, really, really love me?

Roger

Vickie passed me in the family room. Her glance told me Mary had been painful again. I retraced her steps discovering Mary in the living room. "What did you say to your sister? She's upset." Her eyes burned at me.

"I asked a simple question. She answered it."

"What did you say?"

"Why don't you ask her? Listen to what she says." Mary walked away. I grabbed her arm.

"You haven't taken your medicine, have you?"

"It makes me sick and I feel like a zombie." Twisting her arm, she wriggled free. "What do you care anyway? You just want me out of the way."

"If it makes you sick, we'll find another kind." I stepped around her to keep her in check. "All I want is for us to be happy. We have a lovely baby girl to raise. Let's not make a scene at Vickie's party."

She pushed me aside. Returning to the party we promulgated a united, contented front.

Vickie opened the few presents people brought. A new skirt and blouse set, books, a set of keys. "What are these?"

"Your father and I think you're mature enough and ready to drive your own vehicle. Besides, it helps us not to have to transport you everywhere." Screeching by a sixteen year old has the capacity to disrupt hearing for a week.

"Where is it? I want to see it. Is it here somewhere? I didn't see anyone drive up in a new car." Arms splayed around Mom and Dad.

"I had it delivered to my office. You're responsible for the gas. I will care for the insurance and repairs. The rest we'll cover as needed." Vickie took turns thanking each person who festooned her with gifts. Randy gave a small bracelet and received a kiss on his cheek. Andrea presented her with a scarf of many colors and patterns, getting a hug and kiss on the mouth. Strange to watch two girls kiss.

My parents gave her the skirt and blouse. Hugs abounded. Mary and I helped with the car. Marion received a hug as did her dad. Mary endured a long lasting hug and whispers. I received a full body hug and cheek kiss. The party seemed a smash hit. What could go wrong?

48
CHAPTER

Victoria

Mary is so mean to me when I know she doesn't intend to be. Roger had to be suffering since he didn't understand her as I did. Understand her when she suffered bouts of depression. Understand her when her world collapsed into her fantasies. Why did she antagonize me into believing what was not possible?

Randy helped me learn the finer intricacies of driving after each lesson at school. Mom was not a driver so he won my patience by default, never complaining about the strange travesties of parking lot practice.

"Do you think I'm ready for a test?" His raised eyebrows expressed little confidence.

"I suppose you can pass the written test and the eye exam. Driving is more intense." He smiled, winking at me. "I'm kidding. You'll be fine."

I pounded on his shoulder. We sat in the 2004 Honda Civic which I named Gertrude. "Let's go take a test."

"I think you need to have an appointment."

"Let's get an appointment, then." My hands gripped the steering wheel at ten and two until my knuckles turned white.

"Relax, girl or stress will cause failure." Randy drove me to the Department of Licensing office on Aurora. I had money from Mom who encouraged my independence. I took a number from the machine and checked the reader board, five people before me. Randy sat next to me holding my hand. My heart increased its cadence as each number was called. Two people sat at computer terminals answering questions. One left with the driving evaluator. Two renewed licenses.

"Number 64" Randy winked and squeezed my hand.

"Knock it out of the park." Sports references did not ease the heart rate. A bead of moisture formed above my left eye.

My pace to the desk seemed an eternity. A written test came first and after receiving directions, I sat at a terminal staring at the instructions. Once I passed the written, a driving test stood in the way of my mobility.

Each question required an answer from the driving manual I studied as if life depended on it. Driving independence had consequences, but as the test progressed I relaxed recalling information like the book itself rested on the terminal desk. Completing the written part, I closed the program and returned to the clerk.

Instructed to sit awaiting results, I returned to Randy. "Well?"

"I remembered the book as if I had it with me."

"Good. There's nothing wrong with being smart." He held my hand. I wondered why I couldn't, or rather didn't, want him to be my first man. Did I construct a solitary space in my heart for the unavailable?

My name echoed in the room alerting all to my impending sorrow or elation. I walked to the desk, received my piece of paper, turned to Randy, smiling. The clerk scheduled a road test for the next morning. I was half way to freedom.

As time suggested, Randy said, "Let me take you out to eat, a celebration of victory. I'll want a kiss later, or course, for the inestimable amount of help you received from me."

"I'm now a slave to your wanton pleasures for having passed a simple exam?"

"I'll suggest added wantonness for your successful driving on the morrow."

"Who are you?" I planted a kiss on his mouth before another word. "There, payment made." He wrapped an arm around my waist guiding me to my Civic.

"Get in so I may regale you with my epicurean skills of delectable dining." We drove to Dick's Restaurant in Queen Anne for hamburgers and fries. I pondered again the possibility of succumbing to my feminine curiosity with Randy but my fantasy excluded him. Even a hint of possible romance complicated our relationship.

We ate in silence as my mind wandered this entangling path. I missed his comment. "I'm sorry what did you say?"

"I said, I think you are the most beautiful girl in the world." Creases formed between my eyes, my lips parted, a breath escaped.

"Are you wanting something more for the services rendered to this pathetic automobile owner?" A clarification of intent aimed at his heart lest I succumb to his charm.

"There is nothing pathetic about you and yes I wish to bestow the honor of being my girlfriend upon you. I find you irresistible."

"Rather forward of you, don't you think? Does this girlfriend status include sharing certain favors a male might deem appropriate?"

"Such as?"

"Holding hands in public areas, making out in automobiles, liberal handling of said partner's physical anatomy, and an intercourse which, without proper preparation, may result in additional human creation." He roared with delight.

"You sure you're just sixteen? I swear any other guy would still be working on what just transpired." He placed his half-eaten meal on the paper. "Yes, I guess most of it. I'd never demand sex with you as a condition of being your boyfriend. As I told you, it's too important a step to be walked without serious commitment to a future."

My mind reeled with the idea of committing to someone who could as opposed to another who shouldn't. Could I? Could I experience womanhood without love? Could I love without the one who mattered most?

Roger

Mary entered the house office a few months after Vickie's party. "I'm pregnant." We had resumed a convivial life which excluded interacting with extended family. I saw my Dad at work and Mom as often as I could. Mary's family failed to be important enough to include. My sister, Sarah, and Hiram finished their remodeling project which I witnessed without Mary. Billy was away at school.

"How far along are you?" Clouds of anger darkened the atmosphere.

"That's your first question? No comment like...great or fantastic?" She turned to leave the room, stopped and faced me again.

"I'm sorry." My words rang hollow. "What I mean is, I am glad. I just wanted to know how long I had to wait before we got to share this wonder you're growing." She turned and departed. I smashed the palm of my hand to my forehead.

Mary's pregnancy was normal physically and a torture mentally. Her tirades came and went with the quickness of summer storms in the Northwest. I watched for the omens of anger in her eyes, which darkened with alarming speed. Sometimes I remained calm, mostly I reacted. I needed a stabilizer, a way to understand the woman who captivated my heart and broke it.

Telling our families about another child helped calm tempests as mothers involved themselves in our routines. Mary wanted the attention as much as I wanted the serenity. We spent time with my parents as summer edged into autumn. Mary's mother visited on day trips, but her father seemed oblivious.

Vickie and I communicated more than society deemed proper, I suspected. When occasions arose, I took a high seas trip on the ferry to Seattle. We met in obscure places which rattled sensibilities. One trip resulted in our being alone at her parents' house. I wanted advice about another bout of depression the previous night.

"What happened to you?" The evidence consisted of scratch marks on neck and arms. Fury flailed ferocious fingers leaving unhealed proof of my inability to contain the personality residing in Wendlesburg.

"We had a fight about the color of the bedroom. She thinks she's having a boy. I tried to be practical with a more neutral hue." We sat in the living room next to each other on the sofa. Close enough to sense each other, far enough to keep me sane

"Don't you know what you're having?" Her question rocked me. Mary demanded anonymity. I preferred to know. A small squall erupted and died as I accepted her request.

"No, we want to be surprised." Vickie's beauty competed with my sensibility, her mind outpacing her sister, her body attracting an innermost lust.

"Then listen to her when she says it's a boy. Paint is less expensive than the cost of your marriage." I admired her ability to catch the wind and navigate to a safe harbor. I wanted to kiss her and tell her I loved her.

Victoria

Roger hurt so much. I listened, responded, and wanted to hold him. Mary carried the common factor of our feelings for each other and for her. I knew he loved her, loved me, as I loved her and loved him. We finished our liaison with a choice of paint and a sensible conclusive parley to save a marriage and family.

"Thank you, Vickie. You are a wonderful person." Wonderful? All I am is wonderful? I stood speechless. He placed his hand under my chin and kissed my forehead.

I save him and he kisses my head. This was not the moment to press for more and yet I could not stop. I could not resist. I could not have him leave without understanding what he did to me.

I put hands on his shoulders, pressing my lips on his lips. My tongue caressed the rim of his mouth. My body shuddered. Please, don't stop. Now was wrong. I couldn't stop.

Roger

Her mouth tasted of mint tea shared as we talked. Her hands pulled me to her. I gave in to the pleasure she exhibited and put my hands around her pulling her close. I betrayed my vows and cared not. I wanted more. My mind cried out to stop. My body demanded satisfaction. Could I? Should I?

PART
THREE

BETRAYAL

49
CHAPTER

Roger

Her perfect body reminded me of Mary's curves. I pulled away. "We can't." Vickie held my hands as if struggling against a torrential tide. "We can't do this." A noise in the back hall evoked our sanity. She let go.

"I'm sorry." Her tears hurt. Had I disillusioned her?

"I must go." Marion entered the foyer as I walked out of the living room. "Hello, Marion." Did guilt display an ugly face?

"Roger, it is so good to see you. Are you here in Seattle on business?"

An out presented itself. "Yes, so I dropped by to see you." Vickie followed soon after.

"Hi, Mom. Wasn't it nice of Roger to stop by?"

"Yes, I'm sorry I wasn't here to be a proper host." Vickie was, though. Thoughts deceived me. I bid adieu and left.

The ride to Wendlesburg clutched time in what seemed forever. Would Mary question my lengthy work day? What slip of the tongue might unleash another tirade. Why did Vickie have to be so alluring and sensitive to my stricken passions?

I vowed to halt any further time with her. I wanted to see her, though. I wanted her to know the truth which Mary questioned of me. I loved both of them for different reasons. I shouldn't betray the vows said in truth at our wedding. Love, honor, cherish. Until death. Death of our love? I had to make it stay alive.

Arriving home I sat a moment in the garage before going in the house composing my self-worth. Mary deserved better of me, as did I deserve better of her.

Mary entered the kitchen carrying Rebecca. Her pregnancy showed under her blouse. "Sorry I'm late. I got caught up in some business."

"Marion called." Oh, shoot. "She thought it was nice of you to stop in after you did your Seattle business. She invited us for Thanksgiving. Do you have any other business there so we can go?"

I played along. "We can leave on Thursday morning and have dinner with them, but no, I don't have any other business in Seattle during the week. Why? Did they invite us to stay there for the weekend?" Panic rose into my throat. I swallowed.

"I thought you might like to see Garrett and Marion." She knew, and I hadn't done anything worth the guilt I now owned.

"I'd prefer to come home that night to be with you and Rebecca alone for the weekend." Alone with you, not Vickie.

Victoria

Roger was gone. Mom followed me into the kitchen with the dishes from the tea service, a feeble attempt to avoid an inquisition. "When did Roger arrive?" It began.

"A little while ago. He wanted to see us while here." Stop asking questions. Poking around in the refrigerator did not ease the inquest.

"I called and invited them here for Thanksgiving and the weekend." Great another opportunity for disappointment.

"That's nice." My brain elicited no other response. I walked out of the room with my silence and a surging emotional pride. I kissed him and he hadn't retreated. Mary was right, but she could never know.

In my room I called Andrea for advice. Another person to ease me down or be used as a distraction.

"I kissed him." The squawk in the phone thundered. "Ouch."

"Sorry, I'm just so like surprised. I didn't think you had the guts. Spill."

"He came over to see me about my sister. They had a fight over paint for the baby's room. Oh, I guess I should tell you. My sister's pregnant with a boy. I'm losing my guest room."

"That's so cool. But how did you get to kiss him?" I envisioned Andrea cross-legged on her bed, the phone glued to her head.

"He put his hands on my chin and kissed my forehead. I grabbed him and kissed his mouth. I even gave a little tongue."

"You slut, you. So what happened then?"

"He kissed me back and said we couldn't do this again. Then my mother showed up." My eyes rolled as if controlled by another person.

"Your mother. Wow, did she see anything?"

"No, she did ask questions though. I hope she doesn't suspect something." My head shook from side to side.

"Do you want to kiss him again?"

"Duh, of course." Andrea had to be rocking back on her bed to see the clouds on her ceiling.

"When are you going to see him again?"

"Mom called to invite them for Thanksgiving weekend. Three or more days with him around and no alone time. He'll try to stay in a crowd."

"Still, you can walk with him somewhere. How did he feel? All muscular and such? Did he have a woody?"

"Gees, girl, you're nosy. He's firm and yes he was firm there, too."

"You need to get him alone again and see if you can get him to kiss you. I bet he'll crack like a ripe melon. You're going to get your first real soon."

"I think you're over saying it. He's afraid of losing Mary and Rebecca. And now another one coming? He'll be cool for a while." I sat down in my desk chair. A pang of regret stabbed my heart. I unleashed the beast in me and was not certain how to gain control of it. I wasn't even sure I wanted to.

50

CHAPTER

Roger

Thanksgiving Day arrived. Rebecca woke early. I grumbled but retrieved the little darling. In the kitchen I heard her say "Baba, Daddy?" Her noises and grunts grew each day into coherent sounds. I handed her a sippy cup and opened a jar of apple sauce. Standing by her high chair she watched me.

Placing her in the seat, I put a bowl in front of her to watch her mastery of the spoon. With some assistance she finished the apple sauce. "I think you are the smartest little girl in the whole world."

"Of course, she is." My heart raced the short course with Mary's entry into our secret world.

"You startled me." I looked her in the eyes. Nothing showed. Vacuous with sleep. "Did you sleep well?"

"I slept fine. Can we be at Mom and Dad's by noon to help with dinner?" This was not a question as much as a dictum. We meant me.

"Sure." Preparing for a dinner in Seattle involved taking our share of the food. My parents invited us, as well, but the game of alternating holidays endured by couples with families nearby meant we had a trip to Seattle. I did not mind. I liked Mary's brother and his friend. Vickie had Randy and I would not make the mistake of kissing her, but I did want to see her.

"Get Rebecca's things. They're on her bed, ready to go." I complied, leaving Mary to care for her. A small suitcase we bought for these excursions sat on the bed along with the necessary diaper bag. A breeze swirled the rustling leaves which scratched on the concrete of the driveway. I placed the two items in the back of the SUV and retraced my steps.

Entering the kitchen, Mary and Becca engaged in a tug of war over a bowl of cereal. Mary wanted the spoon used. Becca employed her hands with dexterity. "Why can't she be like other little girls and be neat?" She stood from the chair next to the high chair, leaving us alone in our secret world.

"Mommy's getting ready to see Uncle Ben and Aunt Vickie. Grandma and Grandpa want to see you, too. We need to finish eating so we can go across the Sound." Becca continued shoving Cheerios into her mouth by hand. I smiled knowing her life was much easier when Mary was gone.

Clearing the debris left by a small child can be a two person chore. I did what I could with her tray and the floor. Rebecca needed a change and to be dressed after a hosing down. She giggled when I picked her out of the confinement of her highchair.

Prepared for a trip across the Sound, we searched for Mommy, who sat on the side of the bed placing clothes in a small suitcase. "Are we staying for more than a day?" My question evoked no anger but a simple look of disgust. I placed Rebecca on the bed, gathered my own overnight bag and loaded the appropriate articles. Arguing against a protracted stay seemed pointless.

"Roger, you don't have to stay with me at my parents tonight. I think I want to have some time away." Again she avoided the obvious. She wanted me out of her life for the weekend.

"I know, but I want to be with you. Work can wait a few days." I closed my bag "Is your bag ready to go?" An imperceptible nod assured me it was okay to take it to the car with mine. "I'll be right back for Becca."

With the car packed for the weekend, I thought about a time when all was euphoric, when no other person invaded my life. Now I had a hell to accompany me; living, breathing and an enigma.

Returning to the bedroom, Rebecca and Mary remained oblivious to each other, but one had sought the other to no avail and with patience awaited my entry.

Mary stood expressionless, a face watching nothing as she left for the car. "Come, little one. Let's follow Mommy."

I strapped Rebecca into her car seat. Mary sat lost in thought or so it seemed. I drove to the ferry terminal, paid the requisite fare and parked in the line to wait for the ferry to arrive and disgorge its contents.

"Roger, do you love me?" I furrowed my brow wondering which answer would dispel a storm. My hesitation created a repeat of the question. "Do you?"

"Yes, I do. I don't always know what to say or how to react or where your mind is. But I still love you." I looked at her thinking I may have unleashed a hurricane.

"I love you, too. I just don't think I can do what I need to do. I'm so lost."

I had no idea from where this arrived. She acted as though she came from another environment, another world, another lifetime. Vickie would know what to do for her. I sent a text, but could I repel the charm she exuded? Would she even exude the charm I had to repel? Did I want to repel the charm she exuded?

Victoria

Thanksgiving Day is about family and for what we are grateful. I'm grateful for my school year and a new boyfriend. I'm grateful he didn't push me to have sex with him. I'm grateful for my sister and her husband and Rebecca.

I'm so freaking grateful I knew the weekend was going to be a bust. Roger was coming to visit and I had no idea whether time permitted my being alone with him. Randy wanted to go out on Friday after we gorged ourselves on Thursday. Yes, I'm freaking grateful.

Dad had his usual gratitude about money, life, and children. Mom was excited to have all of her brood home. If Ben and Jackson stayed over the weekend, could a little secret escape? I hoped Mary was happy and despondent free.

My phone vibrated on the desk. It lay there after another exchange with Andrea. He sent a text that Mary was not doing well. I thought about calling him but figured they had left for the ferry. I could wait. I departed my room to help finish prepping for the afternoon dinner.

We skipped lunch to save room. Enough food floated around the kitchen to feed several Somalian families or was it Armenians? Smells abounded delighting nostrils and taste buds. Flowers adorned the dining room table and buffet. Purple and pink asters, delphiniums, orange Asiatic lilies and yellow germinis radiated color and fragrances pleasant to behold. All was ready.

I was so grateful. All I wanted was Roger to be alone with me long enough to test his resolve and mine. How could I get him alone for a test? Where could I get him alone? When could I get him alone?

51
CHAPTER

Roger

I watched for Vickie to come out of the house when we arrived. I was not disappointed. Her exuberance showed as she bounded down the steps from the front door. Her locks flew out behind her in waves of gold. I forced my brain to stay on the task of unpacking my family.

"Hi, everyone." Her excitement thrilled Mary, who smiled. Vickie hugged her, holding on for a long moment. I didn't hear any exchange of words, but guessed it calmed the inner turmoil which bubbled on our trip across Puget Sound.

Marion appeared as the scene assembled. "Here, I'll take that." She pointed at the bag in my hand. "You get Rebecca." I did as requested. Before I could unlatch her, Vickie came around the car to me, hugged me and whispered.

"We need some time alone to talk." Her body cried for attention.

"We have to be careful."

"I promise to be good." She released me and unhooked Rebecca from the backseat carrier. We entered the house to aromas of turkey roasting and pumpkin pie. Candles burned in the foyer and living room. Candles awaited lighting on the dining table. Flowers adorned the center of the table. I hadn't seen such opulence for a while. My parents made Thanksgiving a time for giving thanks. I had thanks for many things in my life, a beautiful wife, an adorable daughter, another baby on the way, and families on both sides of Puget Sound.

Vickie carried Becca into the family room. I picked up my bag which Marion deposited on the floor by the stairs. Along with Mary's suitcase and the diaper bag, I ascended the stairs to leave them in our room.

Thinking about what Vickie said, I remembered our last encounter. To kiss her again. To feel her body close to mine. I wanted to engulf her essence, to forget the swirling emotions of her sister.

"What are you thinking?" I turned to see a vision of heaven, a beauty captured on canvas by painters throughout history. I was ready to say I love you then realized who stood before me.

"I was thinking about us." She entered the room illuminating my mood with her presence. I wanted to hold her but knew it was not the time. She had a look in her eyes which sent a chill through my veins. I wanted freedom from the enslaving of my heart and soul by her. She must recognize her power but I doubted it. She captivated and crushed with equal ease. How was I to survive?

Victoria

Rebecca kissed my cheek with an open mouth and plenty of wetness. I squeezed her and buzzed her neck. She squeaked with delight. I placed Becca on the baby floor mat which contained enough stimuli to satisfy any child. Roger had not come in and I suspected he was upstairs. I turned to leave, but Mary intercepted me. "I want to talk with you later." I nodded. She left the room.

Following her I wondered what she wanted, but she climbed the staircase to the second floor. I stayed down to be away from any confrontation which might occur. I prayed for Roger to know she was on her way to him.

I returned to the family room and played with my niece. She would be an excellent diversion to get alone with Roger. We could take her on a walk in the park. Although the weather was cooler, the sun cooperated by shining on our part of the world for the weekend. I plotted an escape.

"Vickie, come here and help me, please." My intrigue, put on hold for the moment, nevertheless remained my goal. "Mary told me the vegetables and hors d'oeuvres they brought are still in their car. Please go out and get them."

"All right." I left for the front door but detoured up the stairs. Curiosity consumed me. Had Mary gone to confront Roger? Was he handling her emotions well enough? A sneak peak could be excused if I was caught.

As I came near to Mary's room, where they stayed, I sensed a lull in storms. As I peered into the room, Mary and Roger were embracing and kissing. I turned away and ran downstairs and out the front door. My heart died for a moment. Why did he captivate me and then crush my soul?

52
CHAPTER

Roger

Mary's entrance into the bedroom quelled an inner turmoil. Both of these women confounded my common sense thinking. Both women offered themselves to me, albeit in different ways. Both their personalities generated conflicting emotions. I loved Mary for reasons which her current mental state challenged. I loved Vickie, or rather was infatuated, because she reminded me of the girl I met at college.

"So what about us?" She approached me but the vestige she portrayed alarmed me. What was her mood? My body stiffened, defensive to an unexpected assault as she put her arms around me. "What about us?"

Did she sense my apprehension? Her lips locked onto mine before I could speak. Her tongue explored my lips and my body relaxed. My eyes closed for a moment as she caressed my back with gentle strokes. My arms cradled her body with my hands travelling to her bottom.

For a second I opened my eyes and thought I saw Vickie in the hallway. I dismissed the visage as a mental fabrication. Mary aroused my lurid passions for a quick rendezvous. She stopped kissing and I closed the bedroom door. "Lock the door, and you haven't answered my question." She disrobed to her underwear and stood with hands on hips.

I did as requested and as I stripped, I answered her question. "Let me show you."

The culmination of our sexual fulfillment did nothing to relieve my tension regarding Victoria. Curious about her wanting to talk with me, I dressed to find her. Had she seen us kissing?

Mary donned her clothing as well, saying, "Nothing is better than what we have together." Her sane moments complicated life. I appreciated her comment and loved her for it. I pondered a future of her fighting for sanity as moods changed in a whirlwind of mental instability.

"Nothing is better." I repeated her statement half-hearted in my belief of the words. "I'm going to find our daughter and be sure she has an entourage covering for us." Mary began unpacking her suitcase.

In the family room Rebecca regaled her audience with steps across the room, sipping out of a cup containing water, and repeating words in toddler dialect.

"Where have you been?" Marion was genuine in her caring about familial relations. "Rebecca is so smart. You have done a wonderful job raising her."

"Thanks. She takes after her mother in the brains and beauty department. I had little input." In our absence, Ben and Jackson arrived. They coaxed Becca to walk to each of them. She had her entourage.

Vickie entered the room from the kitchen. "I brought in the rest of your things." Her comment, directed at me, had a sting to it. I figured there was an issue I knew nothing about and she was telling me I failed.

My option to answer her was sweetly as possible. "Vickie, you are the best." I smiled to add to the postulate I was not mad at her. "Is there anything else in the car, such as the Play N Pak?"

After a moment, thinking, her eyes widened and a grin formed. "I do believe I forgot it and her toy bag." I'll go out right now." She left the room.

As she walked out I offered to help. "We'll be right back." Outside I confronted her about her attitude in the house. "Are you mad at me for some reason?"

"No." A tear welled up in her left eye as she pulled the Play N Pak out of the back of the car. "I saw you and Mary upstairs. You have every right." She reached in the car and grabbed the toys which were in a canvas bag.

We stood out of sight of the house behind the car. I turned her toward me with hands on her shoulders. "Is this what's upsetting you?" Before she could speak I kissed her on the mouth. "I'm as infatuated with you as I am in love with your sister." I kissed her again. "However, we are not in any position to start something we'll both regret." I picked up the playpen, winked at her, and started for the house. A mine field laid with imprecise patterns now separated me from any hope of a simple future. And I didn't care.

Victoria

Why did he kiss me? What would Mary think if she knew? I was bewildered. He did like me. Mary was correct

I grasped the bag of toys, closed the back of the van and returned to the house. My heart pounded, my breathing quickened, my body reacted in a most embarrassing manner.

In the foyer I stood a moment to quiet my nerves. I dropped the toys on the floor by the stairs and went up to my room. I closed the door locking out intruders. My breathing shallow and rapid preceded the flood of tears. I was happy, scared, excited, and disappointed for unfathomable reasons. Why now? How could he kiss my sister one moment and kiss me another?

"Get it together. Calm down. Breathe." I swiped at the tears cascading across my cheeks. I grabbed my hair pulling it tight above my ears. No pain, just taut enough to gain control of emotions. "I must get time with him." I sat on the bed. "I must get time." I released my hair. "I must." I stood again. "Calm down." I inhaled deeply and long, holding, and with a slow deliberate rhythm, exhaled.

"Roger, you have some serious explaining to do." I closed my eyes recalling the kisses. A crooked grin covered my face. "You are so my first conquest. I don't know when, or where, or how. But you will teach me to be a woman." I inhaled slow and steady, and relaxed. Was I ready to rejoin the festivities? I had to find out if I could pull off the charade of my life.

53
CHAPTER

Roger

A wickedness gained, an honesty lost. My heart and mind conflictions escalated kissing Vickie. Her tender lips and magnetic body lured me nearer an ever deeper chasm bridged by an authentic love for Mary. I wondered if Vickie understood we had no future together as long as Mary lived.

In the family room I picked up Becca and sat on the couch next to Mary. Our daughter climbed on us as if we were playthings. "Did you get everything you were after?" I looked at Mary with wide eyes.

"What?" My brain constructed strange scenarios of what she knew or suspected. "Yes, yes I brought in the Play N Pak and put it in our room. Vickie was bringing in the toy bag." I scanned the room. "I don't know what happened to her, though."

Ben crossed the room. "I'll get her." He walked out alone. Jackson stayed in the kitchen working on dinner with Marion. I leaned over to Mary, kissed her cheek and tickled Becca as she crawled on her mother's lap.

She wrestled a smile, her temperament exhibiting a casualness to what she may be thinking about me and my trip outside with Vickie. I grinned at her to assure her nothing happened. My attention returned to Becca who crawled into my lap slobbering a kiss on me.

"Are you having fun?" I asked an innocent question loaded with plenty of explosive answers which could detonate our future.

"Yes, dear, I am. I do hope you're having fun as well." Mary stood, mussed my hair, and strolled to the kitchen. I couldn't decide whether she was mad at me or still in love. She had no tell for me to play her game.

Ben returned from his hunting trip. "What happened with you two outside?" He looked confused, not angry or disappointed or ready to rip my head off. "Vickie's in her room and won't come out. Did you say something to her?"

"No. I got the playpen, put it in our room and came down. Why, did she say something?"

"No, but I heard her crying and my sister almost never cries. She is one of the toughest kids I know."

"Do you think she got hurt, somehow?" I picked myself up with Rebecca in arms and looked back toward the hallway. "Maybe we should check on her." I put my baby on her blanket, spread out so she had a place to play. I started for the foray, but Ben put a hand on my shoulder.

"Let her figure out what she's doing. She'll fix it and join us soon. If she doesn't, we can check on her then." My heart kicked up its rate a notch. My neck throbbed to the increasing rhythm. I nodded. Ben returned to the kitchen and Jackson engaging him in conversation.

My eyes closed and my breath deepened. As I opened them and exhaled, I realized no one paid any attention to the drama started with the automobile's opening scene. The play was a one act affair and I was its only audience.

I glanced at Rebecca who was nibbling the cloth ears of her dinosaur, and then followed Mary into the kitchen, to predict stormy weather or calm sailing. I needed to see for my own sanity, which Mary walked this Magnolia Eden. Vickie was my radar and out of commission. How did Mary perceive our day, and when was Vickie joining me in this drama?

Victoria

Roger was not winning a war of attrition with me. No one controlled me and no one would stop me. I redid my make-up after drying eyes and combing hair.

He had the right to be intimate with Mary. I wanted only to share my first experience with him, not destroy the happiness my sister gained by her marriage to him.

"Hi, everyone." My voice faltered for control of words. "Rebecca, you sweet child, come to Aunt Vickie." She toddled over to me to be picked up.

Ben stood and whispered in my ear away from prying parents. "What's the matter? I heard you crying upstairs."

My mind concocted a tale of injury fraught by a wayward chair. "I'm sorry. I didn't want anyone to know. I'm okay." Rebecca rotated her head from Ben to me and back to Ben. She couldn't understand but made it seem as if she knew the truth.

"Okay, as long as nothing upset you outside with Roger."

"What would he do to upset me?" Everything was fine for now. I could wait for when he could no longer act like he was in control. I entered the kitchen with my little charge and sat on a stool. The aromas of dinner lightened my mood. Roger stationed himself on the other side of the bar counter as a barrier. Mary came to reclaim her child.

"Thank you, Vickie." She took Rebecca. "I do hope you're okay." Her mood was somber without threat of a meltdown.

The final preparations finished, we sat and enjoyed a lavish dinner of turkey, potatoes, vegetables, and rolls. Dessert had a postponement for our stomach digestions. Conversations consisted of school, another baby, and workloads. Jackson spoke when addressed but remained mute for much of the evening. Garrett commented least, seeming to ignore anyone's existence.

Mom asked me to clean up the table as Mary and she gathered dirty dishes, rinsing before placing them into the dishwasher. Rebecca remained confined to her highchair. I thought about the division of labor and how male/female roles had not matured in this household.

Commencing with dessert, we gathered again in the family room, ate our fill of pie and ice cream, drank coffee or tea and called it a successful evening.

Ben and Jackson left for Capitol Hill. Dad still seemed oblivious or just ignored their relationship. Mary took Rebecca, asleep in her arms, and went to bed. Mom and Dad said good-night leaving me alone with Roger. I hoped he was not going to be a spoil sport and depart, as well.

With Roger sitting reading a magazine he found on the coffee table the quiet unnerved me. I placed the remainder of the dessert dishes in the sink to await entry to the dishwasher in the morning. Looking out the family room sliding glass door at the backyard with darkness enveloping it, my thoughts were not about yard duty.

"You still mad about this afternoon?" I jumped at the comment.

"Roger, you scared me."

"Sorry about that. I just wondered about what happened."

I turned to face him. "No, I guess it was a surprise, that's all." He approached me but I had no flutter in my heart or blush in my face. No emotion. "Why did you kiss me?"

"I wanted to, I wanted to taste your sweetness. Compare it to Mary, I guess. Remember, you surprised me the last time."

Now the flutter came and my face warmed. "I wanted to know if Mary was right about how you thought of me. I wanted to find out what it was like to kiss a man."

"She has problems I don't know how to help, but you always get her back. I love you for that." Roger came closer. "If something happened to her...."

"She's not going anywhere. Her moods are controllable and she does love you."

"Do you love me?" The silence of the room made it echo in my ears as if a public address system announced to the world.

"Shh. Somebody may hear us." I looked into his eyes, tears forming and falling. "I don't know what love is. I want what Mary has with you. I want to experience and know what she has. It can't destroy her, though."

"You're a brilliant young lady, beautiful beyond your years, understanding of people's needs before they even know them. That said, I want to experience what life is like with you." He scanned the room, then turned to me and kissed my mouth, wrapping his arms around me. Pulling me to him I encountered his firm body. Arms guided hands to his protuberance. His hands slid to my bottom which he squeezed with a gentleness arousing my body, pushing me against his organ.

He separated from me after an eternity lasting a few seconds. "I can't do this. We have to be careful and plan our meetings so we're not caught." He confirmed and laid hope in front of me to savor and enjoy.

"Do you want me?" My question raised my ethical alert system but I disregarded my head for a happier heart.

"I cannot disappoint your sister. If she found out about my kissing you? If she killed herself, I don't know what I'd do. I can't have that on my conscience."

"Can a person love two people at the same time?"

He looked at me, kissed me a tender goodnight and left for Mary's bed. His physical needs would be sated soon if not tonight. How was I to satisfy my emotional and physical needs?

54
CHAPTER

Roger

Morning came with no squalls, storms, or hurricanes. Mary rose from our bed as the sun hinted its existence. I sat up as she stood. "Was your night restful?" Assessing what the day had in store for us, last night's arousal remained a memory.

"I slept very well." Rebecca stayed asleep but I presumed our time was short. "Are you interested in a shower?" A smile enticed me to rise as well and join her. Fair weather provided festive times.

As I dried my body, I watched Mary complete her bathing. We had pleasantly shared our morning and now had a little girl who needed attention. "You finish here, I'll get Becca." I put on underwear, pants and a shirt, modesty must prevail for my daughter's sake, and left the bathroom to free her from her crib.

"Did you sleep well, my angel? She blinked, raised her arms and smiled. I picked her up, hugging her. "Grow up like Aunt Vickie. Mommy loves you, but she needs help coping with life. We'll help her."

Checking her clothing for leakage revealed a dry night. "Good for you. You are the best little girl in the world." I changed her into play clothes expecting a diaper change to come soon.

We left the bedroom to get something to eat. As we entered the hall, Victoria opened her bedroom door. "Good morning," she said. Rebecca reached out for her. Vickie leaned in to kiss her head. I left the idea of a kiss alone.

"We're going for breakfast. Join us." Becca and I continued our quest for food.

The kitchen was alive to the preparation of a kingly breakfast. Marion stirred pancake batter while bacon sizzled in a pan. I put Becca in her highchair and asked, "What can I do to help?"

"Set the table, please." She pointed to a drawer which I opened for utensils. Mary arrived as I put a place setting at Vickie's seat. I smiled, but she just looked at me. Our dalliance in the shower had not brightened her day. She sat in her chair for me to serve her like a waiter at a fine restaurant. What happened between then and now for her to act pretentious and haughty.

Resentment was wrong. I knew it was wrong but at the moment...We had a good start to morning and now she acted pompous like I didn't exist.

Vickie came in as I finished getting out plates. The first batch of pancakes were placed on the table along with bacon. Vickie got out the syrup and butter. She was cheerful and vibrant, a contrast of attitudes.

We ate our meal, Becca eating a whole pancake cut into pieces. Apple sauce augmented the meal. Coffee and orange juice rounded out the food. Garrett joined us when all was ready. His lack of conviviality killed off all conversation. Mary remained stoic exhibiting neither anger nor remorse.

Vickie sparkled without saying a word. Her face radiated a healthy, happy mood making it difficult to avert my gaze.

After Breakfast Mary returned to our bedroom; I following to assess her attitude. Did I offend her, something misplaced by me?

"What happened at breakfast? You ignored me like I was the plague. Are we okay?"

She looked at me, blank, emotionless. "We're fine. I'm just tired, I guess. Did it bother you?"

A darkness in her eyes indicated I tramped on a minefield. "I was just curious. We had a great morning in the shower. I thought you were happy. I was. Then in the kitchen, it was like we had a fight and you weren't speaking to me."

A mine exploded. "You're such a hypocrite. Do you need validation of how wonderful you are when we have sex? You're not that great."

"How would you know? Were you lying to me in Pullman about being a virgin? Have you been seeing someone on the side in Wendlesburg?" I stepped on another mine. "All those other girls I slept with were satisfied."

"Does that include Monica? Maybe she's still available. Why don't you go find her?"

"Where is this coming from? I love you. What do you want from me?"

As sudden as the attitude detonated, a silence commenced. Tears formed in her eyes. I moved toward her.

"Don't. Take Rebecca and leave." She lay on the bed facing away from me. I walked out, downstairs to the kitchen. Vickie and Rebecca were playing pat a cake. Marion was finishing kitchen duty. I watched this beautiful teenager whose exuberance for life contrasted her sister. What happened? Where was the woman I met in college?

Victoria

Roger didn't look happy during breakfast. Mary seemed distant. Their relationship couldn't survive her mental swings. Rebecca was happy, ate well, and never complained. I cleaned her up after her parents left the kitchen. I guessed they figured she was in good hands. We began playing games, when Roger came back. He looked like a puppy disciplined with a newspaper.

"Roger, let's take Rebecca for a walk." Time with him now seemed appropriate.

Marion wiped her hands on a towel, finished with the tidying. "That sounds like a wonderful idea. The weather is cooperating for the moment. Outdoors will do her some good." Mom was clueless and I wanted her to stay that way.

"Let me get my daughter dressed. Then we can go to the park." My heart fluttered.

I had to dress as well and followed them to the second story. "I'm so glad you stayed for the weekend. It's so much more enjoyable to have you and Mary here." I watched them enter Mary's room. In mine I pulled off my robe and pajamas, and stared at my body and thought, *He wants this.*

Putting on matching lacy underwear, jeans, and a nice blouse, I wore a sweater to counter Thanksgiving's cooler weather. Looking in the mirror I was not pleased with the sweater. A coat would suffice.

I bounded down the stairs. Waiting for Roger and Becca, I paced in the foyer. Did going into the bedroom start problems? I looked at the staircase as they were coming. His face looked hard as if fighting back anger. Rebecca's eyes stared at her daddy with apprehension. What happened?

We left for the park without a word between us. I suspected my sister had confronted him again. Half way there he spoke. "I don't understand her. We start the day great and then it's like a switch is thrown and I don't know who she is." I pushed the carriage while he vented. "I think she's happy, then boom, all's collapsing. What can I do?"

Silence commenced, which I broke. "She needs help, counseling, psychiatric care, and medicine. She's getting worse."

"She has medicine to help with the moodiness, but I don't think she takes it. I can't monitor her or she gets on me about not trusting her. I don't and it's causing real strain. I don't want to leave her, but I need something for me."

"I'm here for you." He scrunched his face. "Seriously, I can be like a partner for you when Mary's crashed and you're frustrated. Besides, I'll come over and stay with her so you can work or do what you need. We can help, together."

"You and I cannot start something we'll regret."

"I'd never regret it. I don't want to break up your marriage. I just want to experience what you and Mary have. If you want to be able to help her, you need to be happy, satisfied. You need someone to enhance your life."

"What is it about you which makes me want to say yes?" We arrived at the park. I put Rebecca in the baby seat swing and sat in the swing next her. Roger pushed her gentle as a lamb. I swung my feet out to start a slow methodical rhythm.

"Maybe it's more about what you think I want than what I do or who I am. I want you to want me. No obligations, no promises, no long term commitments. Mary was happy with you. I want to experience the same."

"What you're asking of me violates a promise I made to your sister when we married."

"I know. I wouldn't ask you if I didn't understand the implications of her discovering our liaisons. Kiss me here and now. Let me know you will think about us. I can give you what Mary is withholding."

"And what do you think she's withholding? We had sex this morning."

"Maybe, but there was something wrong at breakfast and again when you came down from dressing Rebecca." He stopped pushing the swing, and I stopped my slow progress. He stood in front of me placing his hands on my cheeks. I stood as he pressed forward to meet my lips with his. We explored our tongues and clasped our clothing laden bodies together.

55
CHAPTER

Roger

Thanksgiving weekend ended with no more distractions. I made peace with Mary. We came home to rebuild our relationship.

"I am sorry for my attitude in Seattle." Mary meant each word. "I know I should be taking my medications, but being pregnant changes things. I don't go the doctor for another two weeks."

"I get it. I don't want you to jeopardize our child either. I love you more than anything and so we'll work it out." I meant each word and when a challenge stormed in I listened without responding.

Her doctor's appointment arrived and I promised to take her and watch Rebecca, rescheduling three appointments and a closing to be there. She was given a clean bill of health as far as the pregnancy went. Her mental anguish required changes to psychotic medicines which were less potent but safe for the fetus.

A promise to take her medicine encouraged me to seek no other comfort. Life for a while returned to the idyllic time I remembered.

As November moved into December the storms abated for the next week. Mary and Vickie spoke with regularity. I asked for advice occasionally when depression overcame sanity.

More than once I picked up my cell to call Victoria for help and comfort. She was right about the lack of emotional bonding with Mary. Each day slipped deeper into an empty chasm of loneliness.

The verbal assaults grew into bodily attacks, more like Mary's frustrations needed a punching bag. I held her while she struggled with her fears, advice I read about in an anti-depression article at the psychiatrist's office.

During winter break Victoria spent a week with us muddling my vow of leaving her alone for Mary's sake.

"Where can we go to be alone to talk about my sister?" Her innocent question rendered guilty because of past conduct.

"I have a couple of vacant properties." Uncovering a vulnerability in me, I could not resist her sanity. "Should we leave Mary alone with Becca?"

"Can your mom come over for a little while, so I can do some shopping?" I nodded a 'yes' knowing shopping was an excuse. When I was at work, Mary relied on my mother for help when she wanted it. I arranged my schedules to be sure I was home most evenings. Sometimes I couldn't be there and storms arose. I sought my own help. A tryst with Vickie became more probable with each day and week and month.

In late spring after several innocent liaisons, I asked, "Vickie, are you sure about what we're doing? I don't want to ruin our friendship or your relationship with Mary." She accepted my condition of meeting with her, without an affair. What we had left me frustrated but I could work through it with Mary until her pregnancy entered the last weeks.

Physical attacks became more intolerable as the year's end progressed. I parted from my family to save me harming Mary. Irrational thinking triggered a feral beast which I quelled by spending time with Vickie.

Victoria

Roger's calls for help broke my heart. Mary cascaded through a canyon of despair. I talked with her as much as I could supporting her through the rough days when medication failed to work or life seemed unnecessary to her. She talked of suicide but wasn't compelled to another attempt. Her pregnancy proceeded with no harmful effects other than her depression and anxiety about raising two children.

Roger and I spoke after Thanksgiving and I agreed to spend a week with them in Wendlesburg during my school's winter vacation. Dad and Mom planned a get-away for themselves during the same week. Being sixteen was not old enough for my father to allow me freedom of being alone in the house. Randy understood my desire to be with Mary.

Our boyfriend-girlfriend thing had not progressed to any permanency. We dated, went to dances and movies. Parties with friends made for a duly disguised affair. He expressed an ice princess remark after one such date. I guaranteed him he was the only one for me, a fabrication not yet befuddled by actions with Roger.

As the New Year moved into spring we met in Seattle as well as my spending time in Wendlesburg. Each excuse became a game of inventiveness. We met as regularly as possible. My heart fell deeper in love with him which complicated my promise not to destroy Mary's sanity and their marriage.

I came over to visit on spring break. He came outside when I drove into the driveway. "Vickie, I don't want to ruin anything."

"I'm okay. Let's not worry about it too much. How's Mary?"

"She's better today. She wants this pregnancy over. I guess the last month is the most difficult." He took my suitcase from me. "She's looking forward to seeing you." I smiled, wanting to see her, as well.

We entered the house where Rebecca ran up to me saying, "Aunt Vee." I hugged her tight and kissed her head.

Roger put my suitcase in the bedroom while I hunted for Mary in the kitchen. She carried her baby high and looked large enough for delivery. She had another month. "Hi, sis. How are you?" An innocent question.

"I feel like a balloon filled with cement." I laughed. "Oh, you think that's funny?"

"No, but it sounded funny. I've missed you. I'm glad I had time to come over." We hugged. "Can I help?" She was fixing lunch for us.

"Thanks. Can you finish? I need to sit down." I took over the final prep work for the sandwiches. Chips, pickles, and soup made for a tasty and satisfying meal. Becca ate much the same food. She was getting taller every time I saw her.

"I have a closing this afternoon. I'll be home around four." Roger cleared his dishes as he spoke.

I answered him. "Don't worry about us. We'll be fine." He left for his office before leaving the house.

"He works a lot." Mary stayed seated as I bussed the remaining dishes. "Sometimes I think he's avoiding us." My guilt factor rose since some of his appointments were with me.

"He takes good care of you."

"Money isn't the answer to everything." She struggled to rise from the chair. I reached for her. "Thanks." I retrieved Becca from the highchair and we moved into the family room.

"You're right, money isn't all there is. Dad hasn't learned that yet. But you have everything you need to make a fine home. I sometimes envy you for what you have."

"Envy me? I find that surprising since you have no obligations tying you down. I envy your freedom." I didn't have a sentient answer. I wanted what she had and would gladly have switched. Irony clashed with reality.

"I'm going to take Rebecca to the park. You rest. Call me if you need help. Mary, you are my shining star. I love you." Each word spoken originated deep from my heart. Any emotional tie to Roger was a matter separate but equal to my ties to her.

The warmth of the day forecast spring's arrival at last. The equinox had occurred three weeks before but the northwest almost always ran a month behind. Spring started in late April, summer in the middle of July, and autumn held off until the middle of October.

"Rebecca, Mommy needs some rest so we're going to the park." I bundled her into a jacket with a hood. I wore my coat and we strolled to our favorite swing set, Roger occupying my mind.

Rebecca watched as I sat in the seat next to her, in my daydream, obsessed, ignoring her. "Push." Her plea tore me from my trance.

"I'm sorry, baby, I was thinking about your father. He is so nice and kind and wonderful." She smiled but my attention to her caused it; at least my hope was for her not to understand my words and repeat them.

I pushed the chair as gentle as a breeze. Her eyes focused on the ground as it moved before her. I kept my focus on her with stray thoughts of Roger sneaking in and out.

56
CHAPTER

Roger

Vickie became my savior as Mary reached her due date. The assaults waned as her movements were restricted in the final month. I came to Seattle often, engaged in a ritual of non-intercourse contact. I realized the futility of our relationship but did not halt our trysts.

One day she asked me a question for which I had no sane answer. "Roger, why do you want to see me when you really want Mary, the person you met in college?"

I had no words for the longest minute. Admit an obsession with her body and mind? Instead I said, "You're so much like her. I guess I see you as a form of her lost to me. I hope you aren't offended."

Vickie stared at me and shook her head as slow as a pendulum in a grandfather clock. "You don't know what you want, do you?" She kissed me and continued, "I'm my own person. I desire to experience what my sister had when she met you. I am not interested in destroying what you and she have. If you turn down my request, my own life will not be destroyed. I guarantee the same with you."

I stared at her without a thought in my head as to how to respond. What could I say which might be interpreted as rational. Everything I was doing made little sense other than I was a selfish oaf living in a dream.

"Well?" She stood next to me, hands on her hips. "What do you want?"

"I don't know." Yet, I did know, Mary, the woman I loved and Victoria, the fantasy made up to satisfy a lost passion. I saw in her the same woman I had met in college and lost to depression and anxiety.

"My sister is about to give birth to another child and you must decide what you want from this life of yours."

"I know. I know. We should not see each other like this." We sat on the sparse furniture of one of my houses in Wendlesburg. Vickie had come over on the afternoon ferry because school released early as it did on Wednesday each week.

"If you weren't married to my sister, would you be interested in me?"

"Your age is an impediment." My eyes cast downward to the floor. "I could go to jail and be labeled a sex offender."

"If I wanted you to be my boyfriend wouldn't a court understand?"

"Probably not." I placed my hands in hers. "You're not legal for a man of my age."

"I'll be seventeen soon."

I smiled. "Vickie, it wouldn't matter. People frown on perverts. I'd be labeled one."

"Then we need to be discreet." Her hands pulled me from my seat as she stood. "I want more from you." I feared what was to come in the near future.

Victoria

Roger's fears of being labeled a pervert made me laugh, not aloud but privately inside, in my brain, in my heart. He wanted me and freedom eluded him. I accepted my plight as an unfulfilled girl wanting to be a woman. Occasionally, I contacted Andrea to assess her life and compare it to my own. We were fettered in the same unrequited love; me with Roger, her companionless.

In early May Mary produced a beautiful baby boy named Samuel Roger Waite. I was able to see the latest addition the weekend after the Friday morning birth. My family made a ferry ride without protest from my father. He was proud to be a grandfather again. I didn't appreciate his state of mind until I watched him hold his new grandson. Had he held me as a baby with the same affection?

Mary declined into a morose funk. Roger's mood was upbeat, his delight with Sam apparent for anyone who asked about his newest child.

"Mary, what can I do?" The gravity of her attitude frightened me.

"I don't know. Just stay with me."

"What about the rest of us?"

"I don't want Mom or Dad here right now."

"And Roger?"

"He has his son now, so I guess he'll be fine."

She turned away from me and pulled the covers over her head, hiding in a cocoon out of which no butterfly was to emerge. I sat and watched, waiting for her depression to ebb.

Roger followed a nurse into the room. She held Samuel. "Time for feeding," she said. Mary groaned accepting her duty.

"Mary, he's so beautiful." I sought any cheerfulness hiding within the mask she portrayed, her stare as empty as a statue watching over an Olympiad forum. She nodded, but refused to smile. Her eyes reflected the blackness in her heart. Roger sat stoic beside me.

He smiled with his mouth, eyes, trying to express a gladness lacking in the room. My heart hurt for him knowing Mary was not recovering from the post-partum blues prevalent in many mothers. "He is good looking, isn't he?"

"He's adorable. You must be very proud." My words were hollow but meant to encourage Roger to recognize I understood. We sat in silence as Mary completed the feeding. Roger retrieved this young man and held him close providing security for self and son.

Sam slept and Roger placed him in the bassinet inside the hospital room. Mary turned on her side, covering her head again and pretended to sleep.

Nancy and Marion took turns watching Mary for telltale signs of a spirit revitalization. Roger and I left for a walk.

"Will she come out of it?" He begged for an affirmative from me which I assured him was possible. I wasn't certain.

"Let's see what happens over the next couple of weeks."

He touched my hand gentle and sweet. I flushed. "Let's relieve our mothers of daughter duty." Retracing our footsteps I thought of the days we had spent together and the happiness generated by our inconspicuous actions. Someone had to discover or soon would.

Entering the room Mary spewed forth expletives for little reason other than to vent invective instructions of how she wanted everyone to leave and remove the infant. The room chilled to an icy winter day in the middle of spring. We complied to reassure her we were not incompetent of grasping her request.

Walker had Rebecca with him but expected a reprieve from child care. Roger's cell phone buzzed on cue. I volunteered to go to the Waite house and care for my niece. I left before argument could build to dissuade me. Would Roger follow soon after? Would we be alone for a time to spawn a change of heart from him?

57
CHAPTER

Roger

I watched Vickie as she left for my parent's house. I stayed with Mary, stayed with my future, stayed with my son. For now my focus depended on a complete recovery, on recouping her sanity.

"Mom, can you go help Vickie with Rebecca?" Better she go than I abandon the current circumstances.

"Will you be alright here?" Nancy looked back into the room we vacated.

"Marion's here and we can call for a nurse. Go help at home." Nancy left.

"Marion, we should go in and see if she's better." We looked in to be positive she was amenable to our entry.

Marion breached the silence. "Honey, can we come in?" Mary rolled over staring at us as if we were strangers. Her mother crept in apprehensive after witnessing her daughter's tirade. I waited in the hall, to soften the atmosphere with her mother's presence.

"I'm sorry, Mom." She saw me standing aside. "Roger, don't be shy. I won't bite." Her humor returned at the strangest times.

"Vickie's gone to help with Rebecca. Dad had to return to the office for an appointment. Mom went with her." I sat in a chair next to the bed watching for telltale signs of a storm. Different minutes provided different atmospheres. She offered her hand as if nothing had happened.

"Roger, get me some water, please." I retrieved her glass and poured fresh into it.

"Here." I handed her the glass. She drank greedily and handed it to me empty.

"Is Vickie going to be okay at home?" I wondered about her concern so absent a few minutes ago.

"She's very good with our daughter and Becca loves her." Vickie's emotional stability contrasted Mary's mentality. Who was I to question, though? I married this woman for better or worse.

"Where's Sam?"

"I'll get him." I lifted him from the bassinet handing him to her. He squirmed with the interruption but settled into her arms. They seemed so peaceful together. I smiled forgetting Vickie. I leaned in to kiss Sam and then Mary. She accepted without question. What was her mind doing to her?

Victoria

Nancy caught me in the parking lot before I entered my parent's car. Dad gave me the keys when I entered the waiting areas where he sat reading a magazine away from the fray in the maternity wing.

"Roger sent me after you. Let's take my car." I did not need a baby sitter. What was he thinking?

"I have to return my Dad's keys to him." I left her standing in the lot as I fumed into the hospital.

In Nancy's car I asked about Roger and Mary gauging her involvement in their lives.

"Are you worried about Mary or Roger?" My brow furrowed at her question.

"I'm thinking about both of them. My sister had a rough life growing up. She was so happy to meet Roger."

"He's doing fine. I go to their house whenever he needs me. Rebecca loves to have me come over." Her defensive attitude surprised me. I hadn't thought of our various relationships as a competition for affection.

"Glad to know it. I worry Mary and he aren't as happy as when they met. She can be a challenge at times, if you know what I mean."

Her glower froze any further inquiry. We continued to the house.

Walker came out with Rebecca in tow, greeting Nancy with a kiss and me with a 'hi' which I acknowledged with a head nod. Rebecca toddled to me with arms raised. The competition undertaken without either of us declaring a start to it.

I carried her into the house while the grandparents exchanged good-byes and Walker left for his office and appointment.

For different reasons I missed Roger as much as I missed Mary. Nancy entered the house and began to fix food for Becca. I placed her in the highchair and wandered down the hall to the bedrooms. I stood in the master room doorway thinking of the two of them living lives of bliss.

I went into Becca's room gathering toys she might want. I returned to the kitchen to find a sandwich for me as well as food for Nancy and Becca.

"Thank you. You didn't have to do that."

"You're welcome. I figured we hadn't had much nourishment since this morning and food might do us some good." She wasn't a bad person. The competition existed in my head not in the world.

The phone rang. Nancy picked it up spoke for a moment and handed it to me. "Hello?"

Roger's voice sounded strained. "How are things at the house?" He could have asked his mom the same question.

"Fine." Short and curt. Let him figure it out. I wanted to ask about having Nancy tag along. I watched her as she fed Becca. "How is Mary doing?"

"She's better. Her attitude has improved."

"Are you with her right now?"

"No, I needed to talk with you, but I didn't want her listening. So I made an excuse about getting something to eat. When you left she was in a foul mood, but we went back in and it was like nothing bad had happened. I don't understand what's going on with her."

Tears welled up in my eyes. I turned away from Nancy, carrying the phone into the hallway. "Maybe you need to see a counselor to help you. I don't know if she will go with you, though. She's been apprehensive in the past."

The silence spoke volumes. Finally, he said, "I can't do that. I need you. I need you to help Mary. I need you to support me through this. I need someone who is not so volatile and unpredictable."

What could I as a sixteen year old teenager do? What did I know? What was it he wanted? I knew what I wanted.

58
CHAPTER

Roger

Marion helped me gather our belongings while Mary and Sam were wheeled out to the waiting area. Garrett drove his car to the entrance. He insisted on providing the ride home. I explained we had the proper carrier in our car which Sam would need to legally be transported. He took Marion after I retrieved my car.

As I drove to our house Mary insisted I devise a plan to have our families leave as soon as possible. "I want quiet and having your mother and my parents offering their advice about things is not what I need right now." I thought about Vickie and the help she provided. It was Saturday and she could stay another day before going home.

"I'll ask them to leave so we can bond as a family. Your dad and mine aren't going to be much help, so it's only the conflicted mothering we need to be rid of." Mary chuckled. I hadn't understood it as humorous. I relaxed.

We arrived to a throng of people cooing over our latest addition. Mary's eyes narrowed, intensified by the fuss. I helped her out of the car. Rebecca hugged her mother's leg. Vickie opened the back door to get Samuel. "I'll do that." I said. "Get your sister into the house." Nancy and Marion were directing traffic as to who was to do what. They emptied the car of Mary's suitcase and baby paraphernalia. Vickie picked up Rebecca and walked with Mary into the house. I followed with Samuel.

"I'm fine. Just let me sit in the family room and give me my baby." Mary's words were passionate, not threatening, but I heard the anxiety in them, as if a crisis had begun and no one was in control.

"Everybody, listen." I used a firm voice not wishing to offend but needing the authority. "I am glad you all came to meet Samuel and I know you want to help. However, I am asking you all to leave for a while so we can settle in and get some rest. Go get lunch or something and come back later. I'll fix a light dinner for us before you go to your respective homes."

The atmosphere cooled. I was sure Garrett wanted to say something. Marion looked hurt, and my mother began to open her mouth but I mimed a 'No' to her.

Mary interceded, "I just need to rest and this crowd is not what I want right now. Vickie can stay to help with Rebecca."

At least we could have help for Sunday. My mother huffed out the door while Mary's parents said their good-byes and departed soon after. Vickie stood in the living room window smiling. I wondered what she was thinking.

"Sis, can you change Sam while I rest. I fed him so he just needs a change and a nap if you can get him to sleep." Rebecca had toddled in with me.

"Sure thing."

"Anything I can do for you?" My inquiry invoked a smile but nothing more. Mary left for our room and some sleep. Rebecca and I followed Vickie who carried Sam as if he was a cracked egg.

"He won't break."

She grinned. "I know." Rebecca walked over to her crib and asked to be put in it. While Vickie worked on Sam, I lifted Becca into her sanctuary. She lay down holding her rabbit. I covered her with a blanket. Sam closed his eyes and slept while being changed. Vickie placed him in the bassinet we still had from Becca's infancy. We left after engaging the monitoring system.

"You have two of the nicest kids."

"Thanks. What were you thinking when your parents left. You had a Cheshire cat look on your face." We were standing on the deck for privacy. She turned and stared me eye for eye, a serious bent to her look.

Victoria

I had a weekend with Roger, Mary, Sam and Rebecca and they wanted me around. Nothing could have been better. He wanted to know what I was thinking as we stood together on the deck.

My eyes met his. I smelled the anxiety of my idea, felt the roughness of my plan, heard the silence of his question, and tasted the success of his possible agreement.

"I was thinking how compassionate my sister is about my staying here. She wants me here as much as I want to be here." I stroked his hair. He took my hand and kissed it.

"I'm glad, too. When Mary exploded in the hospital with us there, I thought it might be the end of me. After you came here. She was sweet again." He placed my hand on his heart. "Keep this healthy."

I kissed his lips, "I will." We separated looking around for telltale hints observed. No one was near.

Returning to the family room, I sat on the couch. He went to the hallway listening for movement from his bedroom. The baby monitor was quiet. He sat with me. "Roger, I was also thinking about us. I can't see you any more unless I know something is possible."

"Vickie, I can't promise you that." Beholding me as a lecherous man might, he smiled. "I can't not promise either." He moved closer. "I want to. But betray your sister?" His head rocked back and forth in a slow swing.

"I don't want her hurt. I just want you as my first." I stroked his upper thigh. "Think about it. My birthday is coming." I stood, leaving him with a bulge. "Just think about it." I went to my room, closed the door, and released the breath I held. My heart pounded. My brow moistened.

59
CHAPTER

Roger

Our weekend finished with no more conversation about Vickie's hungers. Mary remained stable which I attributed to her sister. Rebecca wanted to play with Sam, so we explained he wasn't old enough. She brought him her favorite items as an offering.

I took Vickie to the ferry Sunday as late as the afternoon allowed. She kissed me with a passion I needed. I returned the favor pressing her right breast with my left hand. She massaged my crotch. I wanted more but the openness of our fondling was not fitting. Her body encouraged exploration. "No," I said. "Stop. You have to get on the ferry. Someone could see us."

"I look like my sister. They won't know." Her statement bold and daring had merit. Except Mary was not the person leaving town.

"I agree, but you have to leave. I'll contact you later this week about meeting in Seattle." She left after a ceremonial kiss goodbye. I drove directly home.

"You were gone a long time." Mary questioned me as I entered the house.

"We talked for a while before the ferry boarded. She's concerned about you."

"Are you concerned about me?"

"I want you happy and able to care for our children with me." Her eyes remained bright.

"She is the one person I trust most. She's been with me and for me ever since I was a teenager. I don't know what I would do without her"

I wanted to ask if I was trusted but thought better about raising snakes I couldn't kill.

Victoria

"Andrea, I called to see if we could meet after school one day this week." My message recorded, it surprised me she was not home on a Sunday evening. In Seattle Randy waited to drive me home.

"Randy, thank you."

"It's what we boyfriends do. I am your boyfriend, right?" He had a right to be concerned.

"Yes."

He drove into my neighborhood and pulled into the Magnolia Park lot. I figured this day was coming. "What are you doing?"

"I need to know where we are with this relationship. Sometimes you act like you want to be serious, but most of the time we seem to be playing a game. What do you want?"

I sat quiet as a mouse, scared to tell the truth, knowing he needed something from me so I could at least get home.

He must have sensed my fear. "I'm not going to hurt you. I just want to know if you like me." He got out of the car and strode to a nearby table. I followed.

"I haven't been with a lot of girls. You know that. I was hoping we had something which ended all the crap of dating and rejection."

"I know. I haven't been the most attentive girlfriend to your...needs. I don't mean to be disrespectful. I'm just not ready to commit to a sexual relationship."

"That I understand. But you don't even seem committed to our being together." He was right.

My silence said much. "I'll take you home, now, but I think we're through as a couple." He acted the gentleman even to the end. I deserved a broken heart but sensed nothing. He did not deserve his.

The school year was coming to another inglorious end with grades high and social life low. I kept to myself, meeting with Roger for short stints, working magic to entice and enjoy a seventeenth birthday.

One day I asked a simple question to gauge my situation. "Roger, do you find me attractive like Mary was in college?"

"What? Of course you're attractive."

"I don't mean to push you into anything, but we have been doing things which can lead one to think maybe more will happen."

"You want to have sex with me, don't you?"

"Think about it. I'm not pushing you to do it, but you need me and I hope you want me." He shook his head.

"You are persistent. I'll give you that." He kissed me. "You wish for something which causes more problems than you can handle."

"Have you wished for something which caused you problems?"

"Are you talking about your sister?"

"Look, I love her as much as anyone can love a person. She has problems which hinder her from being a better person. If we...you...can help her get the best therapy, maybe she can fulfill her dreams and yours. I've told you before, I do not want to destroy your life with her. I just want you to show me what you gave Mary."

Roger smiled. "I don't believe you. How can you know enough at your age to understand what life is like as an adult?" He raised my right hand, looking at it like a new toy.

"This is an instrument for the satisfaction of a man as well as your own body. Have you ever used it to satisfy someone?" I lowered my hand to his area.

"Like this?" Wide eyes revealed a new understanding of my ability.

Before any explosive activity, I stopped. "Where did you learn..." A grin crossed from left to right growing to a wide smile to a chuckle.

"You've been practicing with your boyfriend. Have you...? No. No. You're waiting for me." He stood from the couch in the house in which we met. "I have to get home before it looks bad. I love you much like I love your sister. That said, realize the gravity of your request." He turned, leaving me alone in the house. I secured our lair before returning home.

Mary had moments of sanity offsetting moments of depression and moments of anxiety. Roger's lack of physical gratification raised the possibility I would be a woman in another month or two. Where and when lingered in my mind.

Rebecca's second birthday came with a fun party in Wendlesburg at her parent's house. I had visited on two occasions to help Mary with preparations. Guilt is such a monstrous emotion when allowed to reign. Roger and I had no time alone, but each minute near him roused my fantasy birthday.

Mary involved us in her own fantasy of sanity for the sake of Rebecca. Samuel burdened her life with feedings and diaper changings, naps not long enough or at convenient times. But she took her medicine as prescribed and acted better than anyone thought possible.

The weekend before Becca's party sapped her strength driving Roger to call me after I had left for Seattle. "Mary is not doing well. Can't you come back and help?"

"Call her doctor. He's more qualified to help her."

"You always know what to say to her, though."

"I can't be a savior from her neuroses, Roger. If the medicine isn't doing the job, then get the doctor to change it. I have school for another two weeks. I'll make myself available after I'm finished." He endured a hell reserved for me. I suffered knowing he suffered.

60
CHAPTER

Roger

Why would I risk destroying my family for a fling? She made a credible argument, enticing, alluring, and sane. I could show her what Mary discovered, but how could she reciprocate?

I walked the short distance to the park, leaving my children alone with their mother. I had to get out, to escape before I harmed her. The scratches hurt. They needed cleaning.

"Mary, you cannot attack me for no apparent reason." I spoke to trees or sky or any inanimate object pushing the incident out of me, out of my mind, out of my life.

I married her for better or worse. I wanted her sane moments back. I wanted the girl I met in Pullman.

I rubbed my arm where the bowl hit me. "Why? Why can't you be normal?" My eyes blurred as the tears formed. "Why can't you be…normal?" I blinked and they ran down my cheeks. "Vickie is so not like you, and so much your twin."

I sat on one of the park benches, exhausted from the eruption we had. I couldn't remember why it started. I pulled my cell from my pocket. I pushed the numbers for her cell and stared at them. "I can't." I clicked off the dialing app and put it back in my pocket. Standing, I decided I had to go back and be with Rebecca and Samuel. They loved me without condition; I wasn't sure who or what Mary loved.

I rubbed my neck again. The blood clotted, finally. My arm stung to move it. Darkness descended slowly as the summer days approached. Rebecca and Sam had been put to bed. I hoped nothing had alarmed them. My trauma was not to be shared.

As I drew near the house, I paused, reflecting on what to say to her. Words said do not evaporate with time's passage. Her wrath, unprovoked and senseless, pushed me to the brink of my own recklessness.

I headed to the bathroom in the hallway, needing to avoid another confrontation. Mary found me first. She had sheets and a blanket in her arms. Without a word, she tossed them to me, turned and entered our bedroom.

Specious thoughts roiled in my head. Had she hurt the kids? I dropped the linens and headed for the children. They slept as sound as bugs in a rug.

Returning to the bathroom, I washed my neck and winced when the soap and water on the cloth contacted the wounds. The hiss like breath caused by pain reminded me of the struggle brewing in me. I covered the marks with antibacterial ointment and bandages. My arm bruised but the skin was intact. I placed a cold pack on it.

Vickie's calming spirit contrasted the chaos in my house. Should I accede to her request? I didn't know. I didn't want to endure another failure. Vickie and I could converse, exchange pleasantries. I understood exchanging pleasantries with her body, as well. If I planned carefully, could I?

Victoria

Becca's party day approached and I heard nothing from Roger. Was he mad at me? We didn't meet. We didn't talk. We did nothing. On Thursday I called Mary about the party, but when I mentioned Roger she give an impression of indifference. What was happening?

"Mary, has something happened because you're acting weird?"

"Nothing's happened. He's still insensitive and I'm not happy raising two children alone."

"But, sis, he's always there for you. Whenever I'm over at your house, he's taking care of Becca and Sam. He's cleaning. He's attentive. I don't get it?"

"Vickie, he's putting on a show for you. He's still enamored of you."

"Are you jealous?"

"No, you aren't a threat. Maybe in a few years, but then he'll be really old and he'll still be married to me."

"You're funny. Do you love him?"

"Of course. Why?"

"Sometimes you act like he's not important anymore."

"I try to be interested but nothing's good anymore. What's the use? The world is better off without me."

"You've said that before but who's going to teach me about men?" A giggle reassured me of her rationality. "See, you are wonderful."

"You aren't living my life."

"I know, but you let me in most of the time. Anything I need to do for Becca's party?"

"No, we're ready. Can you stay for the weekend?"

"Sure, if you want me to." Then I could unearth Roger's mysterious disappearance. "Can we talk about what is bothering you while I'm at the house?"

"Nothing's bothering me."

"Good. How are Becca and Sam doing?"

"They're fine." The conversation lagged so I said good-bye and clicked off. I gathered some clothing for the weekend stay. One more day of school and then leave. Mom and Dad wouldn't decline. A call to dinner came soon after I started homework. I closed my computer and went down to eat. Requesting at dinner seemed a good time to ask.

We ate in silence as we usually did until dessert. "Mom, Dad, I spoke with Mary just before dinner and she wants me to come over early for the party and stay for the weekend. I want to leave after school tomorrow. I can help her with any last minute things."

My father interjected his lack of sympathy. "You spend a lot of time in Wendlesburg. Don't you want to be here anymore?"

"Of course I do, but Mary needs help. I relieve her of some of the things she has to do, like for Becca's birthday."

"Garrett, Mary loves to have Vickie help her. I see no reason for her to be held back by us when she can help her sister." He grunted, surrender signaled. Mom continued, "You have fun and we'll be there on Saturday afternoon. Let me know if we can bring anything." I nodded.

I finished my piece of apple pie. "May I be excused?" Without waiting I rose, cleared the table of my dishes and left to finish homework. One day before uncovering Roger's lack of attention. What had happened? I didn't know, but he had to explain himself.

Sleep came in fits as strange dreams of unrequited love haunted me. Did he no longer hunger for me? Had my perceptions failed? Saturday materialized as I dreamed us naked, embarking on my quest for womanhood. Then he declined my advances. Was reality to shatter my hopes?

Classes crawled through the day leaving me more restless. I planned on driving to the ferry directly after school, thought about skipping my final class and dismissed the idea. Roger could wait. I had to be patient, controlled, reserved. Appearing over-anxious might expose my desire for Roger to Mary.

As the last bell rang, Randy approached. "Not now," I thought.

"Vickie, I'm sorry about how it ended with us. Can we start over? I have tickets to the Falling Blind concert next week." A furrowed brow and narrowed eyes answered his question.

"Randy, I'm heading to Wendlesburg. I can't answer now. I have to catch a ferry."

"Call me when you're on the boat." He walked away as I wondered how lonely he was for a woman or how much he had fallen for me. I dismissed it, threw my backpack over one shoulder and headed to my car.

As the ferry swayed through waves on Puget Sound, I thought about Roger and Randy, speculating the possibility of two men, intimate with me at different times, convinced neither would like the other. I thought about Andrea's sharing Raphael. Not what I wanted. I loved Roger for reasons best described as lust, easily assuaged by Randy or Connor or any guy, but not intense as Mary had described.

She found her man and I wanted to know how he was capable of seducing, or rather being seduced by my sister. He exhibited a willing seduction by me and I wanted it. Randy had not enticed the same hunger in me. Nor had Connor.

A phone call, not obligated or wanted, was an easy way to say no to a date and not face Randy. I made it and crushed his plans. As the ferry docked my heart fluttered and breathing quickened. Why does he affect me so?

61
CHAPTER

Roger

"Mary, we have to talk." It never sounds good when someone says 'we have to talk' but I wanted to clear the air before Vickie arrived. I found her in the kitchen constructing some concoction of food.

"I know. You're right. I haven't been fair lately. I don't deserve to live." Her prep work stopped.

"Don't say that. You need to live for Rebecca and Sam and me. Vickie would miss you terribly. How would I explain to her?" Her eyes filled with tears. I moved to hold her, but she put an arm out, fingers splayed. I pulled back. "Mary, I love our life together."

"You just say these things to get me to stop. Maybe I don't want to stop. I'm tired. I'm going to bed."

Looking at my watch, "Vickie'll be here soon." Mary turned and walked away.

I glanced at the food unfinished. I tasted it. She had a talent for making the plainest food enticing. I packed the meal into storage containers for the refrigerator. "What a waste."

As I entered my office a car pulled into the driveway. I recognized the Civic and its driver. Now I could relax and be satisfied Mary would not act out. At least for the weekend. Rebecca could have a peaceful birthday.

"Hi, Roger." Romanticism chimed. I took her bag from her brushing against her.

"I'm glad you're here." Her smile unsettled me. How would I resist sweeping her into my arms with Mary so close?

"How's my sister?" A genuine concern belied an underlying wish for deception. I knew what she wanted. All I had to say was 'yes.'

"She's resting in our room. The kids are with my parents. Go say hi to her and then we can go get your niece and nephew."

Vickie trotted off to the bedroom, while I placed her luggage in the guest room. A loud crash shattered the silence. I raced to the master bedroom to find Vickie holding Mary in a tight hug, not restraining her, but keeping her from tossing anything else. A broken Chinese Buddha statue lay on the floor near our bathroom.

"What happened?"

Mary wriggled free. "I thought you were coming in." I waited at the doorway. Vickie picked up the broken pieces. "When are you picking up the children?"

"I was heading to my parents when I heard the statue break. You really wanted to hit me with it?"

"I'm mad at you."

"Why? What did I do?"

No answer. A glare. Vacuous eyes. Then a sparkle. "What?"

"Mary, are you feeling okay?" I was confused?

"I don't know; I don't feel good." She collapsed on the bed. I reached her before she slid to the floor and placed her on it, safe from tumbling off. "Roger, don't leave me."

"I'm here. I won't leave."

Holding the broken statue Vickie said. "I'll get Becca and Sam."

I responded, "Please do. Thank you." She left with the Chinese Buddha pieces.

As I sat Mary moaned about postponing Becca's birthday party. "Don't worry about it. If you're not ready, we'll call and cancel."

"Becca deserves a party. I just don't want to ruin it losing my mind." Sanity? Now?

Victoria

Mary's SUV had the required car seats to transport my precious cargo. I left Roger to fend for himself with my sister. Maybe insanity would bring him around to me.

When I arrived at the Waite's house, Nancy invited me in. Curious, I accepted.

"How have the children been?" I asked, as polite as I hoped she would be. I was not close to Roger's parents, although I had no reason to think they were unreceptive. Nancy spoke with me at family gatherings and Walker was friendly.

"They have been wonderful, so easy to care for." Rebecca trotted to me and grabbed my leg in a hug. "Sam is napping, but should be up soon."

"Roger's helping Mary, so I volunteered to chauffer them back to the house." The day was shifting to evening although the northwest spring-time was nearing 16 hours of light.

"I was about to feed them, but if they are to return home, I can hold off." Thinking about the turmoil in the other Waite house, I pulled out my cell phone.

"Let me call and find out what they want to do." I punched the speed dial number. With a short conversation ended, I looked at Nancy. "Roger thinks feeding them is helpful."

"Okay, then I'll finish. Are you staying?"

"If you don't mind, I'd like to." To gain trust and faith, hanging around for dinner seemed right.

"How has school been?" An innocent question which I thought of as a probe into my relationship with Roger.

"School's fine. I only have a couple of weeks left."

"Isn't your birthday coming soon?"

"In a month. I'm turning seventeen." Why tell her how old I'd be? Maybe she could accept me as a woman instead of an adolescent. Roger could accept me, as well.

We sat at the kitchen table eating a meal of mac and cheese with hot dog chunks, a meal this two year old kid loved. Cole slaw for adults and apple sauce for Rebecca rounded out the dinner. Before we ate, Sam drank his dinner as I held him. He watched me happy to have me cuddle him.

After dinner Nancy collected the minutia which accompanies children. I thanked her. She hugged me.

"You have been a Godsend to Mary and Roger. I don't think he would be succeeding with his marriage as much as he is, except for you." What did she mean?

"Thank you." A twinge of guilt disturbed my serenity. My stomach ached, upset by doubts. I wanted Roger, but not forever. I wanted to experience what Mary did. But not destroy her. I wanted the feel of a man, but not regret the morning after. I left with the children.

"How's Mom? Did she have fun with the kids?" I placed Samuel in his playpen as Rebecca ran through the family room. Roger put the bags on the floor next to the couch.

"She's fine. She loves having them at her house." My chin quivered as I spoke. Tears formed but did not fall.

"What's wrong?" I slumped down on the couch. Roger sat next to me, holding my hands in his. My heart raced.

"Nothing really. It's something your mom said before I left."

"What?" He scooted closer. "What did she say to upset you?"

"Not here." I scanned the room for meddling ears.

"Mary's asleep. Tell me what Mom said to you."

"She said I was a Godsend to you and Mary and you wouldn't have lasted except for me. She meant it as a compliment. But with what we've done…"

His mouth arched upward. "You're feeling guilty. Don't. I'm a big boy and I can make up my own mind." The rest of his mouth finished the smile. "I enjoy your company."

"What about Mary? I'm not sure she would appreciate our involvement with each other."

"Probably not. And yet, she is your sister and you two haven't been in competition for male companionship. Until now."

Rebecca ran up to us. Roger picked her up and hugged her. She leaned toward me. I kissed her head. "Time for bed, little one." I glanced at Sam who slept in the playpen.

We carried the children to their bedroom and prepared them for sleeping. Roger checked on Mary, who slept soundly. When he returned to the children's room, he watched as I finished with Rebecca.

As we left the room, I brushed my hand against his hand and entered the guestroom. "Goodnight, Roger."

He didn't respond but came in with me, closing the door. My heart beat hard. Was this the night? With Mary in the next room?

62
CHAPTER

Roger

"Vickie," I said, as the door isolated us to a fate neither could deny. I pulled her to me, caressing her hair, pressing my lips to hers. "I need you."

She pushed away. "Roger, I want you more than ever, but not here." She turned. "Wait until we can be together somewhere else." She spun around, a gleam in her eye, and kissed me.

"I'll wait." I opened the door and glanced at her. Such beauty in so young a person. Did she enthrall me the same way Mary did? I thought not, for her intrigue enthralled me in a more subtle and subdued way. I smiled and walked out.

Standing outside the bedroom, I leaned on the wall. "I'm such an idiot." Entering our bedroom, I watched Mary sleep. She was so beautiful, so sweet when sane, so romantic. I didn't need to have Vickie's distraction, but I craved it. She provided something missing with Mary. Or was it the thrill of two sisters wanting me.

I prepared for bed. Mary became aware of my presence, groggily making an incoherent comment. I sat next to her. "Hi, baby. How was your sleep?"

"Fine. What's going on?"

"Vickie and I got the kids to bed and she went to her room." I leaned in and kissed her.

"Roger, I can't function without you and Vickie. I'm not good enough anymore." She turned away, quashing my hopes. I guessed it was for the best. I thought about what Vickie had said, not hurting Mary. It was a fair assessment.

I climbed in beside my wife, holding her, letting her collapse into a profound, intense sleep, keeping her safe from her haunting demons. Mary had me for life. The children needed me for living a bright and illustrious future. I desired Vickie to taste the richness of a lost passion, as temporary as it might be.

Saturday morning came with the sound of children and a vacant bed next to me. I rose from the pale blue sheets searching the room for my missing companion. Laughter greeted my ears. Mary's.

Robing my body, I found two remarkable beings engaged in a ritual of dressing small offspring who resisted with glee as mother and aunt prodded the activity to raucousness. I smiled, really smiled, smiled for the flightiness of their behavior and the mirth it provided. Maybe life had meaning again.

Saturday's burst of energy cast a doubt about the sanity of any of us. I enjoyed the evening cuddling with Mary asleep, but needed a more satisfying repartee. It had to wait. I left the children to mother and aunt to fix a morning meal fit for a birthday princess and her entourage.

Vickie entered the kitchen carrying Sam with Rebecca close at hand. "What's for breakfast?" she asked.

"Pancakes and bacon. Special days deserve special meals." *Special in more than one way*, I thought. "Where's Mary?"

"She's getting dressed." Vickie placed Sam in his carrier seat. "What does my sister act like when I'm not here?" An innocent question, but how was I to answer her? I wanted her help and needed it. I wanted her to stay for Mary's sanity, for my lust, for the way she interacted with the children.

"I guess the best way to put it…is she acts more normal when you're here. She gets so depressed at times." A noise in the hall killed the conversation. Mary entered the kitchen.

"I act more normal when Vickie's here? Is that what you think?" Darkened eyes betrayed her mood.

Vickie deflected the onslaught. "Don't be offended. We love you and want what's best." Mary smiled as sky blue replaced dark navy in her irises. "You are the best big sister a little girl can have."

"Why do you always sound like an adult? You need to be that little girl...for me. I should be the adult." She sat next to Vickie. "Neither of you deserve to be haunted by my demons."

"Let's not worry about that right now. Breakfast is ready and we have a party to put on."

Rebecca followed the conversation understanding something happened which we caused but comprehended not the impact on her. It was her day for celebration and the mood repelled happiness for the moment. I noticed her frown as I placed a plate of pancakes in front of her. She lit up like a lamp brightens the darkness.

We devoted the remainder of the morning to prepping the house to entertain a two year old. Baby Sam fidgeted as the activity accelerated. He wanted attention instead of being ignored. A loud scream escaped him, startling Becca, who had been playing with her toys as she sat on the floor next to the playpen entrapping her brother. She added to the cacophony.

I picked her up as Mary plucked Sam from his enclosure. "You're okay. Sam wanted our attention." Her wide eyes and quivering lips did not expel the anguish her brother initiated. I snuggled her, whispering calm words in her ear. Vickie brought a bottle in from the kitchen hoping Sam wanted nourishment. Mary took it and held it to his mouth. He guzzled the contents.

Afternoon replaced morning as we finished preparing the house. Family members arrived and a party commenced. Rebecca tore the wrapping from her gifts with assistance from Aunt Vickie. We ate the macaroni and cheese dinner concocted by Mary, then said goodbye to sisters, brothers, mothers and fathers. I relaxed after cleaning the kitchen while Vickie put the children to bed. Mary disappeared into our sanctum exhausted by the chaos of so many people descending upon us.

Entering my office, I reflected on the day. Mary maintained a stable, civil, attentive attitude which drained her energy. Nobody suffered the storms; common to us without others present. I sat at my desk, clicked on the computer screen, and investigated properties in Seattle which had decent prices and prime locations. If I owned another place, a special birthday rendezvous with Vickie would thrill her and please me.

I had all any man wanted. A beautiful wife, family, secure employment, a bright future, and few worries, except one. Why create an environment with Vickie which threatened it? It made no sense. I wanted the pleasure of giving her what she wanted. I understood not what I took from the young ladies in college because of my selfish lust. Now Vickie wanted me to transform her from girl to woman and I appreciated what it meant. How was I to deny it to her? How could I justify such an act of selfishness? How would such an act alter our relationship?

Victoria

With Rebecca and Samuel in bed, I changed my clothes to a more relaxing outfit. Mary and Roger's bedroom door was ajar. I peeked in to see if they were there, but saw only Mary asleep. I heard no other noise of a body preparing for bed. I closed the door, departing the hall on a quest for companionship.

I found him sitting at his desk, a glow reflecting from the screen he studied. I stood in the doorway, obscured by shadows, studying. He knew my desire. He satisfied my sister's quest for normality at college and now he needed the return to normality, a normality provided by me.

I vacated my shelter of darkness. He did not react to my entry, so I scuffed slippers as an alert to his loss of privacy. He looked up and I smiled.

"Oh, hi. I didn't see you come in." He grinned. "I've been researching property in Seattle near your house." I nodded, not sure of what to say.

I moved to the side of the desk and stroked his hair. Electricity sparked igniting parts of me I wanted enlivened. He pulled me down to his lap, sitting me on it and kissing me soft as a feather caressing my neck. I returned the gesture, stroking his neck. I felt the growth below me. Fearing I would not resist if we continued our fondling, I pushed away and stood. "We can't. Not here." My body whirled with desire, my mind imagining a consummation of it. "I want this to be a time without fear of anything or anyone interrupting us." He stood next to me.

Pulling me close, connecting our bodies in the embrace, he kissed me again. I feigned resistance and melted with his touch. He cupped my breast arousing me. I caressed his back.

Pushing him away, I closed my eyes. "No. Come to me in Seattle when my parents are on their trip. We can be alone then. It won't be long and then we can do what we both want to happen." I turned from him to leave.

"Vickie, I don't want to wait, but I know you're right." I turned back and kissed him.

—— ∞∞∞ ——

The school year ended with no fanfare of excitement. Randy invited me to his graduation. I declined knowing he still held feelings which would not be returned. Other people ignored me like the ice princess I was. No foul, no harm.

Mom and Dad completed preparing for their trip. My birthday placed second to his business. An opportunity for self-indulgence reared its wonderful head. I grinned at the thought.

"Mom, I promise to behave while you and Dad are gone. Don't worry."

"Oh, honey, I never worry about you. If ever a child was to be trusted, it would be you." She hugged me like a person losing a precious jewel. "You are growing up so fast. We'll celebrate your birthday when we get back from San Francisco."

"I know. You have fun and don't worry about me." I left the family room skipping to my room scheming as I went.

63
CHAPTER

Roger

"Mary, what do you want to do for your sister's birthday? It's coming up in a week."

"She said she didn't want us to do anything elaborate and since Mom and Dad won't be home, let it go." Another battle? Not for me. I had the right present and I would deliver it personally.

"Fine, we'll send a card and wait for your parents to come home." We finished with breakfast. I had a meeting with my father about a business property in Poulsbo and a closing on Bainbridge Island. "I'll call you at noon."

"You don't have to check up on me all the time. I'm not going to do anything bad." Mary glared at me, eyes turning to navy. "Just go. I'll take care your precious little children. You amass enough money to make you happy."

Not the time for an argument. I walked out the front door into the peace of being alone. Mary's moods swung like a well-oiled door. It seemed I could touch it as gentle as a feather and ruffle them before I knew it.

"You're such a bitch," I mumbled aloud with no threat of other ears. I drove to the office and sanity. As I parked in the lot, I thought about the difference between the two women who created the chaos in my mind. One I wanted because she captured a moment in my past which I now lived with in hell. The other, my hell, the woman who settled a wild man and saved him from ruination, lived in a dual world of anxiety and

depression while shining through the clouds to thrill me with two beautiful children and flashes of elation.

One I promised to have and to hold, through sickness and through
health, until death us do part. The other promised me a return to para-
dise lost.

As much as they were alike physically, they differed in personality. The
younger grew more mature with age, as her older sibling declined into immature response to reality. I wanted both to be one, one person, one complete entity of humanity, one being to share a lifetime. I could not choose
one over the other. I could only separate my life and compartmentalize
my time into snippets for one and endurance of the other.

I hadn't lost my love for Mary, for the woman who trusted me with
her phobias and relationships and allowed me to prepare her for an adult
life, sharing with other people, interacting as if nothing haunted her. I suffered when storms brewed which only she could see, but exhibited themselves in painful actions. The days were best when away from her tirades,
and the nights were abided for children and managing the manic mania
until sleep arrested her lunacy.

Vickie became the surrogate to whom I willingly succumbed in an effort to maintain my course in life. She provided an atmosphere of summer's
warmth when clouds threatened. Time with her, sharing little physical interplay, talking of life's challenges, keeping a head above the stormy waters,
gave me the willing heart to withstand the anomalies of my household.

What she wanted from me, so easy to say 'yes', to forget promises made
to her sister, was in reality straying. Or could it be I had another from the
same history who finished the puzzle and created a clear picture for me?
I wanted Vickie to know her quest for womanhood was not to be left for
another man. I would fulfill her dream. Would it lead to disaster and ruin?
I cared not. Would the act be once and done? I thought not. Would it
break her heart when it ended? I knew not. All she had to do was ask and
I would comply.

Victoria

"I'll look for a job while you're gone." Work during the school year for
gas money, also gave some say in my own college funding. Scholarships

and grants would cover some of the expense, as well as living at home the first year, but I wanted separation from any fatherly monetary control of my life.

"Get something part-time," my father interjected. "I'll make your tuition payments for college as long as you maintain good grades and don't betray our family name." As usual, his reputation trumped any accomplishment I might have.

"Yes, Father, I understand." I understood more than I wanted to understand. I understood a desire for Roger must be so covert and quiet, nothing about an affair could ever be discovered. Even Andrea would not know I began what we talked about years ago.

Mom and Dad drove away, leaving me to celebrate a birthday and become a woman. When the car disappeared down the street, I turned toward the house, eyes examining the walls, windows, doors. Could I survive the emotional upheaval of the dishonesty soon to be consummated inside these walls?

Walking back into the foyer, my cell chimed in my pocket. Roger's name appeared in the screen. "Hello, Roger."

"Have your parents left, yet?"

"They just drove away. Can you come over?"

"Don't be in a hurry, dear. I have an appointment in Seattle on Thursday. I'll stop by afterward." My heart fluttered. Thursday was my actual birthday. Four days to find employment and prepare for the one man who stirred my soul more deeply than anyone.

"I can wait." Did he remember Thursday? Had he planned the day purposefully? After clicking off the call, I sat in the kitchen thinking about Andrea and her conquests, the boys who knew her, the discovery of her trysts. "I can wait."

As sudden as my brain thought of my past, I awakened to the fact I was alone in the house, a large manse giving comfort and fear concurrently. Roger could fill the void but feeling hungry for food, I scrounged the cupboard and refrigerator for lunch. Mom left enough food for three people but two had left. I fixed a sandwich and went to my room.

"Roger, I will be as good for you as any of the others, including my sister." The phone rang in the hall. *Who could that be?*

"Hello?" A familiar voice calmed my anxiety. "Hi, Mom. Are you at the airport?"

"We're on the shuttle. Are you okay?"

"Fine. Have fun."

"What are you doing right now?"

"Besides talking with you, eating lunch. I'll clean up when I'm done." Checking on me hourly was not what I dreamed as a time of solitude.

"Well, I'll let you go and check in with you when we land in San Francisco." The phone went dead. If she checked on me regularly for the next week, I wasn't sure I wanted to stay here. Maybe Mary and Roger would house me. No, that would interfere with my birthday plans.

I did as promised and cleaned up the kitchen after eating. In my room, I logged on to search for employment knowing chances for a job I might actually enjoy were slim. Could I make enough to keep my parents away from controlling my life? In reality I wanted Dad out of any control. If he had financial influence, I would have no chance of freedom until I graduated from college and found a life.

Roger's ideas about creating a quiet place for us made sense. We could rendezvous, enjoy being together, and return to our regular lives without anyone interfering. We would make it work. Nothing stood in our way.

64
CHAPTER

Roger

As Thursday approached and my trip to Seattle for business, I discussed the needs of property in the Magnolia area and Queen Anne Hill near Seattle Center with my father. His curiosity about holding property outside of Kitsap sparked a debate regarding my future as a broker in Kitsap, partnering with his firm. I hadn't thought that far into my life, concerned with Mary's mental sanity and Victoria's involvement in my existence. Maybe Mary was right about my focus on making money, but I figured it made sense to protect our future, financially.

"Roger, did you finalize the property on Mission Street?" My father had a way of altering conversations to keep me on my toes. He sharpened my instincts as well as my education.

"It's on Marsha's desk." I turned to leave. "Dad," I faced him. "Are you happy with your life?"

Scrunching his forehead, the next words from his mouth surprised me. "Are you and Mary having problems?"

"What? No. I was thinking about you and Mom raising us and what it took to get us grown. I guess I worry if I'm doing enough for my children."

"You have one of the finest minds I've ever met. You remind me of myself when I started out. At least you don't have to fend for yourself."

"I appreciate that. I guess I should stop worrying about things I don't control and focus on what I can." Dad smiled as I turned again to leave. "Thanks."

In my office, rationalizing my actions with Vickie, I decided I had
to let her go. Nothing was worth the complications perverted by actions
such as we contemplated. I had to tell her we'd not be making her into
anything on her birthday. I hoped she would take it well.

Victoria

The week crawled toward Thursday and seeing Roger at my house.
I prepped myself to be the perfect companion, to be alluring without
raunchiness, seductive but not desperate, sensual minus outright animal-
ism; to surprise Roger with my ability to be a friend and confidante.

An empty house can be a weird place. I wandered around the different rooms upstairs, silent and haunting. It felt strange to be alone with
no one to talk to. I had applied for jobs at several retail outlets, expecting
nothing, hoping for nothing. I would be called if anything came up, or so
I was told. On Wednesday I called Andrea about enticing him to accept
my birthday offering.

"What can I expect from him?"

"Guys are dogs." Her comment surprised me. "All they want is to find
a woman and get her in bed. I don't think it matters whether they're married or not."

"Roger says he loves my sister and doesn't want to hurt her, but he
keeps seeing me in secret."

"Do you still want him?"

"I feel guilty. I don't want to hurt my sister. She's fragile."

"Don't worry about her. She doesn't need to know about what you
want from Roger. After all you only want him to be your first. It's not like
you want to steal him away from her." I said nothing. A shriek hurt my
ear. "You aren't sure what you want from him, are you. Do you really want
to steal him away from her? Or just continue having an affair for the next
zillion years."

I paused before answering. "I don't want to do anything stupid."

"But you don't know what to do about Roger, do you?"

"What if he decides to leave her for me?" I started crying.

"He wouldn't be the first guy to break up a family." How did that help
me? Andrea's family was already a single parent group. Her dad left when

she was in third grade. She probably expected Roger to leave. Was I that person? If he did leave Mary for me, how could I justify it?

"Thanks a lot." I wanted to hang up on her. "I am not interested in his leaving Mary. I love my sister and it would be the end of her if he did."

"Then why are you so interested in his being the first guy you sleep with? It doesn't matter who it is, really."

"So I should have done Connor or shared Raphael with you? Should I find a random person on the street?" I thought about the hunk who saved me from walking into traffic. "I want to experience what changed Mary so much when she met Roger. I want to have what she had. I want to be as happy as she was with Roger when she met him in college."

"Then you need to lose the guilt and enjoy the sex."

"I guess." We ended the call. Emotional conflicts obstructed thinking. Were my yearnings greater than Mary's family needs?

65
CHAPTER

Roger

"Mary, I have a closing in Seattle. I'll be home late." I waited for the tirade. Thursday had blossomed with sunshine and warm air. Vickie expected me and this was my last visit with her. I would conclude the house sale and the salacious behavior threatening to unravel my family. I continued dressing.

"Roger, after you close the deal, please stop by my parent's and see if Vickie is doing okay. Today is her birthday and I feel bad about her being alone." Surprised but pleased, she cared about her sister and it brought out the best in her. "Ask her if she wants to come over here and celebrate tonight. We can give her a day to remember. She can spend the night."

"Are you sure?" I didn't need an argument.

"Yes, and be nice to her. She doesn't have many friends and I understand how she feels." I identified with a spider scurrying for cover before being discovered. I still thought about the birthday offering awaiting me. How she responded to rejection could upset her coming to our house to celebrate a lack of gifting her with womanhood. Accepting her request challenged my sense of justice regarding Mary. Her logic in a moment of sanity stabbed me.

"Alright, I'll call her and see if she wants to come over. If she's busy tonight, I'll let you know." We retrieved our children, changed, dressed, and hungry, and proceeded to the kitchen for breakfast. The morning inside arose as warm as the weather forecast to be outside. All shined brightly.

We ate as a family, a family with solidarity, a family built for success. I then left for my office before heading to Seattle and another family of dysfunction and failure. I was grateful for the parents' departure and Victoria's company. Regardless of my options before her, I did enjoy her company. Her mind, her body, her spirit energized my inner nature and self-worth. Mary had produced the same affect in college. I wanted it to return; Vickie had it now.

Driving to the ferry I contemplated what might happen at the Johnson house. I figured Vickie prepared an attractive persona enticing enough to wither my resolve. I had to be strong but loving, forthright and understanding, caring for her emotions as well as mine. On the boat a young couple, younger than Mary and me, kissed and talked and laughed. Older than Vickie, the girl enjoyed the attention of her companion. I knew the unstated appeal.

With business concluded I headed up destiny's course. Another encounter with this vixen worthy of attention and sharing, I feared the worst and believed the best. Would she hold to a standard I wanted or unravel my psyche like a professional?

Victoria

I showered and shaved, even parts not usually shorn. As I dried, I admired the offering I hungered to give. I knew we should not. I cared not. I knew Andrea was correct. I forfeited any guilt and donned a white blouse and black skirt. I left supporting attire on the bed. No need to over dress, I figured. A hint of powdered Allure, and the game was set to play. My prey was to arrive early afternoon. I had the rest of the day to fulfill my fantasy. My mind made up, regardless of the consequences.

Mary and I shared much throughout life. This immersion was another in my quest to find reason in this broken family. I descended the steps from my room entering the living room to wait. Anxiety fluttered my heart, breathing labored and shallow. Roger had the right perspective about us. We were brother and sister because of the law. We could be together and keep a sensible relationship, protecting each other, Mary, and a family worth saving. Rebecca and Samuel needed all of us. My life was not ugly nor did I want it to be. I had not endured my sister's angst. All I wanted was to understand the experience she had with Roger.

The doorbell chimed. I jumped. Racing beats raised a flush in my face. I breathed in deep and slowly. Exhaled slowly, and opened the door. "Hello, Roger. Welcome to my home." Formal? Acting mature? Being proper?

"Hi, may I come in?" I stood like a statue.

"Oh, yes. Come in. I'm sorry." I vacated the doorway as he stepped across the threshold. "Have a seat in the living room." He wandered in while I closed the door. "How have you been?" I sounded nervous. I breathed slowly again.

"Are you alright?"

"Yes, yes. I'm just nervous with you here, ah, alone with you." I sat down on the sofa. He joined me. "Roger, my birthday is not going as I expected. I wanted to have you come over and now you are here, but what am I doing?"

"Are you having second thoughts?" He appeared so calm. I was a wreck.

"Second thoughts? No, I want to. I do. But I'm fearful of destroying Mary."

"It's alright. I've been double checking this, too." He smiled and I changed my mind again. I began to undo the buttons on my blouse.

66

CHAPTER

Roger

The door opened. She looked fantastic. The white blouse shaped around her revealing her lack of underwear. "Hi, may I come in?" She looked nervous. I guessed she still wanted me and I was like a sheep to the slaughter. Invited to the living room, I walked in.

As she followed I asked, "Are you alright?"

"Yes, yes. I'm just nervous with you here, ah, alone with me."

I sat on the sofa with her after she came in and took a seat. Her skirt hiked a bit exposing a shapely thigh. I wondered about my resolve.

"Roger, my birthday is not going as I expected. I wanted to have you come over and now you are here, but what am I doing?" She was nervous and I had to calm her with my announcement of not following through.

"Are you having second thoughts?"

"Second thoughts? No, I want to. I do. But I'm still fearful of destroying Mary." Now, tell her now, before you change your mind.

"It's alright. I've been double checking this, too." Before I could say anything else, she unbuttoned her blouse. My body betrayed me. My brain forgot words. I watched as the blouse slipped open, exposing the reality my mind pretended to know. Was I strong enough to resist?

Mary slithered into my head, a college Mary. Mary from the sane days. Current Mary evaporated as the fog on a Seattle weather convergence day. Sunshine filled my heart as Vickie shed her blouse. My resolve melted, good intentions dissolving as lust expanded. I reached for her happily, eagerly, caressing her hair, cheeks, neck, kissing her lips.

"Are you sure about this?" I asked knowing my answer and changing my mind. She unbuttoned my shirt after slipping the tie from my neck.

"Don't talk," she whispered. I removed my jacket. She took my hand and led me upstairs to her room. The remaining clothing fell to floor and chair. Her body revealed a similarity to her sister, who was lost in my brain for the moment. She stared at my body. For the first time seeing a male stimulated by lust?

I touched her shoulder asking again, "Are you sure?" She nodded and held me tightly. We sat on the bed exploring forbidden fruits. I wanted to make love without any debasing or degradation. The minutes became an hour and then another. Sated I lay back on her bed holding her, warm and perspiring. Her birthday present delivered.

Victoria

Was this the right thing to do? His body responded as Connor's had, now uncovered for me to see what I had only touched through clothing. I held it in my hand and gently caressed it. He moaned. I closed my eyes and we sat on the bed.

I nodded when he asked again if I was sure about this. No words emerged. He was sweet and gentle, teaching me the ways and wiles of making love. We enjoyed each other's bodies. His entry into me hurt but only for the difference the experience gave me. He satisfied my hunger and curiosity. We lay on the bed embracing, my mind a whir of thoughts about what happened. I loved him, as a brother-in-law, a lover, and a man. Andrea and I shared the forbidden tree and survived. No other man was to be the first. I was complete.

We dressed. I put on my underwear and a pair of jeans and the blouse. Roger forego tying his tie stuffing it in his pocket. As he pulled his pants on he said, "Mary wants you to come over with me to the house. She thinks you might be lonely on your birthday. We can have a small celebration tonight. What do you think?" The switch in character of the moment caught me off guard.

"Do you think it is wise, after what we just did?" Doubt invaded. Panic attacked. My actions now mordant.

"She will never know of this and she is expecting you."

"All right." I packed some clothing in my bag, gathered my toiletries, and we left to catch the next ferry to Wendlesburg. Uncertain of Mary's reaction to our delay, imagined or real, I sat silent not wishing conversation. Maybe I should have showered. Does sex have a smell?

67
CHAPTER

Roger

Vickie's silence unsettle me. Had I upset her? Her beauty vying with Mary triggered the guilt I held in abeyance. I feared the worst, the unknown, and the telltale hint of indiscretion.

Our tryst pleased me more than I expected. She was responsive, eager to explore, inquisitive about what thrilled me. Her body replicated memories of my first sexual encounter with Mary. Still, the guilt of betraying my wife wriggled free from my endeavor to sublimate it.

As we drove onto the ferry, Yakima, Vickie broke the silence. "I hope we are normal around Mary. She may act crazy at times, but she senses when something changes." She clasp my hand. "We can't ignore what happened, so we have to be who we were before today."

I nodded, unsure of any ability to do so. "Do you want to go upstairs?" A premonition of someone who knew us, seeing Vickie and me together, troubled me. It was an unfounded fear, but real to me nonetheless.

"Let's stay in the car." Did she carried the same anxiety? I smiled.

"What makes you smile? Thinking of us? The afternoon?"

"I was thinking about the same thing you were, about someone seeing us together." I pulled her to me and kissed her. We both looked around. Alone, we kissed again. The announcement by the ferry PA system of our impending arrival in Wendlesburg, interrupted our osculation.

After docking we watched the cars ahead of us disembark. Our turn came and I drove off the ferry, up the ramp, and to Judgment Day.

Victoria

Roger and I headed to an uncertain destiny. Could Mary accept our assignation if she discovered it? I thought not, and I feared her mental state if such pressure pushed her over the edge of sanity. "Roger, before we get to the house, I need to say something." He pulled the car over to the side of the street.

Looking at me, he asked, "What did you want to say?"

"I can't be alone with you while at your place. Mary needs me and can't suspect anything."

"I agree. I'll figure a way for us communicate without any trace." We continued our journey into an uncertain future.

"Well, it's about time you two got here." Mary appeared calm and controlled. Her smile, genuine and happy, eased my stress. Determining she suspected nothing, I relaxed and hugged her.

"Thanks for inviting me to come over. It was nice of Roger to pick me up." Rebecca came up to me, arms stretched out for a pick-up. I cooperated and nuzzled her. She squealed and slobbered a kiss on my cheek. A sudden sense of depression invaded. What had I done? Mary didn't deserve my betrayal. Was this the end of family and friendship?

68
CHAPTER

Roger

"Roger, is Vickie okay? She seems different somehow." Guilty, I thought. I'm guilty. I'm guilty of changing your sister. I couldn't resist her charms. Her uncanny resemblance to you. Her ability to compose a difficult situation into a serene state.

"She's fine. I asked her about her birthday and she said it was not what she expected. I guess being alone in that house is hard for anyone." I hoped defraying suspicion might keep our secret safe.

"I don't know. How long were you with her at the house?" Not long, I had to say, not long.

"I arrived about an hour before we left to come here."

"What did you do for an hour?" I smiled. Deflect her reservations.

"She fixed some tea and we talked. About you. About her future. I invited her to come here. She packed and we left."

"I'm happy she accepted, but I wasn't doubting her coming. Did your house close?" I nodded. "Something's up with you, too. Did you do something while in Seattle?"

"Like what?"

"I don't know. I wasn't with you." Was a storm brewing? The atmosphere cooled around me, or was I imagining it?

"We closed. I ate lunch, went to see your sister and came here." *Nothing happened, nothing, nothing you need to know.*

Mary walked away, atmospheric change not occurring. I went to my office to file the paperwork and record the sale and reflect on the afternoon.

Vickie received the birthday gift she wanted. How could I continue giving her the same gift? Why? Where? She had to leave me alone and yet now I wanted a relationship with her. She provided what was missing, lately. Why shouldn't I if Mary and her tirades debilitated our marriage?

Victoria

Rebecca and I hunted for Samuel in the children's bedroom. I found him in need of a change and attention. Rebecca watched while I changed him. "How is mommy," I asked no one in particular. Rebecca looked at me, knowing a truth not visible.

"Mommy's sad." I stared at my niece with a new enlightenment of her growth in just a few weeks. Snapping the pants onto Sam, I pick him up and bent down to Rebecca.

"What do you mean, Mommy is sad?" My face must have looked weird because she grimaced.

"Mommy cries." Holding Sam, I hugged Becca. What I did with Roger had no place in this house. My sister's fragile emotional state would not survive my betrayal. I vowed to make my one encounter with him the last. Could I?

"Let's go find Mommy and Daddy." The tears pooled and cascaded across my face.

"Are you sad?" Rebecca displayed a knowledge of the situation without the experience to fathom the intrigue developing around her.

"No, I'm happy to be here with you and Sam." The lie must preserve a sense of wellbeing for these two young charges. Entering the family room, I put Sam in the playpen and Rebecca at her desk. She began scribbling on one of her notebooks with crayons.

"Vickie," Mary entered from the kitchen, "are you okay." I swiped my eyes hoping against hope. Mary seemed happy and I had to maintain her ebullience.

"I'm fine. Becca spoke in a complete sentence. I'm surprised and happy, that's all."

"Good, we are making this day a most special day for you. Happy birthday, sis. You deserve the best of everything." My thoughts sneaked in heating my face and loins. I had the best. I loved Mary, but Roger stirred the beast in me and I was not positive I was willing to re-incarcerate it. I knew I didn't deserve a most special day and yet one was presented in a most special way.

"Thank you. Coming here makes it special. I love you and never want you to think I don't, no matter what happens."

"That's rather a strange thing to say. What possibly could happen to make me think you don't love me?" My mouth ran before my brain engaged.

"Nothing, you and Roger are so content. I want you happy all of the time." The air chilled as Mary held my hands in hers. Her words cooled it more.

"He doesn't love me the way he used to and I know it's my lack of stability. I'm taking my medication, and I fight the demons haunting me, but he is not receiving what he wants. I'm afraid he's going to wander." My guilt bubbled to the surface. Andrea warned me about losing it, but the shackles held tight in my heart.

"He and I talked about you and what he gets or doesn't get. He loves you and is not wandering. No one attracts him like you do." Except for me, your twin, as he put it. "Forget about his leaving you. I'll make him stay if I have to…" Mary interrupted me.

"Thank you, but this is my battle. My fight. In my mind and in my home. Live your life and find the right guy to make love to and enjoy." Tears formed again and spilled down my cheeks. Mary pulled a tissue from a pocket and daubed my face dry. We hugged as if the end of life approached, which for one of us appeared to be a reality.

Roger entered the family room. "What's happening here?"

Mary answered. "We were just catching up on our lives and what drives us to be as happy as possible." He looked at her and then at me.

"I do believe you two are the most complete forms of females ever assembled by God. I love you both. For different reasons, of course." Guilt reared its ugly head again.

"Let's get dinner ready. Vickie, you play with the children. Roger and I will prepare a suitable feast. I already baked a cake and with help from Rebecca frosted it." She turned to leave but stopped when Roger didn't move. Holding out a hand which he clasp, the flight commenced.

Alone with my niece and nephew, tears welled a third time. I received my connived gift. Now I lived with the consequences of my culpability. Innocence lost, I wanted more but had to suspend another encounter. How did Andrea cope with the emotional baggage? How did she sustain an air of innocence without any remorse? I sat next to Becca as she drew a picture. My imagination saw three people with two smaller ones. All were holding hands. Yellow hair on two of the adults surrounding the third dark haired stick figure, reminded me of our closeness. Too close, now. And yet not close enough. Sharing a man? Mary wouldn't, would she?

69
CHAPTER

Roger

Mary stirred a pot of spaghetti noodles on the stove, as I mixed the sauce to pour over them. "Her birthday must be the best she's ever had." I turned on another burner to heat it and the meatballs. A salad bowl, filled with greens and other ingredients, was on the table. "I feel like you and Vickie have a closer link now." What was Mary saying? That she knew what transpired in Seattle? That she didn't care that it happened? Or was she probing because of suspicions?

"Closer link? What do you mean?" I ignored the best birthday comment. Remorse struggled to escape, but I didn't regret what happened.

"You two seem to have had a nice chat in Seattle and I'm happy for you both. She needs a confidante other than me and I trust you have her best interests at heart. So, I want you to be closer. She can teach you about me and how best to be supportive of me. You can help her to trust men and grow to understand their needs."

The education of Victoria began long before today. My mind wandered back to her bedroom and our liaison. "Alright, if I understand what you're saying. She does has a way of helping you cope which I have yet to discover, even after these years of being together. I'm not sure I am the best person to teach her about men, though."

"Our father certainly is not and Mom is naïve about how to answer questions of a masculine nature. So you're stuck with her."

I finished heating the sauce, turned off the burner and faced Mary. "She has a brother."

"If you haven't noticed, he has a different bent."

"I know, but he's family and loves his sister."

"You're family, too, and she is infatuated with you. Treat her with care and help her cope with boyfriends." No storm approached, but the weather had cooled in the heat of the kitchen. My head bounded up and down for I knew her boyfriend intimately.

Mary announced, "Dinner, Vickie." She came in with Sam in arms and Becca trailing. We ate a delicious meal, sang 'Happy birthday', and cut the cake into pieces after a silent wish was made. Mary then produced a package, gift wrapped, which she gave to Vickie.

'I wanted you to know how much Roger and I love you. It's not much, but it shows how we feel." Vickie tore off the paper which revealed a painting of our family.

"When did you do this?" she asked. I sat dumbfounded. She had not hinted at reviving her art work. "It's beautiful."

"Mary, I didn't know you had this kind of talent," I said. "When did you do this?"

"You're away so much, I just sit and paint for short periods of time while the kids nap. It keeps my mind occupied." So you won't go crazy, I figured.

"Do you have any others?" Vickie asked.

"Nothing to show anyone." The celebration was a success. Vickie's birthday, indeed, was the best she ever had. A maiden in the morning, a woman by afternoon, an owner of fine art with evening. Nightfall gave rise to sleeping children and wife. I cleaned the kitchen while Vickie sat watching. She was correct about being alone together. I wanted to hold her, kiss her, and feel the curves of her body. I washed pots and pans with methodical meticulousness, mastering the procrastination so as to avoid what both of us probably wanted. No talk. No interaction. No problems.

Victoria

Admiring the picture of her family, I despised the afternoon. But I couldn't undo it. Guilt revoked any pleasure this evening suggested. I watched as Roger completed cleaning the kitchen, placing pans and pots on the hooks. Dishes were in the dishwasher and it was running. Silence remained my ally for the moment. If he spoke, I'd melt and bare my soul. I rose to leave. He watched as I glanced back at him. He smiled but remained stoic.

In the guest bedroom I removed my clothes and prepared for sleep. I needed the bathroom but wanted to avoid seeing him. I sat on the bed, half dressed in flannel PJs, pants, no top. He wanted these I told myself. I wanted him to have them. I donned the top and headed for the bathroom with my travel kit.

No one interrupted my passage, hallelujah. I finished nightly chores, packed my kit, opened the door to leave, and ran into Roger. My heart fluttered.

"Vickie, do you have a moment?" I wanted to decline but nodded. "Come with me."

I followed him to his office where he closed the door. I shuttered to think about engaging in sex with him here. He sat in a chair by his desk.

"Please sit down." I complied. "Mary said some strange things to me while we were cooking dinner. I wanted you to know in case she brings up the conversation." I remained silent. "She thinks I am the person to help you learn about men and coping with boyfriends."

"I'm well aware of what guys want. I learned more today, but I wanted it, as well. Are you still wanting to teach me about the wiles of the male gender?" I stayed still, holding my toiletries tight as possible.

"I don't regret what we did. I want to know if you regret it." He leaned toward me.

"I can't regret it. I wanted it, but guilt is pervasive. And you must promise me, you will not leave Mary, ever."

"I promise. As to discretion, next week I'll take care of how we communicate without a trace. Then we can schedule times to be together. You won't think it weird for me to have sex with Mary, will you?"

"You can be so stupid at times. Of course, you'll have sex with her. I'm not naïve to think you'll forgo any contact with her. She'd know immediately you were unfaithful. I'm the interference, not you. I have to deal with the sordid nature of our relationship. I'm not sure we should see each other."

"You sister is right when she says you are wise beyond your years." He knelt beside me "Kiss me now, a farewell to our day." A guiltless kiss shouldn't be a problem. I leaned to his face and pressed my lips to his.

After our kiss I stood to leave. "Good-night, Roger." He stood, clasping my body to his. I relented and hugged him. I detected a swelling. Pushing away, I said, "Not here." He released his hold.

"I know. I'm sorry. You're as alluring as anyone could be. You're a goddess, like your sister, a beauty, strong and bold, yet vulnerable and delicate. I cannot endure hurting either of you."

"Love me, Roger. Love Mary. Love what we have, and no more."

"She said you are infatuated with me. I told her once, a teenager explores to uncover what they want to know. If you are infatuated with me, I'm okay with that. If you are in love with me, remember I love you, too." We ended our tryst and went to separate rooms for sleep. I figured he might get another chance for fulfillment. I had to chase it from my head.

As I slept dreams of saturnine sexual encounters drained the spirit from me. I created a hell, an everlasting purgatory from which escape was impossible. I loved him and was trapped.

70
CHAPTER

Roger

Vickie and I enjoyed a week together with Mary and the children. We stayed in a crowd, free of suspicion. I investigated various communications devises and settled on a pair of long range walkie-talkies. Multiple channels seemed to insure privacy.

As the end of the next week approached I gave Vickie her radio. We had Sam with us at the park while Mary and Rebecca attended a Thursday morning children's movie about fairies and frogs.

"We can use these to communicate with each other."

"How do we know when we can talk with each other?" I smiled. She always thought of the contingencies of a plan. Mary exhibited some of the same traits, but not as securely as Vickie.

"Figure a time best for you and I'll fit it in to my schedule." As we practiced using the devices, Sam sat in his stroller watching us play. We became proficient for what we needed.

"Can others with walkie-talkies share our channels, or can we lock them out?"

"I don't know, but to be safe, let's not use our names. We can make believe we're spies and have code handles, and steal secrets."

"You're funny, Roger. All right, I'll be Barbie. You be Ken. I know it sounds stupid, but that's the point. Isn't it?"

I assented and we continued our stroll in silence. The day's sun warmed bodies and heart. I wanted her hand in mine but refrained. Neighbors now understood the difference between these twin-like sisters. No improprieties to start rumors and wagging tongues. As much as Mary alienated people, gossips would report the sighting of improper conduct. Before long, some busy-body would relate to another who would tell Mary.

"Do you think we can pull this off?" I wasn't sure why I asked the question. I just knew if something happened to Mary, Vickie could easily replace her, weird as that would be. My mind reeled at the thought of having a steady, sane version of the woman who captured my soul.

"Pulling it off sounds so insensitive. You and Mary are a couple. I wanted to be with you, not some sordid affair where we argue why we can't get more from the other. If I decide to share my body with another male who I find attractive, you have to let me. No arguments, no tantrums, no depression.

"The classic case of an open marriage, I see." My eyes betrayed me.

"Open marriage? You cannot hope to share more than the two Johnson girls or neither one of us will stay with you. Is that clear?" She didn't sound angry but resolute. I understood from where she was coming.

"And you? You can have all the guys you want?"

"I am still looking for a permanent Mr. Right. I am not staying with you for the rest of your life. When I find the person I want to spend a lifetime with, we are finished. I will love you forever but not physically involve myself with you."

"Am I the current Mr. Right?" She smiled, as I grinned at my own joke.

"For what I wanted, yes. But for my future, not necessarily. Let's get Mary back on track to sanity and then you will be Mr. Right for her, as you were when you married."

Having solved the problems of our world, we reverted to the house to find my other ladies home from the movies. "How was the show?" I asked.

"Rebecca seemed to enjoy it. As a first timer, she sat quiet and attentive." Mary showed no sign of regret for having inflicted theater on our daughter.

The rest of the day passed without incident. Why did Mary remain a sane person, as long as her sister stayed and collapsed into a stupor soon after her departure? At least it seemed so to me.

Victoria

Sam needed a change. I bade my excuse and went to the children's room. "Samuel, your father is funny." He looked at me with adoring eyes understanding nothing and absorbing the attention. Walkie-talkies, clandestine meetings, secrets, all spelled disaster. We had no right to our cravings, and still were compelled to explore hungers. With a clean diaper on Sam and happy attitude reestablished in me, we ventured out to find the rest of the family and interact like nothing happened.

"Roger," I heard Mary ask. "Did you and Vickie have a nice walk with Sam?"

"The day is so beautiful, we could not have enjoyed a better time. Vickie is as much a companion to us as you are. We really do have nice family. I'm very blessed."

"I'll miss her when she goes home tonight, but Mom and Dad are due in tomorrow and we'll be together for her birthday celebration this weekend. Mom called and left a message about it."

"I'm having a party at home? I hope it wasn't supposed to be a surprise for me." We all laughed.

"Just act surprised." Roger tried to be funny, but we sisters guffawed the comment. "All right, don't be, but your parents might have a big San Francisco present for you."

"That would be a surprise," I said. I had placed the radio in my travel bag when Sam and I went to his room. Roger gave me the big surprise, and I thought nothing could top it.

We ate a simple lunch of sandwiches and soup. I packed my clothing in the bag with the spy device and waited for Roger to finish cleaning the kitchen with Mary. He had to return to his office, so Mary packed the kids in her car and drove me downtown to the ferry terminal.

"Thanks for taking me to the ferry." We were at a stop light while pedestrians meandered on the cross street.

"I like having you around, and I know Becca and Sam enjoy you." Guilt reared an ugly head. "You and Roger are good for each other, also."

"How do you mean?" Fear of her knowing something happened last week on my birthday, rattled me. "We're good for each other?"

"He's more pleasant when you're staying with us. I know he sees you as another version of me. I guess it gives him satisfaction knowing you and I are so much alike." *More than you might want to know*, I thought. "He can be an example to you of what we missed growing up. The father figure we don't have. The type of male who is responsive and caring." *And those times when you call him insensitive?* My brain attempted to wrap itself around the conversation. What was she saying? Would she condone his having sex with me? Would she be all right if she discovered my reasoning for his being my first experience?

The ferry loaded passengers and cars. I left them unsure of what happened during the week since my birthday. The gift from Roger and the painting from Mary were given to me with heartfelt love. I deserved neither and treasured both. How could I accept a future knowing each wanted something from me for a lifetime that I might not be able to give?

—∞—

As summer sped on to autumn, Roger and I practiced communicating our pseudonyms and meeting at locations in Seattle and Wendlesburg. Employment, as a goal prior to summer, collapsed as a house of cards. Three places expected openings when college students left in the fall. I would be contacted.

Between moments of flight in fantasy, our families gathered for picnics and outings. Mary and I visited the Woodland Park Zoo, Seattle Aquarium, and Pacific Science Center with Rebecca and Sam. Her emotions remained in check, although reports from Roger were sketchier. As expected, when I was with her, Mary exhibited a more well-mannered nature. What was it about Roger which ignited a firestorm?

With the beginning of school I obtained the elusive job at a retail clothing store in Ballard. Close enough to school and a parking spot led to my early departure from home and a leisure walk to the high school.

Andrea and her mother moved into a new condo in Ballard when a marriage to an influential businessman raised their standard of living and access to amenities I ignored most of my life. My friend and I now hung out more often and exchanged stories of our disreputable lives. She was celibate, her term, for the last year, as I plunged into the depths of fornication. We no longer desired the satiation of licentious physical pleasures, but our harmony made for great theater.

My ice princess reputation remained intact and Andrea joined the club. We were two of the best looking and physically attractive females in school, but accusations of playing for the other team came about because of our closeness and lack of heterosexual interaction. It mattered not. We exuded a happiness and contentedness others envied.

"So when are you and Roger seeing each other again?" Andrea approved of the madness of my behavior with him. She understood the attraction to intercourse, if not the closeness one has for another person. We were walking from Ballard High School to the dress shop which was near where she lived. Fridays had nothing to offer either of us, so I worked.

"He's contacting me on Wednesdays at 5 in the afternoon. I make sure to be away from my house so prying ears don't hear telltale evidence. Then we plan our rendezvous. Sometimes we miss opportunities since work and travel become obstacles."

"Is he as good as you wanted him to be?" She asked this question several times since our hooking up again.

"It is what it is. We have a great time together and I'm happy. We experiment which Mary doesn't do. I ask him what pleases him, and he does the same for me."

"Remember all the research we did when we were kids? Have you done any of it with him?" Her prurient inquest embarrassed me.

"None of your business." Arriving at her condo we said good-bye and I went to work. The day plodded to evening and closing of the store at 8 PM. The drive home produced no drama greater than the Ballard Bridge being open, which it wasn't.

The school year plodded like my evenings at the shop. Grades remained my focus as did beginning the search for colleges to attend after graduation. Each paycheck provided money for fueling my Civic and saving for an apartment while in college. Although, my parents' promised to provide tuition and housing, my independence from them was a goal worth any sacrifices endured now.

71
CHAPTER

Roger

Days, weeks, months passed without serious conflict. Mary and I visited with her parents and my parents, and we traveled with our two darlings to Ocean Shores for a fall retreat. Each occasion provided opportunity for closeness and refreshing our lives together. Business prospered better than expected as the housing boom continued, a bubble forming which had to burst at some point. I prepared for the inevitable collapse with income producing properties which need not be sold low after buying high.

Vickie and I communicated regularly on Wednesdays, planning when and where to meet. Summer proved to be the best time as her school year interfered with more contact. We agreed to less time engaging in our lurid affair and more time with families. All was right with the world and I feared the destruction of my life from unknown or non-forecastable disasters.

Mary continued seeing a therapist who seemed to being making headway. However, storms persisted whenever I suggested something different or challenging to her reserve of strength. As autumn and shorter daylight hours commenced the darkness was not only in the sky. Routines confounded her sensibilities and mannerisms more often. I feared a tirade and walked the eggshells the best I could. Lack of Victoria visits deepened the chasm between Mary's lucid and incoherent periods.

Late in November on the Monday as Thanksgiving approached and no plans for a festive day of family gathering commenced, a terrible, physical fight caused bruised arms and broken dishes. I took the children to my parents, returning to find a contrite wife.

"Roger, I'm sorry. Bring the children home. I won't hurt them."

"I don't think you would, but it's not good for them to hear us fighting and throwing things. So I need a promise from you to stop."

Mary approached contrite as a pardoned nun with broken vows. "I promise." I left to retrieve our children for dinner and a quiet evening.

As I sat at my desk after dinner, perusing a land contract, Mary entered, sat at my side on an ottoman, and said, "We have much to be grateful for, you more so than I. Accept my sincerest apology for all the wrongs I have inflicted on you over the years we've been together."

"Thank you. I accept, and I apologize for any wrong I've done to you." She stood, reaching for me, placing a hug around my neck, and a kiss on my mouth.

'Good night, Roger. Good-bye." She walked from the room without looking back at me. I wished she had. I returned to my work, forgetting the moment, losing myself in real estate deals and investment properties. As I completed the tasks, I thought of Victoria and what she freely and willingly gave to me, an advantage taken more carelessly than prudent. She had all of the same physical qualities and looks, the same sharp mind and wit as her sister. She lacked the one injurious deficit of instability which so festered my life as a cancer, suspected to be fatal, over which one fights to conquer regardless of the consequences.

The evening had played its role as well as any thespian on stage, occupying my mind against the afternoon assaults and abuses. I forgave and forgot. Looking at my watch the night became morning. Midnight passed and the stress of previous assignations with Mary, parents, and children wore me to grogginess.

I prepared for bed as quietly as a mouse on Christmas Eve is reported. I lay next to her reaching to be with her. My arm wrapped around her though she stirred not at the intrusion. I slumbered without recalling any time passing.

In the morning darkness, I woke as early as usual but without an alarm ringing in my ears. Mary lay as she had been hours before. I did not think waking her was best, so I prepared for the day and fixed a quick, quiet meal after dressing and left to find better market trends and properties ripe for the picking. I entered the real estate office before any others arrived. I sat in my office reading trade journals and advertisements of other firms.

A noise in the hall jolted me to reality. Janet, my secretary, brought me a cup of tea, a morning libation overlooked until now.

"Thanks."

"How long have you been here?" Her question had no malice but genuine concern for my health.

"I woke early. Mary and the kids were still asleep, so I left them."

"Let me know when you need something." She was the main reason for my success since my organizational skills were worthy of ridicule and abuse. She produced papers needed before requested, brought the proper forms for filling out as needed, and provided the clean desk syndrome of a successful business person.

"Thanks, again." She vacated the room to my momentary isolation. Another sound alerted my senses to another invasion.

The door closed as my father entered and took a seat in front of my desk. "You want to talk about yesterday, son?"

"Not really."

"Your mother was concerned all was not right at your house. She noticed the marks on your arms and Rebecca related in her best language skills that you and Mary were yelling and breaking things."

"It's nothing. We had a fight. That's all. We made up last night. Mary promised to be a better mother and wife and I promised to be more responsive." My lie was historically correct, if not from the previous night, then other nights.

"Are you getting counseling? Is Mary?"

"It's taken care of. She takes her medications regularly and has adjusted to being who she is. We're fine. If something happens. I'll let you know."

"Is her sister around anymore?" My thoughts of Vickie around me rather than us cheated me into another lie.

"We aren't in contact with her as much." I looked away and down. "She's in school and working, so no time is available." He nodded as if accepting my explanations. After he left, I blanked out the reasons for working and left. As I drove my car away to unknown destinations, random in their course, I wondered if I wanted the end of this hell or to continue with the marriage so I could see Vickie and rebuild my own sanity.

Sitting in a parking lot near the local Safeway store, I checked my cell phone, left on buzz, to find two missed calls from the office. Figuring my secretary solved another mystery of mine, I ignored the calls. A voice mail accompanied each call. I retrieved the messages, both of which implored me to contact the office as soon as possible or to return post haste.

I called Vickie's cell instead. I had to have a calming voice clear my head so I could defray the onslaught of work. Her cell went to voice, but I listened to her speech absorbing the sweetness of the sound I treasured for unacceptable reasons.

As I clicked off without leaving a message, my phone buzzed again. Without delay, I answered.

"Roger, I am glad I caught you." Janet sounded frantic as if the world relayed the inevitable bad news of the housing market's collapse.

"What's up?" My innocence concealed any concern.

"You're needed at home, immediately."

"Why? Has something happened?" Fear attacked as no beast of Mary could.

"A sheriff's deputy has been trying to reach you. He's at your house. Oh, Roger I hope nothing's wrong."

"What, when, did he say anything to you?"

"No, he said you need to come home."

"Okay. I'm leaving for there now. Tell my father where I'm going."

I started the car, a foreboding feeling creeping in where loathing my current life had rested. She promised not the hurt the children. What had Mary done now? Guilt for many reasons reared an ugly head.

Victoria

Roger's message scared me. He simply said Mary was in the hospital. Nothing about what happened. Nothing about the children or where they were. Nothing. I raced from school missing my afternoon classes. Running to the parking lot by the dress shop, I sat in my car shaking. Dialing Roger's number was hard, small buttons, fidgeting fingers.

No answer. Panic set in. What happened to Mary? I had to get home. No work for me. Home to pack. To Wendlesburg.

I called the store. "Something's happened to my sister. I have to get to Wendlesburg. Please forgive me. I'll be in tomorrow." My boss griped but I didn't care. "Fire me, if you want, but I'm going." I clicked off and headed home.

Racing into the house, to avoid my parents, I ran up the stairs to my room and pulled a few items out of drawers and into a bag. As I left to catch the next ferry to Wendlesburg, my mother stopped me.

"Where are going in such a hurry?"

"Something's happened to Mary. Roger called and left a message; she's in the hospital."

"I know. Roger called earlier today. She is recovering from an overdose."

"How can you be so calm? How can you just stand there and act like nothing's happened?" I pulled away, but she halted my leaving.

"You must calm down. I was waiting for you to get home from work so we could decide if we are needed."

"Of course, we're needed. Roger has to have help with the kids. He needs me for support. Mary needs me."

"She may have taken too many sleeping pills, deliberately. You have to be ready for that." I dropped my bag.

"Don't say that. She's not trying to kill herself anymore." I wanted to slap my mother, but deep inside me recognition of the possibility ripped my heart in two. One part ached for Mary's disorientation. The other part sought sharing a friend and companion, releasing him from the hell he endured with her.

"Vickie, let me call Roger and see what he wants us to do." My eyes shed the despair with large globules cascading down my cheeks.

"Mom, why would she do it? Why would she desert her family and us…me?" I swiped my sleeve across my face. "She was happy when we saw her, wasn't she?" Remembering the pamphlets from the seminar a year ago, I realized the façade she created for us because she formulated a plan, made a decision, and executed the idea. She was relieved to know and want the end of pain and suffering, endured and caused by her. My mother wrapped her arms around me, holding me during my suffering for Roger and Mary, as much as for me.

"Is she going to be all right?" I asked, not sure of my acceptance of a negative answer.

"Roger says she will have to stay in the hospital until she stabilizes, but she will live. I imagine a psychiatric evaluation will be required."

Picking up my bag I returned to my room to wait. I wished I hadn't listened to his message. I freaked for valid reasons, and reacted confused in how to be attendant to them. Work was the distraction needed, now forfeited. I lay on my bed and closed my eyes. Pictures of Mary cut and bleeding occupied my head, of her taking pills from a bottle, emptied to her hand, and swallowing more than requisite for dying slow and agonized. Or maybe she just went to sleep and never awakened. I wanted to join her, now, and ease the suffering with her. I wanted Roger to make love to me distracting me from the waste my sister revealed.

Tomorrow, I had to be at my sister's side so she knew I was a rock for her. I had to be with Roger to alleviate the misery he must be enduring. I had to hug my nephew and niece who comprehended nothing of the events, just as I was ill-suited to understand at my age of five.

Sleep robbed me of time and grief. I remembered nothing of any dreams bewitching me during the hour or so. I bolted up, anxiety gripping me.

Racing to the door, I flung it open. "Mom. Dad. Is anyone here?" They abandoned me? Had they gone without me? "Mom? Dad? Where are you?" The volume swelled.

"Vickie, why are you shouting?" Mom exited her room. She glared at me as if I was the perpetrator of a massive scam.

"I thought you left me here."

"I looked in on you. You fell asleep. I thought it best for you. I wouldn't go without you. Mary needs you, but not right now. Tomorrow, I'll call Ballard and excuse you from class until after Thanksgiving. You help Roger with the children and we'll forget about a big dinner on Thursday." I acquiesced slinking into my room. The clock reported dinner time about to occur. I checked my mirror for telltale signs of grief, cleaning my face as best I could.

We ate a simple meal together. Dad called to say he would be late and to continue without him. My mind reviled the notion he practiced the same deception as me, a justification for my mother leaving him and becoming the woman she should have been all along.

After dinner I returned to my room and grabbed my bag. I was seventeen and a woman. I could decide for myself what and when I would do something. Let them kick me out of the house, I had alternative places to stay. At least, I hoped I did.

Downstairs, I deposited the bag by the door. "I'm going to Wendlesburg and help Roger." My pronouncement met with disrespect. My father had returned from whatever delayed him.

"You will not leave this house." His edict held no sway with me.

"You cannot stop me from helping your daughter and grandchildren. I have a right to be there where she knows I want to be. I will not abandon her, like you."

"You're an ungrateful person. If you leave, I will cut you off financially and ruin your life. Do you hear me?"

"I hear you. But wouldn't that soil your precious reputation as a respectable parent. I'll tell the world about you abusing Mary and not caring about her suicides. I'm leaving." Mom made no attempt to counter the volume of the quarrel. I opened the door, looked back, and slammed it as I walked away. I wanted never to return, but realized as I drove to downtown Seattle, I still needed them for money, shelter, food, and insurances I did not possess.

I also needed a Roger of my own, so I could live the life I wanted for Mary. She had it, but the psychological remnants of growing up in the Johnson household grabbed on, crippling the success of their marriage.

72

CHAPTER

Roger

Another suicide attempt. I didn't need this. Why does she collapse so deeply and harmfully? I wanted Vickie right now. Just to hold, to love, to hear her lucid voice, to give her what Mary rejected.

"How is she?" I asked a nurse after another examination of her vitals.

"She resting. We'll know more in the morning. You should go home and get some rest of your own." What was at the house to attract me to go there? The children were at my parents for the night. Loneliness did not entice me. If Vickie were here, maybe I would be more inclined to leave. I wanted to call. She was not awaiting a radio call, since it was Monday night. I paced the floor in the hall when my cell buzzed. Vickie? I reached into my pocket, frantic I might miss the call.

"Hello?" The familiar number and name relieved my tension. "Where are you?"

"I'm on the ferry. My parents didn't want me to come, but I left anyway. I probably don't have a home to return to after this." She had a place with me, with Mary and me, as long as she needed.

"I'm sorry. What happened?"

"My Dad and I had a big fight and he threatened to cut me off, so I threatened to tell the world about his sordid behavior with Mary when she was a teenager." As I listened my mind planned a rendezvous which had not occurred for over a month. "Where are you?"

"I'm at the hospital. The kids are with my parents."

"I'll be there as soon as the ferry lands."

"Can you meet me at the house?" Rapacious thoughts overcame sensibility.

"I want to see Mary, first. I'll come there and then we can go to the house." My heart pranced with rapid excitement, the events of the day now mitigated because of a young teenage woman. Would she relent without Mary present? Would other people suspect if we remained alone together the entire night? I didn't care.

In the reception area other people awaited transportation or visitors or any of a variety of events. I waited for one reason. Each clanking of doors captured my attention, but no one arrived or departed for me. How long did it take to drive from the ferry dock to here? I figured fifteen minutes. Then she needed to park the car, a task truly difficult from the sheer volume of visitors and patients. A walk from the external parking garage or lot took time.

I checked my watch again. Fifteen minutes had elapsed since her call. But had the ferry departed Seattle? Or was she half way to here at the time of the call? I didn't know. I turned to catch an elevator to Mary's floor, but the door whirred again. I turned hoping. The person entering was young, blond, beautiful, and not Vickie. I punched the button and waited for an eternity. The young woman waited with me.

"Are you seeing someone in the hospital?" Her question caught me off guard.

"What, oh, yes. I am."

"I hope nothing is seriously wrong." Was she flirting with me? Another time, another place, I could be attracted to her. I glanced at her hands, no rings. I slid my left hand out of sight. Why?

"Nothing serious. My wife is sick. That's all."

"Oh, you're married." She sounded disappointed. Was I? The elevator arrived and we entered. Further conversation suffered a humiliating strangle. As my floor arrived and I walked out, I turned back to a genuine smile and a mouthed good-bye. If I cheated on Mary, could I cheat on Vickie? "Not going to happen." Two ladies were enough.

Mary still slept, resting for the evening. No drugs administered for any assistance with sleep. The doctor in charge didn't want to tempt fate,

I guess. As I strolled back to the elevator, I thought about the woman who rode up with me. What did she want from me as she visited someone else? I pushed the button, watching the numbers flash from floor to floor. As the ding sounded and the doors opened I bumped into Vickie.

"Oh, you're here. Good." We hugged. Her body pressed to mine felt so right. "Let's go see Mary. She's asleep but I know you'll be happy to see she is going to recover."

"Roger, before we go in, did she try to kill herself?"

"Yes. According to the sheriff's deputy, she called 911 saying she couldn't function and take care of her children. I had left for the office. She and the kids were still sleeping. I didn't think she wanted to kill herself. Everything was peaceful."

She turned toward the nurse's station. "What room?"

I led her to Mary. We sat in the two chairs in the room watching the monitor pulse her heart beats, a steady rhythm absent in her conscious state. Exchanging gazes at each other, I smiled at her. She looked away toward her sister.

"If she dies, what are you going to do?" Her question left me empty for a moment.

"She's not dying. She took too many sleeping pills and couldn't function this morning. If she wanted to die, wouldn't she take enough to finish the job?"

"It's a cry for help, but she wants to be free of her manic state."

"She has a psychiatric review tomorrow before she comes home. I don't know what to expect. What if the doctor finds her unfit to be a mother or wife? What if she has to be incarcerated?"

"I think you have some say in whether or not she goes to a nut house."

"You know, if you're going to talk about someone who is in the room, you might want to see if I am listening." Mary sat up in bed a little more watching the surprised expressions on our faces.

'Sweetheart, I'm glad to see you awake." I stood to hug her.

"Vickie, I'm surprised to see you here."

"Sis, I would not abandon you for anything." I stood as well.

"Why am I here?" She watched her machines chirp and whir? "I feel like I've been run over by a truck."

"Do you remember anything about this morning?" Roger sat on the bed and held her hand. Mary's dazed expression explained her lack of information.

"I tried getting the kids up. I couldn't stand up." Her tears puddled. Was she setting a scene or truly distressed? Vickie sat on the other side. Kissing her sister's cheek as a tear dropped from a lash dam, she wrapped an arm around Mary's neck.

"Hey, I'm here for you. Mom and Dad didn't want me to come, but I left home anyway. Dad threatened to cut me off. I don't care. You're more important."

"Thanks, I love you." Ignored by them, I smiled at Vickie's ability to affect transformation in her sister. I wanted to share a night with one and a life with the other. How selfish was I? How selfish were they?

Mary rested at the hospital, reassured about life with her sister in town. I wanted to have the same effect but did not possess the same relationship. We sat in the family room at my house, without children, without anyone aware of our situation. Her car resided in the garage for the evening away from visual confirmation.

"Mary looked good." Delaying the inevitable seemed prudent. "I hope her review goes well." I wanted the woman I met in college to be home.

"She'll be fine when she gets here." Vickie stood and turned to me. Holding out a hand, she said, "Come with me. I want you while Mary is not here, and this will be the only time."

"I don't want you regretting it." I stood and clasped her hand. We proceeded to the bedrooms and stopped in the hall in front of the guest room.

"Would it be weird to sleep in your bed with me instead of Mary? If so, we can sleep in here." Looking at the master bedroom containing an unmade bed and clothes scattered on the floor, I acquiesced to sleeping in the guest room.

The oddness of holding her all evening muddled my sense of proper etiquette. They were so much alike, I dismissed it as baggage unnecessary on this wayward journey. We opted for an affair against our better judgments and the consequences of discovery. Our first night together contained ingredients for abject catastrophe and blissful attainment.

I regretted leaving Mary at the hospital but seized this opportunity to bond with Vickie more deeply than the quickies we tolerated beforehand.

She led me to the bed laying on it clothed but tempting. I joined her and we embraced. Kissing her aroused my physical as well as my emotional elements. I wanted her more than ever before and yet twinges of guilt troubled me. This house was the sacred bond established between husband and wife, now to be cleaved as easily as cutting a ham at dinner. Vickie stroked my neck and shoulders, rolled me on my back and climbed onto me. She kissed me again on the lips, cheeks, eyes, and neck. Her body pressed to mine mingling clothing which restricted sensation of her warmth. I craved the freedom of nakedness and reached to pull off her cardigan. She unbuttoned my shirt letting the front halves lay open, my bare chest exposed.

I reached behind her unclipping her bra which slid off her shoulders and down her arms. I caressed her; she moaned, delighted to embrace the moment. We held each other close with a fervor attained by the absence of a time restraint.

"Take your clothes off. I want to touch your skin and embrace your body." Her words added enthusiasm for making love to her as I had with her sister. They were twins my muddled brain invented. Nothing separated them. I plotted to share them for as long as I could.

Standing naked, we embraced, kissed and made love. In bed we continued our carnal action, exhausting our bodies with the physical endeavors. I wrapped my arms around her, both of us naked and sweaty. We slept until morning awakened us. Did anyone suspect? Did anyone realize what we did?

Victoria

We had broken the bond of man and woman in the house of their making. I coerced Roger to violate a sacred oath to Mary and yet did not regret our union to satisfy a curiosity about Mary's initial transformation from a shy introvert to a sexually fulfilled woman. She piqued my interest in men and one in particular. I wanted it and created the scenario for it to occur. I did not regret his love-making, which fired my attentiveness to venturing into more salacious, wanton sex than Andrea and I had, sexual activity which stimulated his interest in me. I wanted to share all aspects of my curiosity with him.

I did not regret the evening and sleeping with him in his own house. This was the one and only time it would happen. I wanted our affair to continue now because the bond of being with a man aroused my mind and well as my heart.

I regretted that Mary was sharing without knowing, but I knew I could never reveal this secret. And I probably needed to stop. Mary would collapse and finish the deed started this morning if she discovered my unfaithfulness to her. I regretted that I was a selfish, lustful, sane, alternative for Roger.

And yet, I was not willing to quit.

As morning blossomed and I awoke, Roger lay beside me sleeping soundly, like a baby content with his surroundings, not hungry, not wet, not ignored. I watched his chest rise and fall with each breath. His eyes fluttered as he dreamed. Was his dream about us? Mary? His children and family?

My first night with a man pleased me. I received the coveted prize. I wanted his touch again, his body pressing into mine, his member entering me. I wanted and now had what Mary explained to me which ignited the fire burning in me now.

He opened his eyes, blinked and smiled. "Good morning, sunshine. I presume you slept well."

I returned his smile. "I must admit. I am more rested than I expected. I loved sleeping with a man, with you." I sidled to him stroking his chest. Pushing my leg over his legs, I said, "Make love to me again."

"I'm not very clean."

"We'll shower afterward." He rolled me onto my back, kissing me, stroking me, arousing me. He entered and moved with grace as I responded with muscles twitching, aching for another eruption.

As we lay refreshed, but spent, I cuddled into his shoulder. "I never want to lose this. I want to share it with you whenever we can without remorse or shame."

"Let's shower and get breakfast. I'll clean-up around here and then I'll go to the hospital and get Mary. You go to my parents and get the kids."

I rolled away as I answered him. "Alright." My heart ached for attention I did not deserve, but had stolen from my sister while she lay in a hospital bed.

The soap and water washed away the remnants of the night and morning, disguising our activity. We ate a quick breakfast and attended to our assigned duties like soldiers marching to battle.

Roger left before me as I straightened the guestroom, making the bed and picking up discarded male clothing. He made his bed and picked up his room. I took his remaining garments into his room, placing them on a chair.

At Nancy and Walker Waite's house, I rang the bell, awaiting the uncovering of my guilt. Nancy opened the door.

"Well, hello, Vickie. I didn't expect to see you this morning. When did you arrive in town?" Now was my uncovering.

"I came over last night after I heard about Mary."

"Come in, come in. We're planning to go to the hospital and see her today."

"Roger went there to see if she's ready to be discharged." How would I know that? My guilty conscience activated my heart and lungs.

"Really? Did you come from the hospital just now?" My answer had to be honest but not revealing.

"No, I stayed at Roger and Mary's last night. Roger offered the guestroom and I accepted."

"He's very thoughtful. And I bet you have come for Becca and Sam. Again, you display the best of humanity by being there for your sister and for Roger." Maybe for Roger, but this time not for my sister.

"Thank you, I appreciate your comments." One hurdle met and cleared.

"Have you had breakfast?"

"Yes." I relaxed a little with each minute of calm.

"I was feeding the children when you arrived." We entered the kitchen where Sam sat in a highchair and Becca gobbled cereal. Each smiled at me. I relaxed some more.

After satisfying their hunger, I drove with them back to the house to await the return of their parents, or parent, as the case might be. We played with toys and I read them books. Sam took another bottle and slept. Becca and I watched a cartoon movie about fish and crustaceans. I loved these children but was not ready to be a mother. Had preventive treatment mastered its role?

73
CHAPTER

Roger

Mary was awake when I arrived at her room. I watched a moment, remembering our first days and weeks together, our first time, our honeymoon. She had it all, except for one serious deficit.

Victoria possessed no deficit. "Hi, how are you doing this morning?"

Looking at me as if I was accountable for a wrongdoing, which I was, she asked, "How is my sister?" Why was it she could ask a question without knowing the truth of it?

"She's fine. She went to Mom's to get the kids. Are you able to leave, soon?"

"A psychiatrist is coming to evaluate me. The doctor said it's required since I attempted to kill myself. I didn't mean to take some many pills. I really don't remember doing it." Her eyes puddled. "I'm sorry, Roger." Could I hug her? Or be rejected? I had to try.

"Mary, it's okay. It is okay." I accomplished my goal, hugging her, loving her. She relaxed a bit. "Any idea what the psych is looking for?"

"My sanity. The same thing you're trying to figure out. Vickie knows. Ask her, but keep the doc away from her."

"Okay." My own nervousness manifested as a chasm between authenticity and fantasy.

"Where did Vickie sleep last night?" Suspicious?

"In the guest room. Why?"

"Just curious. I figured she came for the night, but I didn't know she stayed here. Doesn't she have school today?"

"She not going back until next week. Your mother's coming today." Watching her descend from a happy person to a conflicted creature, hurt. Could psychology uncover the demons and exorcise them?

"What about Thanksgiving? I've ruined it. I don't deserve anything or anyone. I should've died last night. I can't even make that happen."

"Don't say those things. You and I have a good life. We'll fix it." Her eyes deepened like lapis lazuli. I scanned the room for projectiles near her.

"You can't just take a pill and everything gets better. You need to grow up. I'm not worthy of living. Maybe you and Vickie can have a life together. She's sane. She's my twin, remember?" The storm ruled her, so I retreated to the hall looking for help. I grabbed a nurse who saw the fear in my face.

I stayed by the nurse's station and let them perform magic, if any existed. Did she realize what she said to me? She was not coming home, today. I figured the evaluation might result in her confinement at a facility for the mentally ill. Why did she have these tantrums?

The nurse returned. "She'll be okay. I gave her mild sedative."

"I thought she couldn't have anything like that?"

"She's past the danger point of last night. The doctor ordered it for situations such as this." She sat in her chair and began writing her report in Mary's chart.

I peeked in. Mary lay on her side facing away from the door. I pulled out my cell, walking to an area for privacy and punched in Vickie's number.

Victoria

"Becca, I have a call to answer. I'll finish the book when I'm done. Will you play with your toys, please?" She trundled to her special area and maneuvered blocks.

"Hello, Roger, what's up?"

His speech quivered as if frightening events happened. "I don't think she's ready to come home."

"Why, what happened. I can hear it in your voice."

"A psych is evaluating her this afternoon. She's afraid he might judge her to be crazy."

"Did she say that?"

"Not exactly, but I heard it in what she did say. Vickie, she said she doesn't deserve anything or anyone. That she wanted to die last night. She even said you and I should have a life together because you and she are twins, only you're not insane."

"Can you come home?"

"I don't think I should leave her right now. I don't know if I can continue to do this?"

"Do what, Roger? Stay married to her, or have an affair with me? Or both?"

"I don't know how to help her. You do. You've always helped her. She needs you more than she needs me or the children or anybody." Silence followed as I listened to the defeat of a strong rational man by an assailant never experienced by him growing up.

"We'll help her. Together. We can bring her home and provide a sanctuary for her. I'll finish high school this next year, then I can be more available."

"You can't do that. I'm not ready for you to ruin your life taking care of the two of us."

The phone died as he ended the call. I sat holding it to my ear in disbelief. He was right. He couldn't continue to be married to my sister and survive. He couldn't continue sneaking around to see me, even if it was his only salvation. He couldn't continue to pretend all was going to be better.

I called my mother. "Mom, are you coming over soon?" The message I left whispered a plea for deliverance from children so I could rush to Roger, to reassure him, to reassure Mary. I turned to Becca who remained enthralled by blocks. Sam remained asleep, but I knew the time was short. Checking my phone, it approached nine-thirty. It seemed so much later.

The phone's screen changed indicating a call. I answered. "Mom, where are you?"

"I'm on the ferry. I'll be there in half an hour. How's your sister?"

"Roger's at the hospital. He says she's okay. But a psychiatrist is coming to do an evaluation, and I want to be there when it happens."

"What can you do? She needs her husband. Leave them alone so they can mend each other's hearts." *Gees, sometimes you say the stupidest things.* I understood what my mother was saying. She was right, except for the part which saw Mary's happiness influenced by me, not Roger. And Roger's happiness dependent on me. And my happiness dependent on Roger. I didn't mean to love him. It grew with each contact, each touch, and each moment in his arms.

The call ended. Did she suspect we had a closeness more aligned with matrimony than mere family ties?

74
CHAPTER

Roger

Vickie understood more than any other person I knew. How she understood remained a mystery. I had to make a decision, fateful and lamentable. One of these sisters, beautiful, smart, and distracting, had to be cut loose. I sat in Mary's room waiting for a Doctor Conley, the psychiatrist who would evaluate her. I expected nothing but feared the worst.

"What are you thinking?" Mary lay looking at me as if I was lost in a dream. I was, but it seemed more of a nightmare.

"Nothing really. Just wondering about the psych coming to see you."

"I don't want to do this. Take me home. I have to get out of here." The panic reminded me how she stepped away from reality, how fragile her mind was.

"We'll leave as soon as the doctor says okay. I want to know what I have to do to help you get better."

"So I'm crazy now?" Her stare blazed a hole in me. "You're a bastard. Get me out of here now." A slight nod of my head calmed her. I left for the nurses' station and help for keeping her in the hospital. I hated deceiving her, but that ship sailed with Vickie's birthday.

When I reentered her room, she was dressing in the clothes I brought for her trip home. "Wait a sec, Mary. The nurse said the doctor is coming with the psych within the hour. Can't we just see them and then go?"

She picked up a glass to use against me, then thought better of it. Rationality must have overcome the insanity. She put it on the tray table.

"I should be on my best behavior or they'll send me to Western State." Her laughter hid her fear.

"No reason to be crazy now when we're so close to freedom." My attempted levity flopped. She frowned.

Two white coats entered. "Mrs. Waite, this is Doctor Conley. He's here to administer a battery of tests as required by law. They will be administered so you can be discharged. He will explain the procedure to you and your husband.

"Mr. Waite, I would like some time alone with your wife." Conley held the door open. I looked at Mary and back at Conley. Leaving her with him, I wondered what transpired in her mind. She was not to be taken for someone who was crazy. Her problems were better defined as a mix of anxiety and depression. If this psychiatrist was any good could he unmask her demons and prescribe a cure?

A quick call to Vickie to check on the home fires seemed reasonable. Her phone went to voice mail. "Vickie, call me when you get this." I wondered who occupied her time and how the kids were doing. I wondered if Mary was right about not wanting to live. I wondered about myself forfeiting my marriage vows for the sake of my own sanity with a woman not yet old enough.

I called my mother to assuage my doubts. She usually knew what to say. As I thought about it, I changed my mind. Mom was not to know my doubts. What rumbled around in my brain about leaving Mary for Victoria would not be acceptable to either family, but I had to understand my options. I had to contact an attorney.

As my pacing became intolerable to me and probably the hospital staff, the door to Mary's room opened and Conley signaled to me. I entered and looked at Mary who stared out the window.

"Mr. Waite, please have a seat." I sat next to the bed. "Mr. Waite, your wife is undergoing a mild trauma caused by her belief she has little or no value to herself or society. I am setting up a series of sessions with her to guide her through these mental trials. I hope you will be supportive so she can begin immediately as an outpatient. I want to start tomorrow at 10 AM. I understand you have children. Is someone available to watch them while she comes to my office?"

I stared at him as if he was a statue in a museum. He waited for an answer. "Her sister is here from Seattle and my mother is in town. I'll arrange something. Does she need me to come with her or drive her?"

"I do not need you right now, but it's probably best if she does not drive." My thoughts plowed into a scenario of her deliberately crashing into something.

"I'll see she gets to your office." Dr. Conley left an address in the medical building downtown. As he departed Mary turned to me.

"I'm not crazy. I just don't have the will to fight. I don't want to. You don't love me. I'm alone again. So what's the use of trying?"

"You are not alone. I do love you and you know the kids love you. You have a wonderful sister who adores you. She's at home right now watching Becca and Sam. Can you leave?" She nodded. "Let's get out of here. I'll drive you to Conley's office tomorrow and we'll fix this." Fix this. What a lame comment. Like Mary's a broken doll. I wondered though. Is she broken? Can she be fixed? Did I break her? Would her sister be able to put Mary back together again?

Victoria

I listened to Roger's voice mail. Mom was due to arrive any time, so I punched in the speed dial hoping he'd answer. "Roger, what's up?"

"We're on our way home. I'll tell you about it later. Want to talk with your sister?"

"Yes." Mary spoke in muted tones reflecting the ordeal she endured.

"Hello, Vickie, how are the kids?" I wanted to cry and felt a tear form.

"They're fine. Becca and I have been reading books. She's so smart. Sam is sleeping but will be awake soon. I miss you."

Her silence alarmed me. Her depth of depression seemed greater than before. I wasn't sure I had any helpful ideas to pull her through. Roger returned.

"We'll be home in a few minutes. Call Mom and let her know I need her to help me this week."

"I can stay. And my mother is on her way here. She'll be here as soon as the ferry lands."

"All right, we'll arrange things when I get there." The call ended. Nothing was right. Could Mary get better? My sister had to be my focus. But what could I offer?

Sam awakened as the doorbell rang. Carrying Sam with Rebecca in tow I opened the door. "Hi, Mom. Welcome to the crazy place."

She stared at me. "That isn't very funny." Becca clamped on to her grandmother's leg destabilizing her. "Careful, sweetie." Mom reached out to the door frame for support.

"Becca, let go of Grandma." I reached for her. "Are you okay?"

Steadiness regained, she answered, "Yes, let's go into the family room." I picked up her bag which she dropped. We made our way down the hall and sat on the couch. "How is your sister?" I felt relief she hadn't berated me for leaving without permission the previous evening.

"She's fine. They're on their way here as we speak." I placed Sam on his play mat. Becca sat near him stacking blocks.

"Did you stay here last night?"

"Yes." The inquisition began.

"I'm glad you were here to help Roger with the children." A half-truth was better than an outright lie.

"I love being with them. I know Roger appreciated my being here."

"Have you planned dinner, yet?"

"No. I figured we could order something in and not worry about messing up the house."

"That is not what your sister needs to experience when she gets here. We will prepared a nice casserole and salad. What's in the kitchen?" She scoured the pantry for dry ingredients her mind required for a meal residing in her brain's memory. I watched her many times in awe of her ability to create fine dinners from nothing. Today would be no different.

"What do you need for this?" I opened the refrigerator looking at the bare shelves. No one had shopped lately.

"Look in the freezer for some hamburger."

I found a package marked as 2 pounds of ground sirloin. Noodles and sauces magically blended with thawed meat became a delicious meal. Enough salad materials remained for the finishing touch. No dessert but it was okay.

Roger and Mary arrived during the construction of the repast fit for a patient released to the care of loving family members. I wished for her to comprehend the love we shared and the need for her to be a part of it.

As the evening progressed, children were prepared for sleep and adults tipped toes around the events of the last two days. What was I doing to help Mary remain stable and sane? Our mother provided an environment which fed us physically. Roger demonstrated restraint around me. What did Mary need from us? What did we want from her?

75
CHAPTER

Roger

The next few months challenged Mary and me, as we worked through the madness of a mental syndrome labeled MADD. Mixed Anxiety Depressive Disorder. Days and weeks went well. I continued to meet with Vickie every week or two. Often we talked without engaging in what we both enjoyed.

"Roger, if my sister doesn't get better, what are you going to do?" I didn't want to discuss the unescapable truth of her malady. Her medications had side effects placing demands on her body and spirit.

"Nothing will happen to her." Believing in a miracle gave me the hope I needed for my own sanity to remain. We sat in the park with Becca and Sam. Another spring afternoon, cool but sunny, a weekend before Vickie's spring break from high school.

"How can you be so sure? I've never seen her this way."

"What do you want from me?" I knew what she wanted. I wanted the same thing but nothing about what we wanted made any sense.

"Nothing, if you aren't here for my sister. What we're doing will end. You and Mary will rebuild a stable relationship. I want what you and she had before this collapse. I will find it on my own and leave you to care for my niece and nephew with my sister. Let's get back to the house. Your mom is not going to be happy if we leave her alone for too long."

We gathered our cherubs and walked slowly back to our new universe.

"Mary? Mom?" Entering the kitchen we discovered two women engrossed in food preparation. "What's for dinner?" The scene appeared normal, no anomalies in either person.

My mother responded, "Salmon filets and rice. How were the children?"

"They had fun." I watched Vickie take them to the bedroom, checking Sam for dryness and directing Becca to her potty chair. How did a girl so young have so much maturity? My attraction to her confounded any sensibility I possessed.

"So have you and my sister cooked up some conspiracy against me?" Mary sounded light-hearted but I wondered if she suspected my infidelity.

"A conspiracy? Why no, I don't remember any. Vickie does want to help you with the children this summer after she graduates. She says her job is not an interference." Mary's face reminded me of college when Monica Atherton tried to break us apart.

"I wasn't being serious with you. Why are you being so obtuse?" She turned away, continuing with dinner preparations. I left for the shelter of my office. The years of marriage had not allowed for any education how to deal with her. Vickie worked out the history of her sister's decline. I was an idiot about helping make this marriage work, investigating alternatives which challenged me. I was losing ground and the frustration wore heavily on my soul.

Mom entered my sanctuary. "Roger, what is with you and Mary? She needs you right now and you act like it's a chore you can't stomach." She understood me as much as I did not understand Mary. Was I to be discovered as a fraud?

"I know she does, but sometimes I don't have anything to say to her. She reacts to me like I'm some kind of pariah, someone to claw at and destroy." I looked away from her, perplexed. Real estate sales were straightforward. Find the right property for the right person and get the deal done. No problem. I could not find the right words for the right answer to construct the proper environs of my marriage.

She approached, touching my shoulder. "Maybe your father can talk with you. I know what I want from a husband, but that's only half the battle."

My quiet did not release me from the inquisition. "Are you having an affair?"

"What? No, that's not what troubles me. Mary can switch from wonderful to wondering what happened to her. You've seen it, haven't you? Her mood swing from high to low. I don't know if I can survive it."

"Maybe you need to go to counseling with her."

"I have been. I'm not sure it helps. I don't know what she says to Conley when I'm not there and she doesn't say anything against me when I am. It's like I live with two different people." Mary entered before anything more was said.

"What are you two talking about?" Our faces must have exhibited doubt for her next words surprised me. "I'm not a crazy person. Why does everyone think I can't handle things? Roger, you and your family are no better than mine. No wonder I want out of this life." She stormed out bumping into Vickie, who almost dropped Sam. Rebecca scrutinized her mother run down the hall.

"What was that all about?" Vickie glanced after her sister and back at Roger. "What'd you say to her?"

"Nothing. Mom and I were talking and she came in accusing us of thinking her crazy." I retrieved Becca, hugging her. Mom took Sam from Vickie. "Go. Maybe you can get through to her." Vickie left us. I shrugged my shoulders wondering if I should be doing something, anything. What can a husband do? I had no clue.

Victoria

"What do you want?" Her eyes burned into my heart as I watched my sister retreat into her dark world of despair. I watched her many times traverse this world to which she bolted.

"They didn't mean anything." I sat on the bed beside her. She leaned in hugging me, desperate for contact with an empathetic human she knew growing up.

"What am I to do?" I stroked her hair, leaning on her shoulder. Her darkness abated. "I'm not happy. I can't keep fighting when nothing is going right. I feel alone and no one wants to be with me."

"I'm here and I can be with you as long as you need."

"It's not fair. You need your own life. Find someone. Have sex. Run away with him. Get away from my mad and meaningless life." She disconnected and wandered into the bathroom. I followed until she closed the door. The lock clicked and despair of my own rose thinking she might harm herself again.

"Mary, open the door. Please. I want to talk with you."

"Go away."

"Please, don't do anything." My fists shook in the air. My teeth gritted. That's the first thing out of my mouth? What an idiotic thing to say. "I'm sorry? Did I offend you?"

"No, I need to pee. Go away."

"Alright, but I'll be here when you come out." I waited for a few minutes, then approached the door. A click greeted me before I said a word.

"You still here?" Mary sparkled again, like nothing happened. "Dinner should be ready by now." I had forgotten about the time. She interlaced her fingers in mine, dragging me down the hall to the kitchen. I wondered how her mind fluctuated so widely in so little time.

"Okay." The only word which escaped from the plethora in my head. I was numb.

At dinner our conversation consisted of children, Waite family experiences, but nothing regarding Mary's mental challenges...

"Can we go to Seattle tomorrow? I want the kids to see the aquarium." Mary's question caught us off guard.

Roger reacted first. "Great idea. We can make a day of it." His face blanked for a moment. "I have an appointment at 9, but we can leave after that, have lunch on the waterfront and then walk to the aquarium." Mary smiled. Why? I didn't comprehend the change. In our history no transformation like this had occurred. Was she getting better? Truly better?

—⊙⊗⊙—

Roger never complained, as much as he explained, his interactions with Mary over the weeks before my graduation. Fights and arguments became more commonplace and contentious. I witnessed one over Memorial weekend. My sister acted as if someone was stalking her. She skipped outings to the park and stores. She deserted the Kitsap Mall, a favorite escape haven.

I spent the weekend with them to help plan Rebecca's and Sam's birthday party. My eighteenth birthday celebration lost appeal when Mary attacked Roger over a trivial loss of time. He needed to be out completing two house closings. I took Mary and the children to the mall shopping for gifts and party supplies. She complained about Roger's lack of attention.

"Mary, he is taking wonderful care of you and the kids." I held her arm as she pushed the carriage with two cherubs sleeping.

"I know you believe he's wonderful, but I want more than money and things. Someone to love me without using me for his own needs."

"Do you still think about what Dad did to you?"

"Sometimes, but it's more like he says he loves me and then wants to get away as fast as possible."

"Are you having sex with him?"

"Still curious about that? Not as often. He leaves when I'm interested and he acts like I'm a bitch when I don't want it and he does." I unhooked my arm aware of the reason for his lack of interest.

"He's probably working too hard, Maybe he can give up more to be with you."

"You are naïve to think he's more interested in me than money. He's just like Dad when it comes to it."

"Is he abusive?"

"Like hitting me? No, but the lack of attention is worse than being molested. At least Dad paid attention to me. Roger ignores me."

"Do you still love him?"

"I don't know. I'm mad at him more than hating him." Her words stabbed me in the heart. He admitted his waning feelings to me. I begged him not to give up on her. To love her. To use me and not love me. But I wanted his love. I wanted to feel and share what my sister experienced. Guilt hurt, and yet nothing changed.

"I love you, Mary. Keeping loving him and he'll keep loving you. Don't let anything stop what you have."

We finished acquiring our purchases and headed home. As we drove beside the water inlets of Puget Sound admiring the beauty of the scene, Mary's mood declined the closer to home we got. What happened when they were alone which created a fear of being home?

76
CHAPTER

Roger

Filling in forms bored me. I plugged away at them thinking of Victoria and her graduation. Mary's comment about my absence and focus on work irked me. Why would I destroy my children's future? Yet Mary constituted an enigma to me. Should I divorce her? Could I get custody of Sam and Becca? Only by destroying Mary. And I promised Vickie I wouldn't.

"Roger, the Chastains are here for their appointment." Janet's entry broke my mental excursion. "Are you all right?" I was caught.

"Yeah, send them in." I finished the paperwork with my clients and decided to return to the house and face the music. Nothing was worth fighting with Mary or Vickie or anyone.

As I walked past my father's office, I peaked in. "Dad, I have nothing more on my calendar for today, I'm heading home."

"Is everything okay?" He stood waving me into the room. As he closed the door he continued, "Be frank with me. What's happening between you and Mary? Is she doing alright?"

"Yeah, but she thinks I work too much. Money is not the end all be all with her. She came from a wealthy family and does not see it as the answer to happiness."

"Your mother says the same thing. Find the balance between making a living and living a good life." He hugged me longer than expected. "Go home. I can take care of everything here."

I nodded and left his office. The ride through town strengthen my resolve to make our marriage better, but contacting an attorney was not out of the question. If I couldn't handle the outbursts, I had to leave. Should I take the children with me? What about alimony and property splits.

I devised a plan to hide some of my holdings in other names to secure them for my future if a breakup occurred. Vickie and I needed a rendez-vous spot. Maybe she could live in it when she moved from her parents' house. Would she move to a dorm on a college campus? Where was she going to college? Was she going to college?

Having one's mind bounce from one idea to another didn't lend itself to thinking straight. "Mary needs me." Words to no one, words for me to believe. I drove through the city with care which was how I wanted my life to be from now on.

Nothing should derail the world I created when I met Mary. Vickie, a distraction but not easy to give away, had a life as much as I had with any-one in my past. And her relationship to Mary complicated her dismissal. But a dismantling of marriage had greater complications. Contacting an attorney meant a serious step for me. I didn't feel ready. Fear of what oth-ers might think? Maybe. I wasn't sure.

So I drove. Not home but around the neighborhood. Around the cen-ter of my life and the abstract construct of complications unintended and unwanted. I made some, but so much of my current situation arrived with Mary and her decline into hell.

Time to face my situation. I arrived as Vickie and Mary exited our SUV with two wonderful children and several packages. How was Vickie able to convince Mary to leave the house? So many times she accomplished that which I wanted and failed at so miserably.

I parked beside them, smiling as I exited the car, hoping both women were happy with me and children excited to see me.

"I see you two dented the bank account again. Can I help with any-thing?" Each handed me a package which I carried to the house.

Inside I placed my burdens on the kitchen table and turned to relieve Mary of hers. Sam was easy to gather but how was I to help her remove mental burdens?

"How was shopping?" An innocent question with guilt written into it. Sam wriggled to be free. I placed him on the floor and watched as he crawled to his highchair. Vickie picked him up as I listened for an answer. Mary left the room ignoring my inquiry.

"We had fun. We got what we needed for the party and a few other surprises." Becca sat in a chair at the table expectant of her own treasure. I placed a sliced apple next to her.

"Did the kids behave?" I wanted to ask more pertinent questions but feared an explosion if the object of the questions happened to return.

"Yes, they are the best children in the world." Vickie snuggled Sam as he sat. She had a jar of pears in hand, opened the lid and sat to feed him. I sat next to her. With her hands occupied, I placed my foot next to hers, our knees touching. She did not retreat.

Victoria

My high school graduation came and went as did Sam and Becca's birthdays. I was accepted as a freshman at Seattle Pacific University on the north side of Queen Anne Hill, close enough to home to see family. I wanted a place of my own, an apartment for me to get out of the house and experience my new found adulthood. I hoped Roger would visit me, but he said he and I should not be seen together where my mother or father might drop by unexpectedly. He was right. A small house in Fremont across the ship canal from school became our rendezvous spot.

Mary's routine visits to see Dr. Conley faded as the days of summer began to shorten. Roger and she did not fight but co-existed, neither wanting to harm the children mentally. Family gatherings at Mom and Dad's house in Seattle or at the Waite's house in Wendlesburg belied the torment burning in Roger like a smoldering fire.

"I can't do this anymore." We sat in the park near his house in late August. I came over to stay on weekends to help Mary when my job allowed the opportunity. Sam toddled around the bench we sat on while Becca climbed the ladder of the slide and squealed with each descent.

I wanted to touch him, embrace his pain, to ease the conflict destroying his dream. I witnessed one battle in the war raging at home. Mary stormed with little apparent cause for her anger. She lashed out at me for being an interference. I couldn't dispute her argument although she did not proffer any reason for it.

"Please, see Dr. Conley with her. See him alone. Find a way to make it work. Getting angry with her is not going to solve anything." He picked up my hands in his.

"You are so much like her. You fill my life as she did before these demons. I want to leave her but I can't leave Sam and Becca. I want us to have a chance of finding the elusive golden ring." I pulled my hands from his.

"Roger, I will not destroy my sister to be with you. No one in our two families would ever accept our being a couple unless Mary died." I thought of her killing herself and Roger finding his elusive happiness with me. But dreams can be nightmares and any scenario involving suicide created it for me.

"Yeah, if she had been successful with one of her attempts at dying, this conversation would be very different. I don't foresee her trying again. All I see these days is her anger and irrational behavior."

"So, you need to be strong for her. Forgive her. Love her." His countenance bore no support for my premise. "Listen, I'll come over on weekends as much as I can."

"You keep me sane." He leaned close. "I want to make love to you. I ache to touch you. I miss you touching me." A twinge of guilt and desire mingled with his words.

"Mary might not want to kill herself now, but I'm not sure she would refrain from harming us if she discovered our secret."

"I have an apartment complex on Maple that has an empty unit. Meet me there in an hour."

"You're insane if you think she wouldn't suspect something if both of us left the house. You are already suspected of not being faithful. She's told me so."

He collapsed as Becca squealed again and Sam abruptly sat down next to the swing set. "I'm trapped. I'm unfaithful because you are as alluring and desirable as she used to be. I don't want to return to my college philosophy of sex. I really want a family as stable as my parents."

"Mary wants the same thing. She wants what you had from your childhood. She missed out on normal."

"So why are you normal? Why are you what I want in a woman, which I thought I had with Mary? Why can't it come back to me?" I had no response. Silence quelled further investigation.

We collected our charges and returned to the house. Each of us burned for the other and the embers of a marriage running out of fuel to sustain it haunted the situation. How could I want Mary to die so I could be with Roger? Was I selfish enough to ignore the next attempt and let her accomplish finality? What if Roger broke her and made it happen? Could I be with such a man? Would Becca and Sam understand?

Roger

As we walked back to the house and an uncertain climate, I wanted to hold Vickie's hand. Becca became a proxy. Sam rode in the comfort of his carriage. As the silence continued my thoughts wandered out of control.

How would Mary killing herself solve any of the dilemma in which I lived? Why would I push her to the brink and force an attempt? When did this situation become so complex, so convoluted, so impossible?

I stopped walking. "Vickie, we have to help Mary get better. What we're doing is out of control, and she deserves better from us."

"Are you breaking up with me?" Her smile belied the felicity of her question.

"Stop making fun of me. I meant what I said. I need Mary to be healthy. We need her healthy. These kids need her."

"I get it. I didn't mean to be flip." She pushed the cart toward home.

Picking up Becca, I caught up to her. "I'm not afraid of getting the right help for her. She deserves it."

"Yes, she does. So do it and I'll help any way I'm able." She kept going. I wasn't losing her. I had two women who loved me and whom I loved. One needed assistance to live a normal life. The other supported me so I could live a normal life. How was I skillful enough to accomplish both objectives without being honest to myself?

PART
FOUR

REDEMPTION

77
CHAPTER

Victoria

Seattle Pacific University offered residence dormitories but an apartment was my goal. A place for me to be an adult. A place for me to be who I wanted to be. A place where I could act my way without explanations.

Andrea and I met downtown to celebrate my eighteenth birthday. She still lived in Ballard with her mother and new step-father. She remained free of male influences, an idea which I knew I should review.

"I hope you get what you want. Maybe you and Roger can hook up more often if you have an apartment."

"We talked about it.

"Does your sister still have mental problems?"

"Yeah, I think she's getting worse. Roger and she are seeing a shrink, trying to save their marriage, but I don't know how he stands the abuse when she is in one of her moods."

"If he broke up with her, you two could be together."

"Not something either of us want to happen. I love him, but it would be too weird." We sat silent as food arrived at the table outside on the Red Robin veranda, a rare occasion in June. The sun spilled across the water creating sparkles on the extraordinarily calm Puget Sound. A Washington State ferry plied its way to the Colman Dock, as a jet approached SeaTac Airport.

"Is your family celebrating your birthday?"

"They're combining graduation with it. I'm getting a trip to Hawaii as a present. It should be fun, in spite of their traveling with me." I grinned. "At least I have a room to myself."

"I'm jealous."

"Want to come along? They might accept my bringing a friend so I stay out of trouble."

"Yeah, two hot eighteen year olds, staying out of trouble." We laughed. As we finished consuming burgers, I thought about us together, hanging out, enjoying being friends. We didn't have to pick up guys. We understood our needs and desires and sex was not part of it.

The wait staff gathered at the table with a piece of Mud Pie adorned with a candle. They sang happy birthday to me and we savored each bite. I felt contented. I didn't need a distraction or inducement to be happy. I needed a healthy sister and a wonderful brother-in-law. Roger and I had to stop.

Andrea and I promised to meet again before summer passed. My parents hadn't extended the same practice of gifting to my brother and sister. I was included in this journey to abrogate any reason for leaving me home alone. I negotiated for Andrea to be a companion for me, to keep me occupied, out of trouble. He acquiesced and paid for Andrea as I requested. The trip came off without a hitch.

Ben congratulated me, and exhibited no jealousy. Mary reacted with happiness, but I sensed a resentment, something given without grievance, without reluctance. Her New York adventure as a teenager had failed.

When college began in September, I agreed to live at home for the first semester, learning to be a student on a university campus. A move into an apartment for the second half of my freshman year, agreed to by Mom and Dad, to be close to home, seemed to endear me to my father for reasons I missed.

As summer came to a close, Roger and I sat on the queen bed of a one room apartment in a building near the Seattle Center which he had procured seven months ago. Ten of the twelve units were occupied and rents more than covered the mortgage and reparations requirements. He kept the small loft unoccupied.

"Mary's not any easier to live with." Roger cast his vision toward the floor. Our rendezvous was only the third time we met during a frustrating summer of seeing each other, but we only talked.

"Don't give up on her." I placed a hand in his. "She can surprise you just when you think she's finished."

"It's just hard to be near her and have her ramble on about something which makes no sense. I try to help and she hits me or throws stuff." I raised his hand to my mouth and kissed it. "I want you and know I can't have you. You've made that clear enough."

"I'm sorry. You know how I feel about you and why I can't hurt my sister. Throwing her away like a broken toy isn't an option." I placed his hand on my left breast. "My heart is yours. My soul. My everything."

"Can we forget about her for now? I want a person who loves me without conditions. A person I love without reservations." He unbuttoned the top three buttons, leaning in to kiss my bared skin.

I pushed him away. "Promise. Mary is your first priority." He nodded and we consummated our liaison. Had he agreed so he could have sex or did he mean what he promised and truly wanted Mary to get well?

Roger

Lying on the bed next to Victoria, I envisioned Mary as a college student, fresh, alive, lucid, no abrogation of mental stability. Vickie occupied space in my brain for the young woman who enthralled me then and frustrated me now. Extracting a promise from me regarding her sister didn't relieve a feeling of impending doom. My personality was disappearing in the maelstrom of her sister's tirades.

"I have to be in Wendlesburg before three." My watch indicated noon's approach. If I missed the ferry, a long drive through Tacoma awaited. "I have to leave." I rose from the bed and dressed. Vickie lay on the bed, her naked body enticing me to stay.

"I'll lock up. You go to Mary and the kids. Love them as much as you love me."

I picked up my valise containing the early morning meeting's paperwork and departed.

On the ferry I sat in my car on the auto deck unwilling to observe prying eyes who might know me. I was risking everything to satisfy a lust for a mind and body lost in one woman and found in another. A conversation with our attorney, Jeff Woodbury, merited attention. Although a criminal defense attorney, my father and he had established a rapport when they were students at the University of Washington.

I called his office as the boat made its final turn into the inlet where Wendlesburg existed. Jeff agreed to see me at the end of the week.

At the office I filed the sales agreement with Janet, picked up messages from clients and went to my cubicle. Nothing in my life had returned a profit from investment except for the acquisition of land and buildings. They provided financial stability but failed to fill the emptiness in my existence. I understood less about Mary's life each time I thought about my own. I had to find meaning for being the person I was and wanted to be. Conley kept asking the same questions: 'What does it mean to you?', and 'How does that make you feel?' I wanted to slap him, force answers out of him. He was the psych. Did he learn anything while getting his doctorate in meaningless questions?

I read an article about real estate sales approaches and wondered if any of the tips for closing deals might work with Mary or Victoria. I smirked and flipped the ideas out of my head. Clients were one thing, but trying to use sales language at home would only lead to suffering more humiliating confrontations. My children deserved better. The tension affected them as they clamored for calm amidst the storms of our adult conflicts.

As the day waned, I bolstered my spirit to face the onslaught of another evening with Mary and her insane way of communicating. I drove slowly and deliberately, delaying the inevitable.

Remembering my morning, I smiled. She lived life as if nothing could impede her. What happened to her sister plunged our marriage into a canyon of despair. In our driveway euphoria faded as fast as a fogged window on a warm day.

Entering the kitchen I announce my presence. "Mary, I'm home." A disturbing silence answered me. I explored the house but found no one. Clothes were scattered around the children's bedroom. I entered our room and found a suitcase on the floor with some clothing in it. Had she left, taking my family with her? Where could she have gone?

I hastened to the garage, checking for her car. It was missing. I investigated the family room and the kitchen. Panic churned my brain to incoherent mush. Had she followed me to Seattle? Had she uncovered my lies or conversations with Vickie?

"Where are you?" I shouted at the walls. A yellow sheet of paper, stuck on the refrigerator, caught my attention. Reading it, I recognized what Mary had done.

78

CHAPTER

Victoria

"This is such a surprise." Returning home. I discovered my nephew, niece, and sister entertaining Mom in the family room. "Does Roger know you're here?"

"I left him a note. I wanted to get out of the house and this seemed the best place to come." Mary acted without concerns or demons. She appeared calm, although something roiled within her.

"How long are you staying?" Mary suspected Roger's infidelity and came to investigate what I might know.

"We're staying for the weekend. After that I don't know." I dragged her away from Mom into the hallway, away from prying ears, and an inquisitive parent.

"What's going on? Are you leaving Roger? What's he done to you?" Words flew out, vindictive, accusing?

"No, I'm not leaving him. I just needed to get out of the house while I think through my life." She whispered, glancing around as if Mom might be listening. "I can't keep living this lie of me being a worthwhile person. I'm taking a short vacation." She looked me in the eyes as she continued. "You cannot tell him where I'm going."

'That's easy. You haven't told me."

"Come with me."

"What? I can't leave right now. I'm starting college in less than a month. I have lots to do to get ready. I have a job."

"Vickie, are you hearing me?"

"Uh, yeah. What?" I felt slapped back to reality. Now Mary worked to keep me on an even keel. "You were saying."

"I was saying you can quit your job early, since I know you planned to quit before school started. You have no financial worries because of Mom and Dad. And I can front you money anytime you need it." My brain fried with the information inundating it.

I walked into the living room from the foyer. "When are you going to inform Roger you no longer want him?" Thinking of taking her place in his life can make the mind play crazy games when evidence belies the truth.

"That's not what I said. I merely want some time alone, well actually, with you." I slumped into an overstuffed wing chair.

"Where to, then?" Resigning my life to an insane sister while involved with her husband didn't make any sense. What in my life was making any sense of late? Maybe a vacation with Mary was what we both needed. Maybe I needed consideration of what I was doing.

"I was thinking about San Francisco."

"Have you asked Mom to watch Becca and Sam?"

"Not yet, but if you're not willing to go, will you help her?"

"You know I will." Getting away from Roger and complications with consequences no person should endure seemed like the best action. "Let's ask Mom. We'd have a better time together in San Francisco."

We returned to the family room. Mary spoke before I could. "Mom, if Vickie and I take a short vacation, would you be willing to take care of Becca and Sam?" Her lucidity came at the most advantageous times.

"What are you planning to do? And by short, what do you mean?" Mom stepped closer to us ignoring Sam's pleas for more attention. "Is there something you two have done?"

Mary answered her question. "No. I need to get away for a while and I want Vickie with me. She isn't working right now and doesn't start school for another month."

"Have you spoken to Roger about this?" I remained silent; nothing about this exchange required my interplay.

"No, but he knows I came here with the children. He should be contacting me soon."

"What then? What if he doesn't agree to let you travel?"

The dark storm eyes brewed quick as a magic spell conjured by the wicked witch of the west. "He cannot stop me. He is not my master."

"You promised to love and obey him when you married."

"I promise to love him; obeying was never part of the deal." A fight about marriage vows had little sway for now.

"Mary needs to get away, Mom. I'll go with her to keep things level. Please, watch the kids." Mary's storm abated as I spoke. The phone rang casting a pall on the room.

Marion picked up the receiver in the kitchen. "Hello?" Silence followed. "She's here. Do you want to speak with her?" More silence and a reappearance of stormy eyes. Mary shook her head slowly staring at her mother with daggers. "I'll see what I can do." She hung up the phone.

"What does he want?" Mary's atmosphere chilled as a winter day darkened by heavy gray clouds.

Roger

Mary's note was clear. She wanted to be free of me. Forever? Or for now. She took the kids, not for vengeance, but for safety. I hated her and loved her. She loved our children in a convoluted way, but did she love me?

Calling the Johnson family home, I expected Marion, hoped for Mary, and wanted Vickie to answer. "Hi, Marion. It's Roger. Is Mary there?" Confirming my suspicion. "I want her to return home. She has taken the children and made it clear she is not returning. I want my children back. If she wants to run away, that's her choice. Stealing my children is not. Will you put her on the phone?" I waited. "Listen, I figure she's detracting your conversation. So, please let me know when she leaves. I'll come over and get the kids. Can you do this? Just say, 'I'll see what I can do.' I expect to hear from you."

I clicked off my cell. Looking at the note, I reread Mary's words. 'Roger, I know you and I aren't doing well together. I need to get away for a little while. I have taken Becca and Sam to my parents. Please don't contact me or try to find me. I will return when I want and we can figure out what we want to do. As much as I say I hate you, I do still love you. You found me when I was a lost soul and saved me from my own destruction. Attempts to harm to myself are not who I really am. Please take care of yourself. Mary.'

I clicked on my cell and called Woodbury's office again. After the usual banter I said, "Have him call me as soon as he returns from court."

"Damn it, Mary." In my home office I investigated protecting assets which Mary might want if we divorced. A wall safe could be installed while she was gone. I looked up the best installer in Wendlesburg from a recommendation in an online rating site. "*Better safe than sorry*," I thought. The pun made me laugh.

After arranging for the installer to have entry to the house the next day, I clicked on my cell again and dialed my Dad.

"I need some time to follow up on a situation at home."

"Are you and Mary in trouble?" Not desiring to reveal her deserting our home, I lied.

"Mary and I want to leave town for a while, to be together without kids. Marion's agreed to watch them. I just wanted you and Mom to not worry about us."

"Are you sure nothing is wrong?"

"Yeah, I'm sure." Gritting my teeth, I finished. "We're heading over to Spokane. She has a couple of friends from Wazzu there and we want to see them." My lie dug into my heart. I hadn't lied to my parents before now. Omission of any confession of sins, notwithstanding. Mary was running and I had to catch her before she crushed my future. "I'll let you know when I get back." I ended the call before any more words pierced the façade I created.

Packing a few clothes in the suitcase left by Mary, I departed the house for my car. At the ferry terminal, I watched the boat depart for Seattle. The next scheduled departure was an hour later. Waiting in line gave me time to reflect on Mary's exploit. I had to get to her before she disappeared. Vickie might be my best option for understanding why her sister was running.

Afternoon traded into a nap in the warmth of the day. Dreams of a woman running in a crowd, a man chasing her, leaving a trail of broken people, crashed into my brain. I heard the man yelling but was unable to hear what he said. The woman screamed to be left alone. The other people stared and whispered about another woman. The man stopped, returned the stare of the people, and yelled he was not cheating. A loud whistle awaken me to the arrival of the Seattle ferry.

My brain reeled from the memory of the strangeness created from the shattered pieces of my life. I had to get to Mary before anything untoward happened to us. I needed Vickie to steady her sister's mental escapade to whatever or wherever she was headed.

As I approached the Johnson home in Magnolia, I wondered how many triggers existed to fire Mary's irrational thoughts. If I could understand her reasons for tirades, I knew they could be ameliorated and our future secured. Vickie would understand. After all, she insisted on me staying with Mary. But could I?

79
CHAPTER

Victoria

"Come on, Vickie. Let's go."

"Are you serious? We're driving to San Francisco? Do you know how far it is?" We stood in the middle of the living room, bags in hand. "I thought you might want to take the train or fly or something. But drive?"

"Oh come on. It's not like you can't. You're the strong one, remember? You can do anything. I've heard you say it." The radiance emanating from my sister's face glowed with the expectance of a yellow sunrise shimmering through the new growth on trees in spring. I could not recall an exuberance for doing something irrational, insane, and crazy without involving morbid thinking. Mary radiated life. I had to follow to see if she maintained it. I knew I was accompanying her because I didn't trust the vision.

"Well, then let's get going." We bounded to her car, placing bags in the back and releasing child car seats from backseat constrains, which were left for use by Marion. "You drive. I'll take over when you want me to."

As we headed down Magnolia Boulevard to Western Avenue, I wondered what Mary thought. This unexpected lark, did she want to leave him? Would she run from raising her children? Was she chasing rainbows, looking for an elusive pot of gold? I couldn't figure her motivation for this illogical act.

Leaving Seattle's downtown we drove the Viaduct to Highway 519, bypassing Interstate 5. The route took us by SeaTac International Airport, but we didn't stop. Mary drove past South Center Mall and headed for Tacoma. I watched the radiance expand as if, for the first time in her life, she escaped a prison holding her away from her true self. She relaxed and enjoyed the moments of traveling away from her doldrums.

"How far do you want to get today?" My question raised no storms or angry eyes. She smiled.

"As far as we want. Maybe Portland." I closed my eyes and napped. Three hours passed with nary a whimper of regret from the driver.

"Hey, sis, wake up. I need food."

"Where are we?" Groggy eyes struggled to focus on the scenery along the highway.

"Just crossed the Columbia River. Do you know of any place to eat?"

"No, I've never been to Portland. Get off the highway and drive around. It's getting late." The sun rode low in the sky, casting long shadows. "Maybe we should find a place to stay." Mary took an exit labeled 'Downtown'. We found an upscale Hyatt along the Willamette River.

After settling in to our room, we explored the area for a restaurant. Mary's attitude remained upbeat. I had a new sister I didn't recognize, but appreciated. I wanted to explore how deep her calm exterior penetrated. Maybe a trip away had been the needed therapy her psychiatrist missed.

"Maybe we should pick up guys and take them back to the room." Mary glinted with excitement. I didn't know if she was serious. My visage exposed concerns. "Oh, relax. I'm kidding. Your virginity shall remain intact until you give it up, willingly."

Embarrassment must have caused a blush. My cheeks experienced a warming. "*If you only knew.*" My thoughts ran to Roger and the anguish he must have experienced upon reading the note left for him.

"I don't think you're kidding. Roger's been your only partner. I bet you want another man to know whether he is the one. Isn't that it?"

"I guess."

"I'm not up to finding someone. Besides, I want someone who loves me and cares about what I want. I don't need to have sex just to lose my virginity in such a tawdry manner."

"Gees, you sound like some old fogey with a moral stick up her ass. Remember, you're eighteen now and legal."

"Would you cheat on Roger?" My question welled up in my throat as a bad taste.

"He's cheating on me."

Panic assaulted my brain. "How do you know? With whom?"

"He's gone a lot and I'm not much of a companion when I'm stressed out and yelling at him. I don't know." A sadness appeared on her face. Tears fell from her eyes. Mary held my hand.

"He loves you. He's a good man, you've said so. Trust him. I do." My thoughts rambled on about my morning escapade. No one knew and it had to be kept secret.

"Come on, I'll buy us some wine, my new drug of choice. I'm avoiding pills for now." She headed into a small grocery shop. I followed to keep her out of trouble.

In the room she found a corkscrew and pulled the cork, pouring two glasses. Handing one to me, she made a toast. "Here's to freedom, if only for a short period of time." She drank all of the contents in a single swallow. I placed my glass on the table.

Silence separated us as I prepared for bed. Mary followed suit. I had nothing to say as she drained the bottle of its contents. I climbed into one of the queen beds, pretending to sleep. Instead of finishing nightly actions, she lay on the other bed and passed out, half undressed. Her dreams had to haunt her about Roger's fidelity and her future as a married woman. I hoped my dreams left me alone. What would tomorrow bring?

Roger

"Where are they?" Marion remained silent. "Please tell me."

"Roger, they're on a trip and I'm not sure where they went." I picked up Sam from his play area, sitting down next to Rebecca on a chair at her play table.

"I worry Mary has left for good." Nothing made sense to me. My lie, notwithstanding, I now had to be gone away from family, children, work, and common sense just to make my ruse believable. Any contact by my parents, with Mary's parents, shattered the illusion.

"Mary and Vickie are fine. They drove away vowing to return in a few days. Do you want the children back with you?"

"No, I have to find them. I'll call and locate where they've gone. I know this is an imposition."

"Go find them. I'll be okay with the children." I left the house and drove to my apartment building loft. At least I had a place to hide for the time they were gone.

Dialing Vickie's phone, I hoped for a truthful answer to my inquiry of their escape, but it went to voice mail. "Vickie, when you hear this please send me a message telling me where you are." Next I called Mary's number realizing a storm could arise from my invading her plans. The phone went to voice mail as well. Neither wanted discovery, I concluded.

Alone in the apartment I thought about my years with Mary and producing two children. My life was good, even with Mary's rants and raves against me. She was a beautiful, intelligent woman with a problem which together we could solve. Vickie was a beautiful, intelligent woman without a problem whose adolescent infatuation captured my imagination and complicated life. I thought about how these two persons were alike in looks, but so different in temperament. Each had an outlook on life which contrasted their family upbringing. I wanted one because she captured my heart, hanging me on her every moment in college. The other gave freely of herself to uncover what love meant when physically expressed. Now both were running from my selfish wanton lusts and expectations.

Evening and hunger spurred me to prepare a simple meal from the inadequate supplies stocked by me when I bought the building. Never imagining to live in the room, I forewent the requirements of occupation. I ate a meager sandwich and drank a diet soda. Hunger was assuaged for the moment. Where were they?

80
CHAPTER

Victoria

Watching Mary, I wondered if she truly wanted out of her marriage. She had much to gain from staying but tirades drove a wedge between her and Roger. Drove him to me. Drove me away from her.

I loved her but she was not easy to love. I thought I knew best how to help, but recent behavior challenged my precepts about her. I woke her, helped her complete her undressing, and helped her lie under covers. Barely conscious, she cooperated and returned to sleeping.

Picking up my phone, I realized I had no way to recharge it. To save what energy was left I decided to turn it off, first checking for messages. Roger's face popped up. My heart fluttered, a tingle entwining my body. I dialed his number, but stopped before clicking the send button. Mary wanted to be free for now. To honor her request, I powered off. I climbed into bed and hoped for peace.

In the morning we continued our drive south into northern California. "Let's drive down 101 through the redwoods." We stayed another night in Crescent City, California, in a moderate hotel with two double beds over-looking the Pacific Ocean. On our way the next morning we took a side trip to one of the large trees which can be driven through. The scenery was spectacular. Mary was so relaxed and happy, I dared not ask her if she missed her children or Roger.

We arrived in Marin County and parked on the north side of the Golden Gate Bridge. Clouds shrouded the upper stanchions but the view was outstanding. After a stroll around the area, we returned to the car and completed the trip into the city. Unbeknownst to me, Mary had arranged several nights at one of the finest hotels. Could she continue her happiness and enthusiastic attitude when she returned to Wendlesburg? I hoped she would keep it while in San Francisco.

Roger
I dialed Mary's cell with no response. Vickie's phone went right to voice mail. I left another message asking her to contact me. Night and frustration persuaded me to sleep.

Stripping off clothing, I climbed into the bed occupied by Vickie and me only hours earlier. I missed her. She responded to my love-making with gusto and satisfied me in a way I did not experience with Mary. "Where are you?" I echoed as Morpheus waved across my wakefulness.

Morning broke with no news or messages. My hideout reverberated the emptiness. I had nowhere to go and nothing to do. I could drive around Seattle but to no avail. Anticipation of a call from either sister gave me some hope. I turned on the television mindlessly listening to the banter of news personnel. After dressing I rummaged around the kitchen, but nothing attracted attention. Dare I venture out to a nearby restaurant?

My deception had not been thought through. I remained marooned in an apartment while two ladies ventured freely somewhere in the nearby world. Checking my phone, I noticed the battery warning symbol. I plugged in the charger to the phone and wall. No need to start my quest without any contact possibility.

Who did I miss most? My children, certainly. Vickie? Definitely. Mary? I wanted to miss her. I wanted to think of life without her as a miserable life. I wanted my wife to be the most important person, but insanity challenged that attitude. I had to wait. I had nothing to gain from continuing an affair with Victoria. I knew staying with Mary was correct, but how long could I endure the misery she felt and I experienced.

Throwing caution to the wind as hunger overcame fear, breakfast tasted good at the Denny's near the apartment building. No one looked familiar as I sneaked peeks expecting a tail Mary hired to prove my infidelity. She had never accused me directly, imagination fueled this absurdity. Finished eating I paid and returned to my detention. Another day of empty worry and non-action. I checked my phone to see how the charging progressed. I noticed a message from Vickie.

"Roger, Mary and I are on a road trip to San Francisco. She is a different person right now and I don't know why. Please be happy for her and stay put in Wendlesburg. I'll call you as soon as I can be away from her. Love you."

San Francisco? Driving? Fly there on the off chance Mary would accept my being present? I had to chance it. If Vickie wanted to see me, I would be ecstatic.

How would I handle both woman in the same place? Vickie understood any relationship had to be with Mary. Clicking on my laptop, I checked for flights. Alaska Airlines flew just about every hour. I booked an early afternoon excursion.

As I packed the few possessions I carried with me, I thought how stupid this trip was. I had no reason to chase either of them and ruin any possibility for stability in my life. But chase I would. Was I being irrational? I thought Mary had been. And now I wanted to get away from it all and enjoy the same freedom. Was I being rash?

81
CHAPTER

Victoria

Calling Roger was foolish. I had no idea what he might do but feared he could show up. Mary would not forgive me. My phone's power waned so no more calls. I needed to buy a power cord.

Ordering breakfast while Mary still slept, I sat on the veranda of our rooms overlooking downtown and San Francisco Bay thinking about the previous evening's arrival. The room came equipped with all of the amenities expected in an upscale suite. I had made coffee in the kitchenette, a pleasant change from my usual tea.

"Why did you book such an expensive room?" It had a living room with a mini-kitchen off to one side. One bedroom adjoined the main room with its own bathroom. Another room was accessed by way of a double lock set of doors, available for larger parties of vacationers. Mary booked it for me. The veranda, large enough for a table and four chairs, was accessed through French doors.

"Why not. I can afford this and I want to play. Creature comforts come first." She tipped the bellman a twenty and asked for directions to a swank restaurant for dinner. He suggested Scoma's on Fisherman's Wharf and arranged a reservation. Our journey into fantasyland started.

A knock back to reality, announced the arrival of breakfast. I accepted the cart and tipped the young lady. The bedroom door opened and Mary emerged in underwear and open bathrobe.

"I thought I heard a knock at the door." She closed and tied her robed. I grinned at her modesty with me.

"I ordered breakfast. Thought you might like some waffles and bacon. I got scramble eggs, also. And orange juice. Coffee is in the kitchenette." I rolled the cart to the veranda, placed the dishes on the table and sat down to eat. Mary retrieved a cup of coffee and joined me, her mood euphoric again.

"I could eat a horse."

"Yeah? You wouldn't like it. Want a waffle? There's enough here for several people."

We consumed all of the food which seemed meant for a family of four. I hadn't looked at the charge but assumed it to be large. Roger would hit the ceiling when he found out. The vacation lark was setting their finances back. It had to be. Mom and Dad could easily afford to stay in a hotel like this one and not hurt later. Mary dented Roger's income, but the dent was probably fixable.

Throughout the day we visited the tourist traps by way of the trolley car system which traversed the hills. My sister acted like a kid in a candy store with no limit. We even went to one near Ghirardelli Square. Her mood flashed a freedom from the restraints, real and imagined, which confined her life as a wife and parent. She had no one to impress or family values to uphold. I was happy for her.

"I need to stop in an electronics store to get a charging cable for my phone." I avoided a shop which looked like it ripped off tourists with over-priced items marked down and on sale at a regular price in another place.

"I brought one. Does it work with your cell?" We compared phones but the different style plug prevented its use.

A Radio Shack on Lombard carried my charge cord. "Let's go back to the hotel. I'm tired."

"I guess. We've had a lot of fun today. What shall we do for dinner?"

"Let's eat in the room. We can order from the menu and relax on the veranda." I hailed a cab since I didn't want to wait for the cable car "How much is this trip costing you?" My question, asked while we rode to the hotel, invoked curiosity as to what Mary expected when Roger uncovered the charges.

"I don't know, but I haven't exceeded the credit limit, yet." After an order of Pacific salmon grilled on cedar plank and steamed vegetables with wild rice at the hotel's restaurant, we prepared for bed and a restful sleep. Mary drank several of the small liquor bottles with the soda mixers and passed into slumber with ease, her new source of medicines.

After my phone finished charging, I checked for messages from Roger or anyone wondering what we were doing. No one had called. Perplexed, I dared myself to find out what Roger thought, I click his number and waited for a fateful response.

Roger

The flight to the Bay area lasted just over two hours with snacks and drinks. Unable to contact Mary or Victoria my anxiety increased about their escapade and what it meant for our futures. The late afternoon sun cast shadows extending across the runway as we taxied to the gate. I clicked the power button starting my phone. I expected nothing and was not surprised when no message or missed call showed.

I caught the shuttle to the rental car building. With a compact car I drove into the city. First, I wanted a place to stay and a restaurant to satisfy my hunger. Airplane snacks did not fill the need.

Traffic on Highway 101 was heavy, frustrating. I had no idea where to stay or how to find Mary and Vickie without a call from one of them. The cars stopped so I clicked the browser of my phone to search an inexpensive place which didn't have bed bugs or a low rating. A honk from behind reminded me to move forward a few feet and close the space.

Checking again when stopped, I scrolled down and found a Hilton near the Embarcadero. I punched the GPS tracker, having no idea how to get to the hotel.

As I approached San Francisco, traffic opened up and I made better time. After checking in to a small room, I found a place to eat where I washed down a burger and fries with a lager. With the bill paid I started to walk back to my room when my phone rang.

"Vickie?" I checked the number to be sure. "Where are you?"

"I don't think I should tell you."

"I'm in San Francisco at the Hilton near Union Square. Where can we meet?"

"Look, I called to let you know Mary is doing well. She's free of any pressures to perform as wife and mother. She has not had any breakdowns or fits." I heard the stress of fighting back tears.

"Is she planning to leave me or come home?" I dreaded the answered. Neither one held a satisfying conclusion, but Vickie wanted me to stay with Mary. Silence answered my question. I didn't want to raise my children alone, and I knew Vickie would not fill the void. "I need to see you. Tell me where you are so I can come to you, or you come to the Hilton."

"Roger, it's not possible. If she wakes up and I'm not here, I don't know what she'll do."

"Then I'll come to you. I promise to behave." I began returning to the hotel. "I rented a car. I'll be to you as soon as I can."

"She not leaving you. I convinced her she needed you and the kids more than she needed to run away. She wants to get the help you and I both want for her." I stopped. At least I understood my position, now. Vickie and I had little time left. We had to end it. Mary would be away for a while, but Vickie would be busy in school. Mom could provide the child care while I worked. I acquiesced.

"Vickie, call me in the morning. Let me talk to Mary. I won't tell her I'm here, but I want her to know I love her and need her to return home. I glad she wants to get help, but I don't know how to help her like you do. You're an amazing woman."

The phone clicked off. I kept it to my ear thinking about what transpired. I scared her. I might have lost her telling her I loved her, but I couldn't lie. I loved both women for reasons as different and as alike as any tabloid rag sheet could create and promulgate. My life shattered before me, and now I had no way out. Locked into a fragile marriage and chained to an illicit affair.

I returned to my room. The double bed beckoned me to collapse and sleep. I prepared for a fitful night hoping for rest. Night overtook day without so much as a hint of it happening. Clouds obscured the sun as twilight darkened the sky. I climbed in, closing my eyes, wishing.

82
CHAPTER

Victoria

Roger followed us. I thought he might and he told me where he was. Checking on Mary, who remained quiet and peaceful-looking, her demons exorcised for now, I went to my room to sleep.

"Why did you call him?" My whispered voice echoed back from the mirror. I wanted to see him, tell him I loved him. Mary had to share him whether she discerned or not. No, I had to stop this irrational behavior. I'm the stable one. I fulfilled my fantasy and sated his lust, but I had the ability to distinguish between reality and make-believe. I had to end meeting with Roger. Mary had the right to call him husband and expect his loyalty. I could not. I was the problem who mucked up the operation. I climbed into bed.

As I stared at the ceiling through the darkness a movie played with scenes which tortured and frightened me. Mary wanted to be dead. Why couldn't I help her? The characters on the ceiling played out as if real and connected to me. Odd music beset my ears. One female cried out to be killed. Another female pulled out a revolver and pulled the trigger. The loudness of the silence shook me awake. My breathing labored as my heart raced.

Morpheus betrayed me. I got out of bed, went out on the veranda to clear my head. I realized the falseness of my dream and feared the reality of what I might be capable of doing. Could I kill someone? My sister? Roger? The prospects of such acts sobered me. I wanted it clear of me. I decided to do the one thing I shouldn't. I returned to my room and dressed, gathered my wallet and room key and left for the lobby. Standing in front of the elevator, I hesitated pushing the button. What was I doing? I can't leave her. What if she needs me?

The bell for the elevator dinged its arrival. I hadn't punched the button. The door opened and a man smiled at me as he passed. He walked toward our rooms. I wanted to run after him, telling him to leave us alone. Mary wasn't ready. He unlocked a door and disappeared. It wasn't Roger. Imagination is a tricky thing.

The doors began to close. I plunged my arm into the void. In the car, I pushed L and rode to a destination to be avoided.

As I checked the map on my cell phone, I had second thoughts about what I was doing. The lateness of the night and unfamiliarity of the city shouted for caution. But the warm air revived my intention of seeing Roger. He had chased us here and it meant a lot to me that he wanted to be where I was. I had to see him. Tell him I dreamed he wanted to be with me.

In front of the hotel I stared at the doors. One of the bellmen spoke. "May I help you?" I jumped, startled by his comment.

"Yes. A friend of mine is staying here, I think, and I want to contact him. I don't know what his room number is."

"Miss, we don't condone any salacious activity in our hotel. Do I need to call the police?"

"What? No. I'm from Seattle and drove here with my sister. He flew in this afternoon."

He led me to the concierge's desk. There I found a house phone and dialed the operator who connected me with Roger's room as requested. My heart pounded as if to explode. I was sure others heard the thunder in my chest. What if he wasn't there? What if he refused to see me? Deciding I was being a foolish teenager, I started to hang up.

"Hello?" I heard from the receiver. "Is anyone there?"

"Roger?" My voice must have been louder than needed as several people turned to look.

"Vickie. Where are you? How did you get this number?"

"I'm in the lobby. Can I come up?" The plea escaped much as begging, not asking.

"I'll be right down." He didn't want me in his room? He didn't want me. He didn't. Want. Me. Streams ran from the blue pools of my face. I turned to leave. I couldn't face him if he rejected me.

Roger

The phone's ring shocked me awake. "Hello? Is anyone there?"

"Roger?"

"Vickie. Where are you? How did you get this number?"

"I'm in the lobby. Can I come up?"

What did she want? "I'll be right down." I hung up and dressed as fast as I could. Knowing her she would leave and I would miss her.

In the lobby she stood by the entrance, a lost lamb not knowing which way to go. I approached and stood behind her.

"Roger." She turned having seen me in the glass's reflection. The darkness outside created a mirror. She set her jaw.

"I'm sorry. I panicked. You caught me off guard." I reached for her. She cringed. "Come on, let's go outside and talk."

"Are you afraid to be alone with me in your room? Afraid I'll seduce you? Afraid you'll want me instead of my sister?" Her venom scared me. She was acting so much like Mary and yet the turbulence did not exist. People stared. A bellman approached.

"Okay. My room." I grabbed her arm and led her to the elevator. In the elevator she leaned in to kiss me. I flinched.

The doors opened and I guided her to my room. Inside she tried again and I reciprocated. She reached for the buttons of her blouse. I placed my hands on hers.

"No, explain this madcap dash to escape."

"Mary had enough of her life. This has been therapeutic for her. She's relaxed and happy." I released her hands and sat in a chair. "She's not leaving you, but this time has to be hers to enjoy alone, without you or Rebecca or Sam."

"She should have told me she wanted some time alone. I would have granted it."

Vickie's head rocked back and forth. "That's the problem. You think you're allowed to run her life and grant her things. She can make up her own mind. Just like me." Vickie moved toward the door. "I wanted to be with you for a little while. I guess I don't have permission." She opened the door, turned to look at me and started out.

"I'm sorry. Please. Stay." I rose from the chair and went to her. Vickie closed the door. "We need to evaluate what we're doing. I came after both of you for different reasons. Mary deserves my fidelity. You deserve someone who can be with you long term." She sat on the bed.

"What are you saying? Don't you love me?"

"You got what you wanted from me."

"You got from me what you wanted. So, do you love me?"

"I love you," were the last words I uttered.

83
CHAPTER

Victoria

Sitting on the bed, I wondered if Roger meant what he said. I feared he did and had transferred his love for Mary. I didn't care but he had to still love her, as well.

"Roger, do you still love my sister?"

"I think so. It's getting complicated, though. You're complete, whole. Nothing fazes you. You handle everything with maturity and wisdom I seldom have in me. Mary is the first woman who captured my heart and soul. Her mental state is a challenge and that's why it gets complicated. If she sought the necessary help to cure or at least control her mental gymnastics, it would make life more tolerable." I stood and opened the door. He stood and moved next to me. I wanted to strip off clothes and seduce him, but I now knew we were finished. His loyalty was to Mary.

"Don't leave her. Something will happen to fix all of this. Be sure of that. You and I love her and will find a solution." I opened the door and ran to the elevator. Tears formed. I betrayed her in heart and mind. If she uncovered our past activities, she'd kill me, or worse, herself. I had to act before she did.

As I hurried back to my hotel, the earliness of the morning, and the danger of being exposed to crime as a single female on a San Francisco street, hit me. Eyes widened as I realized possible peril awaited me around every corner. I should have hailed a cab, but none appeared for my rescue. I was alone in the world for the moment and alone in my soul for a lifetime.

Turning the last street corner offered our hotel entry and my relief. I sighed. My next encounter with danger slept in a suite near the top floor. The sky remained black illumined by artificial means. Dawn was a couple of hours away, yet an impending doom haunted my mind, thinking of Mary in a tirade because I snuck out on her and met someone.

I scurried to the elevators pressing the up button. I wanted to see Roger again, to hold him, and caress him. I wanted him hold me and caress me. I wanted him each day and night. My sister's trauma prevented his happiness with her. If she left him…

The elevator arrived at my floor. The man who been on it when I left my room was in the hall again with a full ice bucket in hand.

"Hello, we meet again." His comment caught me off guard. I did not want to speak with anyone, but politeness is best.

"Hello. Yes, I remember."

"I guess we're neighbors. I'm across the hall from you." He didn't need to inform me of his whereabouts as if he wanted to engage in a pick-up line I rejected. I nodded acknowledgment and continued to my room. He wasn't repulsive but his age was at least twice mine and a woman probably awaited his return. I pressed the key card into the slot and opened my door. Quietude was an ally. I closed it with care.

Stripping off my clothing, I went to the bathroom and washed all traces of sordidness from my body. Naked and damp, I climbed into bed. Hoping to sleep soon, I plunged deep into the covers curling the pillow around my head.

The man across the hall was active at an odd hour. His seeing me at the same time presented a problem. He could alert her to my escapade and ruin the rest of the trip. We had to begin our return to normality soon, the sooner the better. I dozed as I wondered about Roger and Mary and me and the man across the hall.

"Hey, sleepy head. Are you getting up soon? It's almost eight o'clock. Let's go out for breakfast to that little café down the street." Eight? I got three hours sleep. I stirred in the bed forgetting my lack of pajamas.

"Let me sleep a little longer. Take a shower or something."

Mary yanked the covers before I could stop her. "Well, when did you begin sleeping in the raw?" I pulled them back to cover my humility and embarrassment.

"None of your business. Get out and I'll get up."

"What did you do last night after I drank myself into a stupor?" I had no real answer for her which would keep her from knowing.

"After helping you, I watched some TV, showered, and went to bed." Well, at least all of that was true. Leaving out the night sojourn wasn't really a lie. "When did you start drinking so much?"

"I am having a week long party."

"A week? How can you afford a week in this place?" I jumped out of bed despite my exposure. "Seriously, Roger's going to blow when he gets the bill. I thought we could start back tomorrow."

"You want to leave, go ahead. Take the car. I'll fly home when I'm ready." She moved toward the common doors, then turned. "You really do have a better body than I did at eighteen. I should be jealous and don't show it to Roger." She winked and left my room. I blushed.

I dressed in jeans and a tee with a blouse over it. Entering the suite I asked again, "Who's paying for this? Did you ask Mom for money or a credit card? Roger will have a fit."

"What do I care if he's upset? Mom gave me some cash and her credit card. Dad can pony up for his history with me."

"Mom's going to throw her own fit, then. And Dad? He's so tight he'll let you go broke rather than help."

"You let me worry about it. Let's get some breakfast." I had to admit, Mary was as calm and sane as ever I had seen. She was becoming a new person, relaxed and assured. Why should I stop it? My concern was Roger and how he would react to his new and improved wife. My life with him now ended, I had to be real.

After breakfast we rode the cable cars to the Embarcadero Center for some shopping. I had no plans to contact Roger or inform Mary of his having followed us because of my contacting him. But I wanted some assurance of how she was going to conclude this irrational romp from everyday living.

"Sis, I have to admit this has been fun." Before I could say more she stopped me with a finger on my lips.

"But, we need to get back to my children and reality, is that it?"

I nodded. "I don't know how Roger is going to accept this. I don't want you and him to break up over this." Guilt permeated.

"Then let me handle it. For the first time in my life I am free to be who I want to be. I have no responsibilities and certainly no cares. I love my husband and I will fight for my marriage. I needed this getaway and counseling with Conley helped me decide to do it. Since I now know I can be this person, I can be the other without the drama."

"Alright, I get it. You're different, so I guess all is okay. Roger better love the new you or I'll break his legs."

"Little sister, such violence. I thought you were a pacifist."

"You better love him, too."

"Or more violence?" She smiled and hooked her arm in mine. "I do and will. You should find someone like him." More guilt.

Our trip concluded after another three days. Roger flew back to Seattle to await our return. How were we all going to explain the diversity of our stories? Roger and I discussed it, but he and Mary passed as ships in the night.

Roger

Mary had changed after her trip to San Francisco and for the better, as far as I was concerned. Our marriage was better and the children sensed the calmer seas of life. After tallying the expenses, I decided the therapeutic value was less than the cost of continual counselling and medications. Mary's parents had covered the charges on her mother's credit card. Garrett was not happy but accepted it.

I met with Woodbury about divorcing her and concluded the expense of it to be far more than I was willing to pay, monetarily and emotionally. He gave me a copy of the decree which I stored in my desk for future reference if needed. I marked the document for changes I saw as prudent.

Vickie and I communicated every couple of weeks mostly discussing the new and improved sister and wife. Although sex ended with the impromptu vacation, I had all I wanted.

Counseling helped us both until the stress of building a family and interactions with her father caused a slide in Mary's temperament. Vickie and I planned for weekends to help her cope. I was taking the kids to church each week and Vickie came to stay with her sister and help her deal with the return of stormy atmospheres.

Business continued to improve as property values rose and Wendlesburg grew in population. I amassed a small fortune which I thought I needed for Mary's future. We discussed seeking help from professionals in Seattle, but she balked.

She grew more distant as days became weeks, and then months. Another year passed and I feared old demons had invaded her mind. In spring an opportunity for me to advance my career came up.

"Mary, I have to be out of town for a week at a real estate convention with my father. If you want me to stay I'll cancel. Dad will understand."

"Sure he will. He'll think I can't handle things, like before and he'll get you on his side. You go. I want you out of my life for now. I can handle it."

"Call your sister, and see if she can come over. Contact Mom for help, if you need it."

"When is the conference?" Her question was empty of real interest and concern. I feigned excitement for her sake.

"We leave next week on Tuesday and will be back Sunday night."

"Go. Have fun and forget about me for a while."

"You sound upset. I won't be gone long and it is a valuable experience for me, for us." The chill of depressing atmosphere ended further conversation. A return to physical fights was not going to happen.

Sitting in my office at home, I wondered if I lost my wife a second time. Vickie agreed to help convince her to get professional help and we strategized how to accomplish it. Now I needed her to help me with the current low pressure zone. I pulled out the radio we used to contact each other. Our prearranged time wasn't for another two days. I had to wait.

"Roger," Mary appeared at my door. "I'm sorry. I didn't mean to sound mad. You need to go and enjoy time with your dad." I relaxed and got up to hug her. She did not resist but returned it with affection. With Rebecca and Sam asleep the evening settled into a romantic conclusion. Why was she so different with each different minute of the day or night?

84
CHAPTER

Victoria

"Vickie, with Roger at his conference can you stay with me this weekend?" Mary sounded like anxiety controlled her mind. Roger left on Tuesday and now on Thursday she was falling apart. I knew she wanted help with Becca and Sam more than she wanted me, but I loved my niece and nephew.

"I have to finish my classes tomorrow, but I can be there by four. Are you okay?"

"I miss having an adult around. Maybe I made a mistake not finding a job when I graduated. I don't know. I'll see you tomorrow; I'll be fine until then." Something in her voice told me another concern was eating at her.

Mary, what's wrong? You can tell me. If nobody is to know, I can keep a secret." Even from you. Silence reigned for the moment.

"I'll tell you tomorrow." She clicked off leaving me wondering if she knew and wanted to confront me in person. My enthusiasm for studying waned as I pondered her words. Although Roger and I spoke regularly, a history of contact did not exist as the radio communications worked like a charm. But the charm would sour if Mary suspected infidelity involving me. I slept a fitful, tossing night with hallucinations haunting my dreams.

In classes I heard little of the teachers' lectures or directions. My scribbles did not stand the scrutiny of study patterns for testing.

Since moving into my own apartment, my parental contacts were confined to weekends. I explained to Mom about Mary's request and my being absent this Saturday and Sunday. After completing my psychology class I was free to head west. I went to the apartment, gathered my travel bag, and headed to the ferry terminal.

Anxiety of my own rose as the boat approached the dock in Wendlesburg. What did she know about us? How much damage had we inflicted on an already fragile psyche? I wished Roger was home, but his absence would help me to ameliorate any confrontation which arose.

In front of their house I pondered my words. Sighing, I resigned myself to accepting whatever Mary had to say. My apology was engrained in my head.

Becca came bounding out the front door as I exited my car. "Aunt Vickie, hi." Her language skills had become remarkable for a four year old. We hugged and she guided me with her hand to the entryway. Mary greeted us as if nothing bothered her. We hugged, as well, longer than usual.

"Thanks for coming. Is Mom alright with it?"

"Yes, I explained you wanting help with the kids. She understands." I placed my bag by the staircase. "What's for dinner?"

"You're always hungry. I thought I was bad when pregnant." She paused, looking at me funny. "Are you...?"

"What? Pregnant? No. That would take an immaculate conception and I know of only one of those." My head shook in disbelief. "Is that what you were worried about last night? Being pregnant?"

"I'm not pregnant. I just finished my period. And Roger and I aren't exactly priming the pump." My familiarity with her sex life popped the guilt mood again. She had something else on her mind.

"So what is for dinner, then?" A raised eyebrow and a tilted head elevated the importance of the question.

"You make me laugh. I'm ordering pizza from D 'Angelo's. If you're really good we can have beer with it. I won't tell anyone you're underage."

"Good." Her mood contradicted my theory of betrayal, so I dropped it and my apology. We entered the family room where Sam smiled at me and ran over to clasp my legs in love.

Dinner's arrival came shortly after and we ate in peace. I still wondered what troubled Mary, but no longer feared it was me. After preparing Becca and Sam for bed, we sat in the family room and talked about raising kids and our parents. Bursting with curiosity, I asked, "What's on your mind? You said you'd tell me. And I will keep it a secret."

She hesitated, stood, walked away, and turned. "I think Roger's cheating on me." The words stabbed me deeply. She did suspect us. My face heated, my heart raced, breathing became shallow.

"What…why do you think he's cheating?" My word sneaked out in terror of her answer.

"He's not attentive to me and sometimes he comes home with another scent on him." My body powder betrayed me. "He works all the time."

"That doesn't prove anything. Maybe his clients hug him because they are so pleased with the deals he makes for them." I had to deflect from my concupiscence for him. "Maybe he wants to please you with his success."

"Maybe, but the real kicker here is I saw someone, or think I saw someone, from his past."

"Who?" I hadn't been in Wendlesburg lately, but this brush with Mary's suspicions left me doubting my own sanity. Did she see me as competition for Roger's affections?

"It doesn't matter, but she was part of his life before me, and with our problems, or rather my problems, maybe he's hooked up with her again."

I relaxed, not being the other woman. "Maybe this other lady is here on business. Do you have any proof?"

"No, and I don't want any. He would deny it, anyway." Mary sat again.

"I'm so sorry. Maybe I can find out something for you. He and I get along pretty well. Maybe I can get him to open up and spill the beans."

"I don't want you involved in this. Except, I do want you to do me a favor." She fidgeted as she spoke.

"Sure, anything."

"I'm not sure about how safe I am. I want you to get me a gun. I'll give you my ID and the money. You can fill out the paperwork and pick it up when registered."

My hackles raised with this request. "Why do you need a gun? Are you afraid of what Roger might do? Or this woman you saw?" She was not stable enough to use a gun and her history of mental problems ought to intercede. "I don't think I should do this."

"Please, I wouldn't ask if it was not important. I'll feel better knowing I have a way of stopping an intruder." *Killing Roger or committing suicide,* I thought.

"Let me think about it. I just worry having it in the house might end up with something bad happening." What was she up to? She didn't need a weapon. Or was she threatened? Was this other woman from Roger's past a problem? Did Mary want to eliminate her and needed the gun to do it?

Roger

I arrived back from the conference with a mountain of information and an out-of-state client list. Excited to share my new learning, I called from the airport.

"Vickie? What are doing in Wendlesburg?" My surprise answerer floored me. "It's good to hear your voice."

"Mary asked me to come over while you were gone. I've been here since Friday afternoon."

"Is she available?"

"Just minute." The phone clinked on the counter. In the background I heard the TV and Rebecca's laughter. Calm prevailed at home. I relaxed.

"Hello, Roger." Mary sounded great. Vickie worked wonders with her sister, which I wanted to recreate.

"I called to say we landed a little while ago and as soon as we get the car we'll be home. I've missed you and the kids. I learned a lot."

"I am glad to hear the trip was worth your time. See you when you get here." No 'I love you' from her.

"Alright, then, I love you. See you soon." I clicked off. We started on the hour long drive from SeaTac to Wendlesburg.

"How are things at home?" My father's inquiry could have been innocent but I assumed he was probing again.

"Fine. I heard Becca laughing in the background. Vickie came over to stay with Mary for the weekend. I'm glad those two get along so well. It helps Mary a lot."

"I want you to have a life like your mother and me. She is my ally, friend, and dare I say, lover. Can you say the same about you and Mary?

If you can, then I applaud what you have." I kept driving, not responding but contemplating his comments. Did Mary and I have an ally, friend type of marriage? The lover part suffered from her depression. But my ally and friend was in reality, Vickie. No longer my lover, though.

As we approached home I thought about the ladies who confounded my life. One in turmoil. One a youth. I stopped in front of my parents' house, said good-bye to Dad, and started to my house. What was I going to find?

"Daddy," Rebecca squealed. I picked her up, kissed her and walked into the house with her. Vickie stood in the doorway with a sheepish smile coursing her face.

"Hello, you," she said. We walked into the family room to find Mary with Sam. Rebecca wiggled to get down. I approached hoping a calm prevailed.

"I'm so glad to be home." I hugged Sam and Mary. No rejection. The atmosphere remained warm with no storms. I relaxed.

"I'm glad you're home. I missed you." She kissed me a second time and placed Sam in my hands. "I have a dinner to finish." She wandered off to the kitchen. Vickie and I sat on the sofa watching the kids play.

"I'm glad you came over help. How's it been?"

"Mary's fine. She and I've been running errands and shopping. You have the nicest children. So tell me about the conference?"

"It was fine. I learned more about real estate and how to gain market share." Vickie stifled a yawn. "I'm boring you, aren't I?"

'No, I've been up a lot with Sam at night so Mary can sleep. He's been cranky." Her hand slid over to mine, just touching my fingers. My heart beat hurried.

I whispered "careful," drawing attention from Becca. Looking at her I winked. Vickie withdrew her hand. In stillness we watched the kids again while they continued playing.

85
CHAPTER

Victoria

He looked so fine when he returned. I wanted him but Mary had first right. Dinner had been delicious and my weekend with Mary and the kids had been fun. I didn't know what to make of her request of me to buy her a gun. If somebody was in town who knew Roger before Mary snagged him, it could be an old girlfriend.

The announcement to return to our cars shook me back to reality. The ferry horn announced our arrival in Seattle. I walked down the stairs to the deck and readied for the signal to drive off. Mary's mind plays tricks on her. Maybe nobody was in town. So why get a weapon? I drove off, turning onto Alaska Way to head to Queen Anne Hill and my apartment. Should I tell Roger about the request?

The lateness of the night made for fewer cars to impede traffic flow. I arrived within ten minutes of leaving the ferry. I was tired and thinking about Mary's wish, and what implications existed if she wanted Roger dead, increased the fatigue. If she knew about what I had done, I could be the target of her delirium.

My fidgety sleep left me unwilling to attend the one class on my schedule for Monday. My job didn't start until afternoon so the several hours of morning, misallocated as they were, raised my angst. Mary thought Roger was cheating. He had. She thought she saw another woman who knew Roger. I did not know. She suspected this woman was the object of

Roger's attention. She was not. She wanted a weapon to protect her from an unknown rival. I was the rival.

What possible need does she have for a gun? I could buy it for her. Keep it from her. Use it against her, if needed. She cannot harm Roger or her children and I will protect them. If Roger is seeing this illusory woman, then he cheated on me, as well.

I had no hold on him. He is free to see anyone he wanted, but he made a promise to my sister to love her until death. His or hers? Did it matter? Work distracted my mental gymnastics until evening and another bout with sleep rang into uncertainty. I dreamt of several grotesque entities who attacked each other. No one survived the onslaughts when I awoke unrefreshed and irritable.

I skipped no classes today. But my notes were doodles of stick figures fighting for liberty and freedom from the neighborhood gossip mongers. I decided Mary was right. I was going to help her out by obtaining a weapon so she could have the illusion of protection. She had to have firearms training if she wanted me to do her dastardly deed. I could train with her, if Roger's mother watched the children. Better I know what to do in case of a slip by Mary.

"Mary, I'll take care of it for you." I called that Tuesday evening to set an agenda for my sojourn into ill-advised purchases.

"Thank you. You are the best sister a person could have."

"I don't know why you can't do it yourself."

"I don't think I would be able to go through with it. I'd chicken out and I want to have protection because I'm alone most of the time with the kids. Can't you understand? If someone broke into the house to rob it or worse, I want to defend myself from being attacked."

"Well, I'm not going to attack you, and Roger's not going to. So that leaves your mysterious woman. Why are you afraid of her?"

"Don't worry about her. I guess I was delusional."

"Don't put yourself down. A lot of people look alike." We arranged for my travel to Kitsap County to complete the deal. My hesitations remained but her sanity seemed hinged to it. I hoped she was not planning to finish what she tried throughout her life.

Roger

"Vickie, can you come over on Sunday mornings and stay with Mary while I go with the kids to church? She refuses to go and I don't want to leave her alone. I know this is an inconvenience and you have to leave Seattle early."

"Are you sure she needs help? What about the sanitarium you and she discussed with Dr. Conley?"

"She hasn't decided, yet." The tremor in my voice exposed my dilemma. I thought the children needed a church experience, but Mary wanted no part of it. I did not understand. Her mind seemed less able to fight her depression and her anxiety levels of being in public muted her desire to leave the house.

"Don't worry about the distance. There's a 7:40 ferry. I can be at your place by nine."

"Thank you. When is spring break? It would be nice to have you stay with us, me, to help Mary with the kids. My mom is not able to be here as much, lately." Vickie's love for me sustained me more than I wanted, but without her I wanted to eliminate the problem in my head. Church offered me the chance to redeem myself and find reconciliation of my sinful thoughts.

"It's in three weeks. I'll see what I can do, but my job at the boutique might interfere a little. I'll get some time off. I want to see you and the kids and help my sister." We ended the call. My imagination rendered a dream of living with Vickie instead of her sister. Of having Vickie raising her niece and nephew. Of our having children together. I shook it out of my head.

Another suicide would only complicate things. She had to be watched so as to obstruct her destructiveness.

"Mary, your sister has agreed to come over on Sunday morning to stay with you while I go to church with the children. I wish you'd come with us."

Dark eyes pervaded the room as I spoke. "I can't be seen in public. It's dangerous for me. There's someone who wants me dead."

"Honey, I know you think that's true, but nobody is stalking you. You're safe with me and I don't think staying cooped up in the house all the time is good for you." Her face screwed into a wicked grimace.

"You don't know and besides you lie to me about people you see. They want me gone so you're free to do what you want with them."

This unrealistic fear scared me more than I needed. Did she suspect Vickie and me? Or was she just delusional and not facing her mental illness? I couldn't leave her. I promised Vickie, and I couldn't continue living with this insanity. My thinking about her killing herself was a sin which I asked forgiveness each week. I couldn't do away with her which was an even graver sin.

My work was suffering, and my father quizzed me continuously about my life. I had to have the burden lifted from my shoulders.

"What is it you think I want to do? I'm not leaving you. I love you. I want you to get the help you need to get better. So we can get back to living the life we had at first, before the kids were born."

"So Rebecca and Sam are in the way. They have nothing to do with this. You're the one who's not fulfilling your obligation to me. I don't believe you love me as much as you say you do." She stormed out of the house office. I pulled out the divorce papers rewritten by Woodbury to include some changes. If I continued processing them, would I have what I wanted?

86
CHAPTER

Victoria

Roger sounded so depressed about Mary. I cried, his pain hurting me. I had gone to Wendlesburg two weeks before and purchased a small 9 millimeter revolver for Mary from a local gun shop. She had given me her identification and several hundred dollars in cash. Wearing a large hat to hide from prying cameras, I hoped to be subtle and calm, but feared exposure as a fraud. The background information page asked for information about Mary. I filled in the paper and handed it to the clerk.

A week later, I heard from Mary. The gun could be picked up. Her anxiety about seeing the unknown dark haired woman required my helping her again. I returned to the store and retrieved her weapon. I didn't know what the woman looked like and never felt anyone following me. Her paranoia fueled her depression.

"Roger must not know about this," Mary admonished me. "This is between you and me." I agreed and like a spy in a cheap movie I left her without seeing Roger or the children. But I had extracted a promise from her not to use it on herself. I didn't trust she would keep her promise. I feared for Roger's safety.

I rearranged my schedule at work so I could leave the boutique early. If I couldn't have all of the week off, at least I could spend evenings with Roger and Mary. Many people commuted every day from Seattle to Wendlesburg and vice versa. I joined the throngs of workers claiming their benches and tables as if they had ownership of them.

At the house I played with Becca and Sam in the kitchen while Mary fixed dinner. Roger had yet to return from his real estate office.

"Mary, have you seen your mystery woman again?"

"I haven't left the house since you and I were out a couple of weeks ago." Her voice expressed no concern or fear. Her home was her castle and she was safe.

"We can take the kids out after dinner for a trek to the park." Would she appreciate her freedom from the house or fear her vulnerability in public?

"You take them." She continued prepping as she spoke. "Roger can go with you." I wanted time with him, and I debated telling him about the revolver. What good was it to have him angry with me and fearful of Mary? I had to retain the secret.

"If you wish. Is there anything I can do to help with dinner?" The door opened in the garage signaling Roger's return. Becca got off the chair in which she sat and stood by the door, waiting for her daddy. She was so cute and the turmoil of the parents had not fazed her. In an atmosphere of anxiety and depression she maintained high spirits and a sunny outlook. Sam wriggled in his chair wanting to escape and join his sister.

"Set the table, please." She handed me silverware and opened the cupboard containing plates and cups. Roger opened the door and encountered an assault from a little adorning fan. He reached down to pick her up with briefcase still in hand. His love for his children inspired me to stay faithful to my sister and brother-in-law in spite of the extracurricular shenanigans.

"So what have you two connived to regale our taste buds this evening?" He handed me his case which I placed by the door to the hall and his office.

"A simple meat loaf with potatoes and red beets. Your treat is taking our daughter, son, and Vickie to the park for a stroll." Her calm alluded to an underlying hesitancy for joining our troop. Roger missed the momentary quirk.

"Sounds great. I'll put my things and away and be right back." He picked up the briefcase and disappeared down the hall to his office. Upon his return, we enjoyed a restrained moment of happiness as we ate dinner.

At the park Roger and I sat on a bench watching Becca and Sam dig in a sandbox. "Does Mary still love you?" My question evoked an odd stare from Roger.

"Of course, she does. At least that's what she says. Why?" I wanted him to touch me, kiss me, hold me until morning light broke our sleep.

"I don't want her to leave you and you cannot leave her for me. I'm sorry we had this attraction. It complicated our lives. Is she willing to seek help in Seattle?"

"We've talked about it. She seems to want it, but I wonder. Something is troubling her. I think she may suspect us of having been more than family."

"Us? Or you of infidelity?" Her suspicious other woman was not a conversation piece between them as it was between Mary and me. If Roger was seeing another woman, I would know. At least I hoped I would. "Mary has no proof of you cheating on her."

"How do you know? Has she said something?" Roger's gaze at me burned like the hell I was destined to be assigned in the afterlife.

"She does not like it when you're gone for long periods of time. I try to convince her you're at work despite our time together. She said your sex life is not as active." I looked down hiding any blush I could.

He laughed. "She cuts right to the point. No, we are not as intimate these days. I guess I'm to blame."

"Are you seeing someone else? And don't lie to me. I can take it if you are. It's Mary whose sanity is at stake."

He clasped my hands although I did not look at him. "I am not involved with any other person. Circumstances are complicated enough, as it is." The children shrieked as a large dog approached them. The woman holding the leash looked at us before pulling her dog back. She was familiar, but I couldn't place where I had seen her. Dark tresses surrounded a stunning face. Her sleek frame must have attracted approval from men nearby. She turned away before Roger had a chance to see her.

Roger

On a Sunday morning in late spring I waited for Vickie to arrive before leaving for church with the children. She had been coming over on

Sundays to stay with Mary and I appreciated her more than ever. This particular Sunday was no different, except we planned a trip to Seattle. Mary had agreed to enter a facility to receive help with depression and anxiety. All of us were leaving after lunch. Vickie had been instrumental in convincing her sister to seek the needed support.

"Mary, Vickie should be here soon. I'll get the kids ready for church. You finish packing. I love you very much." Her smile hid the trepidation lingering within her.

"Hello, anyone here?" Vickie's voice echoed in the hall.

"We're in the bedroom." I answered.

"Aunt Vickie." Rebecca ran to her.

"Hello, sweetie. How are you today?" She placed her sweater on the hall table, and then bent down and picked up her niece. "Are you ready for church?"

"Yes and Sam is ready, too."

"Good. You have fun there and I will take care of mommy until you get back."

"Okay. Just like last week." Vickie smiled and placed her on the floor.

Turning to me she asked, "Is everything set for Seattle?" I nodded.

"Help Mary finish packing and I'll head to church." She entered the bedroom. I picked up Sam and called to Becca who followed me out to the car.

As I buckled them in, Vickie showed up with Sam's travel bag. "You might need this."

"Thanks. I don't know what I would have done without you all these years. I do love you."

"I know and I feel the same, but we vowed not to continue. Your priority is Mary."

Tears formed in her eyes. I hugged her and said good-bye. She reentered the house as I opened the garage door and backed out. I knew she was right. We had our last chance together and dismissed it for a better happiness.

At church the children went to the play area for the first part of the service. I sat with my parents and listened to the preacher give a sermon about forgiveness for perceived wrongs we created or endured. I thought of Mary and her troubles. She didn't ask for any of them. Yet she now allowed for a chance at redemption and I had a chance at forgiveness. Vickie had done nothing wrong except fall in love with a grateful man who had no right to accept her love. How was I so blessed to love two women, so alike and so different, and be able to live without guilt or remorse consuming me?

After church we were leaving to begin a new life. Mary was getting help. Vickie would finish her education and do remarkable things. My children would have all of the benefits of a happy family with two parents who loved them and an aunt who shared more with them than most children get from their parents. I would be able to support all for the world's benefit and not have to worry about my frailties? What could possibly go wrong?

87
CHAPTER

Victoria

"Did Roger and the kids get off to church?" Mary looked apprehensive as she spoke. We sat in the bedroom together looking at the suitcase and a small pile of clothes.

"Yes. Are you alright with what you're doing?"

"Don't worry about me. I've needed help for years. It's about time I did something about it; before I do something I'll regret. Or worse that Roger has to live to regret. You have been so good to me. Listen, I need you to do me a favor." She stood and from the bottom drawer of her dresser she retrieved the revolver and the box of bullets.

"You were wonderful to get this for me. Now that I'm going to be busy for the next few weeks, I want you to hold on to this for me. I don't want Roger finding out about it. And I certainly don't want the kids discovering it and harming themselves or Roger." She handed me the gun. I placed it on the bed.

"That's a good idea. Do you want me to dispose of it?" I put the box of shells with the gun. I dreaded the idea of it being in the house. Temptation could rear an ugly head and seek vengeance on innocent people.

"No, keep it at your place until I return."

"Okay. Do want you anything?"

"Would you get me some tea? I'll finish in here." I picked up the weapon and shells to place them with my sweater. I planned to move them to my car before Roger returned.

In the kitchen I thought about all the times he and I had shared our bodies and thoughts. It was over and I held no regrets. He taught me about a man's love. I showed him how to care about another person without creating a tragedy. I was truly happy. Nothing was wrong. Nothing was going to be wrong.

A noise in the hall attracted my attention. "Mary, is that you?" No one responded so I finished fixing the tea. I placed the cup on a tray and got out crackers in case hunger prevailed. I decided to have a cup myself and placed a second cup beside the first.

An itchy sensation of another presence alerted me to investigate the hall. Looking, I saw no one. Mary was in her room, packing. I shook my head and grimaced. I had been in the house many times alone with the children and nothing bad happened. What could happen, now?

Picking up the tray I walked down the hall, past the table with my sweater. I noticed the gun was missing. The box of shells was there. Mary must have picked it up. A panic set in as I realized what she was about to do. I felt moisture on my neck and figured adrenalin caused a sweat. Putting the tray on the table I ran to Mary. Why now? She had made a good decision. This was not right. My heart raced as I entered her room to find her closing the suitcase.

"There, that's all done." Turning toward me, an astonishment crossed her face. "Vickie, are you alright? Where's my tea?" I took a deep breath, holding it.

"I'm fine. Are you okay?"

"Never better. But you look like shit. What's wrong?"

"I thought you were going to…." I couldn't think of what to say.

"What?" A puzzling look stared at me. "What did you think I was going to do?"

I steadied my body against the door frame. "I thought you had picked up the gun and were going to use it." I closed my eyes as the room began swirling and thinking became jumbled.

"Use the gun? On me? You thought I was going to kill myself." She helped me sit on the bed. "I gave the gun to you. Where is it?"

"I put it on the hall table and when I came back it was gone. Did you pick it up?"

I blinked and tried to gather my thoughts but I didn't remember. It had been 10:30 in the kitchen. I remembered the missing gun from the table. Now the clock on the nightstand read 11:23.

I looked at Mary and the blood on my hands. What had happened?

Roger

I hung up the phone confused by Vickie's call. Don't bring the kids home. I arranged for my parents to take Becca and Sam with them, making up an excuse about surprising Mary with a gift for Seattle. They agreed and I left for home. What happened?

Entering through the front door I found Vickie sitting on the floor in the hall, bloody hands, and tears streaming down her cheeks. "What's wrong?" I picked her up and she pointed down the hall toward the bedrooms.

"She's dead."

"What? I asked you to watch her." I ran to our bedroom. The scene brought bile to my mouth. Swallowing, I entered to find a gun on the bed, blood spattered on walls and floor, and Mary slumped next to the closet. Vickie followed me into the room. "Dammit, Vickie, where did she get a gun?"

"I'm sorry, Roger, so sorry. She asked me to buy to for her. I didn't think she would really do it." I looked at the gun on the bed, too far away from Mary.

"Tell me what happened. Tell me." I grasped her shoulders. "What did you do?"

"I don't know. I can't remember anything after I got tea for her."

"You have to remember. Did she shoot herself or did you?" Shaking Vickie, I asked again. "What happened?"

"We were finishing packing and she asked me to get her some tea. I went to the kitchen. No wait. She gave me the gun and box of shells, asking me to get rid of it." Vickie wriggled free of me and walked out to the hallway. I followed. "I put the gun here on the table." Only a box and a tray holding two cups of tea and a plate of crackers was there. "I thought I heard Mary in the hall and she had come out picked it up. I put the tray down and I went to your bedroom. I don't remember anything after that."

"How can you forget?" Mary hadn't done this. She wanted to get help. The only other possibility was Vickie. This was not right. Yet, I couldn't let her go to prison.

"Roger, I killed my sister, didn't I? Why can't I remember?" She slumped to the floor again.

"Get up. You have to get out of here. Go in the kitchen and wash the blood off your hands. Then go home. Drive around since it's faster than waiting for a ferry. I'll get this mess fixed up so you don't go to prison." I loved them both and now one was dead and the other claimed amnesia. "Vickie, if Mary wanted to get help, I don't think she would have done this. I don't understand why you thought it a good idea to kill her." My eyes glared at her. "Now get cleaned up and go home."

"I couldn't kill her. I couldn't. Could I?" She washed her hands and scoured the sink clean. I left to prepare a story for the police. I heard the front door close. With fists tight and held near my chest, I returned to the bedroom. I had lost two women in a single misfortune. Now I had to make the best of the situation.

Victoria

Driving on the highway south through Tacoma, my mind whirled trying to recall what happened at Roger and Mary's house. I had arrived as usual before Roger left for church with the children. Mary and I were having a nice chat while she packed. I made her tea. Then Roger is home and Mary is dead.

Tears blurred my vision as I turned onto Interstate 5 for Seattle. All I could recall was Mary lying on the floor. She had been so happy. What did I do? The gun. I took it and placed it on the table. The noise. The gun was gone from the table. Nothing. I can't remember what happened. Why?

Arriving home I entered my apartment. The blood on my blouse told a tale I had to dismiss. I stripped off my clothes and placed everything in the washing machine. I wanted a shower to remove any evidence of my crime. Or had I done anything? Mary was suicidal. I wasn't violent or homicidal. Was I? Did I want Roger so badly, I would kill my own sister? Did we have a fight? Was it an accident? Did I try to stop her from shooting herself?

I collapsed on the floor naked and vulnerable. Nothing had gone right. My sins had consequences I couldn't tolerate. I should have finished the scene as murder-suicide. How was I going to live with this memory?

The phone rang. Roger. "Hello?" My mother's voice quivered as she related her call from him. I had lost a sister to suicide. Could I come over to the house as soon as possible? I relented. After showering without success at washing away the guilt of being Roger's lover and Mary's confidante who failed her, I changed the laundry to the dryer and left for my parents' house. I had to be strong. I had to remain ignorant of the facts. I had to win a Tony for the play in which I was about to perform.

My future depended on circumstances I no longer controlled or understood. We had to invent a story neither of us collaborated to create. Roger and I were finished. Someone was going to prison. That person was me. Could Roger concoct a scenario believable enough to convince people of Mary's guilt? Of my not being present?

Another scenario blazed across my thoughts. I wasn't supposed to be at the house. Only Mary and Roger. The police would arrest him for killing his wife. Breathing sharpened, eyes widened. I wasn't to be incarcerated. Roger would be. My stomach churned, but I had to be silent and let him control the situation. He was smart. He knew how to arrange it for Mary to be the victim and perpetrator. We would be okay, as long as, I kept quiet.

I had to be available when Roger needed me. Our future? Together? No one would accept it. His children had to cope with the loss of their mother, what fate, what chance, did they have without parents?

I sat in my car in front of my family home and cried.

ACKNOWLEDGEMENTS

Writing a book involves many people who interact for the benefit of the story's author. After completing the manuscript I asked several people to peruse it for readability and interest. With feedback from my friends and associates I realized how a manuscript which seems to be acceptable is not what it seems.

Sheila Curwen, Maggie Scott, Susan Wall, and my wife, Sandy Stockwell read first drafts and gave sagacious advice for making the story more interesting and less monotonous.

J. Stephen Lay of Epicenter Press contacted me about providing services for cover design, editing, formatting the interior, printing, and distribution. He and I went to Shattuck School in Faribault, Minnesota, a residential preparatory high school. We hadn't seen each other for 40 years and had a great reunion at the office of Epicenter Press. He introduced me to Marcia Breece who introduced me to Marsha Slomowitz, a graphic designer. I contracted with Marsha to design the cover. She agreed to format the interior for printing, as well.

Phil Garrett, head of marketing and sales at Epicenter Press, helped get this latest publication off the ground. Getting the book into stores and holding reading and signing events is a critical element in the success of a book.

Everyone who reads this book and other stories I concoct are the basis for my continuing this career. Without you, authors work in obscurity leaving manuscripts to die ignoble deaths. Thank you for trusting me to entertain and inform. Disappointing you is an anathema I aspire to avoid.